Praise for *Angel*
'A page-turner . . . it is brilliant. Genuinely amusing
and readable. This summer, every beach in Spain
will be polka-dotted with its neon pink covers'
Evening Standard

'The perfect post-modern fairy tale' *Glamour*

'*Angel* is the perfect sexy summer read' *New Woman*

'A perfect book for the beach' *Sun*

Praise for *Angel Uncovered*
'Glam, glitz, gorgeous people . . . so Jordan!' *Woman*

'A real insight into the celebrity world' *OK!*

'Brilliantly bitchy' *New!*

'Celebrity fans, want the perfect night in? Flick back
those hair extensions, pull on the Juicy Couture
trackie, then join Angel on her rocky ride to WAG
central' *Scottish Daily*

Praise for *Paradise*
'A fabulous guilty holiday pleasure' *heat*

'Go on, run yourself a bath full of bubbles and
indulge in this page-turner.' *Now*

Also by Katie Price

Non-Fiction
Being Jordan
Jordan: A Whole New World
Jordan: Pushed to the Limit
Standing Out
You Only Live Once

Fiction
Crystal
Sapphire
Angel trilogy:
Angel
Angel Uncovered
Paradise

Crystal

Katie Price x

arrow books

This edition published by Arrow Books 2011

2 4 6 8 10 9 7 5 3 1

First published in Great Britain in 2007 by Century
First published in paperback in 2007 by Arrow Books

Arrow Books
Random House, 20 Vauxhall Bridge Road,
London SW1V 2SA

www.rbooks.co.uk

Addresses for companies within The Random House Group Limited can
be found at: www.randomhouse.co.uk/offices.htm

The Random House Group Limited Reg. No. 954009

A CIP catalogue record for this book
is available from the British Library

ISBN 9780099553175

The Random House Group Limited supports The Forest Stewardship
Council (FSC), the leading international forest certification organisation.
All our titles that are printed on Greenpeace approved FSC certified paper
carry the FSC logo. Our paper procurement policy can be found at:
www.rbooks.co.uk/environment

Mixed Sources
Product group from well-managed
forests and other controlled sources
www.fsc.org Cert no. TT-COC-2139
© 1996 Forest Stewardship Council

Typeset by SX Composing DTP, Rayleigh, Essex
Printed and bound in Great Britain by
CPI Bookmarque Ltd, Croydon, CR0 4TD

Chapter 1

The Audition

'Oh my God, look at the queue!' Crystal exclaimed, taking in the long line of wannabes which snaked out of the London hotel and halfway down the road.

'Do you think we'll even get in to see the judges?' Tahlia bit her lip and looked anxious, but Belle replied, 'Sure we will,' confidently flicking her long blonde hair over her shoulders. 'Most of these people look like total losers. I bet they can't even sing a note. Their auditions will be over in seconds. You know what Dallas is like.'

She was right, but Crystal wished she had kept her opinion to herself. Several people had turned round to look at Belle and raise their eyebrows at her bitchy comment. Crystal sighed. She mustn't let Belle get to her. She had to stay calm for the audition. The three girls were going to be singing for a chance of a place in the TV reality show, *Band Ambition*, which aimed to find the perfect pop

1

group and turn them into stars and had shamelessly ripped off *The X Factor* format.

The girls saw the show as their last chance to launch their singing careers. They'd met at stage school more than six years ago when they were sixteen and formed their band Lost Angels, united in their dream of making it as singers. They definitely had talent and had worked hard but their big break just hadn't come – no matter how many clubs and pubs they'd performed at (and some of them had been real dives) and however many CDs and letters they'd sent off to record companies. They'd even met an A&R man from a leading record label who claimed he could get them a deal. He was dressed in a tight denim shirt and jeans, which was fine if you were Heath Ledger but not such a great look for a man in his late forties, with moobs and a comb over. But it quickly became all too clear that he was more interested in getting into their knickers than helping them get into the charts. For a start he'd insisted on meeting them in a club rather than his office, which immediately set off alarm bells in Crystal's mind. 'There are hundreds of wannabe girl bands out there – all with talent, all good-looking and you need to have your USP,' he declared, plying them with champagne and perving over them. 'I can help you work on yours. So how about we finish the champagne and go back to my place. I can play you some of my other artists' tracks and you can see what I can do for you.' As Crystal looked at him, lounging back on the sofa, thinking that he was in for some action, his arms round a very uncomfortable Tahlia and a pissed-off Belle, something inside her snapped. She desperately wanted a break but not if it meant shagging some jaded old letch. 'How about you fuck off!' Crystal shot back at him. 'We don't need your kind of help. Come on you two, let's go.'

'Yeah, right back to oblivion,' he shouted after them. 'You'll never make it.'

Belle was almost ready to give up after that, but Crystal and Tahlia stayed strong, keeping the dream alive. But it was hard for them. Belle was fortunate because her parents were wealthy enough to support her and she didn't have to work, though she occasionally helped out in her aunt's boutique, but Tahlia and Crystal had no choice but to work, often in dead-end jobs. Tahlia's CV included waitressing (working in a fast-food chain) and modelling (handing out promotional flyers for a new mobile, dressed as a banana). Crystal's included several 'acting' roles: working as an elf in Santa's grotto (but being sacked for swearing when one obnoxious brat stamped on her toe) and a major part in Panto (playing the Cat in *Dick Whittington* in Croydon and being sexually harassed by King Rat). She didn't include all the other crap jobs – working in a supermarket and behind a bar.

Band Ambition was it, they had decided; either

they make it this time or they would give up and go their separate ways. But none of them, least of all Crystal, wanted to abandon their dream. All she had ever wanted to do was to be a singer. It was the first thing she thought about when she woke up and the last thing before she fell asleep at night.

The girls worked brilliantly as a group, even though the three of them couldn't have been more different – Crystal, with her exotic Mediterranean beauty, black hair and green eyes, was confident and outspoken; Belle (yes, her parents really *had* named her after the character in *Beauty and the Beast*), blonde, petite, extremely pretty and bubbly, but something of a spoilt princess who always liked to have her own way; and Tahlia, the quietest of the trio, a beautiful, mixed-race, sensitive girl, frowning too often, when, with looks like hers – huge brown eyes, flawless skin, a size eight figure to die for – most women would have been smiling all the time. She and Crystal were the strongest singers. Belle wasn't in their league, but she was still good and she was a superb dancer. Crystal and Tahlia were best friends and although they got on okay with Belle there were tensions. Crystal and Belle often clashed, usually when Crystal didn't think Belle had pulled her weight in the group or over her prima donna attitude to life, which got on Crystal's nerves. If it hadn't been for the group Crystal doubted she would have had anything to do with Belle. But now their destinies were linked even though Crystal frequently wished that Belle wasn't part of Lost Angels.

Outside the hotel it had started raining and the three girls huddled under one umbrella, practising their song. They had been queuing for two hours, and Belle had moaned practically non-stop that she was bound to get a cold. Tahlia was too stricken with nerves to say much so it was down to Crystal to keep everyone's spirits up. But finally they were in the hotel, they'd registered with the production company and they could rehearse their song properly. As they did so, one of the producers listened in, and Crystal felt a surge of optimism when he gave them the thumbs up. 'You sound great,' he told them. 'One of the best groups *I've* heard all day.' They'd chosen the Sugababes' 'Hole in the Head', knowing it showed off their voices really well. They were equally good at singing pop or R&B. As for their image, they each had very different tastes. Crystal nearly always wore black; Belle wasn't seen in anything but designer labels and it was practically impossible to prise Tahlia out of her jeans even though she looked amazing in skirts. They'd argued endlessly about what to wear for the audition. Belle had wanted them to wear matching outfits, but Crystal had resisted, saying they should wear things that showed off their different personalities, otherwise they'd look too manufactured and a cringe. In the end Tahlia wore jeans and a white vest trimmed with sequins,

Crystal wore a black mini with leggings and black vest, and Belle wore a leopard-print tunic and leggings. Now, as they checked their make-up in the mirror in the ladies, jostling for space with the other hopefuls, Crystal thought they'd made the right choice. They looked good, relaxed and confident, in contrast to many of the other acts who had gone for revealing outfits, and full-on make-up that made them look like hookers. One such girl, in layers of slap and a black leather dress, turned to Belle and said, 'I like your tunic, is it from Primark?'

'No,' Belle hissed back. 'It's Gucci. Where's your dress from? Whores-R-Us?'

Suddenly Crystal, Tahlia and Belle found themselves surrounded by the girl's band members, who looked equally slutty and hard-faced. 'Nobody disses us like that,' one of them said, her dyed auburn hair scraped back into a Croydon face-lift, huge gold earrings hanging from her ears, that looked as if they could double as offensive weapons. Was it ironic chav chic, Crystal wondered or just Vicky Pollard chav?

'It was just a joke,' Belle shrugged. Crystal bit her lip, infuriated by her attitude: *like they needed this before the audition*.

'Well, we didn't think it was very funny,' the girl persisted, advancing on Belle.

God knows what would have happened next, Crystal thought, but luckily the door opened and someone called out the girls' number, telling them their audition would be in twenty minutes and immediately the four of them tottered out, not before giving Belle the finger.

'Nice one, Belle,' Crystal said sarcastically.

'Whatever,' Belle answered, rolling her eyes and sauntering out of the door.

Crystal started to follow her. 'Are you coming?' she asked Tahlia, but her friend shook her head, then dashed into a cubicle and bolted the door.

'I'll see you out there, then,' Crystal called, used to Tahlia's pre-performance nerves – she always threw up before they sang live.

Outside Belle was leaning against the wall, examining her perfectly manicured nails. 'Is Tahlia being sick again?' she muttered. 'God, I hope she's not going to fuck it up for us.'

'You know she won't!' Crystal answered back hotly, hating any criticism of her friend. 'She's the best singer out of all of us, you know that.'

Belle did know that, but she didn't like hearing it and she flicked her hair back dismissively.

'How are you feeling?' Crystal asked as Tahlia emerged from the ladies a few minutes later looking pale.

'I'll be okay now,' Tahlia replied. Crystal put her arm round her friend and hugged her, then, because after all they were a group, she gave Belle a hug too.

'Come on, we can do this,' she told them. 'And

anyway it can't be as bad as the gig we did at that wedding.' The girls all smiled at the memory. By the time they had got on stage, the wedding guests were all caned and instead of dancing to the girls' repertoire of disco hits, which included 'It's Raining Men', 'Dancing Queen' and 'Celebration', songs usually guaranteed to get everyone on the dance floor, one of the very pissed bridesmaids had demanded they sing 'Lady in Red'. When Belle asked sarcastically if they looked like Chris de Burgh, all hell broke loose. Some of the guests started pelting the girls with food and when they made their escape the guests turned on each other.

'Yeah,' Belle said dryly, 'I don't imagine Dallas ever loses control.'

Dallas (he was always known simply as Dallas; no one ever used his second name) was the most feared of the judges on *Band Ambition* – a tough-talking American with an acid tongue capable of making grown men weep. Dallas told it like it was and took no prisoners. He had taken Simon Cowell as his role model and was frequently even more straight-talking than *The X Factor* judge. He was in his late twenties and boyishly good-looking, but seemed much older as he was so ambitious and driven. He had been an extremely successful A&R man for a leading record label but when they refused to sign up two of his newest discoveries he had resigned and started his own label. The two groups his old label didn't have faith in went on to be massive in the States. A year later he'd made his first million and now his label was one of the most successful in America; five years since he started up he was a multimillionaire.

Just then a girl wearing a headset and carrying a clipboard came their way. 'Number 275?' she asked briskly. 'You need to move to the pre-audition area. You'll be on soon.' As the three of them made their way there, Crystal felt more nervous than she had in her life. This had to go well for them; if it didn't they may as well take it as a sign to jack it in – they'd tried everything else. They sat down in the corridor, taking their place next to the two acts waiting in front of them. Everyone was subdued, whispering occasional comments, straining to hear the act performing behind the huge double doors at the end of the corridor.

'Girls – how are you feeling?'

They looked up to see Tess, the bubbly red-haired presenter clutching a microphone, standing with a cameraman pointing a camera right at them. *Wow*, Crystal thought, *this is the real deal. They were going to be on TV*. She was about to answer when Belle got in first.

'Really nervous,' Belle replied, flashing her best stage-school smile.

'Well, good luck!' Tess replied. 'Though I should warn you that you're the hundredth act the judges are going to see today and so far they've only put one act through!'

'Cheers for that,' Crystal muttered when Tess had trotted off to deliver a blow to another nervous group of contestants.

'Come on,' Tahlia said. 'We can do this!'

And then, after a further agonising twenty-minute wait, it was their turn and the three of them were walking into the huge conference room, empty except for a large table, where the three judges – Sadie Park, Dallas and Charlie Reynolds – sat in a row. All three stared at the girls and Crystal had to fight her nerves. *Come on*, she told herself sternly, *you've wanted this all your life, don't fuck up now*.

'Hiya,' she called out much more confidently than she felt, remembering from watching past contestants how important it was to give off a star-quality vibe and not look as if they were apologising for even being there and taking up the judges' time.

'And who are you?' asked Sadie Park. She was a forty-something ex-singer who'd been massive in the eighties and then reinvented herself as a manager of several very successful boy bands. Her image hadn't evolved since her singing days and she still dressed like a rock chick – wild blonde hair, heavy black eye make-up, tight jeans and T-shirts. She was as tough-talking as Dallas, but was known to have a sweeter side too.

'We're Lost Angels,' Crystal replied.

'Oh, I like it!' Sadie answered smiling. Dallas

10

remained stony-faced. 'And what are you going to sing for us?' she went on.

'"Hole in the Head",' Belle replied.

'Off you go then,' Sadie said.

Crystal softly counted them in 'One, two, three.' And then they were singing – a little tentatively at first, but gaining confidence and strength. Just as they'd started the third verse and were well into their stride Dallas shouted out, 'Stop! We've heard enough.'

The girls looked at each other in dismay; had he really thought it was bad? Crystal squeezed Tahlia's hand as she saw her friend's eyes had filled with tears.

'So how did you think that went, girls?' Dallas addressed them in his LA drawl.

'I think it was okay,' Crystal replied. 'The beginning was a little weak, but we picked up and, yeah, I think we did all right. Better than all right.'

'Well, you're correct about the start,' Dallas replied dismissively. *God he was mean*, Crystal thought.

'Sadie, Charlie, what did you think of Lost Angels?' he demanded, saying *Lost Angels* as if it was some kind of infectious disease. Crystal had never quite understood why people so often hated Dallas before, as she'd always thought he was fair and could recognise talent. But standing in front of him, with her dreams in the balance, and him looking as if it was all too tedious for words, she

11

totally got it. He enjoyed playing the role of a total 100 per cent bastard! To him this was entertainment.

Sadie was the first to speak. 'I have to say that I really liked you, girls. I thought you were great!' *That was more like it*, Crystal thought.

'Okay, what about you Charlie?' Dallas asked the third judge. Charlie was an attractive blonde in her early thirties and had been in a very successful girl band that broke up three years ago after some bitter in-fighting between the girls and their management. There were rumours that she and Dallas had been an item a year earlier, a rumour which neither had confirmed or denied, but the fact was that she hated him now.

Charlie seemed unimpressed and without looking at Dallas replied, 'Girls, you were okay, but I feel I've heard it all before. You just weren't particularly special. It's a no from me.'

Bitch! Crystal thought, hardly believing her ears. So now it was all down to Dallas. There was a pause – Dallas liked making people wait and Crystal stared at him, willing him to put them through. His face was totally unreadable as he looked at each of them in turn. Ever since Simon Cowell had perfected his deadpan look, it seemed that one of the judges on each of the other reality TV shows always tried to copy him. Dallas was the best yet. Finally, just as Crystal thought she would have to make a plea, he spoke. 'Well done, you're through.'

The girls screamed and hugged each other, then thanked the judges and raced out of the room.

'We've *got* to celebrate tonight!' Belle declared as they left the hotel. 'You should come and meet Max. I'll get him to reserve us a table in the VIP lounge.' Max was Belle's new boyfriend. She'd met him a month ago when she was out clubbing and had become completely besotted. Belle liked her men rich and good-looking and Max ticked both of those boxes. He had been a top Formula One racing driver but two years ago had been involved in a serious crash. He was in a coma for a month, and when he recovered he suffered from recurrent blackouts which ended his career. Instead he'd turned to business and opened a club in London that had become the latest celeb hangout.

'Okay,' Tahlia replied happily, while Crystal frowned – meeting Belle's new boyfriend was not her idea of a fun night out, she'd much rather be with the girls. She could guarantee Max would be arrogant and full of himself. And she didn't like the prospect of Belle showing off her new man when she, Crystal, had been single for five months after ending a year-long relationship that had been going nowhere.

'Well, Crystal?' Belle demanded, 'Max knows loads of hot single men.'

Crystal shrugged. 'Okay,' she mumbled. 'But I don't need fixing up with anyone, I'm perfectly happy being on my own.'

'Yeah right,' Belle shot back. 'You wouldn't say that if you'd been getting the kind of sex I've been getting lately.'

Four hours later Crystal was sharing a taxi with Tahlia to Max's club in Covent Garden, called Max's.

'God, how egotistical naming a club after yourself,' Crystal sniped.

'Chill, babe, we'll drink champagne and then leave them to it; we deserve a treat after today,' Tahlia replied and Crystal couldn't help smiling. *She was right, they were through! It was so exciting.* There was a queue of people already waiting to get into Max's and for the first time in her life Crystal marched to the front and told the doorman that they were on the guest list. Once inside they looked round for Belle but there was no sign of her.

'She's probably having a celebration shag,' Crystal muttered darkly. 'Come on, let's go to the bar, I'll buy you a drink.' She had just ordered a vodka and cranberry for herself and Bacardi and Coke for Tahlia when a confident male voice behind her said, 'No, that won't do; these ladies have got to have champagne and by champagne I mean vintage Cristal!' She turned round ready to tell the man that they could buy their own drinks when she found herself face to face with one of the most drop-dead gorgeous men she had ever seen. He smiled at her and said, 'Hi, you must be Crystal.

14

I'm Max. Belle's still getting ready. And hi. Tahlia, right?' He moved forward and lightly kissed them both on each cheek and Crystal found herself thinking *lucky Belle!* He was dark-haired, with such deep-brown eyes they almost looked black, a sexy mouth and the kind of classically good-looking features male models usually have. But she'd been right in the taxi; there was something arrogant about him. 'Come on,' he said, 'I'll take you through to the VIP area; we need to toast your amazing success!'

For the next hour the three of them chatted away. Max was charming and easy to talk to, with a dry sense of humour Crystal immediately got. He seemed confident, totally at ease with himself and the world – the confidence Crystal had seen before in people who'd always had money and who'd never known what it was like to struggle to pay the bills. He was wearing an expensive-looking black suit, and the cufflinks on his white shirt looked as if they were real diamonds. *A bit flash*, she thought, *but tasteful flash*. He had a London accent but every now and then would slip into talking proper. He intrigued her. She couldn't remember enjoying a man's company this much in ages, or being so instantly attracted to one. And was it her imagination or did his eyes seem to seek hers out? She found herself engaging in classic flirtatious behaviour, flicking back her hair, and straightening her back so her breasts stood out more. She was pleased that she'd made an effort and worn one of her favourite dresses, a short black silk one, showing off her long slim legs, low cut at the back to reveal more tanned skin. And then she stopped herself: *this was Belle's boyfriend for fucksake!*

Max pulled out a packet of cigarettes and offered them to Tahlia and Crystal and Crystal found herself accepting one, even though she had promised the girls that she would give up.

'Ah, come on!' Max said to Tahlia's protests. 'One won't hurt, will it?'

'You're bad,' Crystal said, smiling at him as he lit her cigarette.

'Yes, I'm the big bad wolf, didn't Belle tell you?'

Crystal's stomach flipped and she took a drag of her cigarette, resisting the urge she had to reply, '*And I'm Little Red Riding Hood, why don't you eat me all up?*' God what was happening to her? Had five months of celibacy turned her into a nympho who wanted to shag her friend's boyfriend? Of course she didn't! She tried her best to tell herself that it was purely the excitement of the day's events that was making her feel like this. Probably even if Max looked like Shrek she'd have fancied him. But then again, maybe not . . .

She was saved from her thoughts by the arrival of Belle, looking way too gorgeous in a silver Biba mini dress. 'Sorry I'm late,' she said, throwing her arms round Max, then sliding on to his lap, making

Crystal feel quite faint with jealousy. After that Crystal just wanted to go home, but Max continued to look at her and she detected more than a flicker of interest in his eyes.

So what? she told herself, *he's a player, he's probably like that with all women,* but she was unable to resist sneaking glances at him when she thought no one noticed. Their eyes locked and his seemed to say *I want you as much as you want me.* Crystal was the first to look away.

That night in bed he was all she could think of. She let her imagination run away with her, taking her to a place where he wasn't with Belle, where he was free to be with her, and they were free to do what they wanted to each other . . . It was a delicious fantasy, but frustrating because that's all it was, and that was all it could be, right?

Chapter 2

Boot Camp

'Oh my God, do you think this is it?!' Belle was pointing out of the coach window at what looked like a stately home – a grand, imposing building set in several acres of beautifully landscaped garden. It looked to Crystal like the kind of place you'd see in films. She couldn't imagine anyone actually living there. She was just about to reply 'No way' when the coach turned into the drive. So this really *was* Dallas's house – the venue for the second stage of the competition. The contestants had been divided into three groups – each made up of eight acts. Charlie had taken her bands somewhere in Surrey, Sadie's were in Spain and Dallas's category were in Oxfordshire. All the acts would have a week to impress their judge.

Everyone filed off the coach and hung around outside it looking nervous, unsure of what to do next. Crystal wondered if she should go and knock on the door. But then a woman in an expensive-looking suit, who Crystal recognised as Dallas's PA Jenny, opened it and invited them inside. Lost Angels were the first in. Crystal felt like a little girl in a fairy tale – she had never been anywhere like this in her life – okay, she had been round a couple of stately homes on school trips but that was as a visitor, not a guest. The entrance hall was vast, with an ornate stone fireplace at one end and a large, elaborately carved wooden staircase at the other. Richly coloured rugs covered the stone floor.

'This is well posh,' Tahlia whispered to Crystal, her eyes wide with astonishment.

'We're meeting in the dining room,' Jenny's voice echoed through the hall as she indicated the room they should go into.

'Some dining room,' Crystal whispered to Tahlia as they walked into a room the size of small football pitch. Dallas was standing by the fireplace.

'Come and find a seat,' he called out, gesturing at the rows of chairs that had been arranged to form a semicircle in front of him. Waiting only a few minutes for everyone to get settled, he began his speech.

'Welcome to Phoenix Manor, your home for the next week. I hope you'll have everything you need, but don't make yourselves too comfortable – you're here to work!' Dallas addressed the eight bands that would become four in five days' time. 'At the end of the week I will be deciding who I want to keep in my category and I'll be judging that on the

19

performance you give on Friday. Good luck everybody.'

Crystal, Belle and Tahlia looked at each other; they all knew how important this week was. Their first audition had been two months ago and since then they'd been rehearsing harder than ever, determined to get through to the next round. Crystal had mixed feelings about having Dallas as their mentor. He was an extremely hard man to please and she knew if they were to get picked they would have to excel.

Dallas strode out of the room, leaving his staff to show the groups around. Lost Angels were sharing a large bedroom on the first floor. It was more luxurious and spacious than any room Crystal had ever stayed in but as soon as the door closed Belle started moaning: 'God, I always have my own room, I hate sharing, I *must* have my beauty sleep.'

'For God's sake, Belle, it's only for a week!' Crystal replied in exasperation. 'Tahlia and me will share the double and you can have the single bed.'

Belle curled her lip. 'I really wanted the double, actually.'

'Well, you'll have to share it with one of us and, as you hate sharing, that's not a great idea, is it?' Tahlia said patiently.

'Actually, I'm going to ask Dallas if I can have my own room,' Belle replied petulantly.

'Come on, Belle, don't piss him off!' Crystal exclaimed.

'I won't piss him off, he likes me,' Belle snapped back. 'And there's no harm in asking', and to Crystal's astonishment she applied another layer of gloss to her already glossed lips, brushed her hair and sauntered out of the room.

'Bollocks!' Crystal exclaimed, throwing herself on to the bed. 'That's all we need! Dallas is hard enough to impress without him thinking that we're a bunch of spoilt prima donnas.'

'Oh, don't worry, Crystal. Come on, let's go and look round, we've got a few hours before we have to meet for cocktails with Dallas,' Tahlia answered, checking through the itinerary they'd been given. 'We could always go for a swim if you like.'

'Good idea,' Crystal answered, rummaging through her suitcase for her bikini.

She and Tahlia spent the next few hours hanging out by Dallas's fabulous indoor pool and fending off the three members of a boy band who were flirting outrageously with them. They were sweet enough lads but neither Crystal nor Tahlia had the slightest bit of interest in them.

'They just remind me of my kid brother,' Crystal confided as they watched the boys showing off by diving flashily into the pool and wrestling with each other. 'They're just boys. And frankly I need a man.' As she said that an image of Max rose up in her head. She'd met him a few times now and every time the attraction she felt for him had grown stronger, until it had reached a point where it was such sweet torture to be near him that she almost couldn't bear it. She had cried off on the last occasion when they were all supposed to meet up. Max had wanted to give the girls a send-off from the club, before they went to boot camp. Crystal invented a bout of food poisoning and was stunned when her mobile rang and it was Max.

'Are you really ill?' he demanded.

'Yeah, I feel terrible.' Crystal tried to put on a croaky voice.

'Well, that's a pity. I wanted to see you.' He paused, and Crystal's stomach flipped. 'I'm disappointed you're not here.' Another pause where Crystal nearly said, *So am I.* 'Good luck, Crystal. I'll be thinking of you.'

He was obviously waiting for Crystal to say that she would be thinking of *him*, but much as she was tempted to, she simply thanked him and said goodbye. She knew she'd made the right decision not going to the club; somehow she had to beat her obsession with Max.

'Oh, there you are,' Belle called over to them from the other side of the pool. 'I just wanted to let you know that I'm going to be in the suite next door to you, so come up and I'll show you round.' And with that she turned and walked away, her high-heeled sandals clicking loudly against the marble.

'She obviously didn't piss Dallas off then,' Crystal muttered, then had a thought. 'You don't think she did anything with him do you?'

'What do you mean?' Tahlia asked.

'Like a blowjob-for-suite scenario?' Crystal whispered, not wanting the boy band members to overhear.

'No way!' Tahlia shook her head, too sweetly naïve to imagine such a thing, but Crystal couldn't help wondering. Dallas was known to prefer blondes and Belle was quite capable of giving the odd favour if it got her what she wanted . . .

And when the two girls saw Belle's suite Crystal wondered even more. It was palatial – high, moulded ceilings, glittering chandeliers, an ornate four-poster bed in the bedroom, an imposing stone fireplace. Adjoining the bedroom was an elegant living room with yet another impressive fireplace; an HD TV set, several huge vases of lilies giving off a heady perfume, and a well-stocked drink cabinet. It was the kind of suite Crystal expected a fully-fledged pop star to have.

'So how the hell did you get him to give you this?' she exclaimed.

'I just explained how badly I sleep if there are other people in the room,' Belle replied, 'and he was very sympathetic.'

'I bet you manage when you're with Max,' Crystal said dryly.

'We don't sleep much when we're together, know what I mean?' Belle said smugly. And Crystal shut up, not wanting to hear any more.

23

'And Dallas didn't mind you asking?' Tahlia said.

'No, he was an absolute sweetie about it,' Belle replied, flicking back her hair but avoiding eye contact with the others. 'Anyway, I'm going to get ready now. I want to look my best for tonight as I think we're being filmed.'

'How was your first day?' It was Max on the phone. Tahlia was in the shower. Crystal's heart raced as it always did at the sound of his voice.

'Great,' she replied, wondering why he was calling her.

'I've just spoken to Belle but she's too busy getting ready to talk so I thought I'd call you,' Max continued. 'Are you feeling better?'

'I'm fine,' Crystal replied, having totally forgotten that she'd invented an illness.

'Yeah, I thought so,' Max said laughing. 'There was nothing wrong with you, was there?'

Crystal suddenly remembered and tried to protest, but Max wouldn't have any of it. 'Just make sure you see me when you finish boot camp.'

'I'm sure we'll all meet up soon,' Crystal replied, trying to play it cool. 'See you, Max.'

She felt distracted for the rest of the night, obsessing over Max when she should have been focusing on what she was here for. Mind you, if there were any prizes to be won for sucking up to Dallas, it looked like Belle was on course to get one. She stayed by his side, hanging on his every word

throughout the champagne cocktails and three-
course dinner that Dallas had laid on. While he
didn't give much away he seemed to enjoy the
attention; Belle was extremely pretty and an
accomplished flirt when she wanted to be. Crystal
did not think this was a good thing. She had overheard several of the other groups gossiping about
Belle's behaviour round Dallas and knew it would
make Lost Angels extremely unpopular with the
other contestants, who were bound to think they
would have an unfair advantage with Dallas. The
boy band kept trying to flirt with Tahlia and Crystal
– the vast amounts of alcohol they'd knocked back
had made them bolder. But Crystal and Tahlia
were watching their intake – limiting themselves to
a couple of glasses of champagne, wanting to be
fresh in the morning. Also Crystal didn't want to
look pissed as they were all being filmed for the
show. The other groups apparently didn't have the
same concerns; they were drinking like it was going
out of fashion. At midnight the two girls decided to
go to bed; by now all the other groups were
hammered, singing and dancing along to the
Scissor Sisters blasting out of the stereo. Belle and
Dallas were nowhere to be seen.

'God, I hope she knows what she's doing,'
Crystal muttered to Tahlia as they made their way
up the staircase.

They were woken at seven by a loud knocking at
the door. Crystal dragged herself out of bed to

25

open it and was handed a piece of paper by one of the production team. Yawning, she quickly read it. They had to be downstairs in fifteen minutes, ready to start rehearsing their songs.

'Shit!' she exclaimed, telling Tahlia to go and wake up Belle and running into the shower. When she emerged five minutes later, Tahlia said, 'I knocked and knocked for Belle but there was no answer, and when I tried to open the door it was locked.'

'Well, maybe she's gone jogging,' Crystal answered, thinking it highly unlikely; Belle was not known to be an early riser.

She and Tahlia were the first downstairs. Coffee and croissants were laid out and the two girls helped themselves and watched as the other contestants staggered in, stinking of booze, bleary-eyed and looking as if they'd hardly slept.

'Jesus, I'm wasted!' one of the boy band members – she couldn't tell them apart, they all looked the same – said to Crystal, sinking into a chair next to her. 'We didn't get to bed until four.'

Crystal smiled sympathetically but inside she couldn't help thinking *one up to Lost Angels*. Except where was Belle? Next Dallas marched in. He stood at the door surveying them all and then he let rip: 'So you guys have been dreaming all your lives of being singers. So much so that at the first chance of free booze you lose it? It's pathetic!' he barked. He looked round the room, and seeing Tahlia and

Crystal looking so fresh he added, 'Well, not everyone, I see. Well done, girls, you passed my first test. Now where's that other band member of yours?'

'Here,' Belle called out from the doorway and everyone turned to look at her. She was dressed in a white Juicy Couture tracksuit and looked glowing. 'Sorry I'm late; I've just been doing Pilates. Nice gym, Dallas.' If it had been anyone else Dallas would have hit the roof, but as it was Belle he just smiled and told her to sit down.

'Yeah, right, I bet the only Pilates she's been doing was on his face,' the boy band member whispered to Crystal. He may well be right, but Crystal told him to be quiet – whatever she might feel, she had to show solidarity with Belle.

'Were you really in the gym?' Crystal asked as the three of them made their way to the rehearsal room where they were going to meet Kathy, the singing coach.

'Of course! Where else would I be?' Belle snapped.

'Well, everyone noticed you flirting with Dallas last night,' Crystal carried on.

'I was *not* flirting,' Belle replied, turning bright red. 'I like Dallas and he likes me but it's a strictly professional relationship. Anyway, if he likes me then he'll like Lost Angels and that can't be bad, can it?'

Belle was right, Dallas did seem to like Lost

Angels – or at least he didn't give them as hard a time as he gave the other acts and every now and then he even praised them. But being his favourites meant the other acts hated them – the boy band had even stopped flirting with Tahlia and Crystal. They obviously felt that the girls were bound to get through on Friday because of Dallas's relationship with Belle, regardless of their performance. She kept denying there was anything going on, but she often disappeared in the afternoon during their break, claiming she wanted to have a lie-down.

'It's who she's gone to have a lie-down with that worries me,' Crystal muttered when she and Tahlia were sunbathing outside on the immaculately cut lawn, enjoying a few minutes' relaxation before they returned to rehearsing their song.

'Do you think we should say something to Dallas?' Tahlia asked.

Crystal shook her head. 'Like what? "Don't shag her".'

'No, I meant about the way the other bands think that he's going to favour us,' Tahlia answered.

Crystal sighed. 'I just don't think that's a good idea. Maybe we're worrying too much; hopefully it will all blow over.'

But she was wrong and two days before they were due to perform the song that would decide their fate, all hell broke loose. They were mid-rehearsal when a member of the production team burst into the room and told them to go straight to the dining room. The other acts were already there, and they all turned to stare at Lost Angels when they walked in; their stares weren't friendly. 'Do you know why we're here?' Crystal asked one of the boy band members, but he just shrugged and turned away, blanking her. Some twenty awkward minutes passed for Crystal and Tahlia; they were aware of people whispering about them. Not so Belle, who was oblivious and kept going on about what they should wear for their performance. Finally Dallas walked in, flanked by the director of the show and one of the producers – all looking serious.

Dallas was the first to speak and his tone was pure ice. 'I've just had an interesting conversation with a journalist friend of mine. Apparently someone in this room has seen fit to try and sell a story – a story about me and one of the contestants.' He paused and surveyed the room and he looked colder and harder than Crystal had ever seen him look before.

'That person needs to know that we will find out who they are and when we do they had better have an explanation.'

The director now spoke. 'Dallas has assured me that there is absolutely no truth in the story and we will be issuing a denial when the story is published tomorrow. This kind of muck-raking is not what this competition is about and whoever did this should be ashamed of themselves. Now all of you get back to work. Anyone who has a problem with that knows where the door is: believe me, there are plenty of other people who want your place.'

Everyone filed silently out of the room. Crystal didn't dare say anything until she was sure they couldn't be overheard. Once they were back in the rehearsal room she turned to Belle, who looked pale, and said, 'Well, is there something you need to tell us?'

Belle was just about to reply when the door swung open and Dallas strode in. 'Sit down, girls, we need to talk. First of all, Crystal and Tahlia you need to know that there is nothing going on between me and Belle. She has a boyfriend, I have a girlfriend, and as far as I'm concerned she's just another contestant; that's it. I give you my word.'

Crystal looked at him closely. Was he telling the truth? She didn't know for sure, but she had a pretty good idea that Dallas would be perfectly capable of lying in the interests of self-preservation.

'But I'm afraid it is going to be harder for you now to get through to the next stage.'

'What!' the girls exclaimed in unison.

'You are going to have to give the performance of your lives on Friday – you've got to be better than the others by the widest of margins. It cannot look as though I am favouring you. I've got my reputation to think of. People can't think I favour pretty girls.'

'But you've just said there's nothing going on!'

Crystal couldn't stop herself from saying.

'And that's the truth,' Dallas answered coldly. 'I'm just giving you the facts; we've got to consider what people will think.' With that he got up, and just as he was leaving the room he added, 'You'll also be doing a photo shoot tomorrow with Max and I want you all to stress how much Belle and he are in love. It will look good.'

Crystal, Tahlia and Belle stared at each other as Dallas shut the door. Crystal felt too wound up to speak, afraid that if she opened her mouth she would lay into Belle and say something she might regret.

'Okay, Crystal, can you get in closer to Max, and Max put your arm round her.' The tabloid photographer barked out instructions to Lost Angels and Max as they posed in Dallas's beautiful walled rose garden. The whole experience was torture for Crystal. Max was his usual charming self, flirting with her and telling her how beautiful she looked, when he thought no one could hear, but the rest of the time he was all over Belle. They'd had to do group photos and then she and Tahlia had to watch while Max and Belle posed together for the photographs that were supposed to tell the world how much they were in love. So there were shots of the couple kissing, of them in each other's arms, of Belle sitting on Max's knee.

'Are you sure this isn't going to backfire?' Crystal

31

asked Dallas who had come along to watch. 'I mean, isn't all this lovey-dovey stuff a bit sickly?'

Dallas laughed. 'Crystal, I had no idea you were such a cynic. Trust me, it won't. People will just see a couple who are in love; they'll think it's romantic.'

Crystal wasn't so sure and she couldn't help wondering why Max was so keen to play the role of the loving boyfriend. Didn't he suspect Belle at all? Wasn't *he* worried about the story? She made an excuse that she needed a drink and headed back to the mansion. Soon the journalist would be interviewing them, and she and Tahlia were supposed to enthuse about how much Belle and Max were in love. It wasn't something she was looking forward to. She'd almost reached the house when Max called out to her as he strode after her through the grounds, 'Hey, are you okay? You've hardly said a word.'

She turned and Max was so close to her that their bodies were almost touching. *God he was so fucking sexy.* She longed to get closer still, to slide her hands under his shirt, touch his golden-brown skin, kiss those lips . . . She shook her head, trying to get a grip. 'I don't know, this whole thing just seems so corny to me.'

'So, you don't buy into the whole fairy-tale romance between me and Belle?' He asked mockingly.

'I don't know,' she replied, staring back at him. 'Should I?'

'For practical reasons, yes, you should.' He paused and reached out to brush back a lock of hair that had fallen on to her face, and Crystal felt a spark of desire at his touch. 'I don't know what Belle got up to with Dallas, probably nothing, but I'm doing this for Lost Angels. If I don't, you'll be screwed, the public will hate you and I want you to do well. But I'm doing it for me as well. I've got a proposition – I'd like to manage the group. I've got some great contacts. You're the really talented one, Crystal, and I think we'd make a good team. If you go with Dallas you know he'll end up ripping you off; his kind always do. And just how long do you think he'll be interested in you? It'll last a few months, you'll churn out the album and then he'll forget all about you and be on to the next reality show winner. Whereas I would be with you one hundred per cent. What do you think?'

For a moment Crystal was lost for words, trying to figure out her feelings – was Max interested in *her* or just the group, and did he have true feelings for Belle? Then she spoke. 'It's an interesting thought, Max. I'd need to talk to the others and I'd need to know what you could offer us.'

'I think I could take you all the way, Crystal,' Max replied, staring into her eyes, and Crystal found herself thinking *God yes*. Then Belle called him and the spell was broken. 'Just think about it,' he said to her as he turned to go.

*

The story about Dallas's alleged special relationship with Belle came out the next day and was front-page news in one of the more downmarket tabloids. Crystal had got up at six, dressed in her gym kit and run to the newsagents in the nearby village to buy the paper – she'd hardly slept the night before worrying about what it was going to say. The article was short on facts and big on rumour; its only source an anonymous contestant who claimed that Dallas and Belle had been spending a lot of time together *alone*, and that Dallas was therefore bound to favour Lost Angels. The paper had used one of the girls' early publicity shots and Crystal felt horribly pessimistic as she looked at their smiling, hopeful faces. Was this going to be the end of them? Before they'd even had a chance to prove themselves? But by the time she had walked back to the mansion, anger and determination had taken over. She was not going to let this defeat her.

Belle went mad when Crystal showed her the paper, throwing it across the room and shouting that it was all 'bollocks'. But just as Crystal couldn't read Dallas, so she couldn't tell if Belle was lying or not. However, she knew that worrying about it would get them nowhere. So after letting Belle moan about the unfairness of it all for half an hour and listening to Tahlia worry, Crystal insisted that they put it behind them and get back to rehearsing. And for the next two days she was the one who held them together, made them continue rehearsing long into the night when they were all knackered, and told them to ignore the other acts who continued to give them the cold shoulder. It was so ironic, she thought, that the song which Dallas had given them to perform was Destiny's Child's 'Survivor'.

'We've got to be perfect,' she insisted when Belle complained. 'Anything less and we just won't get through, you heard what Dallas said.'

Crystal woke at six on Friday and couldn't get back to sleep. Today would decide their whole future. She lay in bed willing herself to be strong, trying to push everything out of her head except the performance later that day. Max had texted her the night before, wishing her luck and suggesting they meet the following week to discuss his proposal. As usual the prospect of meeting him sent her emotions into free fall. At eight all the contestants had to assemble in the dining room where they would be given the instructions for the day. They were expecting to perform in one of the mansion's vast rooms but Dallas, being Dallas, had a little surprise for them. 'In half an hour you'll be getting on a coach to London. You're going to perform your song on stage at Earl's Court with a full orchestra. Each group will have an hour to rehearse. Then at two it will be the real thing and I'll be deciding which four groups will be going on to the next round of the competition and which will be going home.'

Crystal looked at Tahlia and Belle – they all looked shocked at the prospect.

'I expect *you* knew that already,' one of the other contestants said snidely to them as they left the room.

'Fuck off, of course we didn't,' Belle snapped back.

'Yeah, right,' the girl answered, shooting Belle a filthy look. Belle was about to answer back but Crystal grabbed her arm and whispered, 'Just leave it, Belle.'

They arrived at Earl's Court at midday. Crystal walked into the vast auditorium, feeling completely overwhelmed. Lost Angels had never performed at such a venue, nor had they ever been backed by an orchestra. True, none of the other bands had either but then Lost Angels were under pressure to be nothing less than the best. They didn't perform very well during the rehearsal. Belle forgot her words, Tahlia came in too early and Crystal failed to hit a note, something that had never been a problem before.

'It can't end here!' Crystal said as they sat in the dressing room, trying to stop them all feeling pessimistic and downhearted about their chances. 'We've worked so hard to get here. I know the rehearsal didn't go well, but we're better than the other acts. Let's just go through the song one more time.'

Lost Angels were the last act on stage. Crystal walked on with a lot more confidence than she felt. The lights were shining directly on them so she couldn't see anyone in the auditorium, but she knew Dallas was there, joined by his two singing coaches Kathy and Frank. Then the music started up. *This was it.* As Crystal began singing, the nerves suddenly left her. She could do this; she was a good singer and so were the others – they deserved to go through. It seemed that Tahlia and Belle felt the same way and this time they gave as close to a perfect performance as Crystal thought was possible. Surely it had been enough to secure their place? At the end Dallas simply said, 'Wait on the stage, girls, the other acts will be joining you and I'll be telling you who's in and who's out.'

The other acts walked on in silence – everyone was too apprehensive to speak. *Please let us get through*, Crystal found herself thinking over and over, digging her fingernails into her palms. She knew the cameras were on her, recording everything for the TV, but she was past caring about looking cool. She wanted this more than she had ever wanted anything and if she didn't get it, she didn't know what she would do. But then her thoughts were interrupted by Dallas's voice: 'I've made my decision and I've decided that—' he reeled off the names of three of the other acts and Lost Angels, Crystal took a sharp intake of breath, waiting to hear their fate – 'will not' – he paused for effect and Crystal thought she would scream with the tension – 'will not be going home. You're all staying with me.'

Crystal didn't hear anything else, as she found herself whooping with delight and hugging Tahlia and Belle. *They'd done it!*

'It's a fucking stitch-up,' one of the contestants whose group hadn't made it said loudly, bringing Crystal brutally back down to earth. 'Come on,' she said to the others, 'let's go to the dressing room.' She wanted to celebrate their success without being watched and without having to hear the snide remarks.

'Well done, girls!' Kathy, their singing coach, walked into the room and hugged them all. 'You were fantastic, by far the best.' She was followed by Dallas who actually smiled at them. 'You were great, well done.' Belle ran over and threw her arms round his neck and hugged him while Crystal and Tahlia stood awkwardly to one side. Then Dallas walked over to them and gave each of them a kiss on the cheek. But just as Crystal was thinking that he wouldn't give them such a hard time now they'd proved themselves, he delivered another of his bombshells.

'Okay, so you're through but I can guarantee it's going to be harder for you. You're going to have to work extra hard so that the public don't think I've favoured you. And you've all got to have whiter than white images – there can't be any more scandal attached to the group. So that means no shagging around, no going out drinking and partying. If there are any skeletons I need to know now so I'm prepared. The press are bound to go digging around. So, Belle, is there anything I need to know?'

Belle shook her head and said confidently, 'No, Dallas, there's nothing.'

'Tahlia?'

Tahlia shook her head and whispered, 'No.'

'And you, Crystal?'

'I have no skeletons,' Crystal replied.

Chapter 3

Temptation

Three months later . . .

'*Please*, Dallas, can't we stop now? We're all knackered!' Crystal was so exhausted she didn't think she could sing another note. Her throat hurt, her eyes were sore and she could feel the beginnings of a spot on her chin and Crystal *never* got spots. She looked pleadingly at Dallas. But as usual he didn't budge. Immediately he was on talk-back through the studio glass in his best sarcastic LA drawl. 'Listen, cupcake, if you want to stand any chance of winning this competition stop whining and concentrate on getting this song right. At the moment it sounds shit.'

'Come on, Crystal,' Tahlia said encouragingly. 'We can do this.'

Belle rolled her eyes at Crystal and muttered, 'Let's get it over with.'

Trust them to toe the line, Crystal thought bitterly; she was always the one who stood up to Dallas and spoke up for the band. They'd made it through to the semi-final but had had to fight for their place all the way through the live shows and consistently outsing the other acts. There had been no more rumours about Belle and Dallas's relationship, but you know what they say about mud sticking . . . and the public didn't like it, nor did the other acts. It had felt like a very lonely three months for the girls, constantly trying to prove themselves.

The music started up in their headphones, Crystal closed her eyes, took a deep breath and for what seemed like the hundredth time that day began singing 'When Will I See You Again?'

This time when they'd finished Dallas actually looked at least a tiny bit pleased. A minor miracle, Crystal thought because he rarely cracked his face. The other mentors – Charlie and Sadie – were pussycats compared to him and didn't seem to work their groups half as hard as Dallas pushed the girls.

'Do that on Saturday night and you'll be in with a chance of a place in the finals. Right, you can get off to the hotel now, but remember the golden rules – no drinking, no partying, no shagging, straight to bed.'

Crystal knew better than to answer back. 'Okay, Dallas,' she said sweetly, thinking longingly of the large glass of white wine she was planning to drink the minute she was in her hotel room. She was just walking out of the door when Dallas called her back.

41

'Oh, I almost forgot, Crystal, we need to record a short film with your mum about you. Can you let Jenny have her number?'

Crystal's face fell. 'Do you have to, Dallas? My brother's going to be in the audience this week with his girlfriend and lots of my mates. Isn't that enough?'

'No, it's not,' Dallas said firmly. 'All the other acts have got family in the audience cheering them on and it will look odd if yours aren't there as well. I know you don't see your dad any more but I want your mum to give an emotional message of support for you, to say how much she loves you blah blah blah and how even though she can't be in the audience she'll be watching you and voting for you.'

Crystal sighed and muttered 'Okay,' hating the thought of her mum being involved. She did not have a good relationship with her mum and didn't want to pretend that she did. Her parents had divorced when she was eight and Luke, her brother, was six. Her dad married a younger woman and had a new baby within a year. And the new wife made it very clear that she didn't want stroppy little Crystal and Luke ruining her new family life. And so gradually the weekend visits to his house stopped until Crystal and Luke weren't seeing their dad at all, something which had devastated Crystal. For years she thought she must have done something wrong to drive him away and her mum was so bitter about the divorce she never tried to understand Crystal's feelings. She focused only on herself and if she loved Crystal and her brother she kept it well hidden. Her dad eventually moved away and lost touch with his children. When Crystal was sixteen her mum announced that she'd met someone else and was moving to Spain with him to open a restaurant. She offered to take Luke but he didn't want to leave his sister behind and she wasn't included in the invitation. Suddenly Crystal found herself responsible for a thirteen-year-old. Her mum left her the flat and sent back a little bit of money each month, but it wasn't enough and Crystal was forced to take on two jobs – one in a supermarket, and one in a bar – to support her brother and herself. It wasn't easy. She and Luke were very close and he tried to help out as much as he could, doing a paper round, learning to cook, instead of hanging out with his mates, but Crystal could have done with someone else to share the responsibility of raising a teenage boy and someone to take care of her.

Never mind a glass of wine, she needed a bottle to get over this news! She trailed after Tahlia and Belle who had already raced out of the studio, desperate to be free after eight hours in there. Outside the chauffeur-driven Mercedes was waiting to take them to the hotel. One thing you couldn't fault Dallas for, Crystal thought, was his generosity. He always made sure that his girls were well looked after. He'd put them up in a five-star hotel and he always provided chauffeur-driven cars to ferry them to and from the studio. Though he warned them not to get too used to the luxury: if they didn't win they'd be straight back to using public transport.

'I thought we did really well today,' Belle said, flicking back her long blonde hair and examining her immaculate French polished nails. 'What do you reckon?'

'Yeah, we weren't too bad,' Tahlia answered. Crystal smiled to herself about her friend. Tahlia was always the cautious one. 'We were shit-hot,' Crystal put in bluntly. 'The best we've been. If we do that on Saturday night we're in with a really good chance.'

'Yeah, but you know how it's worked out before. The women are the ones who vote so the lads are always safe. Plus Sadie doesn't like us,' Tahlia answered.

Crystal sighed. Tahlia was right, for some reason Sadie didn't like the girls. Crystal was convinced that she had taken against them because of the Dallas/Belle rumours, and she had been quoted as saying that she made a point of never having favourites among her acts – a direct dig at Dallas. She also seemed to prefer the good-looking, 'bit of rough' lads who she could mother, or the older singers who, let's face it, were never going to make it. Crystal and the girls had struggled to get where they were. Only Belle had been fortunate enough to come from a comfortable background. But Sadie seemed to think they were overconfident, good-looking girls who had it all and didn't need the public's vote.

'Stop being so negative!' Crystal said in exasperation and asked the driver to put on some music. She didn't want to be sent on a downer now; the session had gone well and there was no point worrying about Sadie.

Back at the hotel Belle said she was going to crash out straightaway.

'D'you want to come to my room, Crystal? We can watch a DVD and get something to eat?' Tahlia asked after they'd said goodnight to Belle.

'Sure, and I'll order some wine.'

'Don't let Dallas find out!' Tahlia said anxiously.

'Don't worry, Tahlia,' Crystal replied, 'I've already got a separate tab running at the hotel for emergency alcohol. Dallas need never know.'

Chilling out with Tahlia was just what Crystal needed. The two girls were so close and Tahlia was one of the few people she felt she could really be herself with and let down her guard. Tahlia had been the one who insisted she change her name. Her real name was Christina. As soon as they formed the group Tahlia was on her case. 'There's already one famous Christina in the pop world and when we make it we don't want there to be any confusion.'

Crystal had laughed at her friend, telling her

that she had a long way to go before she was in Christina Aguilera's league but Tahlia kept on at her and every day came up with yet more suggestions, none of which felt right. But one day when Crystal was working behind the bar, bored out of her mind and longing to be somewhere else, the name Crystal came to her. She had grabbed a pen and written it down on her hand and Crystal was born. Tahlia loved the name, but Belle hadn't been at all happy, saying she didn't think it sounded right. Crystal was sure it was because she worried it might upstage her – Belle loved being the centre of attention, she really didn't like sharing the limelight with anyone else.

When Belle was with them, Crystal never felt quite as relaxed – the way she had behaved with Dallas had increased the distance between them and of course there was Max . . . Over the last three months Crystal had done her best to resist him, however much he came on to her. She was always cool with him and she'd even gone out on a couple of dates with other men, desperate to break the hold he had over her. True, she wasn't that close to Belle but they were still supposed to be friends and while they might not always see eye to eye she didn't want to hurt her. After all, there was the unwritten rule that you didn't shag your friend's boyfriend . . . The trouble was, Max was getting to her, wearing down her defences.

Recently she'd bumped into him when she was

shopping in Covent Garden and he'd insisted they have a drink together to discuss business. When she refused to go to his club he suggested a nearby pub. It was Friday afternoon and already packed, but if she thought that would make their meeting less intimate she was wrong as she and Max had to stand dangerously close together.

'Why have you been avoiding me, Crystal?' he demanded, gazing at her, making her feel as if he could read her mind, that he could sense the desire that pumped through her body like a drug, and left her feeling reckless.

'I haven't.' She tried to act dismissive and ignore the battle raging inside her.

He smiled at her, his sexy, big bad, very good-looking wolf smile, that said he didn't believe her for a second.

'Well, I've got some news. I've been talking to several labels and there's definitely interest in you.'

So this is just about business, Crystal thought, disappointed.

'Great,' she replied, not very enthusiastically.

'And my other news is more personal.'

Christ please don't let him say that he's moving in with Belle.

'You probably know that Belle and me haven't been getting on so well lately – bit of a rough patch.'

Crystal shook her head. She hadn't known.

'I just wondered if you knew anyone who might be interested in that information?'

Crystal's body screamed yes but her head tried to take control and to avoid answering she took a sip of her drink. *Play it cool*, she told herself, even though she felt on fire. *Of course she was interested! If Max was going to be single soon that put a whole different perspective on things*. Max moved still closer to her, ducking his head down to her face, so his skin grazed hers as he whispered, 'I was hoping *you* would be.'

Crystal stared at him and knew she didn't need to answer. Her eyes said it all. Max smiled, 'Anyway, back to business. I know if I manage you I can get you a really great deal – much better than any that Dallas is going to come up with.'

Crystal struggled with the change of subject. She couldn't concentrate.

'Okay, but Dallas mustn't find out yet that you want to manage us.'

'And that you want me to manage the group,' Max prompted.

'Yeah,' Crystal answered, not really thinking about what she was saying – she was too busy thinking about the prospect of Max being single . . .

'I thought Belle sang better today,' Tahlia said, dragging Crystal back to the present.

Crystal agreed. 'But,' Tahlia continued, 'I'm getting so sick of the way she sucks up to Dallas.'

'Yeah, but I often think I should suck up to him,' Crystal said.

Tahlia laughed. 'Crystal, I can't imagine you

sucking up to anyone, least of all Dallas. And anyway, if you started now he'd only think you were taking the piss. You're way too honest for that kind of bullshit.'

Not that honest, thought Crystal. She longed to confide in Tahlia about her feelings for Max but knew her friend wouldn't approve one little bit.

The girls stayed up till eleven watching *Mr and Mrs Smith*. Crystal was too preoccupied with thoughts of Max to really pay attention to the film. She wondered what he was doing, who he was with, wondered if he was thinking about her. After the film and several glasses of wine she wandered back to her room. She was just falling asleep when her phone beeped. She had a text. Sleepily she reached for her mobile, thinking it might be from her brother. It was from Max. Suddenly she was wide awake.

Hi Gorgeous, can u come over 2morrow nite? I need to talk. Max x

Crystal bit her lip as she agonised about what to do. *It was probably about business; maybe he had news about one of the deals.* The trouble was that in her heart she didn't want it to be just about business.

She was about to text back yes, when she decided to call him instead. That way, she wouldn't have to see him; she could steer clear of temptation. But when she rang him Max insisted that he did need to see her. 'Listen, Crystal, it's not something I can talk about now, I really need to see you, please meet me.'

Just hearing his sexy voice weakened her resolve and she found herself agreeing. After that it took her ages to get back to sleep and when she did she had the recurrent nightmare about her dad walking out on her. She could never remember exactly what happened in the dream when she woke up, she just knew that she was waiting for her dad to come and pick her up for the weekend and he never came. Then she'd be searching for him on a busy street, with people pushing past her, ignoring the lost little girl. And she was left thinking that she'd done something wrong to drive her dad away.

She felt like the bad dream was hanging over her for the rest of the morning. She wished she could talk to Tahlia about it – telling her friend always helped the nightmare go away – but they were meeting Jessica, the stylist, to go through their outfits for Saturday night's show and there was no opportunity to talk in private.

'So what have you got for us Jessica?' Belle demanded, examining her nails. (Belle was obsessed with every bit of her appearance: her hair, skin, weight and, of course, her nails. Her personal grooming regime included weekly manicures, pedicures, blow dries and fortnightly facials and spray tans.) 'Hope it's better than last week's. My tits nearly popped out of the top.'

'That's because you insisted on wearing one that was a size too small,' Crystal put in bluntly. She was coming to hate the way Belle spoke to people she thought she was superior to – stylists, make-up artists, hairdressers, waiters, shop assistants, Belle treated them all as her servants, and it wasn't pleasant to be around. Crystal tried to keep Belle in her place, taking the piss out of her and telling her that she was turning into a proper diva, that soon she'd be demanding she bathed only in mineral water and could only eat food prepared by her personal chef. But Belle had no sense of irony.

'Don't talk crap. Why would I want to have a bath in mineral water? You know I only ever use Space NK bath oil.'

Now Belle turned on Crystal. 'Fuck off, I'm a size six.'

Crystal sighed. She couldn't be bothered arguing with Belle, who was definitely a size eight. Jessica was busy getting out various outfits and holding them up. This week she wanted the girls to wear fifties-style dresses and both Tahlia and Crystal were more than happy to go along with her ideas. As far as Crystal was concerned Jessica was a really good stylist who knew her stuff and she trusted her. As Crystal always wore black she chose a black satin dress, with a corset top that nipped in at the waist and had a full skirt with several layers of black tulle petticoats. Tahlia went for a similar design in green, which left Belle a choice of a red or pink dress.

'The red would look great on you,' Jessica said, holding the dress against Belle. But Belle pushed the dress away petulantly.

'The material's so cheap, it looks really tacky.'

'Actually it's from a really chic boutique, and it *is* a designer label, just not one that you've heard of, Belle,' said Jessica trying to stay calm.

'Yeah, I don't know if you're aware, Belle,' Crystal said sarcastically, 'but we haven't made it yet and we haven't got designers queuing up to dress us. Maybe if and when we do Dolce & Gabbana and Roberto Cavalli will be begging us to wear their designs. Until then I think we should go with what Jessica's got for us.'

Belle glared at her, while Jessica tried her luck with the pink dress.

'Beyond vile!' Belle exclaimed. 'I hate both of them.'

'Come off it, Belle, stop being such a bitch. Both of those dresses will look really good on you.' Crystal was really pissed off. This was wasting valuable rehearsal time. But Belle had got out her mobile and was calling Dallas: 'I need to see you urgently, there's a major problem with our outfits.'

Her call over, she turned round and said smugly, 'Dallas is coming by in twenty minutes. While we wait, will you get me a skinny decaf latte, Jessica?'

Jessica was about to say yes, when Crystal said, 'No, she bloody well can't. Get your own coffee.'

Belle tutted and without offering to buy anybody else a drink she flounced out of the room. Jessica was obviously trying not to show how upset she was as she asked Crystal and Tahlia to try on their dresses so she could see if they needed altering.

'Don't let her get to you,' Crystal said warmly, putting her arm round Jessica. 'She can be a complete bitch.'

'I just don't want Dallas to get involved,' Jessica said anxiously. 'He'll probably end up firing me.'

'No, he won't,' Crystal said. 'You know his bark is worse than his bite. It's all an act, he so loves playing the tough guy on the show that he thinks he has to do it in real life, but he doesn't mean it really.' Unfortunately Dallas was obviously having a bad day because when he turned up he took one look at the dresses and laid into Jessica: 'No way can Belle wear these. I don't know what you were thinking. They look way too cheap.'

'They look great.' Crystal tried to stand up for Jessica but Dallas cut across her.

'Just stay out of this, Crystal. I wasn't happy with last week's outfits either, Jessica, so I'm giving you one more chance. You've got until the end of the day to come up with a classier outfit for Belle.' And as an afterthought, he muttered, 'And for Tahlia and Crystal as well. If you have to throw money at it, do it. Now if you'll excuse me, I've got a record label to run.' And with that he marched purposefully out of the room.

'Has he been watching too many episodes of *The Apprentice* or what?' Crystal commented, trying to lighten the atmosphere.

Belle smiled sweetly at Jessica. 'Sorry to drop you

in it, Jess, but I really couldn't wear those dresses. I've called one of my favourite boutiques and they're expecting you. I asked them to pull out some things for me and the girls so why don't you come and find us at the studio when you've picked them up?'

'But I really wanted to go with the fifties look,' Jessica said. 'Dallas had approved it as well; I thought it would look really good.'

'I'm sure the boutique will have things that will fit your plan,' Belle said, all sweetness and light now she had her own way.

They spent the rest of the day rehearsing in the studio. Crystal was seething over Belle's treatment of Jessica. It didn't help that when Jessica turned up with the dresses from Belle's boutique Dallas was there and couldn't stop praising Belle for her taste. Jessica had managed to find some fifties-style dresses and, as before, Crystal had the black one, but this time Tahlia had to settle for purple, which wasn't her favourite colour. Belle was over the moon with her gold dress. She held it up against her and spun round the studio, making Crystal long to slap her. Then she remembered what she was doing that night. She was seeing Max. When it came down to it she was no better than Belle – Belle just wanted her own way over a dress whereas Crystal wanted her own way with someone who was not hers . . . With just a few hours to go the butterflies were starting up inside her. The last time she'd met Max she was sure he'd been about to kiss her. And if she was honest, she wanted him to kiss her, wanted him to do so much more to her . . .

Dallas's voice cut through her fantasy. 'Before you go tonight, girls, I want you to take a look at the contract I've drawn up.' He handed them each a copy of the document. 'It's very straightforward. I just need you all to sign it and then we can start thinking about your album. If I am going to manage you then we need to get this signed and sealed now.'

Belle and Tahlia picked up their pens and were about to sign without even checking the paperwork, but Crystal held up her hand. 'Hang on a minute, Dallas, we really need to go through this properly.'

Dallas tutted. 'It's just a formality, Crystal, there's nothing in it that we haven't talked about already.'

But when Crystal started reading through the contract, it was anything but straightforward and the terms sucked. As far as she could tell, picking her way through the convoluted phrasing, the girls would barely get any royalties from their records, and even if they wrote their own songs they wouldn't own the copyright; if they got any advertising deals, gave any PAs and went on tour, the lion's share of the money would go to Dallas. He would own them lock, stock and barrel. He leaned over Crystal, waiting for her to finish reading, and when he saw that she had, he held out his

Montblanc pen, clearly expecting her to sign on the dotted line there and then.

She shook her head. 'We can't sign this, Dallas, the terms aren't good enough. If we do well in the competition we need a better deal than this.'

'And that's why this deal is so great; I'm offering you the chance to make an album even if you don't win,' Dallas said smoothly.

'This is a really good deal,' Belle said sharply. 'We should sign.'

'Well, I want much better terms, just because we are starting out doesn't mean we have to take the short straw. We want a much larger share of the royalties and we have to own the copyright of our own material,' Crystal said determinedly.

'Are you sure about this?' Tahlia asked anxiously. And Dallas smiled, obviously thinking that with two against one the deal was in the bag.

'I'm sure,' Crystal said.

'Okay, I agree with Crystal,' Tahlia said, handing the contract back to Dallas, unsigned.

Dallas laughed mockingly, but he looked furious. 'You're making a big mistake. If you don't win, you'll have nothing. But that's your choice. I'm not prepared to alter the terms now. I'll review it if you win but you know that's a big *if*.' And with that he left the studio.

'Christ, I hope you haven't fucked it up for us, *Christina*,' Belle said crossly. She always called her by her real name when she was annoyed with her.

'You heard what Dallas said, I don't want to end up with nothing after all this.'

'Dallas isn't the only person who wants to manage us. You know that Max wants to as well. In fact,' Crystal took a deep breath and tried to keep her voice steady, 'he wants to see me tonight to go through some of the deals he's been working on. D'you want to come too?'

'No chance!' Belle exclaimed, 'I'm knackered, and I've got a massage booked. You go and see what he's got lined up. And remind him he's taking me out on Saturday. I want to go somewhere lush.'

See, Crystal told herself as she got dressed after her shower later that night, *Belle knows I'm seeing Max. It's all above board, and it's just business.* But she spent longer than usual deciding what to wear, trying on several different outfits before finally settling for tight black jeans, a black vest, a short black jacket and the black patent-leather Christian Louboutin Yo yo slingbacks that she'd saved up for months to buy. She hoped that she looked sexy, but not as if she was trying too hard. While she was putting on an extra layer of mascara Tahlia wandered in to her room.

'Are you sure you don't want to come too?' Crystal asked, praying that she didn't.

'I'm way too tired,' Tahlia said, yawning. 'And, anyway, you're much better at the business side than me and Belle.' She paused, then went on, 'But do you seriously think that Max could be a manager? He hasn't exactly got Dallas's experience, has he?'

'No,' Crystal agreed reluctantly, 'but he might be able to get us a better deal than Dallas. I think we should keep our options open.'

'You know best, babe,' Tahlia answered.

'Okay then.' Crystal took one last look in the mirror; her heart racing wildly at the prospect of being alone again with Max.

'How come you still look good even though you're knackered?' Tahlia demanded. Crystal shook her head. For someone so beautiful, she wasn't at all vain. And so when she looked in the mirror she didn't see what everyone else saw – didn't see that she was jaw-droppingly beautiful, a one-off. Her beauty was exotic, striking, she definitely wasn't a pretty, pretty girl. Her grandmother was Spanish and Crystal had inherited her flawless olive skin and jet-black hair. She had incredible cheekbones, sensuous lips and huge green eyes, fringed with thick black lashes. Her long silky black hair fell halfway down her back. She was still brown from the summer and hardly needed any make-up.

Crystal laughed dismissively. 'Can't you see that spot on my chin? I look rough.'

'Hmm,' said Tahlia. 'If that's rough, God help the rest of us.'

'Don't wait up,' Crystal said, heading for the door.

'And if Dallas calls, I'm in bed with a migraine.'

There was already a queue outside Max's. Crystal walked to the front and spoke to the doorman: 'Max is expecting me, tell him it's Crystal.' And all the while her heart was racing. A phone call later she was in and walking towards the bar in the VIP area where she knew Max would be. 'Hey, Crystal!' Max had seen her. Immediately he walked over and kissed her on each cheek.

'So glad you could make it,' he murmured, his hand lightly touching the small of her back. 'I'll get us some champagne. We need to celebrate.'

'What are we celebrating?' Crystal dared herself to ask.

Max couldn't keep the naughty little glint out of his gorgeous brown eyes. 'Oh, I don't know, we just are.'

A few minutes later they were sitting at one of the private tables, screened off from the rest of the club, and Crystal was doing her very best not to stare at Max. God, she wanted him so much. It just wasn't fair. Why had Belle met him first? *He's much more my type*, she thought wistfully, loving his unpredictable, slightly dangerous edge and, if she was honest, she couldn't help being attracted to him because she knew he was a bit of a bastard.

'You said you needed to talk to me. Is it about one of the deals?' Crystal asked, trying to cover up the surge of attraction and adrenaline he always provoked in her.

He nodded. 'All in good time; how have the rehearsals been going?'

Crystal shrugged. 'Well, I think. The others are being pessimistic but I reckon we've got a chance.'

'There's definitely interest in you out there. I've had another meeting with one of the labels. I'm just waiting for the paperwork to be drawn up.'

'We'll need to go through it together,' Crystal said quickly. Infatuated as she had become with Max, she knew she couldn't trust anybody in the business she was in. The group had worked so hard to get where they were and she wasn't about to let anyone take that away from them.

Max lit a cigarette. 'You're right to be cautious, babe, but you know I'd never rip you off.'

Crystal covered her face with her hands and groaned. 'Max, you're smoking in front of me, and you promised you wouldn't.' She'd finally given up a month ago, at Dallas's insistence and she was finding it extremely difficult, regardless of how many nicotine patches she used and how much gum she went through.

Max gave her one of his sexy smiles, blew a perfect smoke ring at her face, then held out the cigarette. 'One little puff won't hurt, will it? I won't tell if you won't.'

For a few seconds Crystal hesitated, then reached out for the cigarette, took a deep drag, immediately getting the nicotine hit that she'd been missing. 'Oh my God, you're such a bastard!'

'And that's exactly why you like me, isn't it?' Max said quietly, staring directly at her, his brown eyes serious for a change.

She quickly looked away, half loving what was happening, half knowing it was wrong. Max was off limits, she should leave. Right now.

'I only put up with you because of Belle.' She tried to sound as if she believed what she was saying, but she knew she lacked conviction. Max gave her that sexy smile again that turned her willpower to dust: 'Okay, Crystal, we can play this game if you want, or you can admit that you like me as much as I like you.'

Crystal looked down. *This was definitely the moment to leave.* But still she couldn't. 'You're the one who's going out with someone.' She couldn't bring herself to say Belle's name.

'Shall I tell you why I like you, then?' Max asked softly.

Now Max had Crystal's full attention. She raised her face and he was looking at her, definitely not in the way you were supposed to look at your girlfriend's friend.

'I like you for your eyes, they know more than you let on; for your smile; for your ambition; for being the sexiest woman I've ever met; for your mouth.' Max reached over and gently traced the outline of Crystal's lips. She closed her eyes, willing herself to be strong but it was a battle she was losing fast. She couldn't resist him any more, couldn't stop herself, didn't want to stop herself. She kissed his finger and then he was kissing her and she was kissing him back. No kiss had ever felt so good, so sweet . . . Crystal forgot everything but the feel of his lips, the taste of him. She closed her eyes again, but Max was pulling away, whispering, 'Let's go upstairs.'

He stood up and held out his hand. Crystal hesitated, torn between desire and guilt. She knew that upstairs meant Max's office, where he sometimes stayed the night. She knew there was a bed . . . Somehow she managed to blurt out, 'No, I can't.' And before Max even had a chance to try and stop her, she got up and ran for the door, pushing her way through the clubbers and out into the cold November air.

Chapter 4

Guilty

'Christina, get up! You've only got ten minutes before the car picks us up.' Belle was standing by the side of Crystal's bed looking extremely pissed off. 'Dallas will go ape if we're late.'

Groaning, Crystal sat up. She picked up her watch. Eight o'clock. 'Okay, okay,' she muttered, hardly able to look Belle in the face. She was the very last person she wanted to see this morning.

Belle walked over to the door. She looked pretty and fresh in her tight white cashmere cardigan and denim mini, her long blonde hair pulled back into a sleek ponytail. 'And don't think I don't know what you did last night,' she called out as she opened the door.

Crystal's stomach lurched, *Oh my God, how could she know?*

'You were smoking!' Belle called out. 'I can smell it. For God's sake, Crystal, you promised you'd given up.'

Crystal collapsed back on the bed, feeling a mixture of guilt and relief. 'I know Belle, I'm a bad person.'

Belle laughed. 'You've got no willpower, just like Max. Now get your arse into the shower and put some slap on, you look like shit. What did he have to say, by the way?'

'Oh, er, it's still a bit vague; he's hoping for some news in a couple of days,' Crystal lied, hating herself for doing it.

Dallas had meetings all morning so, to Crystal's relief, it was just Kathy, their singing coach, rehearsing with them. The girls adored her; she was laid back and had been in the business for years and never worked them quite as hard as Dallas, who often left them feeling on edge and stressed. Crystal tried to push what had happened the night before out of her head and concentrate on her singing. But she couldn't stop the images flooding back, the feel of Max's lips on hers, his body against hers . . . *It can't ever happen again. Ever.* She told herself sternly. But when she checked her phone during a break there was a text from Max asking her to meet him again that night, which triggered the all-too-familiar feeling of desire. She wanted to text back no, to tell him to leave her alone. Instead she ignored the text and turned her phone off.

Don't fuck up, she urged herself. Winning the competition could change her life and she couldn't allow herself to be distracted like this. For as long as she could remember all she had ever wanted to be was a singer. Singing had always been her escape. When she sang she was at her happiest; she knew she was doing something she was good at. She could block out the pain of her dad leaving her, her mother's lack of interest, the responsibility of looking after her brother, and lose herself in the music. It made her feel alive like nothing else ever had and she loved every minute in front of the mic. People like Belle wanted to win the competition because they longed to be famous and to live the life of a celebrity, to be photographed in the celeb mags, to go the parties, to hang out with other celebs. But to Crystal winning the competition wasn't about fame; it was about being a singer.

After their singing rehearsal came a three-hour session with dance instructor Tash. She was petite and ravishingly pretty but as tough as old boots and pushed them to nail their dance routines spot on. Luckily they were all good movers, though Crystal knew she was the weakest and Belle was the best dancer – a fact which she was frequently fond of pointing out. By five, Crystal was flagging, the lack of sleep was catching up with her and she kept making mistakes.

'Come on, Crystal!' Tash shouted, 'You've got two left feet at the moment. Get with the pro-gramme, or I'll be telling Dallas.'

Crystal immediately pulled herself together and

mentally shook off her tiredness. A bollocking from Dallas wasn't something she could handle right now on top of everything else on her mind.

'Do you want me to show you the moves again?' Belle said in her most patronising voice, and Crystal had to grit her teeth to stop herself from telling her where to go.

After dance it was straight back to the hotel to be interviewed for the TV show. She was dying to check her messages to see if Max had called again, but couldn't risk doing it in front of Belle. Crystal dreaded these interviews more than the live show itself. Having a camera stuck in her face made Tahlia even sweeter than she usually was, Belle came across as bubbly and fun, but it had the opposite effect on Crystal and she worried that she came across as a right hard bitch. Belle had agreed to do most of the talking and Crystal did her very best to sound sweet and humble, when really she was thinking, *vote for us, we're the bollocks!*

'So how's this week been for you girls?' asked Hadley, the very attractive black co-presenter of *Band Ambition*. Crystal and Belle were convinced he fancied Tahlia, but she wouldn't have any of it.

'It's been great, Hadley,' answered Belle, as Crystal worked on her sweet look.

'It was a tough one last week when you and Trick or Treat were in the final two and had to sing your songs again, wasn't it?'

66

'Yeah, thanks for reminding us,' Crystal couldn't stop herself blurting out.

'It was hard,' Tahlia added, 'and we felt really sorry for the guys going out.'

Like fuck we did, thought Crystal, doing her best to look sympathetic.

'Crystal, do you think you are ready for this week's performance?' Hadley pointed the mic at her.

'We've been working our arses off and the song's sounding shit-hot.'

Hadley frowned. 'Crystal, I did ask you not to swear if possible; this programme goes out before nine. Can we have the same question again?'

Crystal tried not to giggle; he took himself so seriously. He was very good-looking, but not in a raunchy get-your-kit-off, let's-have-sex-against-the-wall-now kind of way. He was more like a clean-cut member of a boy band – definitely not Crystal's type.

'Sorry, Hadley. We've been working really hard and we're really hoping that everyone's going to like the song. We've put everything we've got into it.'

Hadley seemed happy with that and the cameras stopped filming. As the girls were filing out of the room, Hadley walked over to Tahlia. Looking a little awkward, he asked, 'Um, Tahlia, I was wondering if you fancied going out for a drink sometime?'

67

'Okay,' Tahlia said shyly. 'But would it be okay if we waited until after the competition?'

Belle and Crystal gave each other meaningful looks and walked out of the room, giving Tahlia and Hadley the chance to swap numbers.

'Lucky Tahlia,' Belle said outside. 'He's fit.'

'What are you up to now?' Crystal asked, longing to get to her hotel room to check her mobile.

'Oh, I'm meeting Mum and Dad for dinner. What about you?'

'Having an early night,' Crystal replied forcing a yawn. 'See you in the morning.'

She was just opening the door to her hotel room when Tahlia walked along the corridor with a huge smile on her face.

'Well?' Crystal asked, raising her eyebrows.

'What do you think of him?' Tahlia asked.

'He's very sweet; you should definitely go out with him. Do you want to come in and talk?' she asked, praying the answer would be no as she thought she might explode if she couldn't check her messages.

'Thanks, but I'm going to babysit for Mum,' Tahlia answered.

Tahlia was always babysitting her little sister and Crystal had given up telling her that her mum should bloody well find her own babysitter. Tahlia had enough on her plate with the competition.

'Okay, see you in the morning then.'

Finally Crystal was alone. She reached for her

phone. There were five texts from Max and ten voice mails. The first message simply said, 'Crystal, please call me. I need to talk to you. You know why.' And the following were all variations of that until the last: 'Crystal, I haven't been able to stop thinking about you, about that kiss. Babe, please, I never beg, but I'm begging you now. I've got to see you.'

Crystal played the final message several times, agonising about what to do, but each time she heard Max's voice, her resolve to ignore him weakened until she knew she would have to speak to him.

'I can't see you Max,' she said, her voice sounding more certain than she felt.

'*Please*, Crystal, I've got to see you, babe,' he replied passionately.

Crystal took a deep breath. 'I can't. You're with Belle.'

There was a pause and Max said, 'So if I wasn't with Belle you'd see me?'

Crystal hesitated, 'Yes. No. I don't know! ' She felt so torn, she wanted Max so badly but she didn't want to hurt Belle.

'We can't do this over the phone; please come to the club. We'll talk, that's all.'

An hour later Crystal was sitting at one of the private tables next to Max, smoking (her willpower had totally crumbled) and sipping her drink, trying hard to play it cool.

'You know I can't finish with Belle until after the competition. I don't want to do anything to jeopardise the group's chances, but as soon as it's over I will. I want to be with *you*, Crystal,' Max said urgently. 'I want you, Crystal, I've wanted you since the first time I saw you.' He reached over and took her hand, 'We could be so good together, I know we could.'

Hearing the words that she'd been dying to hear Max say for so long Crystal felt something inside her give. She looked at him. 'So after the competition, you promise?'

He nodded, and Crystal continued, 'And you won't tell her it's because of me? I don't want to hurt her.'

'I won't, babe, I promise', and he put his arms round Crystal and pulled her to him, kissing her deeply.

'No running away,' he murmured. As Crystal lost herself in the kiss, she had never felt less like running away. And this time when Max suggested they went upstairs, she didn't resist.

She held his hand and the two of them walked quickly through the bar and up the private staircase. Max had brought the bottle of champagne with him and as soon as they were in the room he poured them each a glass and locked the door. They both drained their glasses, unable to take their eyes off each other in anticipation. They were suddenly in each other's arms, kissing. He was running his hands over her body, unbuttoning her jacket and letting it slip to the floor, caressing her breasts, kissing them as he led her to the bed, taking off her jeans,

'No underwear, Crystal, you are a naughty girl.' He pulled off his T-shirt, revealing his toned chest and his perfect tanned skin. She unbuttoned his jeans and slipped them off. Max was pinning Crystal to the bed, kissing her all over, caressing her with his tongue, sending shivers of pleasure through her. She kissed him, moving down his body, slipping off his black Hugo Boss boxer shorts, teasing him with her mouth. And then they were fucking, and Crystal wasn't thinking about anything else except how good it felt, how it felt the best ever. And when she came she cried because it had been *so* good and because she knew that she should have waited.

She closed her eyes, not wanting Max to see the tears, but he already had and was kissing them gently away. 'Oh Crystal, what have you done to me?'

The next morning when she woke up she couldn't help but feel guilty even though Max had told her that he was going to finish with Belle. What if Belle really loved him? Then it would destroy her if he split up with her. It was, admittedly, hard to tell what Belle thought of Max – she definitely seemed to enjoy the glamour of their relationship, going

71

out with a famous ex-racing driver, hanging out in all the hip clubs, being taken out to expensive restaurants. But, then, it hadn't stopped her flirting with Dallas and doing God knows what else . . . Crystal tried to remember if she'd ever actually heard Belle say that she loved Max. She never had, had she?

She spent the rest of the day in a loved-up haze. Last night had been the most intense sex of her life and she couldn't stop thinking about Max even though she knew she should have been putting 100 per cent into her work. Everyone noticed she was distracted and she got several ear bashings from Dallas.

'Sorry,' she told him, after a particularly weak performance, 'I guess it's nerves.'

Dallas looked disgusted: he despised it if his performers showed any kind of weakness.

'If you're nervous now, what the fuck are you going to feel like on Saturday? Get a grip, Crystal; I don't have any time for losers.'

Crystal tried her best to pull herself together for the remainder of the rehearsal and by the end of the day she had managed to get out of Dallas's bad books. When she checked her phone at the end of the session Max had texted her, asking her to go over. Crystal didn't hesitate this time in saying yes. When Belle and Tahlia asked her what she was doing, she lied, saying she was meeting one of her friends in town for a quick drink.

This time when she arrived at the club she went straight to the back door. She felt breathless with desire, anticipation and guilt. She rang the bell and a few minutes later Max opened the door.

'Hey, gorgeous,' he said as he pulled her towards him by her jacket and kissed her.

Crystal wriggled away from him, trying to shut the door, paranoid that they would be seen, but Max just laughed. 'There's no one outside, babe.'

Upstairs in his office was a rerun of the night before. Champagne, kisses, feverishly pulling off each other's clothes and tumbling on to the bed. The sex was even better now they knew a little about each other's bodies. Crystal loved what he was doing to her with his hands, with his tongue, but she liked it best when they were fucking, when it felt like he was part of her, when she could pretend that he belonged to her . . .

Afterwards she demanded, 'Give me a cigarette then.'

Smiling, he lit a cigarette and passed it to her.

'That was amazing, babe,' he whispered stroking her hair. '*You're* amazing.'

Crystal enjoyed the compliment for a moment, then asked the question that wouldn't go away, even after the mind-blowing sex.

'Have you worked out what you're going to say to Belle yet?'

Max frowned. 'I don't know, I guess I'll say that

73

we were drifting apart, that I need my own space, that kind of bollocks.'

That wasn't good enough for Crystal. 'Do you love her?' she found herself asking.

Max looked annoyed. 'Do we have to talk about Belle? Do you think I'd be with you, if I loved her?'

'But do you think she loves you?' Crystal persisted.

Instead of answering he took his cigarette and hers and placed them in the ashtray; he pulled her back down beside him and kissed her. She kissed him back, hoping the kiss would block out the questions in her head. Max broke away first and reached once more for his cigarette. 'Don't look so worried, babe, we'll be okay. You've just got to be patient.'

Crystal felt a surge of anxiety and guilt run through her. She lay down, her head on his shoulder, Max lightly caressing her back. *Would it really work out okay? Would she and Max be together?*

'Anyway, I almost forgot. I bought you something today.' He reached under the pillow and pulled out a small velvet box and handed it to Crystal. She opened it to discover a diamond stud.

'It's for here,' Max said, caressing her stomach and lightly touching the piercing on her naval. 'Will you wear it from now on? And then every time I see you I can think of you wearing it, think of kissing your sweet skin.'

Crystal smiled and, pulling out the silver skull

and crossbones stud she was wearing, replaced it with the diamond. She lay back on the bed.

'Perfect,' Max said and, reaching for his phone, took a picture of her.

'No way, Max!' Crystal protested, trying to grab the phone from him, but he held it out of reach. Then he gently, teasingly kissed her neck, moved down to her breasts, then her stomach, then further still. And Crystal stopped thinking about the phone, stopped thinking about anything except how Max was making her feel . . .

Chapter 5

Saturday Night

'How are you feeling now?' Crystal gave Tahlia a sympathetic look, as she returned from the bathroom. Even though they'd made it to the semi-finals, Tahlia's pre-stage nerves hadn't got any better. Crystal felt nervous, too, but also excited. She wanted to get out there and prove what they could do.

'A bit better now I've been sick,' Tahlia answered, looking pale and sorry for herself. 'Come back to the dressing room,' Crystal said. 'I'll touch up your make-up.'

'Thanks, Crystal,' Tahlia said gratefully. 'Sorry I always get like this.'

Crystal laughed. 'Don't be daft, it doesn't matter, your singing's always fantastic. I'd think there was something wrong if you weren't throwing up before we went on.'

In the dressing room Belle was glued to the rest of the competition on the TV. They were up against four other groups. The favourites to win were Northern Dreams, a boy band from Manchester led by Tyler, a rough-diamond, good-looking lad, who all the girls fancied. Bijoux was a group of three women, all over thirty, who were great singers but they lacked a certain something. It was probably sex appeal, Crystal thought – you couldn't imagine anyone pinning posters of them on their bedroom walls and lusting after them, they just looked like someone's mum. X & Y were a squeaky-clean group of two boys and two girls who made Bucks Fizz look cutting edge, and who always chose to sing sentimental songs that Crystal couldn't believe would be enough to win it for them. @ttitude was another girl band – they weren't bad singers but they were arrogant, they hated taking any direction and Belle always said that they dressed like hos. They were the girls that they'd had the confrontation with at their very first audition. @ttitude had clearly not forgotten Belle's bitchy comments and they had gone out of their way to be as vile as possible about Lost Angels. @ttitude were quoted often, slagging Lost Angels off, saying they had more talent in their little fingers and they would never make it, hinting that they had only got as far as they had because of Dallas's special relationship with them. Tahlia and Crystal refused to comment when tabloid journalists pestered them for a reply but Belle didn't hold back and called @ttitude a bunch of hard-faced slappers, who looked as if they should be living in a trailer park. The tabloids loved it and had a field day superimposing the four girls' heads on pictures of some fat white trailer-park women. More insults followed from @ttitude and war was well and truly declared.

Tonight each act had to perform two songs – one contemporary and one classic. The Lost Angels were singing the Sugababes' 'Too Lost in You', and The Three Degrees' hit, 'When Will I See You Again?'. They were appearing last which was a good place to be, Crystal assured the others. 'We'll be the ones that the viewers remember.' Northern Dreams had just finished their first song and the audience were screaming their heads off in appreciation. Sexy Tyler had stripped off his shirt to reveal a tight white vest and some pretty impressive pecs which had added to the audience's appreciation.

'They're *so* going to win,' Tahlia said gloomily.

'Don't be so sure,' Crystal answered, 'They were flat and I reckon they're getting too cocky for their own good.'

Dallas was the first judge to comment and as usual he wasn't one to tread softly. 'Tyler, you know I think you're a nice enough guy but that wasn't up to scratch, was it? You were flat in at least five places. I think you're losing it; maybe it's time to go back to your day job.' (Rough-diamond Tyler had worked as a scaffolder, hence the pecs and abs that all the girls, and Sadie, lusted after.)

From beside him their mentor Sadie exploded. 'Absolute rubbish, Dallas! They were all perfect, especially Tyler.' She appealed to the audience, who cheered along with her and booed Dallas. Northern Dreams were her babies and she was fiercely protective of them. Dallas shrugged dismissively and said, 'Letting his pecs influence your judgement, Sadie?'

Sadie was clearly about to let rip, but Tess, the bubbly red-haired presenter, obviously wanted to move things on. She managed to cut across Sadie and ask Charlie for her comments. During the show she was generally the good cop to Dallas's bad and usually never had an unkind word to say about any of the acts unless they were one of Dallas's. She was full of enthusiasm for the boy band: 'Boys, I predict you're all going to be stars.' The boys blew kisses at her and Tyler shot her a very sultry look that made Crystal think that maybe there was something more to their relationship.

'Bollocks!' Belle shouted at the television. 'They're going to be a one-hit wonder!'

Crystal wasn't quite so sure. Good as she knew Lost Angels were, it was going to be hard to get Sadie to admit it and she knew how the audience could be swayed by her opinion. Dallas was a fantastic mentor but the only problem was that he was so outspoken, it often had the effect of turning people against his acts, to spite him. Bijoux were next, delivering a rousing performance of 'It's

Raining Men'. Crystal thought it was fine but there was nothing special about it – it didn't have that star quality the judges were so often talking about. Cringingly flat, X & Y made little impact and then @ttitude took to the stage. It was hard to concentrate on their singing as their outfits were such an eyesore – they'd gone for the ho look again in a big way and, dressed in white, they wore tiny leather-fringed mini skirts, thigh-high boots, bikini tops, cowboy hats and full-length fake fur coats, and all of them dripped with fake bling.

Belle was disgusted. 'Look what the cat dragged in, it's top of the slags.' And then Lost Angels were told they had five minutes to go. The three girls immediately formed a circle and held hands. This ritual had started off as a total piss take of diva performers they'd seen in concert. Each of the girls had come up with their own ridiculous, over-the-top saying which they would declare in an American accent before they went on stage. Crystal's was: *I promise to deliver my best performance tonight, not just for myself but for all the children in the world*; Tahlia would say: *This is my chance to change the world and I will take that chance*; and Belle always finished: *It's not enough to sing the songs, I will feel the songs in my very soul.* But now it had become part of their pre-stage ritual, something that they *had* to do before they performed.

'If we ever make it we have got to stop doing *this*,' Crystal said afterwards, 'otherwise we're going to look like the twats of the century!' Belle managed to smile but Tahlia was tight-lipped with nerves.

Tess announced their names and they walked on stage to thunderous applause and whistles, as their music was starting up. Crystal took a deep breath and cleared her mind of everything but her voice. At the end of the song, she knew that the three of them had given their strongest performance yet. She felt exhilarated. It was one of those times when they all clicked together and it felt and sounded so right. Surely the judges would have heard that? But of course Sadie wasn't going to make it easy for them.

'Yes, girls, that was really good, and I can't fault you on anything. But do you know what? It was just *too perfect* for me. Where was the edge? It confirms what I've always thought of you. It's all been too easy for you and you come across as too slick, too polished. I look at you and I see three beautiful girls who have never had to struggle for anything in their lives and I just don't know if that's what this competition is about.'

Crystal could feel the anger building up inside her. How dare this multimillionaire tell *them* they hadn't had to struggle? What the fuck did she know? She was sick of the way they were being treated in the competition, just because of something that may or may not have happened between Belle and Dallas. It just wasn't fair. She was supposed to wait until every judge had delivered their verdict before she had her say, but she couldn't stop herself from grabbing the microphone from a stunned Tess.

'We might not have worked on building sites, Sadie, but that doesn't mean we haven't struggled. You don't know *anything* about us. Tahlia's dad died when she was three and her mum had to hold down two jobs to support her.' Crystal's voice was shaking with emotion but she didn't care. 'Belle's gran died two months ago but she decided to carry on with the competition because her gran would have wanted it. We've been trying to make it for the last five years and this competition is our last hope. Don't you dare sit there and waste our chances just because you don't like us.'

She looked defiantly at Sadie who was looking slightly less comfortable than usual. Then Tahlia grabbed the mic from Crystal. 'And Crystal's mum left her to bring up her brother on her own when she was only sixteen. We haven't had it easy, we've struggled every inch of the way to get this far.'

The audience erupted. They were up on their feet cheering, whistling and clapping; they loved a confrontation. Sadie tried to speak but couldn't make herself heard over the noise. Tess had taken the mic back from Tahlia and was also trying to make herself heard. Finally, after what seemed like ages, but was probably only a few minutes, the audience calmed down enough for Tess to ask Sadie for her response.

'Well,' she began awkwardly. 'I have to admit that I had the wrong impression about the girls. I take back what I said earlier; they obviously *do* deserve to be here. And their performance tonight was outstanding.'

Crystal felt her spirits lift; *this could make all the difference*. She looked over at Dallas and he winked at her. Charlie was next. 'Girls, what can I say? You were brilliant.' And when everyone had said their piece, Dallas spoke. 'I'm glad the girls got to have their say. They've been professional and hard-working from the start. They could have played for the sympathy vote, but they never have because they and I believe you should stand and fall by the performance you deliver. And tonight, girls, you did yourselves, and me, proud. You were awesome. You deserve to win.'

Crystal and the girls couldn't stop smiling as they went back to the dressing room. 'Oh my God!' Belle squealed. 'Thank God you did that, Crystal, otherwise that would have been it.'

The three of them couldn't believe what had happened and it took several minutes for them to calm down. Crystal tried to bring them back to reality. 'Come on, we've got to focus on performing our next song.' But it was hard. They all felt wired, longing to get back on stage. Luckily their next song, 'When Will I See You Again?', demanded a full-on performance, no holding back from anyone. In rehearsal it had been the one Dallas nagged them about most, saying that they needed to put more emotion into it. After their exchange with Sadie they had emotion in spades. Dallas stood up to applaud their performance. Sadie and Charlie followed his lead. They were definitely not going home that night. It was a playoff between Bijoux and X & Y and Bijoux were voted out.

'Girls, girls, girls!' Dallas exclaimed walking into the green room at the end of the show. 'You were fabulous. I'm taking you out to celebrate.' As soon as they had finished being interviewed by Hadley, Dallas whisked them off to the swish Blue Bar for vintage Cristal and Beluga caviar. He was full of praise for their performance and for Crystal for having the guts to stand up to Sadie. 'I really think that might swing it for you. But you can't be complacent. I'm going to be working you harder than ever this week. You can have tomorrow off but that's it. We're going to be working flat out from nine o'clock Monday.'

'But we're free tonight, aren't we?' Belle asked. Crystal's heart sank. She'd been so fired up by the night that she'd hardly had time to think about Max but now she was reminded that it was going to be Belle who would be in his arms and kissing him, Belle who would be celebrating their good news with Max. Surely he wouldn't have sex with her, would he? Crystal felt a stab of jealousy so sharp that she had to bite her lip to stop herself saying anything. What the hell would she say, though? *Don't go and see Max. I want him more?*

Dallas laughed. 'Yes, Belle, you're free to see Max. Off you go.'

Crystal looked at her retreating figure and wondered about Dallas and Belle. He was so cool about Belle seeing Max. Could there really have been anything going on between them? It was true that Belle was his favourite, but while she flirted with him he never flirted back. Crystal sighed and took a large swig of champagne.

'What about you two then?' Dallas asked, signalling for the bill.

'I'm just going to go back to Mum's. I'm too tired to do anything else,' Tahlia said.

Dallas raised his eyebrows at Crystal. 'I can't imagine *you're* planning on an early night, are you?'

Crystal shrugged. 'I'm knackered as well. I'll probably just go back to the hotel.'

'Well, I've got a party to go to.' Dallas drained his glass and keyed his pin number into the chip and pin machine the waiter had brought over as he stood up. 'So I'll see you all on Monday.' He pulled out a fifty pound note from his wallet. 'Get yourselves a taxi home.'

'Cheers, Dallas,' Crystal and Tahlia answered together.

'And cheer up, Crystal! You were fabulous tonight, you all were,' Dallas said, slinging his tan leather coat over his shoulder and blowing the girls a kiss goodbye.

'Come back to mine if you want, Crystal,' Tahlia said as they made their way out of the hotel. 'Mum and Leticia would love to see you and we can spend Sunday together, if you haven't any other plans. We can stop off at the hotel to grab your things.'

Crystal hesitated, the prospect of going back to the hotel on her own to spend the night obsessing over Max and Belle together was not an inviting one. She thanked Tahlia and agreed.

Tahlia's mum, Rosie, lived off the Archway Road in north London in a three-bedroomed flat that was always spotless. She might not have much money but her floor was clean enough to eat your dinner off, something Crystal always teased her about. As soon as she and Tahlia walked through the front door Rosie and Leticia came running out of the living room, cheering and clapping. They'd wanted to be in the audience watching the show but Leticia had a high temperature and Rosie thought it best to keep her at home. Leticia was seven years old, a beautiful mixed-race little girl, with startling blue eyes and honey-coloured hair. Usually, Crystal didn't particularly like small children but she made an exception for Leticia because she was so sweet and funny. Rosie was blonde-haired and blue-eyed, warm and feisty, and Crystal adored her. She was like a mum to her. She was in her late forties and Leticia had been a bit of an unexpected arrival. The result, Tahlia told

Crystal, of a two-week fling with a Jamaican music promoter she had met at the Notting Hill Carnival. He had promised to keep in touch but when he left London he never made contact again and Rosie didn't have an address or number for him. Tahlia had always tried to help her mum with Leticia as much as she could.

Crystal envied Tahlia's family life; there might not be much money but there was always laughter in the house, and love – something that had been in very short supply in Crystal's background.

'I saw your mum on TV tonight, Crystal,' Rosie said as they all sat down round the kitchen table.

She'd insisted on making the girls scrambled eggs after hearing that they'd only eaten caviar all day.

'Yeah, I saw the film this afternoon. She sounded really false, I thought,' Crystal answered. Dallas had, of course, got his way and they had filmed a piece with her mum in Spain. To Crystal it was obvious that her mum had been told what to say. All about how proud she was of her baby and how she was sure she would do well. When, in reality, her mum had texted her a couple of times in the last three months to say well done for getting through the audition, but apart from that nothing. Her mum's take was that she had a new life in Spain and it was up to Crystal and her brother to get on with theirs. Crystal always tried to make out that her mother's lack of interest didn't hurt, but of course it did.

'She didn't, Crystal!' Rosie exclaimed, but

Crystal knew that she was only trying to spare her feelings. 'I'm sure she's really proud of you.'

'Yeah, right,' Crystal muttered.

'Will she fly back for the final, do you think?'

'I doubt it, Rosie, you know what she's like.'

Rosie sighed. 'I'm sorry, Crystal, I don't understand why she won't. But I'll be there and you might think this sounds really corny but I think of you as my other daughter.'

Crystal felt her eyes unexpectedly filling with tears. Rosie gave her a hug. 'You look exhausted.'

'We've been working flat out,' Crystal replied, which was true, but the real reason was that she had spent the last two nights with Max and she was feeling emotionally and physically shattered.

'Still no man in your life?' Rosie asked. *Great, this was all she needed.*

Crystal shook her head and avoided meeting Rosie's eye.

'I can't believe a beautiful girl like you doesn't have someone.'

'*Mum!*' exclaimed Tahlia.

'Okay, okay,' Rosie said, smiling. 'You don't mind me asking, do you Crystal?'

''Course not,' Crystal managed to reply, 'but it's Tahlia's love life you should be asking about.'

She wouldn't usually have dropped Tahlia in it, but she couldn't bear having to lie to Rosie. Tahlia blushed and was forced to tell her mum about Hadley asking her out.

Rosie was delighted. 'It's about time!' Crystal had to agree. For as long as she'd known her, Tahlia had hardly dated any lads and she'd never had a serious relationship. It was a total mystery to Crystal as Tahlia was a gorgeous girl and she always had plenty of men asking her out.

They spent the rest of the night on much safer territory – analysing their chances of winning the competition and bitching about the other contestants.

At midnight Rosie ordered both girls to bed. Crystal was on her last legs but she didn't want to go to bed. She knew she wouldn't be able to sleep. She looked at her watch, imagining where Belle and Max would be now or, more to the point, what they'd be getting up to.

'I've not been sleeping very well lately. I'll stay up a bit longer,' Crystal replied, but Rosie was having none of it.

'I'll make you a hot chocolate and brandy; that should knock you out. You need to sleep!'

Ten minutes later Crystal was lying in bed convinced that she wouldn't sleep a wink. She picked up her mobile, hoping for a text from Max, knowing that there wouldn't be one. There was nothing. She finished her drink, switched off the light, and lay back. The next thing she knew it was morning.

Chapter 6

Tahlia's Secret

Crystal pulled an old dressing gown of Tahlia's on and, rubbing the sleep from her eyes, wandered into the kitchen where the others were having breakfast and Tahlia was listening to Leticia read. Rosie jumped up out of her seat to pour Crystal a cup of tea and insisted on making her a bowl of porridge.

Crystal pulled a face; she almost never had breakfast. But once Rosie had set her mind to doing something it was almost impossible to stop her, so she gave in. To her surprise when the bowl was placed in front of her, she realised she was starving and she ate the lot.

Rosie looked at her with satisfaction. 'That's better; you've got a bit of colour in your cheeks now, honey.'

'I'm taking Leticia ice-skating if you fancy coming, Crystal,' Tahlia said.

'Sure,' Crystal answered, not wild about the idea

of falling over all day, but wanting to spend a day on her own brooding about Max even less. 'I'll just have a quick shower.'

She had a better day with Tahlia and Leticia than she'd had in a long time. It was great because she was enjoying herself and the enjoyment was guilt-free. They had such a laugh ice-skating and it was lovely being with Leticia who was so innocently excited and enthusiastic about everything they did. After they had all careered round the ice for a couple of hours they were ready for a drink. Crystal could have done with a vodka but knew Tahlia wouldn't take her sister anywhere near a pub so they ended up in a café drinking hot chocolate with marshmallows.

'I wonder what Belle's doing?' Tahlia asked. Crystal pretended to be helping Leticia scoop out her marshmallows to avoid looking at her.

'Probably having lunch somewhere flash, you know what Max is like.'

Tahlia didn't sound impressed. 'Um, what do you think of him, Crystal?'

Bloody hell, she thought. Max was the last person she wanted to talk about.

'I like him. Why? Do you think there's a problem?' *It would be good if Tahlia thought there was something wrong with Belle and Max's relationship. It would let her off the hook a little bit, wouldn't it?*

'I'm not sure. I just sometimes think he's a bit too smooth, a bit too much of a charmer. And once or twice . . .' Tahlia hesitated, looking embarrassed.

'Go on,' Crystal urged her. 'What is it?'

'I don't want you to think I'm being big-headed or anything' – Crystal couldn't help smiling. Tahlia wasn't the slightest bit big-headed – 'But I've sometimes felt as though Max is coming on to me.'

Crystal's smile vanished. This was not so funny.

'I know you think I'm being stupid, but it definitely felt like that.'

'I don't think you're being stupid. I'm just surprised, that's all.'

'Oh, you mean he's never done that with you?'

Crystal shook her head, but she still couldn't look at Tahlia.

'Maybe I did imagine it then,' Tahlia said, looking puzzled. 'I was sure it would have happened to you as well.'

'Oh, you know Max, he is such a charmer. What with working in the club and everything, he probably doesn't realise he's doing it,' Crystal said breezily, desperate to change the subject, and fast.

'Hey, Leticia, do you want some of my marsh-mallows?' The little girl nodded and Crystal handed them to her.

'Don't say anything to Belle, will you?' Tahlia whispered.

'Of course not! And just forget about it, Tahlia.'

Later, as they caught the bus back to Tahlia's, Crystal found herself obsessing about the situation again. There was sweet Tahlia worrying because Max might have flirted with her, and yet Crystal was sleeping with him. It was not a good comparison.

'Thank God you're back!' Rosie exclaimed as the three of them walked through the door. She looked shaken and pale.

'What's happened?' Tahlia asked, looking alarmed at the state her mum was in.

'Come into the lounge and I'll tell you. But please, Tahlia, promise me you'll stay calm. Crystal, can you take Leticia into the kitchen?'

'Sure,' Crystal answered, wondering what was going on. 'Come on Leticia why don't we draw a picture of some ice-skaters?' As she got out paper and felt pens for Leticia she could hear Tahlia sobbing in the other room. Worried that Leticia would hear as well, she put on the radio. While Leticia concentrated on her drawing, Crystal tried to imagine what on earth had upset Rosie and Tahlia so much. Some twenty minutes later, Rosie came into the kitchen, and seeing that Leticia was still busy with her picture she whispered, 'Crystal, can I have a word?' Silently Crystal got up and followed her into the living room. Tahlia was curled up on the sofa, clutching a cushion. She'd stopped crying but looked as if she might start again at any second. She looked up at Crystal.

'Sorry, Crystal, I've ruined everything. I know we're not going to win now and it's all my fault.'

'What's going on?' Crystal asked, more confused than ever, as she sat down next to Tahlia and put an arm round her.

'I never wanted it to come out like this, nor did Tahlia,' Rosie said quietly, looking at her daughter.

'Never wanted what to come out?' Crystal asked, adding anxiously, 'you're not ill, are you?'

Rosie shook her head, and said, 'Leticia isn't my daughter; she's Tahlia's.'

'Oh.' Crystal was taken aback. She was so close to Tahlia yet she'd had no idea – although she had always been slightly surprised by how much time Tahlia spent with her sister.

'I'm so sorry, Crystal,' Tahlia said tearfully. 'I always meant to tell you and now it's come out in the worst possible way.' She dissolved into tears again and Rosie had to take over.

'What Tahlia's trying to say is that we've not seen or heard from Leticia's dad for seven years but he has just sold his story to the papers. He must have seen Tahlia on the show and thought he'd make some money. He's in prison at the moment for drug dealing.'

Crystal was about to say that didn't make Tahlia a bad person but she was interrupted by the phone. Rosie answered and Crystal could hear Dallas shouting, demanding to speak to her daughter. Tahlia shook her head. 'There's no way I can talk to him! Please don't make me.'

Crystal held out her hand to take the phone from Rosie.

She didn't even have time to say hello before Dallas was shouting, 'Is it true, then? I can't believe you didn't tell me. You've ruined the group's chances now. Didn't I say that the group couldn't afford any more scandals?'

Crystal cut in. 'Dallas, it's Crystal.'

'Put Tahlia on right now!' Dallas shouted back.

Crystal looked over at Tahlia who was still sobbing. 'He wants to talk to you.'

'I really can't, Crystal, *please*.'

Crystal sighed and spoke once more to Dallas, 'She's in no fit state to talk to anyone.'

She could just imagine Dallas pacing furiously up and down his luxurious Knightsbridge house. He hated not being in control, but evidently he realised he wasn't going to get his way this time because he said, 'Did *you* know she had a daughter?'

'No,' Crystal answered, 'I've only just found out, but it doesn't matter, does it?'

'What!' Dallas sounded as if he was about to explode. Crystal resisted the temptation to tell him to calm down. 'Tahlia was only just fifteen when she had the baby. Don't you get it? The show is watched by millions of children, whose parents aren't going to be too happy about having Tahlia as a role model. Plus the child's father is in prison for drug dealing. It's a double whammy. No one is going to vote for you. She's totally blown it.'

'Hang on a minute, Dallas; it's not that bad, surely?' Crystal asked with a sinking feeling that it probably was that bad.

'It's the hypocrisy thing. If she'd been straight from the start, okay it wouldn't have looked so great but we could have handled it, gone for the sympathy vote, but this coming right before the final is a fucking disaster. You're screwed. Sadie fucking Park will be on cloud fucking nine.'

'Well, there must be something we can do?' Crystal said, starting to feel more desperate.

'Tahlia will have to talk to the press, do some TV interviews, maybe try and drum up some sympathy.' Dallas did not sound hopeful and Crystal didn't feel hopeful either. Tahlia was so shy and got so nervous when she was interviewed, she was hardly going to do herself any favours.

'Can I have a think about this, Dallas, and call you back?' Crystal asked.

'I'm sorry Crystal. I really thought you were in with a chance. You'd better prepare your loser faces for Saturday,' Dallas said, ending the call.

Crystal took a deep breath. Somehow she had to salvage something out of the situation. She refused to believe that this was it.

'What did he say?' Tahlia asked anxiously.

Not wanting to reveal how pessimistic Dallas had been, Crystal put a gloss on the conversation she'd just had. 'We're going to have to talk to the press about this, Tahlia, and do some TV interviews.' As she told her friend the news, she saw her shudder then try to pull herself together.

'Okay, I'd better tell you everything.' She looked at Rosie, who nodded her agreement.

Haltingly and tearfully, Tahlia told Crystal the story of how she became a teenage mum. She'd only been going out with her boyfriend for three months when she fell pregnant. At first Tahlia tried to pretend the pregnancy wasn't happening, she didn't want to let her mum down, who was working all hours to pay for her stage-school fees. But it wasn't long before Rosie found out. They both decided that she should keep the baby. Tahlia had just been diagnosed with polycystic ovaries, which could make it harder to conceive naturally and this baby might well be the only one she could have. They didn't tell anyone about the pregnancy except the head teacher, who was sympathetic and agreed to explain Tahlia's absence from school as a bad dose of glandular fever. The boyfriend was not at all sympathetic; as soon as Tahlia told him he made a rapid exit out of her life. He had never met Leticia – Tahlia hadn't seen or heard from him since she told him about the pregnancy. All she'd heard was that he'd been in and out of prison on drug charges. Rosie pretended the baby was hers so Tahlia could pursue her dream of becoming a singer.

'You have a beautiful daughter,' Crystal told Tahlia when she'd finished her story. With tears in her eyes she hugged her friend. She felt deeply moved hearing how Tahlia had kept her secret for so long and how hard it must have been for her. She suddenly thought of her own secret, of the lies she was telling and the lie she was living, and felt such a hypocrite. 'We'll be all right; you haven't ruined anything, I promise,' Crystal reassured Tahlia. 'I just wish you'd told me and then I could have helped you. It must have been so hard pretending.'

'When we became friends there were so many times when I wanted to tell you, Crystal, but I didn't want it to make a difference to our friendship,' Tahlia said. 'It sounds stupid, I know, but I was so used to the lie by then.'

'Tahlia, you're my best friend and nothing will ever change that. I'll always be here for you,' Crystal said warmly. 'Now, I'd better call Belle, and get her to come over so we can work out what to say to the press tomorrow.'

Two hours later they were all feeling calmer, even though the phone had been ringing non-stop with journalists wanting the juicy details. In the end Crystal had disconnected it. Belle had turned up and they'd discussed their strategy and decided how they would tell the story. Crystal had called Dallas and told him that they had to be interviewed as a group by the press and on TV.

When Tahlia had gone to have a bath, Belle

turned to Rosie. 'I still don't understand why Tahlia couldn't tell people that Leticia was hers.'

Rosie sighed. 'You know what Tahlia is like. She's fragile. She worries about what people might think of her. I didn't think she'd cope with everyone knowing. And the father—' mentioning him caused her to grimace, 'was a right little shit and apparently still is.' Rosie looked exhausted.

'I'll order us a takeaway,' Crystal said.

Rosie tried to protest that she was perfectly capable of cooking dinner, but Crystal insisted. While Rosie went to make Leticia her tea, refusing Crystal's offers of help, the two girls sat on the sofa, quietly discussing what had happened. Crystal said that their role was to stand by Tahlia and support her, to stress that she hadn't done anything wrong, that she had a beautiful daughter. Who could criticise her for that?

'I can't help wishing she'd told us,' Belle finally said. 'It would be so crap to lose because of Tahlia being a teenage mum. We've all worked so hard.' She paused, adding thoughtfully, 'I suppose you and I could give it a go together if the shit really hits the fan – see if Dallas would sign us on our own.'

Crystal couldn't believe Belle's lack of concern for Tahlia, but it was fairly typical of Belle. She had a habit of only thinking about herself. And how convenient that she'd forgotten that her little flirtation with Dallas had nearly cost them their place in the competition originally.

'We're not going to lose because of Tahlia! For fucksake don't let her hear you saying things like that, she feels bad enough as it is,' Crystal hissed.

Belle looked sulky, then shrugged, 'Okay, whatever.'

There was a pause before Crystal asked the question that had been haunting her all weekend: 'So how was your night with Max?' She tried to sound as casual as possible.

Belle smiled. 'Fantastic. He took me to Nobu for dinner which was wicked – I've been wanting to go there for ages. Then we went back to his. Absence definitely improves performance!' Belle smiled cheekily. Crystal forced herself to smile back, but she felt as if she'd been punched in the stomach. *Why did he have to sleep with Belle? Surely he could have made an excuse?*

To hide the look of hurt Crystal grabbed the phone book and started flipping through it. 'Indian or pizza?' she asked, her appetite completely gone.

'Nothing, thanks, I'm going to head off to Mum and Dad's. You know I never eat that kind of food. I don't want to get fat.' She rubbed her flat brown stomach exposed by her low-riding jeans and smiled, knowing that she was in top shape, and Crystal found herself staring at the diamond stud in Belle's naval. It was identical to the one Max had given her. *Surely he hadn't given them both the same present, had he?* It was an unsettling thought but she didn't feel up to asking Belle about it.

*

After supper Crystal decided to go back to the hotel. Tahlia had finally calmed down and was curled up in bed with Leticia. The girls should have been rehearsing the next day but instead they were going to be in wall-to-wall interviews and wouldn't be able to get into the studio until the evening. Crystal told herself that she would get an early night, in preparation for what was going to be a very long day. But once she got back into her hotel room all she could think about was Max. She hated the fact that he'd slept with Belle again; she was tormented by jealousy and doubt. Who did he really want – Belle or her? Or was he only interested in having an affair? He'd seemed so into her and she'd believed him when he said he wanted her. She checked her phone; there was a text from him asking her to come to his flat.

In spite of everything she was still tempted, but somehow she found the willpower to text back no, and couldn't help adding, *heard you had a good night with Belle, what's going on?* She sent the message then threw her phone on the bed in frustration. God, she needed a cigarette. She grabbed her bag and went down to the bar where she bought a pack and ordered herself a double vodka. The cigarette hit the spot, but the alcohol increased her longing for Max. She wanted him so much. She had never felt like this about anyone before. What the hell was she going to do?

Half an hour and three cigarettes later she went back upstairs. She checked her phone. No messages. She wandered aimlessly round the room, pulling out clothes from her wardrobe, trying to decide what to wear for the morning. She should have been thinking about the interviews, but she couldn't concentrate on anything. Suddenly there was a knock at the door. Wondering who it could be at this time, she went over and opened it. There, leaning against the doorframe, and looking more wickedly handsome than ever was Max.

'What are you doing here?' she exclaimed, terrified that someone would see him.

He walked in, closing the door behind him. 'Why do you think, Crystal? I haven't been able to stop thinking about you.'

Crystal shook her head in disbelief and took a step backwards. Max walked towards her.

'I know you've missed me too, babe.'

'Oh yeah, you missed me so much that you spent last night shagging Belle,' Crystal said angrily.

He shrugged. 'What else could I do? She'd have thought something was going on if I hadn't. It was a mercy fuck really. I didn't want to.'

'Couldn't you have thought of an excuse?' Crystal demanded.

'What? Like I had a headache? Get real, Crystal, it didn't mean anything and I didn't want her getting wound up before the final. Sometimes you need to look at the bigger picture and keeping

Belle happy at this moment in time is important – I want you girls to win.'

Crystal wasn't convinced. Max seemed too able to switch off his emotions – she couldn't imagine shagging someone just to stop them suspecting something, when she was in love with someone else. Max didn't seem to be taking her feelings seriously. She moved further away from him. As if sensing her mood, Max changed tactics and lost the arrogant edge to his voice. Sounding heartfelt and sincere he said, 'I'm really sorry, Crystal; I feel like a complete shit, I would never do anything to hurt you. Can't we just forget Belle? You're the one I want.' He paused for a beat and said, 'I love you.'

She stood frozen to the spot. *He loved her?* Now Max crossed the room and pulled her into his arms. 'It's true, babe, I love you,' he murmured and leaned down to kiss her. *He loved her? That changed everything, didn't it?* She found herself putting her arms round him and kissing him back. Then he was pulling her on to the bed next to him, running his hands over her body. And instead of saying no, she was whispering, 'I'm yours, fuck me', hopelessly lost in her desire for him.

It was back to reality with a vengeance the next day. By four o'clock the girls had been interviewed by three tabloids and two celebrity mags and now it was Hadley's turn for the TV show. For once, Crystal was glad of his upbeat, boyish attitude – the journalists from the tabloids had all done their best to trip the girls up, make them say something sensational or bitch about each other. They had stuck to their story and to Crystal's surprise Tahlia had been brilliant. Instead of her usual nervousness, she had spoken confidently. Yes, she regretted having lied about the situation, but now it was out in the open she was relieved. She loved her daughter and she had nothing to be ashamed of.

'And what about you two,' Hadley turned to Crystal and Belle. Crystal spoke first. 'It's a shame that the truth had to come out this way, by someone selling a story to make money, but we're happy for Tahlia. Now she can be a mum and she doesn't have to pretend any more.'

'Yeah, we're pleased for Tahlia. Not that we're saying that it's a good idea to have a baby when you're fifteen,' Belle put in.

Trust Belle to put in a negative comment. She was so paranoid about her own image. Swiftly Crystal added, 'But she's a fantastic mum and Leticia is a great kid.'

Dallas had been sitting in on all their interviews, looking like the Grim Reaper, but over the course of the morning he was starting to look a little less foreboding and Crystal allowed herself to feel ever so slightly optimistic. Finally, at five, they were in the studio, rehearsing their two songs for the final – 'Will You Still Love Me Tomorrow?' and 'Independent Women'. They were exhausted, but

Dallas insisted they do at least three hours. Crystal took the fact that he was working them so hard as a good sign. It meant that he hadn't written them off yet and, even though she was knackered, she tried to put her all into the songs.

As Crystal curled up in bed that night, pressing her face against the pillow, she could still smell Max's Dolce & Gabbana aftershave on the pillow and she felt full of guilt, even though Max had repeated his promise that as soon as the competition was over he would finish with Belle. *Just one more week*, she told herself, *then we can be together*. She was determined not to contact Max, but wasn't strong enough to switch her phone off just in case he might call. When it rang at midnight she immediately reached for it.

'Hi, gorgeous, just wanted to say goodnight,' came Max's husky voice. 'I guess it's going to be difficult to see you this week. I don't know if I can wait till next week but I suppose I'll have to. Love you, babe.'

There were so many things Crystal wanted to say. Instead she simply replied, 'Love you too.'

Chapter 7

The Moment of Truth

'Lost Angels, you were absolutely fantastic! I love you!' Sadie exclaimed after their second performance in the final. Crystal felt a rush of excitement. If Sadie was behind them it could make all the difference. 'And, Tahlia, I've seen the pictures of your daughter and she's beautiful!' Sadie actually had tears in her eyes. She'd been unable to have children of her own and had two adopted daughters. Instead of ending their hopes it looked like Tahlia's revelation might swing it for them.

Charlie was next and she simply backed up Sadie – although slightly less emotionally – and then it was Dallas.

'Girls, that was without a shadow of a doubt your best performance of the competition. You deserve to win. You should win!'

'What do you make of those comments, girls?' Tess asked excitedly, thrusting the microphone in front of them. Crystal and Belle had always been the ones who spoke up before, with Tahlia just smiling shyly. But now Tahlia was first to speak. 'I just want to thank all the judges for their comments, especially Dallas for believing in us and Sadie for what she said about my daughter. This has been one of the hardest weeks of my life and I couldn't have got through it without the girls and my mum. Tonight I was singing for my daughter and I'm so proud I can finally say that. So everyone out there, please vote for us!'

The audience erupted. *Please*, thought Crystal, *let us win!* She looked at Belle and Tahlia and they smiled at each other.

They stopped smiling as soon as they got off stage, knowing that they had over an hour to wait before the results were announced. Crystal was unable to sit still. She paced round the green room, dying for a cigarette. Tahlia was surrounded by people congratulating her, including Hadley who didn't seem to be able to take his eyes off her. Crystal was glad; it was about time Tahlia had some male attention and Hadley was such a sweet guy. Crystal noticed that Tahlia looked different tonight too; she was always beautiful but now she had an extra glow about her. She seemed to be carrying herself with more confidence than usual and she didn't look so serious.

A nail-biting hour later they were all back on stage. The viewers, Crystal thought bitterly, probably enjoyed the way Tess deliberately built up the tension, counting down the time left with the audience before the phone lines closed. Crystal felt sick. *Please, please, please, let us win*, she prayed.

Finally, Tess was ready to reveal the results. 'Two million of you have voted! This has been one of the closest competitions ever, with the two runners-up practically neck and neck, but there is a winner. And I can now reveal that the act in third place is—', she paused for dramatic effect, '– *Northern Dreams*!'

Crystal, Belle and Tahlia gripped each other's hands even more tightly.

'In second place—', she paused again. *Please let it be @ttitude*, Crystal prayed, '—is *@attitude!* So that means the winner of *Band Ambition* is *Lost Angels*!'

Crystal, Belle and Tahlia let out screams of delight and hugged each other and then it seemed as if they were hugging everyone – Tess, Dallas, Charlie, Sadie, the other acts, who were all pretending that they were happy for them although it was obvious they were disappointed, particularly the members of @ttitude. And then they were back on stage singing their winning song once again. Crystal had never felt so happy. All her life she had dreamt of this and here she was. She looked at the audience cheering them. *This is where the rest of my life starts*, she thought. *I'm going to be a singer at last and I can be with Max.*

*

The next week passed in a blur of interviews and photo shoots. Crystal barely had a second to think about Max and not even Belle got to see him because their hectic schedule wouldn't allow it. Crystal and Max texted each other every day, several times a day, and he promised that as soon as he could, he would arrange to see Belle. Crystal was on a high from their success but she was desperate to be with Max. Surely there was nothing to stop them from being together now?

But she also had business on her mind. Now Lost Angels had won, Dallas was supposed to be drawing up another record deal for them to consider. After one of their many photo shoots Crystal asked Dallas about it.

'We'll discuss it in Ibiza.'

Crystal looked blank.

'I'm treating you all to a week's holiday at my pad in Ibiza,' Dallas replied, clearly expecting Crystal to be delighted at the news. She managed to smile for his benefit, but inside all she could think was that that would mean another whole week before Max could end his relationship with Belle.

'Dallas, thank you so much!' Tahlia exclaimed as the three of them walked into his stunning beach house. It was easily as luxurious as his Oxfordshire mansion – white marble floors, hi-tech lighting and ultra-modern gadgets. In the living room there was an oil painting of Dallas, looking very self-important, hanging over the marble fireplace, which Crystal had to avoid looking at to stop herself from giggling; a huge bronze sculpture of a female nude, expensive-looking chairs and sofas in pale cream silk, which Crystal was afraid to sit on. And the view out of the floor-to-ceiling windows was of a turquoise infinity pool with the equally turquoise Mediterranean beyond it, forming one glittering expanse of water.

Dallas smiled. 'I just want the three of you to relax, swim, and sunbathe. There's a spa at the hotel up the road which you can have treatments at. Just tell them to bill me.'

'Thanks, Dallas,' Crystal said, echoed by Belle. 'This is amazing!'

'I thought my girls deserved a treat. Make the most of it because I'm going to be working your arses off when you get home. We've got to get that number one!' he replied.

Crystal smiled to herself, remembering how down on them he'd been when he'd found out about Leticia. Now they were his golden girls and long might that continue. It was no fun being on the wrong side of Dallas.

That night, Dallas's chef prepared a delicious seafood barbeque for them by the pool. It was the first time in ages that all three of them felt able to relax – though since she'd started seeing Max, Crystal never felt entirely comfortable round Belle. Dallas stayed with them for dinner and then went to visit a friend of his at a neighbouring beach house, telling the girls they could have anything they wanted. They just had to ring the bell and ask the butler.

'I could get used to this,' Belle said, sipping champagne and looking out over the infinity pool and at the sea beyond. 'There's just one thing missing – it would be so great to have Max here.'

Crystal's stomach lurched. She wasn't prepared for that – it sounded like Belle had strong feelings for Max.

'I know what you mean,' Tahlia answered. 'I'd love it if Mum and Leticia could be here too.'

'And I bet you wouldn't mind if Hadley was here as well!' Belle teased Tahlia, who looked embarrassed but pleased at the same time. Tahlia had been on a date with Hadley on Thursday and finally admitted that she fancied him like mad.

'Who would you like to have here?' Belle asked Crystal.

Fuck, she could hardly tell the truth. 'Jesse Metcalfe,' Crystal lied, although it wasn't that big a lie; who wouldn't want Jesse Metcalfe?

'God, yeah,' Belle replied. 'He's well gorgeous – almost as fit as Max.'

'Who wants some more champagne,' Crystal asked, desperately wanting to change the subject, 'I'm going to ring and ask Jeeves, or whatever his name is, to get us another bottle.'

That night the girls didn't get to bed until after

four – one bottle of champagne became two, became three and by then they were all extremely drunk – even Tahlia, who never usually drank that much. In the morning Crystal woke up with a full-on hangover and was about to turn over and go back to sleep when Tahlia came racing into her room.

'Crystal!' she said excitedly, 'Leticia and Mum are here!'

'What?' Crystal asked blearily

'Dallas flew them over, oh and Max is here, too.'

Crystal's heart raced. This was not what she needed. Not at all. How the hell could she be with Belle and Max and pretend everything was hunkydory? It would be pure torture.

'Isn't it fantastic! I'm going to be in the pool with Leticia; she's dying to see you.'

'I'll be up in a minute,' Crystal muttered, pulling the sheet over her head and trying to gather her thoughts.

Oh my God, what am I going to do? She couldn't stay in bed for the next five days, tempting as that was. She was going to have to get up and face them. She dragged herself out of bed, showered, put on her black bikini and the Dior shades that she'd brought at the airport as a treat for their victory. Then she walked outside, a feeling of dread in the pit of her stomach.

'Crystal!' Leticia shouted excitedly from the pool, 'Are you going to come in?' Tahlia was sitting on the

112

edge, letting the water wash over her long legs, and Rosie was lying on a sun lounger. She called out 'Hello' and Crystal strolled over and hugged her. 'I think I'm dreaming,' Rosie said happily.

I wish I was, thought Crystal.

'The water's gorgeous,' Tahlia said, adding quietly, 'you don't mind about this, do you? I mean, I've got Leticia and Mum and Belle's got Max, and you—'

'Haven't got anyone?' Crystal laughed. 'Of course I don't mind. It's not your fault that my love life's been so shit lately.'

'Dallas said he asked your brother but he couldn't get time off work. But you mustn't feel left out, Crystal, you're part of my family.'

In spite of the situation, Crystal forced herself to smile back. 'Thanks, Tahlia', then she called out to Leticia, 'I'll come in a minute. I just need to have some orange juice.' She walked over to the lavish breakfast buffet which had been laid out for them and was just pouring herself a glass when Max walked up behind her.

'Surprise,' he whispered in her ear.

Spilling the juice in her confusion, Crystal turned round swiftly. Max was so close to her she almost brushed against him. *Damn him for looking so good*. He was only wearing trunks and there was way too much of his sexy, tanned body on display. She longed to touch him. Instead she took a step backwards and whispered, 'Where's Belle?'

Max shrugged casually. 'Having a shower. I said I'd meet her by the pool.'

Crystal searched his face for clues – had he missed her? Did he still want her? But he was wearing sunglasses and she couldn't see his eyes. She could only see herself reflected in the lenses, looking tense.

'I couldn't wait to see you,' Max whispered, giving her bikini-clad body a very appreciative once over. 'Looking good, babe.'

Crystal furtively looked over at Tahlia to make sure she hadn't heard him; luckily she was too busy playing with Leticia. Crystal was about to tell him that he mustn't say things like that, when Max gave her one of his sexy smiles, walked to the edge of the pool and dived in, making Leticia shriek with delight. When he surfaced, he called out, 'Come on, Crystal, it's lovely in here and it will cure that hangover.'

Crystal shook her head. 'I will in a bit, I just need to get rid of this headache.' She piled some fruit salad into a bowl, picked up her juice and went and sat on one of the sun loungers next to Rosie, who was now dozing. It was probably the first holiday she'd had in years. Crystal could see that Max was showing off for her benefit, doing an impressive front crawl up and down the pool, then splashing around with Leticia, and she tried to avoid looking at him.

'Can you believe it?' Belle exclaimed to Crystal as

she walked across the terrace. She was wearing a stylish white bikini and looked stunning. 'It's so cool of Dallas, isn't it?'

Crystal tried to smile. 'It's a lovely surprise,' she lied, and couldn't help staring at the diamond stud in Belle's naval; it was definitely the same as hers. Before Crystal had come out to the pool she'd swapped hers for her skull and crossbones stud again. She was relieved she had.

'Well, I'm going for a swim,' Belle said, sauntering to the pool and climbing elegantly down the steps.

Crystal sipped her juice and watched Belle put her arms round Max and kiss him. She closed her eyes, not wanting to see any more. This whole scenario was a fucking nightmare. She didn't know if she could handle being around Belle and Max – especially a Belle who could hardly keep her hands off Max. It didn't look as if Belle was going off him, in fact quite the opposite. Suddenly, to her horror, she was being picked up by Max and hurled into the pool. She emerged from the water, coughing and spluttering, her sunglasses askew, hair all over the place. She was furious. Everyone else was laughing.

'Couldn't resist it, Crystal,' Max said.

She wanted to tell him to fuck off, but knew she couldn't swear in front of Leticia, so she had to make do with muttering, 'Thanks a lot.' Then, trying to salvage some dignity, she took off her sunglasses, smoothed back her hair and swam a couple of lengths. She was an okay swimmer, but not in the same league as Belle, who was fantastic and had swum for her school and for her county. Crystal completed her lengths then sat at the side watching Belle swim with her effortless front crawl; she could even do tumble turns at the side, something Crystal had never managed to achieve. Max swam over, pulled himself out of the water and sat next to her.

'You're not really cross with me, are you?' he asked, wiping the water from his face. 'Bet it cleared your head.'

She shrugged, not knowing how to behave with him and trying to avoid looking at his body – a body that she ached for, a body that she longed for.

'Listen, I know this isn't an ideal situation,' Max said quietly, 'but Dallas landed it on me, and I couldn't say no.'

Crystal nodded, still not trusting herself to speak.

'There's no way I can tell Belle when we're out here, but I promise I will when we get back to London. And I sorted out the record deal for you last week and I've got the contract ready for you all to sign.'

Now Crystal spoke. 'Hang on a minute, we haven't even looked at it. And we need to see what Dallas has come up with.'

Max clenched his jaw and looked angry. 'For fuck's sake, Crystal, you said you wanted me as your manager. I've spent the last six months busting my balls trying to get a deal for the group.'

'Calm down. We just need to check out both deals,' Crystal answered, taken aback by his aggressive tone. 'You're a businessman, surely you understand that?'

'I don't like being messed around. I've put myself on the line for you guys. The record company are expecting you to sign with me. It's going to put me in the shit if you don't.'

'Oh, come on, Max, don't be like this.'

But Max had got up and was walking away, muttering that he needed a drink.

Belle swam over. 'Is Max okay?'

Crystal sighed. 'He was annoyed because I said we needed to see what deal Dallas was going to offer us. I was right to say that, wasn't I?'

'Totally. You know that Dad doesn't think we should be managed by Max. He's always going on about not mixing business with pleasure. And,' Belle lowered her voice, 'Dallas does have an amazing track record, whereas Max has never managed anyone before.'

'Well, I just think we need to look at both offers, and then decide who we really want to manage us,' Crystal answered, somehow not wanting to be disloyal to Max.

For the rest of the day Crystal didn't see Max or Belle. They'd gone into San Antonio to meet one of the club owners Max knew on the island. Crystal was relieved when the pair left. Max still seemed angry with her and was being snappy with Belle. It was a side to him that Crystal had never seen before.

'What's *his* problem then?' Rosie asked when Belle and Max had left.

'Promise you won't say anything to Dallas but Max really wants to manage us and he doesn't seem to get it that we need the best deal,' Crystal replied.

'To be honest, Crystal,' Tahlia put in, 'I don't know if I want him to manage us any more. It seemed like a good idea before we won the competition, but now, don't you think Dallas would be a better choice?'

Crystal hesitated; despite her feelings for Max, the other more logical side had to agree with Tahlia. 'I think we've got to see both deals and then make up our minds.'

Crystal swam and sunbathed for the rest of the day. It was the first time in ages that she'd had any time off and she needed the break. But as she lay in the sun her thoughts kept returning to Max. Despite his earlier behaviour she couldn't stop herself from fantasising about him, replaying in her head the last time they'd made love. *He probably just felt awkward because Belle was here as well*, she told herself, quick to excuse him.

Max and Belle didn't return until dinner that night and it soon became clear that Max was drunk. Barely acknowledging anyone at the table, he

118

reached for the bottle of wine and poured himself a large glass, not bothering to offer it around. He drained it and poured himself another. Crystal raised her eyebrows at Belle, who looked extremely pissed off. Dallas was having dinner on one of his friend's yachts.

'How was your friend, Max?' Crystal asked to break the awkward silence that had fallen around the table.

Max shrugged. 'Alright.'

Then Belle said, 'Max is thinking of opening a club out here too; that would be so cool, wouldn't it?'

Crystal looked at her. She seemed unusually uptight; clearly she'd had a stressful afternoon with Max.

'Yeah, well, I don't want a bunch of freeloaders hanging out in it. This club would have to pay its way,' Max muttered, sounding surly.

'What do you mean by that?' Crystal asked before she could stop herself. The last thing she needed was a confrontation with Max.

'It means I can't have Belle and her friends ordering champagne on the house, non-stop, like they do in London. I'm running a business, not a fucking charity.' Max shot her a hostile look and Crystal thought it wise to change the subject so she turned and made a comment to Rosie about the food. She was hurt by his tone and snide remarks. *What the hell was going on? Was this because she said she wanted to look at both deals?* She didn't understand; the Max she knew was easy-going and charming. The man in front of her was like a stranger. She'd spent so long fantasising about them being together, but if this was what he was like when he didn't get his own way, she wasn't so sure.

Max didn't say anything for the rest of the meal; he just moodily picked at his food and drank a bottle of wine on his own. It was a relief when he stood up and said he was going to have a cigarette outside. As soon as he was safely out of earshot, Tahlia exclaimed, 'What's his problem?'

'He's been like this all day,' Belle answered. 'He's just been going on and on about how we promised him that he could be our manager and questioning why we want to go through the contract rather than just trust him. He's been a right shit.'

'But we never promised that he could manage us, did we, Crystal?' Tahlia said, looking worried.

'No,' Crystal answered confidently, although she didn't feel it. She remembered meeting him in the pub in Covent Garden, how he been talking about managing them, in a way which suggested he thought it was a foregone conclusion and Crystal had been too loved up to remind him that they had other offers to consider.

After dinner Tahlia put Leticia to bed, Rosie read her book in the living room, Belle went to her room to call her parents and Crystal wandered outside, half wanting to see Max but also hoping that he'd crashed out in bed.

But he was lying on one of the sun loungers by the pool smoking, and drinking yet more wine.

'Don't you think you've had enough?' Crystal asked softly.

'Not nearly enough,' he replied bitterly.

'What's going on, Max?'

'What's going on is that for six months you've all been having a laugh, pretending that I'm your new manager and all the time you've been planning to stay with Dallas.'

'Oh come on, Max, we never promised anything. We've got to look at Dallas's deal but I promise if yours is better we'll go with you.'

Suddenly Max leapt from the chair, grabbed Crystal's arm and pulled her close to him.

Crystal stopped herself from crying out in pain and tried to pull away, but Max only held her tighter and said nastily, 'Too fucking right you will, Crystal. You choose me. Remember, I can ruin this band. All I have to do is let Belle know what we've been up to. And then it's goodbye Lost Angels. You'll just be another reality show band on the scrap heap.'

Crystal felt sick. 'Why are you being like this, Max? I thought you wanted us to be together?'

Max laughed harshly. 'You like me because I'm a bit of a bastard, don't you, Crystal, so just enjoy the suspense.' And before Crystal could stop him he kissed her, forcing his tongue into her mouth. She tried to push him away, dreading that someone would see them, hating what he was doing. Finally he stopped. 'Just remember, Crystal, I can do whatever I like.' And picking up the bottle of wine, he sauntered down the steps and on to the beach.

Crystal stood rooted to the spot for a few minutes, trembling and trying to regain her composure. *I've made a terrible mistake*, she thought. She almost had to stop herself screaming out loud. What the hell had she been thinking getting involved with him? She'd been so caught up in the competition and in what she thought was her love for Max. But now it was clear; she didn't love him, she didn't even know him. It had been a wild infatuation. And judging by his behaviour tonight he'd been using her as a way of getting the girls to sign with him. He didn't love her. He obviously had no intention of ever leaving Belle for her. How could she have been so stupid?

Eventually she forced herself to go back into the house. Rosie, Tahlia and Belle were in the lounge. They started when Crystal walked in.

'Thank Christ it's you. I thought it was Max,' Belle said, sounding on edge. 'Did you see him?'

Crystal shook her head and Belle carried on, 'I hope he's gone to see his mate. I can't deal with him when he gets like this.'

'Does he often get like this?' Tahlia asked, looking concerned.

Belle shrugged. 'Every now and then, it's all to do with his racing accident. He gets really down sometimes because he can't drive any more and the doctors have told him he is suffering from depression, but he won't do anything about it. And he *definitely* has mood swings.'

He didn't seem depressed, Crystal thought, *more like a bully who wanted his own way.*

'God, Belle, I had no idea. How do you handle it?' Tahlia spoke again.

'Oh, it will blow over,' Belle said breezily. 'He'll be lovely again tomorrow, he'll apologise, want to buy me a present and take me out for dinner, and it will all be forgotten.'

Crystal couldn't help thinking that Belle was in denial and that no amount of bling and meals at flash restaurants could make up for having to put up with Max in one of these moods.

He reappeared the following day at around midday. Crystal had been swimming in the sea and emerged from the water to find him looking his usual handsome self, in designer sunglasses, surrounded by several bags from expensive boutiques, smiling and chatting away as if his mood the day before had never happened.

'Crystal!' he exclaimed as soon as he saw her. She nodded and went to pick up her towel. 'I wanted to say sorry about yesterday, I was a total twat and I apologise. I bought you a little something to make up.' And he handed her a small cream bag from a jeweller's. Crystal muttered her thanks and put the bag down and carried on drying her face.

'Aren't you going to open it, Crystal?' Belle asked. 'Look what Max bought me.' She held out her arm and showed off an expensive-looking platinum watch, the face edged with diamonds.

'And look what he bought me,' piped up Leticia, showing off a cute pink bead necklace and matching bracelet, 'and he got Mummy and Tahlia, I mean Rosie and Mummy gold bracelets.'

Crystal looked at the new charm bracelet hanging round Tahlia's slim wrist.

Talk about trying to bribe us, she thought bitterly.

Reluctantly she picked up the cream bag, pulled out a black leather box and opened it to reveal a solid gold love heart on a black leather string. It was gorgeous, exactly Crystal's style.

'Oh, that's so *you*,' Belle said. 'Max has got such great taste hasn't he?'

'Yes, it's lovely,' Crystal replied without enthusiasm.

'Let me put it on you,' Max said.

Crystal shook her head, but Max took the box from her and slipped the necklace over her head anyway. The heavy gold love heart hung between her breasts and Crystal almost winced at the feel of it against her skin. She felt as if Max was trying to buy her.

For the rest of the day Max made it his mission to charm everybody. He played with Leticia, got everyone drinks. Crystal almost thought she must have imagined his outburst the night before, but she knew she hadn't; the vicious look on his face and his threats were burned on her memory forever. And whatever he said to her, she had seen quite clearly that he didn't love her. Belle seemed to have completely forgiven his behaviour but Crystal could tell Tahlia and Rosie were still wary of him. The three of them were all relieved when he and Belle decided to hire a boat and cruise round the island for a couple of hours. Max had tried to persuade them to come but they had all made their excuses.

As soon as they'd left Crystal took off her necklace and Rosie questioned it. 'Don't you like it, Crystal?'

'I don't like what it represents,' Crystal answered.

'Why don't you like it?' Leticia demanded and immediately Crystal back-tracked and said that she didn't want the sand to spoil it.

'Come on, Leticia,' Tahlia said, 'let's go for another swim.'

Crystal watched Tahlia and Leticia walk hand in hand to the sea and sighed.

'That was a heartfelt sigh, Crystal,' Rosie said.

'I'm worried about these deals,' Crystal answered. 'I really want the best for the group and whatever he's saying now we never promised Max that he could manage us.'

'Don't worry, I'm sure it will be okay,' Rosie said reassuringly.

Crystal wasn't so sure. She lay back on the sand and closed her eyes, dreading later that evening when they would have to go through Max's offer. All she wanted to do was get off the island and tell Max that she never wanted to see him again. He wasn't the person she thought he was. She couldn't believe that she'd been so taken in by him.

That night Dallas joined them for dinner. Max was visiting his friend again. He'd told Belle to expect him back at ten when he wanted to go through his contract. And that prospect left Crystal on edge. *What had she got herself into?* But Dallas, though, was on good form and whatever deals he'd been doing that day must have gone his way because he kept insisting that everyone drink champagne. Crystal raised her eyebrows at Tahlia and Belle. They had agreed to go through the contracts that night and Crystal wanted them to have clear heads when they got down to business. They got the message and slowly sipped their drinks. After dinner Dallas wanted them to go out by the pool to discuss the contract.

'Actually, Dallas, can we stay here?' Crystal asked. 'It's easier to make notes.'

Dallas smiled. 'Whatever you say, Crystal.' Rosie took Leticia out and Dallas's staff efficiently cleared the table around them. Dallas waited until everyone was out of the room, then spoke.

'I think you'll find that this contract speaks for itself. I made a mistake with the last one, but I'm sure you'll agree that this one is a hundred times better.'

He caught sight of Crystal's sceptical expression. 'Okay, ninety-nine times better. Jesus, Crystal, I'm a businessman!' He handed each of them a copy of the contract and, whereas before he had hassled them to sign there and then, on this occasion he seemed to have learnt his lesson and went through it clause by clause, answering Crystal's questions. It was a vast improvement on the last one. Not only were they guaranteed more money from the royalties but Dallas had also lined up some of the best songwriters in the business to work on their album as well as giving Crystal and Tahlia the chance to write and record at least three songs of their own. And to cap it all, it was a two-album deal.

'The bottom line is I really want to manage you. I think you've got great potential not just in the UK but in the States as well and I've got all the contacts there to ensure you make it,' Dallas said finally. The three girls looked at each other. Crystal could tell they were swayed by what Dallas had said and so was she. Max was going to have to come up with something pretty damn special to top it.

'Okay, I'll leave you to discuss it. There's just one thing: I need an answer first thing in the morning,' Dallas told them, walking with his usual confidence out of the room.

'Wow,' Tahlia said, echoing what Crystal thought. 'This is an amazing deal, don't you think?'

'It's so much better than the first one,' Crystal agreed. 'What do you think, Belle?'

Belle frowned. 'It's really tempting, but we've got to see what Max has come up with.'

'I bet it won't be half as good as this one,' Tahlia put in. 'Face it, Max has no experience.'

Tahlia was bang on with her prediction. When Max returned and they were sure that Dallas had gone out, they met up with Max in the living room. In contrast to Dallas, Max didn't even have copies of the contract for the girls to read through. It seemed to Crystal as if he was trying to bluff his way through the terms. But they wouldn't let him get away with it. To Crystal's relief Tahlia was the most vocal, insisting Max explain exactly what he could offer them and what money they could expect. It didn't take long for them to discover that Max and the record company would be making all the money. It was only a one-album deal, the song-writers weren't in the same league as the ones Dallas had offered, and the girls would only earn a fraction of the royalties. There was no competition. Sensing that he was losing ground, Max went for emotional blackmail:

'Come on, I was the one who was there for you at the beginning, not Dallas. I was the one who gave you gigs in my club. You'll be my main priority whereas, with Dallas, you'll be one of many groups he manages. He'll get bored of you after a few months, whereas I'll always be there for you.'

Crystal forced herself to speak. 'Thanks, Max, the three of us need to discuss it. We'll have an answer for you in a while.'

Max got up. 'I just want you to know that you'll be making a huge mistake if you go with Dallas. He won't look after you like I will. And I didn't want to say this again but you *did* promise me that I could manage you.' With that, he marched out of the room.

Belle looked pale. 'I can't believe that I'm saying this but we've got to go with Dallas.'

'I agree,' Crystal said, relieved that Belle had said it first.

'So do I,' said Tahlia.

'Shit! I'm not looking forward to telling Max.' Belle put her head in her hands and Tahlia immediately got up to give her a hug.

'It's the right decision,' Tahlia said reassuringly.

'I know, but what the hell is Max going to say?'

Ten minutes later they'd found out exactly what Max would say. He went ballistic when Belle gave him the news. She'd insisted on doing it on her own, and took him into the bedroom. The others sat in the living room, but could hear Max's angry shouting from upstairs.

'God, do you think she's all right?' Crystal asked, feeling anxious about Belle. She'd seen for herself last night how aggressive Max could be.

'I don't like the sound of it,' Rosie put in. 'I'm going up to see if she's okay.'

The others followed her as she walked up the marble staircase, but halfway up Max came running out of the room and angrily pushed past them, 'The show's over,' he shouted angrily as Belle appeared at the top of the stairs, looking upset, pleading with him to stay. 'But you haven't heard the last of this. I know what I was fucking promised.' He shot a warning glance at Crystal as he ran down the stairs and she was gripped with panic. *What if he told Belle about them?*

After Max's sudden departure they all gathered in the living room, Rosie fussing round Belle, insisting she have a brandy, tutting over how badly Max had behaved.

'Don't let him upset you, Belle, you did the right thing. You can't confuse business with your personal life, it will only go belly up.' Crystal and Tahlia agreed but Belle still looked upset and bewildered. 'He was so angry,' she kept saying. 'I don't understand, it was like he'd been pinning all his hopes on us, but I thought his business was going really well.'

Tahlia tried to reassure her but Crystal was feeling too wound up to say anything. All she knew was that in the morning she would tell him that whatever they'd had between them was over, totally finished, and as far as she was concerned it never should have happened.

Max didn't come home that night. In the morning, Belle was red-eyed with crying. 'He never stays out all night after an argument.'

'I'm sure he was just at his mate's,' Tahlia said. 'Just let him calm down, he'll be back.'

At midday Dallas caught up with them by the pool.

'So have you got an answer for me?' he asked, with the look of a man confident he was going to like what he was about to hear.

Crystal looked at Belle and Tahlia, then took a deep breath. 'We agree to the terms of your contract. We'd like you to manage us.'

A smile spread across his tanned face, showing off his gleaming white, perfect teeth. 'You won't regret it, I promise you. As a little treat why don't you all go to the spa and have some treatments on me; whatever you want, just charge me and then we'll go out tonight to celebrate in style.'

Unusually, Belle insisted that Crystal go first, on the off-chance that Max turned up. The last thing Crystal felt like doing was relaxing; she felt totally wired and on edge but thought it might look odd if she didn't. The therapist kept commenting on the tension in Crystal's shoulders as she massaged her. *That's because I am fucking tense*, she was tempted to reply. Crystal thought there was no way she would be able to relax but gradually the therapist's expert massage and the soothing aromatherapy oils took over and she drifted off to sleep.

She was so wiped out after the massage that as soon as she got back to the beach house she collapsed into bed. The emotional rollercoaster she had been on had caught up with her and she fell into a deep sleep. She woke up suddenly to discover Max lying on the bed beside her.

'Did you miss me?' he demanded, grabbing her roughly and kissing her neck, the stubble on his face scratching her skin.

Crystal leapt out of bed, pulling the sheet around her body. 'What the fuck are you doing here?' she hissed.

'Come back to bed, no one's here. It's just you and me, alone at last.'

Crystal ran to the door and tried to open it, but it was locked. She rattled it frantically, desperate to get away from Max. She felt a stab of fear. 'Get out!' she shouted. 'It's over between us!'

'Don't be like that, babe.' Max had got off the bed and was standing in front of her, holding the key. He reeked of alcohol and still seemed drunk

Crystal grabbed at his hand and tried to wrestle the key out of it but he prised her fingers away, causing her to cry out in pain.

'Why don't you come back to bed?'

'No, I don't want to!'

But he ignored her and pulled her back towards the bed, his grip like iron on her wrist. With her free arm she tried to lash out at him but he simply seized her other arm and dragged her along. She was struggling wildly now, kicking out at him. But she was no match for him. And then he had pinned her down on to the bed, forced her arms over her head and was on top of her, trapping her so that she couldn't move.

'God, Crystal, I've missed you,' he panted. 'Even though you've been such a bitch to me over the contract. It's not too late to change your mind.'

'You're hurting me, Max, please, just go. I don't want to do this.' The tears were streaming down her cheeks and she couldn't believe this was happening.

Max laughed, 'Oh come on, Crystal, you don't expect me to believe that, do you?' He put on an absurd imitation of her: 'I want you Max, fuck me, Max.'

Then he snapped out of it. 'Well, here I am, Crystal, and after last night I reckon you owe me one, don't you?'

Crystal tried to push him off with all her strength but he only laughed some more. 'What are you going to do, princess? Scream? I've told you, there's no one here.'

She kept struggling, but it was hopeless; he was so much stronger. She couldn't stop him.

After he'd gone, she stood in the shower for what seemed like ages, the water drowning out the sounds of her sobbing. For the rest of the day she stayed in her room, pretending she had a migraine. Tahlia and Rosie popped in at regular intervals to see if she wanted anything but she sent them away, saying that she needed to sleep. She couldn't face seeing anyone. She didn't know what to do; she couldn't see any way out of the situation. If she told Belle, it would destroy the group and everything they had worked so hard for; but if she didn't, Max would have a hold over her and, as she had just learnt to her cost, he would do whatever he wanted.

He raped me, she said to herself, hardly able to comprehend it, *and there's nothing I can do about it.*

At seven that evening Belle knocked softly on the door and wandered in. She was dressed up for dinner in a red backless designer dress and the scent of her perfume filled the room. 'Are you sure you aren't well enough to come out Crystal? Dallas is going to take us to this amazing restaurant then on to a club.'

'No,' Crystal mumbled, 'I still feel really awful.'

Hardly registering what Crystal had said, Belle continued, 'And I've got something to celebrate as well. Look!'

Crystal looked up as Belle held out her left hand showing off a blingtastic ring – a huge diamond cut in the shape of a love heart.

'It's gorgeous, isn't it? Max got back this morning, took me for a walk on the beach and proposed to me. He got down on one knee and everything.'

Crystal felt sick.

'I'm so happy,' Belle gushed. 'He said he was

really, really sorry about last night. And now he totally understands that we want to go with Dallas.'

'Are you sure about this, Belle? You weren't very happy with him yesterday. He was well out of order.'

Belle curled her lip. 'Yes, I know what Max is like and, anyway, if he doesn't behave himself I'll call off the wedding.'

'Well, congratulations,' Crystal croaked, wishing more than anything in the world that Belle would get out of her room.

'You and Tahlia will have to be my bridesmaids, won't that be cool? I reckon we should be able to get a deal with a magazine now we've won.'

Crystal was saved from answering as Max called for Belle to tell her the car was waiting to take them to the restaurant.

'Okay, see you in the morning and hope you feel better.' Crystal nodded and closed her eyes, as Belle walked out of the room, her heels clicking loudly on the marble floor.

As soon as Crystal was sure that everyone had gone out she got out of bed. Now she really did have a headache, but she needed a drink. She pulled on her white combats and a white long-sleeved T-shirt, as if by covering up her body she could somehow erase the memory of what Max had done to her. She looked in the mirror and was appalled to see how pale and drawn she looked. She felt a sudden jolt of anger: how dare that bastard make her feel like this? Crystal shook back her hair. Whatever else happened he was not going to make her feel like a victim again. Yes, she'd made a mistake, but now she had to put it behind her otherwise she would lose everything she had worked so hard for. She knew that if all of this got out she would run the risk of blowing the group apart. They were on the brink of making it, and she wasn't going to let Max take that away from her. Somehow she would have to find a way of dealing with what had happened and make sure Max could never hurt her again.

Chapter 8

Living the Dream

Six months later . . .

Crystal looked at her watch as the taxi made its way through the London traffic painfully slowly. She was late. She was supposed to have been at the film studios an hour and a half ago to start work on the video for Lost Angel's second single. Their first had gone straight to number one and their album was in the top three. Crystal should have been on top of the world. She was doing what she had dreamt of all her life, her career was going from strength to strength – the public loved Lost Angel's mix of sassy and soulful songs. They had broken away from just being a reality show product and had become artistes in their own right. They were famous! They'd become permanent fixtures in the tabloids and celebrity mags, celebrated for their style and good looks. But there was a dark shadow hanging over Crystal, which stopped her from feeling completely happy – Max. Since winning *Band Ambition* she'd experienced six months of the best and worst times of her life because when Max raped her he didn't just shatter her confidence, he also got her pregnant.

Crystal had been devastated when she found out. She knew what she had to do, knew there was no way she could have Max's baby, but it didn't make the decision any less painful. And she had no one to confide in. She couldn't tell Tahlia or her brother because that would involve an explanation about Max, one which Crystal didn't want to give, and she didn't want to tell any more lies. She felt so alone, she went through with the abortion by herself, cried her tears in private and tried to pull herself together.

If only that could have been the end of Max's involvement in her life but it wasn't. He was a constant, menacing presence. He regularly texted and called her. He kept repeating that he was going to manage Lost Angels and that she had to make the girls leave Dallas. Crystal did her best to stall him. She had no intention of saying anything to the others. She was running late this morning because, when she had left the gym after her morning workout, Max had been waiting outside for her. Crystal shuddered to herself as she remembered.

He had grabbed her arm and said, 'Let's go for a walk, babe, we've got things to discuss.'

'I've got nothing to say to you,' she had exclaimed, horrified at seeing him again, horrified that he'd known where to find her. *Had he been stalking her?* She tried to shake him off, to run away, but he had held on to her.

'Don't be like this babe, I only want a chat. Come on, I'll walk you back to your flat.'

'No! If you want to talk to me, we do it outside.'

'Whatever,' Max had shrugged, steering her towards a bench. They both sat down, Crystal trying to sit as far away as possible from Max, but he moved closer towards her so that she had to move to the very edge of the bench to avoid touching him.

'So, Crystal, it's all going well for you, isn't it?' Max said sarcastically.

Crystal avoided looking at Max and muttered, 'Yeah I thought you'd be pleased for Belle's sake.'

Max snorted with disgust. 'Makes no difference to me. Did you know that her old man's gone and drawn up a pre-nup? I'd get sweet FA if we ever got divorced. He's even put in a clause protecting her assets while we are married.'

Crystal said nothing. She didn't want to show how relieved she was that Belle's dad was defending his daughter. She felt awful knowing what Max was like and she felt worse for not being able to warn Belle. And even though Belle had turned into a full-blown diva lately, who could be a nightmare to work with, Crystal didn't want her to be hurt by Max. She'd promised herself that when the group had finished promoting their first album she would tell Belle *everything*. In her heart she knew that, when she did, Lost Angels would be finished. Belle would never forgive her. Crystal wasn't proud of herself for keeping the truth from her but she didn't want the group to end just yet. *I just need a little more time*, she told herself, *more time for us all to become established, then it won't matter so much when we split.*

'Anyway,' she said abruptly, wanting to get away from Max as quickly as possible, 'what do you want?'

Max smiled, leaning back. 'Ah yes, I thought we could have a little chat about things. Still no boyfriend, Crystal? Are you holding out for me?'

'Just get to the point,' Crystal replied, trying to keep the emotion out of her voice.

Max got up and stood right in front of her. Crystal willed her face not to show the disgust she felt for him. He reached out and stroked her hair, and she couldn't stop herself from flinching. He laughed. 'Oh Crystal, I remember when you couldn't wait for me to touch you, when you were gagging for it. But don't worry, princess. I've got different needs. My plans to manage Lost Angels have eaten up quite a lot of capital and, to put it bluntly, I need more cash.'

'How much?' Crystal asked quietly. She should have seen this one coming.

'Twenty should do it, then I reckon we'll be quits.'

'What? Do you seriously think I can just hand over twenty grand just like that?' Crystal exclaimed.

Suddenly, Max wasn't smiling any more. He narrowed his eyes. 'Yes, I do. And I'm doing this for you, babe, and for the group, so don't be so fucking difficult.'

'And if I don't give you the money?' Crystal said quietly. Max sighed as if he was bored with the whole thing and pulled out his mobile phone. He held it up to show Crystal one of the passionate text messages she'd sent to him during their short and ill-fated affair. How stupid she'd been.

'And just in case that isn't enough to convince you, take a look at this.' Max held up his phone again and Crystal saw a picture of herself, lying naked on Max's bed. He'd taken it when he'd bought her the diamond stud.

'What if I said I don't care, go ahead, show them to Belle? You've got just as much to lose as I have. Belle would leave you for sure,' Crystal said, trying to call his bluff.

'Well, you could, but that would probably be the end of your music career. The tabloids would have a field day with you. Whereas I could say that I'd been feeling suicidal about the end of my racing career and you threw yourself at me. I tried to resist at first, but because I felt so low, I gave in . . . Of course, Belle would be furious at first, but eventually I'd win her round.'

Crystal felt cornered. Max was probably right

about her music career and she was damned if she was going to let him take it all away from her. And when Belle finally got to know the truth, Crystal wanted to make sure she was the one to tell her.

'I'll get you the money by next week,' she said in a flat voice.

'Good girl,' Max answered and kissed her on the cheek as if they were still friends. 'You can go now.'

Crystal wanted to shout that he had no right to tell her what to do, that he could fuck off. But she knew she was powerless. Instead, she got up and, even though her legs felt wobbly from the shock of seeing Max again, she forced herself to run home, turning round every now and then to check he wasn't following her. Back at her flat, she took a long shower, not caring she was already late for filming.

When she walked into the dressing room Belle and Tahlia were already made up and in costume.

'You're late!' Belle exclaimed.

'Is everything okay, Crystal?' Tahlia asked more sympathetically.

'Yeah, sorry, I had a migraine last night and it wiped me out.'

'D'you feel okay now?' Tahlia asked. 'You look a bit pale.'

'I'm fine,' Crystal lied.

'God, if I'd have known how late you were going to be, I'd have had a lie-in,' Belle said, studying her reflection in the mirror.

'How do you think I look?' she demanded.

'Great,' Crystal answered, trying to summon up enthusiasm that she didn't really feel.

Crystal had come up with the concept for the video. The girls were going to be dressed as style icons from five different decades, starting with the sixties and Twiggy. So Belle was wearing a white mini dress with white patent-leather boots, Tahlia was wearing a similar outfit in pink and Crystal's was in black.

Danni, the group's make-up artist, and Jez, their hairdresser, appeared in the doorway of the dressing room. They'd been working with the girls for the last six months. Crystal adored them and they'd become close friends.

'Thank God you're here, Crystal. The director's been going ape shit!' Jez exclaimed dramatically.

'Sorry,' Crystal said. Usually it was Belle who kept everyone waiting.

'No worries, Crystal, it won't take me long to do your face and, as you're wearing a wig, Jez will be quick,' Danni told her. Crystal smiled. Danni and Jez were like chalk and cheese. Aussie Danni was always so calm and laid back, whereas Jez was much more temperamental and flighty. And even though Danni was a make-up artist, she was the least vain person Crystal had ever met. She hardly ever wore make-up herself and jeans and a T-shirt was her usual uniform. Jez, on the other hand, was altogether more high maintenance; he changed his hair colour and hairstyle practically ever other week and at the moment his hair was ash-blond and spiky. He also spent a fortune on fake tan and designer clothes. He rolled his eyes, and muttered, 'Just because it's a wig, there's still a lot of skill involved. I haven't seen it on yet. I might have to trim it.'

'I know, darling, you're an artist,' Crystal soothed him. A slightly calmer Jez offered to go for coffees and Crystal gratefully accepted; she felt emotionally battered from her meeting with Max and in need of a caffeine fix.

She sat down in front of the mirror, and groaned at her reflection, 'Do something, Danni!' she said. 'I look like shit!'

'No, you don't,' Danni reassured her, getting to work. She started with foundation, keeping Crystal's skin pale, with just a hint of blusher. Then she turned her attention to her eyes, giving her huge false lashes, silver eye shadow and dramatic black eyeliner. Finally, she applied pale pink lipstick. Then Jez was let loose on Crystal's hair. He scraped it all back into a tight bun and pinned it into a hair net.

'That's *so* not a good look,' Crystal exclaimed. 'Please hurry up and put the wig on before anyone sees me!'

'Don't worry, sweetie, I'm on the case.' And Jez picked up a jet-black wig styled in a short bob with a long fringe and carefully put in on Crystal's head.

'That looks fantastic!' Tahlia exclaimed. She'd been given a similar wig but in caramel which perfectly complimented her skin. Crystal smiled for the first time all day.

She was just being zipped into a black PVC mini dress, which she was wearing with black patent-leather boots, when an angry male voice called into the dressing room, 'Is she here yet?'

Crystal turned round to see a tall, handsome man with short, dark blond hair, and the most intensely blue eyes she had ever seen. He looked extremely pissed off.

'Yes,' Tahlia called back. 'Crystal, this is Jake Fox, the director.'

Crystal was about to apologise, but she didn't get a chance before Jake muttered, 'You're fucking late,' and walked off.

'Great, just what I need, a stuck-up director with an attitude problem,' Crystal said, riled by his comment.

Tahlia smiled at her. 'Forget about it, he's supposed to be brilliant.'

'He'd better be; I'm not putting up with that for the next week,' Crystal muttered sourly, making one final check of her appearance in the mirror.

'And this is Gavin, Jake's assistant.' Tahlia introduced the cute twenty-something lad who had been hovering behind his boss.

'Hiya, we're ready for you on set now.'

In contrast to Jake, he was smiling. Crystal

smiled back and she, Tahlia and Belle followed him to the studio.

'It's so cool to be working with you guys,' Gavin chattered away in his Liverpudlian accent, pushing his long blond hair out of his eyes. 'We've just done back-to-back shoots with indie bands, who all wanted to look gritty, which gets monotonous after a while.'

'Let's hope your boss feels the same way as you do,' Crystal said wryly, still smarting from Jake's comment.

Gavin laughed. 'Oh, yeah, he hates anyone being late, but he's cool really and I know I'm biased, but he's one of the best in the business.'

The girls had made a video before but this one was far more ambitious, with lots of set and costume changes, nearly twenty extras to work with and intricate dance routines to memorise. For the sixties section the set had been transformed into a sixties-style party. The extras were already in place. Crystal nudged Tahlia and said 'Groovy baby! This looks just like a set from an Austin Powers film!'

The three of them got into position and waited for the music to start up. As she stood, hand on hip, Crystal looked over at the film crew. Jake was staring right at her; he still looked pissed off. Crystal quickly looked away. *Wanker.* Then the music began and she focused on what she was doing instead. They weren't singing live, but miming, which was fortunate because the dance moves were so energetic. She and Tahlia were perfect first time but Belle was struggling and they had to rehearse several times before she got it right – she hadn't been as conscientious lately. She seemed to think that hard graft was beneath her now she had made it, Crystal thought.

Afterwards Danni and Jez came on set to check their make-up and hair. It was extremely hot under the lights and Crystal asked Danni if she could have some water.

She heard Jake tut, and saw him look at his watch. She ignored him and gratefully drank the glass of water Danni brought for her.

'I had an idea as I was watching you just now.' Jake had walked on set and was standing in front of her.

'Oh?' Crystal asked, not wanting Jake to inter-fere with her concept for the film. She was usually open to new ideas but Jake had got her back up.

'Yeah, you're wearing the wrong colours. I think you should be in pink, Belle in black and Tahlia in white.'

'I never wear pink,' Crystal said quietly, annoyed that he was suggesting the change. 'I always wear black. *Always.*'

'The black dress is lost on you because of the wig. Pink would be more of a contrast.'

'Well, maybe I could change wigs then,' Crystal replied, hating the thought of not wearing her favourite colour.

Belle shook her head. 'No way am I wearing that wig! Let's change dresses. I wouldn't mind wearing black.'

'I'll swap so long as you don't mind, Crystal,' Tahlia said quietly.

'Look, come over here, I'll show you what I mean,' Jake said and Crystal reluctantly followed him to one of the cameras. He pressed one of the many buttons and told her to look at the small screen which played back the rehearsal. He was right: black was not showing her to an advantage for once.

'Okay,' she muttered grudgingly, avoiding looking at him, 'I'll change.'

It wasn't as simple as just a change of outfit, though. Danni had to alter their make-up and that took another hour. When she'd finished Crystal nipped outside for a sneaky cigarette. She was just enjoying the feel of the May sunshine on her skin when Jake appeared and said abruptly, 'We've been looking all over for you; we're ready to start. Do you think you might be able to join us?'

God he sounded so arrogant. Crystal was sorely tempted to tell him to fuck off. Instead she ignored him, threw her cigarette on the ground, crushed it with her heel and marched back to the set.

The filming was so much slower than Crystal had imagined. Every two minutes it seemed Jake was shouting cut, telling them to do it again. They didn't call it a day until eight o'clock that night. By then Crystal was exhausted, but she had no desire to go home and spend the night worrying about Max, so when Gavin said that a group of them were going to get something to eat she decided to tag along. She asked Tahlia and Belle but they both had other plans.

Crystal couldn't be bothered to remove her make-up, but it was bliss to take off the wig. Her hair had been completely flattened, so she simply brushed it out and tied it back in a sleek ponytail, and swapped her pink mini dress and boots for a tiny combat print skirt, a black vest, cropped black jacket and black cowboy boots, spraying on her favourite Agent Provocateur perfume.

'Do I look shit?' she asked Jez and Danni as the three of them shared a taxi to the restaurant.

Danni laughed. 'No, you look great.'

'So what did you think of the director?' Jez asked. 'Gorgeous, isn't he?'

Crystal frowned. 'Is he? He was so arsey with me, I didn't notice.'

'Oh, he's delicious!' Jez replied. 'Those stunning blue eyes – passionate one minute, icy the next, that face, that short blond hair that's just begging you to run your fingers through it, that body; I don't know where to begin. Didn't you see those pecs and biceps? And when he reached up to get something I saw his abs and they were perfect,' he sighed heavily. 'But, alas, not gay.'

'He was so arrogant!' Crystal exclaimed. 'I can't believe you think he's attractive.'

'You know me, I love the masterful type,' Jez said, looking dreamily into the distance.

'I'm with Jez,' Danni put in. 'He was hot, hot, hot!' Crystal frowned, thinking that her two friends were deluded.

'And I would have thought Jake was right up your street. It's about time you went out with someone, isn't it? Or if not Jake I know someone who could introduce you to Russell Brand,' said Jez, ever the matchmaker.

'Jez, I'd like to have a relationship with someone, not just a one-off shag. And God knows where those ball bags have been!' Crystal said, laughing.

'Oooh, I know, the swines!' exclaimed Jez.

'No, Jez, I really don't want to be another notch on a very crowded bedpost. And I would never sleep with anyone with bigger hair than me.'

At the Thai restaurant she sat next to Gavin who was like a breath of fresh air; he was so enthusiastic and friendly, wanting to know all about how the group was doing, telling her his younger sister had voted for them when they were on *Band Ambition*. Then Jez insisted on interrogating Gavin about his boss and within a few minutes had established that Jake was single, having split up with his long-term girlfriend three months earlier. Along with directing videos for bands he was a photographer and had just returned from a month in Malawi where he'd been working for a charity, photographing orphans whose parents had died from AIDS.

'Eye candy with a social conscience? He sounds too good to be true, eh Crystal,' Jez winked at her and Crystal rolled her eyes. He was always trying to set her up with men, not realising that she was in no mood for seeing anyone after her experience with Max.

They were halfway through their starters when Jake himself arrived and sat in the empty seat opposite Crystal. He said a general hello to everyone, ordered a beer and drained it in practically one go.

'You look like you needed that,' Jez said, impressed.

'God, yeah,' Jake said ordering another.

'I was just telling everyone about your trip to Malawi,' Gavin said.

'Yeah, it's a bit of a culture shock to be back. Last week I was meeting children who had no family and now here I am—'

'Telling spoilt pop stars what dresses to wear,' Crystal put in dryly.

Jake shrugged. 'Sorry if I was rude today.'

'No problem,' Crystal lied and concentrated on eating her noodles, but she couldn't resist looking up and checking out whether Jez was right in his appraisal of Jake.

Um, beautiful eyes, handsome face, strong features, yes, I suppose he is good-looking. Very good-looking.

She quickly looked away when Jake caught her eye and felt an unexpected flash of desire.

Jez was bang on the money – he really was gorgeous.

'So do you forgive me for making you wear pink?' Jake asked her and Crystal couldn't help thinking that he was taking the piss.

'I suppose so,' she answered. 'Just don't make me do it again.'

'I don't imagine it's usually that easy to persuade you to do something you don't want to.'

'Oh, I'm a pussy cat really,' Crystal answered.

Jake looked at her consideringly. 'Yeah, right. I bet you have a whole list of diva demands – I'm guessing your dressing room has to be full of Diptyque candles, you can only sleep on the purest Egyptian cotton sheets, in restaurants you always order off the menu, you only drink vintage champagne, you have a diamond-encrusted loo seat and people aren't allowed to look you in the eye when they talk to you.'

Crystal laughed. 'That is *so* not true. I draw the line at the diamond-encrusted loo seat.' *Did he really think she was a diva?*

Jake shrugged. 'I've been around performers and models for a long time and, believe me, nothing would surprise me.'

Jez had been listening to their conversation and said loyally, 'Crystal's the least diva-like person I've ever worked with. I've never known her ask for anything, except for a cup of coffee and a bacon sandwich.'

'Yeah, but you came very close to freaking out about the black dress, didn't you?' Jake challenged Crystal.

'Close,' Crystal admitted. 'But I saw reason, didn't I?'

Jake smiled at her and Crystal felt another jolt of desire. 'You did, and for that I thank you.'

For the rest of the meal he was caught up in conversation with Greta, who worked for Dallas and was overseeing the filming to make sure it stayed on budget. Crystal chatted to Gavin, Jez and Danni. But every now and then she found herself sneaking glances at Jake, drawn to his stunning blue eyes, and, she definitely had to admit it – his well fit body. He was pulled back into their conversation at the end of the meal when they were all discussing how to get home. Gavin had discovered that Crystal lived in Westbourne Park and said, 'You could share a taxi with Jake, he lives in Notting Hill.' Crystal wasn't keen. She did find him very attractive, and suddenly felt awkward. It had been so long since she felt like this about a man and she was wary. It was unfamiliar territory.

'Good idea,' Jake said. 'That way I know where you live, and if you're late again, I know where to come and get you.'

Was it her imagination, Crystal wondered, or was he flirting with her?

She scrapped that idea on the taxi ride home when he didn't say a word to her, instead staring moodily out of the window. *Fine by me*, she thought, relieved that she hadn't given any hint that she found him attractive. She was first to be dropped off and, as the taxi pulled over, she reached for her wallet to pay, but Jake refused, saying that he would settle it.

'See you in the morning,' Crystal said getting out of the cab. 'And don't worry: I won't be late tomorrow.'

Now Jake smiled at her. 'Goodnight, Crystal. Sleep well on those Egyptian cotton sheets of yours.'

'I just hope the maid has tidied up,' Crystal bantered back, wondering again whether he was flirting or not?

The following day Crystal arrived on set early. Secretly, she wanted to see Jake and she was disappointed when he seemed too busy to say hello. In fact he barely acknowledged her. For day two the girls were to be dressed as the seventies TV stars Charlie's Angels. Jez had gone to town on their hair, giving them Farrah flicks. All the girls were wearing white trouser suits, with nothing on under their jackets, and Danni spent ages trying to ensure they wouldn't have a wardrobe malfunction by sticking on plenty of tit tape. The routine was slightly easier than the day before and there were fewer retakes. It meant that they were done by four.

Tahlia rushed off to see Leticia and Hadley, and Belle went off for one of her oxygen facials. Danni and Jez had plans and Crystal realised that she was facing an evening on her own, not something she was looking forward to. She would have no excuse but to sort out the money for Max.

As she wandered past the studio, on her way out, Gavin called out, 'See you later, Crystal.'

'Yeah, bye,' Crystal answered. Jake stopped chatting to the crew for a minute and turned round. 'Thanks, Crystal, that was good work today.'

Crystal was not impressed. He sounded patronising and since she had found out about his recent photography for charity she couldn't help thinking that he probably didn't take this work as seriously. So she simply gave a brief smile and carried on walking out of the building, angry with herself for finding him so damned hot. Back home, Max called, demanding to know if she had the money for him.

'I'm in the neighbourhood. I can drop by and collect it.'

Hating the sound of his voice, Crystal snapped, 'No way am I getting twenty grand out in cash. You give me your bank details and I'll transfer it by the end of the week.'

'Okay, that's a deal, babe, I'll text them through in a bit.'

Crystal ended the call and threw her mobile on the sofa in disgust. Then she poured herself a very large vodka. Worried as she was about Max, she found her thoughts returning to Jake and two vodkas down she was on her laptop Googling him.

He'd photographed scores of famous people – film stars, models, musicians: you name them, he'd taken them and the pictures were stunning. He really seemed to capture his subjects in a way they weren't usually seen. But she found her attention focusing more on his private life. There were few details given, but she discovered that he was twenty-nine, his mother was Swedish and his father English. His studio was in London, and he'd dated Eve, the Swedish supermodel, for three years. The only picture of him was one with Eve at some awards function. He was in black tie and looked incredibly handsome, while Eve was in a red silk dress and was breathtakingly beautiful. But according to Gavin they were no longer an item. *Oh, shut up*, she told herself. *He's too serious, not my type*. However, she couldn't deny that he was the sexiest man she'd seen in a *very* long time.

The following day they'd reached the eighties and Madonna was their chosen icon. The girls were paying homage to her *Desperately Seeking Susan* look – short black ra-ra skirts, lace gloves, corsets and footless tights, lots of bangles and beads and wild hair, decorated with ribbons and lace. Tahlia had brought Leticia to the studio as her school was closed and Rosie was at work. Unusually for her, Leticia was playing up, whining that she was bored.

'She's doing my head in,' Tahlia whispered in exasperation as Leticia demanded sweets for the tenth time. Danni was trying to do her make-up but Leticia kept distracting her mum and it was taking Danni much longer than usual.

Seeing how wound up everyone was getting, Crystal stepped in. 'Come on Leticia, we'll go to the café and I'll buy you a treat; but you can only have sweets if you eat an apple as well.'

'Yesss!' Leticia shot out of her chair and grabbed Crystal's hand.

'Thanks, Crystal,' Tahlia said gratefully.

Crystal and Leticia made their way slowly to the café; Crystal wanted to give Danni as much time as possible to finish Tahlia's make-up. Now that sweets had been mentioned Leticia's mood had improved and she was back to her old sunny self. Crystal bought her some chocolate buttons and an apple and for herself a mineral water. They'd just sat down, Leticia had got out her Tamagotchi toy to show Crystal and was explaining how it worked, when Jake walked into the café. He looked sexily rough in faded jeans and a blue T-shirt the colour of his eyes, day-old stubble on his face. Crystal prepared herself for him to ignore her but, to her surprise, he ordered a coffee and asked if he could join them. Leticia immediately asked him if he wanted to see her Tamogotchi and bombarded him with information about how it worked.

'I didn't know you had a daughter,' Jake said, when Leticia finally let him get a word in.

'I haven't,' Crystal answered. 'She's Tahlia's.'

She lowered her voice, and whispered, 'I just needed to get her out of the dressing room so Tahlia could get ready, which has *totally* interrupted my diva routine – usually my personal masseuse would have arrived and be giving me a full body massage before I could even set foot on set.'

Jake smiled. 'Okay, I got you wrong; you're an exception.' His eyes lingered on Crystal and she found herself hoping that he liked her, because she was really starting to like him. She liked him even more when she saw how kind he was to Leticia. She compared his behaviour with Max's, who had never paid Leticia any attention all the times he'd met her – unless he was trying to suck up to everyone. In fact, she doubted that Max even knew what Leticia's name was. Inwardly she shuddered at the thought of Max. Being involved with him had knocked her confidence on so many levels; she used to know when men liked her; now she wasn't so sure of herself.

'You look miles away,' Jake said, pulling her back to the present.

'Sorry, I've got a lot on my mind,' she replied, trying to shake off the unwelcome thoughts of Max.

'What does this say?' Leticia piped up, pointing at a small black tattoo on the inside of Jake's wrist.

Jake frowned and replied. 'It says Eve in Sanskrit.'

'Who's Eve?' Leticia persisted.

'My girlfriend. I mean, my ex-girlfriend. I'm supposed to be getting rid of it.' He didn't look at all comfortable with the direction the conversation was taking.

'Oh well, at least she has a really short name,' Crystal said, trying to keep it light.

'Yes, that's one positive to come out of the whole heap of shit,' Jake said in a voice edged with bitterness.

For a few minutes they were both silent, then Leticia declared, in a voice loud enough to be heard at the other side of the canteen, 'Crystal's got a tattoo of a love heart on her la-la.'

'Leticia!' Crystal exclaimed, her face burning with embarrassment. 'That's *way* too much information.'

'Oh, I don't know,' Jake said, his frown gone. 'It's cheered me up, so that's got to be a good thing. And,' – he added, his tone definitely on the flirtatious side, 'maybe Crystal can show it to me later.'

Leticia giggled while Crystal could hardly bring herself to meet his eye; the old Crystal would have shot back *'I'll show you mine if you show me yours'*, but now she could only look at her watch and mutter something about needing to get back to the dressing room.

'See you later then,' Jake said, giving Crystal a very cheeky grin.

Filming did not get off to a good start. The set – a New York subway station – was proving too small

159

for the number of dancers, and the girls were fighting for space. Several retakes later they were no closer to getting it right and everyone was fed up and hot.

'Okay, let's take a break,' Jake called out, but as Crystal, Belle and Tahlia walked past him, he said, 'can I have a word?'

'I don't think this is working. What do you reckon?' he asked as the girls gathered round him. He looked at Crystal as he spoke, and she replied, 'There's too many people. I think it should just be the three of us on set.'

Jake considered her comment then said, 'Okay, good idea. Could you be ready to film again in half an hour?'

The girls nodded and just as Crystal was about to wander back to the dressing room, Jake lightly touched her arm, and said, 'Thanks, Crystal, that was really helpful.'

They didn't get a chance to talk again for the rest of the day but whenever there was a pause in filming Crystal found herself thinking about Jake again. He was so gorgeous; she was really attracted to him but not just because of his good looks, but because of his personality. And she could see how much everyone else liked and respected him, and how good he was at his job. *It's just a crush*, she tried to tell herself, not very successfully.

That night she went round to Tahlia's for dinner. Hadley was away filming so they'd be able to have a proper girly chat. He'd moved in a month ago and Tahlia couldn't have been happier, telling Crystal that she thought he was *the one*. Crystal was so pleased for her friend, but couldn't help feeling a tiny pang – *was she ever going to meet anyone?*

'Well, at least we're over halfway through,' Tahlia said, examining the blisters on her elegant feet, as they flopped on to the sofa drinking wine.

'Hmm,' Crystal answered, suddenly realising that after Friday she might never see Jake again.

'So what do you think of Jake? He's very sexy, isn't he?'

'Hmm,' Crystal said again, trying to be non-committal. 'I suppose so.'

Tahlia laughed. 'Crystal, I know you think you're the ice queen, but, babe, I can tell that you really like him. And I reckon he likes you.'

'Why do you say that?' Crystal demanded.

'I've seen the way you look at him when you think no one's watching and I've seen the way he looks at you and the way he talks to you.'

'He's hardly talked to me at all,' Crystal said sulkily.

'Well, he's talked to you a hell of a lot more than he's talked to me and Belle. Why don't you ask him out for a drink?'

'God no! I couldn't; what if he doesn't like me and says no?'

Tahlia looked surprised. 'You never used to be afraid to make the first move.'

'I know, it's just that it's been so long since I liked anyone. I'm way out of practice.'

'So you do like him!' Tahlia said triumphantly. 'I knew it.'

'Yeah, but he's just split up with his girlfriend and she was a bloody supermodel. I bet he thinks I'm just a spoilt pop princess.'

'I bet he doesn't, I bet he really fancies you. I bet he wants to see your tattoo,' Tahlia teased her.

'Yeah, right. I've got your daughter to thank for that,' Crystal said, trying to be cool, but inside she felt a flicker of excitement. If Tahlia had noticed him looking at her, then maybe he did fancy her, just a little bit.

By the end of the nineties shoot on Thursday, Crystal was beginning to think there was more than a chance that he was interested. Every time there was a break and she went outside for a cigarette, Jake would come too. His excuse was that he wanted to talk about the filming but they soon moved off that topic and into more personal territory – he asked her about how she'd started in the music business, she asked him about his photography career and there was definite undercurrent of attraction between them that brought a sparkle to Crystal's eyes and a glow to her face and made her look forward to the next break.

'So what are you doing after this?' he asked,

leaning against the wall next to her.

'We'll be promoting the single and I want to write more songs for the next album,' she replied, trying to blow the cigarette smoke away from him.

'So will you be around in London?'

'Yes, we've got interviews in Europe, but we're mainly here.' She paused, thinking and hoping *maybe he wants to know what I'm doing because he's going to ask me out*. But they were interrupted by Gavin telling Jake he had an urgent call.

He sighed. 'Sorry, I'd better go. I'll catch up with you later.' *Did he sound reluctant to end the conversation?* Crystal wondered. God, her ability to understand men's behaviour had completely gone. She felt like a teenager again – uncertain and unsure of herself.

She didn't get to see him later and she had to go straight from the studios to *Style* magazine's annual awards night with Belle and Tahlia. Belle spent the night chatting to as many celebrities as she could, while Crystal and Tahlia hung out together. Crystal could never see the point of talking to people just because they were famous. She liked her friends because of their personalities, rather than what they did, but Belle had taken to the celebrity circuit like a *Big Brother* contestant to a tabloid photo shoot and there was no holding her back when there were celebs around.

'I need to talk to you about Belle,' Tahlia said suddenly, as they both watched her chatting to a group of WAGs, who all looked identical – with their perfectly toned and carbohydrate-starved bodies, fake-bake tans, long hair extensions, all proudly displaying their outrageously expensive designer bags. Crystal did not get why anyone would want to spend three grand on a bag, which would then be out of date the next year – she'd had to worry about money for too long to want to blow it on handbags.

'What about?' Crystal asked

Tahlia shook her head. 'Not here, next time we're on our own together.'

Crystal wondered what was worrying Tahlia. She'd been so preoccupied with thinking about Jake that for the first time in months she'd hardly thought about either Max or Belle.

'So are you going to ask Jake out?' Tahlia said. 'You really should'.

'I don't know,' Crystal said coyly. 'Maybe. Or maybe he'll ask *me* out.'

For the final day of the shoot they were in the present day and Kate Moss was their chosen style icon. Instead of attempting to look like her – after all, who could look like Kate Moss? – they were dressed in the clothes that she'd made fashion must-haves – skinny jeans, black pumps, blue and white striped T-shirts and heavy gold chain necklaces. Make-up was kept minimal and natural, and Jez gave them all that just-rolled-out-of-bed-because-I've-been-shagging-all-night hair.

While Tahlia and Crystal loved the look – the outfit was the kind of thing they'd wear anyway – Belle wasn't happy. She liked her blonde hair blow dried and ironed totally straight, plus she always wore killer heels. She'd taken Victoria Beckham's style advice to heart – that the way to seduce a man was to be kitted out in tight jeans and sky-high heels and, while she didn't always wear jeans, she always wore heels.

'There must be some high boots I can wear,' she moaned on to Jessica. Despite Belle's best efforts Dallas hadn't sacked her yet.

'No,' Jessica said patiently, 'then you'll be too tall and you'll look odd next to Crystal and Tahlia.'

'But I never wear flat shoes,' Belle protested. 'They make my legs look fat.'

'Come on, Belle, you look great in pumps,' Crystal put in, wanting the argument to be over so they could get on with filming.

'No I don't!' Belle snapped. 'And I'm not wearing them! Jessica, you're going to have to go out and get us all high boots that we can wear over the jeans.'

Jessica tried to explain that wasn't the look, but Belle was seriously losing her cool. Crystal and Tahlia looked at each other and raised their eyebrows. *Belle could be such high maintenance*, Crystal thought.

'Belle, we really haven't got time for this,' Crystal started saying.

'I don't fucking care. I'm not wearing those

pumps and that's it.' And to prove her point she picked up the pumps and threw them across the room just as Jake was walking in. One of the shoes hit him just below his eyebrow, the metal buckle nicking his skin.

'Shit!' Jake exclaimed. A thin line of blood trickled down his face. 'What's going on here?'

'We're having a heated debate about shoes,' Crystal said, hoping to defuse the situation. 'By the way, your face is bleeding. I'll get something for it,' and she scrabbled around on the table for some cotton wool.

'We've got to make a start; we've only got the studio 'til three today. There's another booking straight afterwards,' Jake went on.

'Get me the right shoes then,' Belle snapped. 'I'm not going to be filmed looking like a fucking heifer!'

Jake looked furious. Crystal approached him cautiously and attempted to wipe away the blood to see the extent of the cut, but he brushed her arm away impatiently. 'It's fine, thanks.' Then, realising he wasn't going to get anywhere with Belle, he turned to Jessica. 'How quickly can you get the other shoes?'

'A couple of hours, I guess.'

'Okay, just be as quick as you can.' And he marched back out of the room.

Belle gave a satisfied, cat-that-got-the-cream smile.

'Aren't you going to say sorry?' Crystal demanded, shocked by her thoughtless behaviour.

Belle shrugged. 'It was his fault for getting in the way and if I'd been given heels in the first place it wouldn't have happened.'

Not wanting to stay in the same room as Belle while she was in this mood, Crystal left the dressing room and went outside for a cigarette. Gavin was already having one out there. He saw Crystal and smiled. 'How's the shoe diva?'

Crystal shrugged. 'I know, it's a pain in the arse, but she won't budge. I bet Jake's really pissed off?'

'He just wants to get on with filming.'

'Yes, I do.' Crystal and Gavin turned to see Jake leaning against the door. 'You know it's times like this I really wished I smoked, even though I think it's a foul habit.'

Crystal took a drag of her cigarette and blew a smoke ring in his direction.

'I agree, but there are worse things, aren't there?' she said.

'Not really,' Jake said abruptly. 'My gran died of emphysema and it really wasn't a pleasant way to die.'

Bloody hell. First AIDS orphans, now this. What had happened to their flirtatious banter?

'He's a right barrel of laughs, isn't he?' Gavin said, gesturing at his boss.

Jake grimaced. 'Sorry, it's just that time is really tight today and I could have done without the delay.'

'Is your face okay?' Crystal asked.

'I think I'll survive.'

'Let me see', and Crystal threw down her cigarette and stood on tiptoes to get a closer look at the cut, trying to avoid staring into Jake's blue eyes, but very aware that she was standing so close that her breasts were almost touching his chest.

'What's the verdict then?' he asked, seeming amused by her concern.

'I don't think it will scar,' she said, moving away from him.

'That's a pity. I could have sued her and retired on the proceeds. I shouldn't say this, but how the fuck do you put up with her?'

Crystal laughed. 'She isn't like that all the time. She's just got a thing about heels.'

'Like your thing about wearing black?' Jake asked.

'I guess so, but I don't usually resort to violence to get my own way, and anyway, if you remember, I gave in.'

'And when you see the result you will thank me for it. By the way, I like the Kate Moss look. It suits you.'

'Thanks,' Crystal answered, secretly pleased at the compliment.

Jessica was back within the hour with three pairs of black leather boots and Belle seemed satisfied, even though she moaned when she found out that they weren't designer.

'Come off it, Belle, give her a break; she only had an hour to get them,' Crystal said sharply, hating Belle's attitude.

'All right, all right,' Belle grumbled, zipping up the boots. And finally they could get on set.

As the girls got into position Belle called out, 'Sorry for the delay. To make up for it I've arranged with my fiancé that you can all get in free to his club tonight. And there'll be drinks on the house for everyone.' She turned to Tahlia and Crystal. 'You'll come won't you?'

Thinking it would be hard to come up with an excuse not to, Crystal nodded. *Fuck.* She was so thrown by Belle's invitation that it took her several takes to get her first dance sequence right. *Was she ever going to get Max out of her life?*

Chapter 9

A New Flame

A few hours later she was back at her flat, wondering what to wear. Her mood had been dramatically improved by the news that Max was away on business, so he wouldn't be at the club. But Jake would. She'd made a point of seeking him and Gavin out after the filming to thank them and to find out when she could see the first cut of the video. Despite Tahlia nagging her, she just wasn't feeling gutsy enough to ask Jake out for a drink.

'So are you going tonight, Crystal?' Gavin had asked.

'I expect so,' she'd replied, willing herself not to care if Jake wasn't going. 'Are you two?'

'Definitely,' Gavin replied. 'I haven't been to one of those celeb clubs before.'

Crystal looked at Jake, who nodded and said, 'Yeah, I'll drop by.'

Crystal rifled through her wardrobe. She'd been dressing up, and plastered in make-up all week;

really she just wanted to chill out in jeans and a vest. Then she thought of Jake's blue eyes and reconsidered. She reached for her sexy LBD, strapless, with a corset-style top, that gave good cleavage, and slipped on her black velvet Jimmy Choo heels.

She had to steel herself when she arrived at Max's; she was convinced that as she walked past the security guy he gave her a knowing look. Inside the VIP area Belle was playing the hostess with the mostest, ensuring everyone had champagne, making up for her behaviour earlier. Still, it was easy to be generous when it was Max's champagne she was giving out. Crystal scanned the room looking for Jake, but there was no sign of him and she couldn't help feeling disappointed.

'You look gorgeous, Crystal,' Tahlia said, her arms wrapped round Hadley.

'Cheers, Tahlia, so do you. How are you doing, Hadley?'

As Hadley chatted away about his latest TV project, Crystal felt so pleased that Tahlia had found such a sweet guy. He was kind, thoughtful, easy-going and clearly adored Tahlia. He might not have an edge, but, as she had learnt to her cost with Max, having an edge was definitely not always a good thing. She sipped her drink and took another quick look around the room. This time, to her delight, she spotted him deep in conversation with Dallas. Crystal's heart raced just that little bit faster. He was so sexy! She took another sip, willing him to

171

notice her. Dallas was first to see her and he beckoned her over.

'Crystal!' he exclaimed, double-kissing her cheeks, 'I've been hearing from Jake how well the filming has gone. Sounds like you three really pulled it off, despite a few hiccups.'

'Or a pair of pumps, to be precise,' Jake put in, touching his eyebrow.

'Belle can be a bit of a Park Avenue Princess. Fortunately for her she's pretty and successful enough to get away with it. Anyway, I've got business to see to. We'll speak next week, Crystal. Thanks again, Jake.' And with that Dallas swept off through the partygoers.

'Must be nice being Dallas. He never seems to have a second's doubt about anything. He always seems so sure,' Jake said.

'Yeah, he thinks doubts are for losers. Still,' Crystal added not wanting to be disloyal, 'I'm glad he's our manager.'

Jake smiled. 'I just hope Gavin's that generous about me.'

'He told us you were, and I quote, "the best in the business",' Crystal said, pleased that Jake seemed in no hurry to talk to anyone else.

He laughed. 'That's bullshit, but he'll get his bribe later. Can I get you another drink? Champagne again?'

Crystal nodded and handed him her glass. She watched him weave his way to the bar. At six foot three he was easily the tallest man there. *And definitely the sexiest.* She stayed where she was, hoping no one would come and disturb their conversation.

When he returned with their drinks he suggested they find somewhere to sit. *Better and better*, thought Crystal. They were quiet for a few minutes while they sipped their drinks. Tahlia and Hadley wandered by still with their arms round each other and, seeing them, Jake said, 'Is *your* boyfriend busy tonight then, Crystal?'

If he was asking that, surely he must be slightly interested.

'I'm single at the moment, actually,' Crystal replied, trying to sound casual. 'How about your girlfriend?' She wanted to double-check that he really wasn't with Eve any more. She actually felt herself blush and hoped it was dark enough for Jake not to have noticed. She didn't think she was the blushing type, but Jake seemed to be having quite an effect on her.

'I'm single too.' He was looking right at her and Crystal gazed back at him. *This was very promising.*

They spent the next couple of hours locked in conversation. He wanted to know all about her and about the group. As he hadn't watched *Band Ambition* he didn't know much about them until Dallas had booked him for the video.

'To be honest, Crystal, I'm more of a Red Hot Chili Peppers kind of guy, but I can see the attraction of your kind of music.'

'God, that sounds so patronising!' Crystal

answered. 'You're not our target audience anyway, you're way too old!'

'Just how old do you think I am?' Jake demanded.

'Twenty-nine,' Crystal answered confidently, she knew because she'd Googled him.

'Very good, and you're . . .' he paused, moving closer to consider her, so close that Crystal got a delicious hit of his aftershave. 'I can't see any lines, but then you could have been Botoxed.'

Crystal laughed, and he went on, 'Ah, but I can see some now so you obviously haven't yet. I reckon that you're twenty.'

'Twenty-two,' Crystal corrected him.

'A baby then,' he replied.

'No, I'm all grown up and used to looking after myself,' Crystal said cheekily.

They were sitting so close on the sofa that their bodies were almost touching, their heads close together so that they could hear each other speak over the music, and Crystal realised that she wanted him, really wanted him. She thought, after what had happened with Max, that she was immune from finding men attractive, but the way she felt about Jake, the way she longed to kiss him, the way she longed to touch him, told her she most definitely wasn't. And surely she wasn't imagining it? Jake liked her too.

They'd finished their drinks and Crystal offered to get some more.

'There's a great bar near my place in Notting Hill; it's a bit quieter than here. If you like we could go there?' Jake said.

'Sure, I'll just say goodbye to the others,' Crystal replied, feeling a sweet rush of excitement.

But the change of scene seemed to break the intimacy between them and yet again in the taxi Jake was silent, just staring out of the window. Crystal felt awkward and almost said that she would go home. He was still quiet in the bar and when he returned with their drinks Crystal felt compelled to say something.

'Look, if you've changed your mind about having a drink, it's okay. I don't mind calling it a night; we've both had a really long week.'

Jake looked surprised. 'God, have I given that impression? I didn't mean to. I really want you to stay. I'm just a bit out of practice at this kind of thing.'

'Okay, then,' Crystal said softly. 'I'll stay.'

They stayed in the bar for the next two hours. Crystal loved being with Jake. She felt as if she'd been living in the shade for the last six months and now the sun had finally come out and she could be herself again – the Crystal who could flirt and laugh, the Crystal who enjoyed being desirable, the Crystal who men found sexy. And Jake was making it clear that he found her sexy too, from the way he couldn't take his eyes off her, and sat so close to her. At three, the bar finally closed and Jake said he'd walk her home. As they wandered down the elegant, tree-lined streets towards her flat, Crystal hoped that this was the start of something. She shivered in the cool night air in her party dress.

'Are you cold?' Jake asked and when she nodded, he put his arm round her, and pulled her close, causing more butterflies. It felt so good that she wanted their stroll to go on and on, but it wasn't long before they reached her flat.

'This is me,' she said as they drew parallel to a white Georgian mansion that had been converted into flats. Crystal's was on the ground floor.

'Good night then, Crystal,' he said, dipping his head to kiss her lightly on the lips. Was that it? Crystal thought, disappointed at such an innocent kiss. But then it wasn't just a light kiss, it became a deep, hard, sexy kiss that left Crystal wanting so much more . . . She was about to ask if he wanted to come in when Jake pulled away. 'I'll call you tomorrow,' he said softly.

Inside her flat she caught sight of her reflection in the mirror above the fireplace. Her cheeks were flushed, and the sparkle was back in her eyes, her lips looked red and full from their passionate kiss. *Wow*, she thought, *I'm in lust*.

She woke up with a delicious feeling of anticipation. It was such a novelty after the cocktail of anxiety and dread which had been with her since Ibiza. *Jake was going to call her!* She reached for her watch. It was eleven. She took a shower, taking the phone into the bathroom with her; no call. She made herself breakfast with her mobile right next to her on the table, but still there was no call. At midday she had an appointment with Bradley, her personal trainer, which she half thought about cancelling in case Jake called, but she knew that was pathetic and she forced herself to go along to the gym.

Crystal did not like exercise, which was why she had Bradley to motivate her. Unfortunately she was not one of those women who could do zero exercise, eat what they liked and stay in shape. She doubted that such women actually existed and weren't just lying about what they ate, pretending to stuff themselves but in reality living off rice cakes, fags and water. Crystal looked good – had a flat stomach, toned arms, legs and a pert bum – because she worked hard to get her body into shape. And she had to work out because she liked food too much to starve herself to keep slim. Bradley was great because he always knew exactly how far to push her and he didn't let her slack. Today was no exception; he had her doing two hundred sit-ups on the exercise ball, thirty minutes on the treadmill and then half an hour using the weights. Every time she changed activity she sneaked a look at her mobile, but there were no calls.

'Expecting a call, Crystal?' Bradley asked, raising his eyebrow as she checked her phone for what must have been the tenth time.

Mobiles were banned from the gym but Crystal had smuggled hers in under her towel.

She sighed. 'It's on silent, I promise, Bradley, and yes I thought he would have rung by now.' It was half one.

Bradley smiled. 'He'll ring, don't worry. Go and have a swim and a steam and I bet he'll call.'

Crystal did what he suggested, but there was still no message from Jake when she checked. Disappointment was starting to creep in. *Why hadn't he called? Didn't he like her? Maybe she'd misread the signs, but how could she – that kiss had been so damn good. God, it was frustrating!* The pre-Max Crystal would probably have called him herself by now. The post-Max Crystal didn't have the confidence. Outside the gym she hailed a taxi. She had a hair appointment booked with Jez at the trendy Islington salon that he co-owned with his ex – luckily the split had been amicable.

'He's obviously not interested,' she moaned as Jez trimmed her hair. She knew she could trust Jez 100 per cent; she was always teasing him that he was like her shrink and got to hear all her secrets – well, nearly all, she had never told him about Max.

Jez tried to cheer her up. 'Honey, I'm sure he is. What man could be immune to you, unless he was gay? He's probably tied up at work. You saw how frantic it was on set.'

'Oh come on, he could have found the time if he wanted to,' Crystal said sulkily, taking a sip of white wine. She knew she should have been sticking to water after her workout but was feeling too despondent to care about the calories.

Jez looked at his watch. 'It's only four o'clock, perhaps he meant he would call you in the evening, when he had more time to chat.'

Crystal sighed. 'Maybe. It's just he's the first man I've felt anything for in ages.'

'Tell us about it!' Jez replied. 'Danni and I were starting to think that you had gone over to the planet Lesbos.'

'God no, women are far too high maintenance and so much harder to please in bed,' Crystal retorted. 'And I do like a nice bit of cock.'

'Couldn't agree with you more,' Jez answered, blatantly checking out an attractive male passer-by.

That night she and Tahlia had a film premiere to go to. Belle had flown out to see Max in Ibiza so she couldn't make it, though as a rule she never missed them, as she enjoyed flaunting her new-found celebrity far too much. Usually Crystal would have enjoyed getting dressed up in some fabulous designer dress – now that the band had made it, designers had been queuing up to lend the girls their clothes. And if she was honest she enjoyed the attention as well – working the red carpet posing for the paps, signing autographs for fans; who wouldn't? Especially as this time a year ago she was working her arse off being paid a pittance in a bar.

But tonight her heart wasn't in it. All she could think about throughout the film and after party was Jake and why he hadn't phoned. Maybe he hadn't really split up with Eve. Maybe they'd got back together.

'Come on, Crystal!' Tahlia exclaimed when Crystal confided how she felt. 'He wouldn't have kissed you like that if he was planning to get back with his ex.'

'He might have,' Crystal replied gloomily, recalling how easy Max had found it to sleep with two women. She took another sip of her cocktail but the alcohol just made her feel even more depressed.

Her mood wasn't helped when they bumped into the four members of @ttitude. Since Lost Angels had won *Band Ambition*, the feud between the two groups had intensified. Tahlia and Crystal had tried to stay well out of the slanging match but Belle continued to match @ttitude insult for insult. @ttitude's album had flopped and they had been dropped by their record company. Now they spent their time shagging any Z-list celebs that they could get close to before selling their stories. They pretended that another record deal was in the pipeline and that they were going to break into movies. Belle's latest comment about this news had been that the only movies they were likely to break into were porno ones. And now Kimmi, Faith, Paige and Alicia were standing in front of them blocking their way.

A New Flame

'Well, look who it isn't, Crystal Meth and Tahlia Titsout,' sneered Kimmi, the lead singer. Kimmi regularly appeared in *heat* magazine's 'What were you thinking?'. She was infamous for her revealing outfits – if she wore jeans they were so low cut that they barely covered her backside and at the front revealed that she was no stranger to waxing; tops were always low cut giving everyone an eyeful. And the only make-up rules she followed were slap it on thick. Her waist-length, bleached hair always looked in need of a good wash – it gave hair extensions a bad name – and one of her many exes had revealed how they fell out in clumps in bed, a detail that Crystal could have done without knowing. Tonight was no exception and Kimmi seemed to have pulled out all the stops. She was wearing an eye-wateringly tight black-leather bustier that pushed her tits up to her chin with skintight silver trousers which gave her a shocking camel toe.

'Excuse me,' Crystal said. 'Can we get past?'

'Not before we've had a little word,' slurred Faith. She'd obviously been hitting the free bar. Faith unfortunately seemed to take her fashion tips from Kimmi and was wearing a purple lace mini dress, with nothing but a thong on underneath, teamed with purple thigh-length boots. Her dyed auburn hair was pulled back into a Croydon face-lift.

Crystal and Tahlia turned to go the other way

but Paige and Alicia, bleached-blonde clones in denim hot pants and bikini tops, quickly moved and stood in front of them. They looked like porn stars and had obviously been chosen for their looks and not their singing abilities.

Crystal could see the other guests hovering in anticipation to see what was going to happen next. *God it was so school playground.*

'Where's the blonde slag then?' hissed Kimmi.

'You're out of order; just move out of the way. We haven't got a problem with you,' Tahlia replied.

'Well, we've got a problem with you, the way you keep bad-mouthing us, you talentless bitches,' Kimmi again. 'This time next year everyone will have forgotten about you – there'll be some other shit reality band in your place.'

'And shouldn't you be at home with your daughter or have you found some other druggie to look after her and get you up the duff?' Faith joined in.

That did it; no way was Crystal going to stand there and listen to her friend being insulted. She pulled out her phone and dialled up Bill, their driver, who often doubled as their security guy. She didn't say anything – they'd used this routine several times before, usually with fans who wouldn't leave them alone.

'I'll be right down, Crystal,' Bill said.

Crystal snapped her phone shut. Faith laughed. 'Not there, Crystal? You'll just have to stay around a bit longer, we're not finished with you yet.'

Crystal turned to Tahlia and rolled her eyes, 'Whatever.' There were plenty of things she could have said to the girls, but no way was she going to sink to their level. She reckoned it would be two minutes before Bill pitched in. Faith then started on Crystal.

'And what's your problem anyway, Crystal Meth? Not got anyone to shag you yet?'

Crystal pretended to yawn and then, as Faith was about to launch into another tirade, Bill arrived on the scene – all six foot four of him and two hundred pounds of muscle. Bill was an ex-squaddie who looked as rough as boots but who was actually lovely, and bred Persian cats in his spare time.

'We're ready to go now, Bill,' Crystal said to him, as he stood towering over Kimmi.

'Well, we haven't finished,' screeched Kimmi, trying to stop him moving her. But Bill picked her up as easily as if she was a child and lifted her on to one of the tables nearby. She shouted at the other girls to stop him, but they all backed away nervously. Crystal and Tahlia then sauntered past them. Crystal couldn't resist a parting shot; 'I hear *Love Island* are looking for contestants; you should give them a call, you'd be perfect.' Then she and Tahlia walked out of the club without so much as a backward glance.

'Cheers, Bill,' Tahlia said as Bill drove them away from the club.

'That's what I'm here for,' he replied. 'To serve and protect my angels.'

'Belle was right about that lot,' Crystal said. 'They give trash a bad name.'

It was after one by the time she got home. Crystal had a taste for the minimalist when it came to interior design. Her two-bedroom flat was painted white throughout, with stripped wooden floors. She had grown up in a cluttered, claustrophobic flat in Camden, north London, which had never felt warm or inviting and now she loved having the feeling of space. Her living room had high ceilings, an original marble Victorian fireplace, and the only furniture she'd added was two white sofas, an elegant glass coffee table, and a red velvet chair. On the walls hung a giant Andy Warhol screen print of Marilyn Monroe and a black and white photo Crystal had enlarged of her and her brother together, when she was eight and he was six, on one of the few holidays they had ever been taken on. The pair of them were grinning away on Camber Sands in their swimming costumes and sun hats, each clutching an ice cream. Crystal looked at the picture now, trying to imagine what it had felt like to be so blissfully happy. It was after that holiday that their dad had stopped having them to stay at the weekend and saw them less and less frequently, by the time she was ten he had moved away and lost contact with them completely. For years, Crystal hated Saturday mornings, hated knowing that her dad was never going to come and pick her and Luke up.

She was jolted from her thoughts by her mobile. Her heart raced as she fumbled in her bag to locate it. Unknown number flashed on the screen. She flipped her phone open to answer it. It was Jake.

'Have I blown it?' he asked

'No,' she answered, 'I just wondered why you hadn't called.'

'There were so many times when I was going to. I thought about you all day.' He paused then went on, 'I'm just scared of getting involved with someone else, it's so soon after Eve.' He sounded slightly drunk. 'But the thing is, I do want to get involved with *you*.'

Crystal hesitated; she could be cool, or she could say how she really felt. She went for honesty. 'And I want to get involved with you,' she answered softly.

'So would dinner tomorrow make up for me being so crap today?'

'I should play hard to get and say no, shouldn't I?' Crystal replied.

'No, Crystal. No games, that's the deal with me, we have to be honest.' He sounded serious.

'All right, no games,' she answered, equally serious. 'I'll see you tomorrow night.'

Chapter 10

Crazy for You

'So you like him then, Chrissy?' Her brother Luke asked, as the two of them caught up over lunch in one of the many cafés in Brighton's Lanes. He was the only person she would allow to call her that. Crystal had planned the trip to see her brother several weeks ago – they didn't get to meet up as often as she would have liked because of her work and because Luke's business was taking off. He'd been running his own garden design company for a year and was doing well, but competition was tough and as a result he rarely had a day off. So Crystal really didn't think she could cancel even though she wanted to prepare for her first date with Jake that night.

Crystal nodded and smiled. 'I really do.'

Luke raised his coffee cup and declared, 'Here's to him then. I just hope he's good enough for my big sis.'

Crystal looked at her brother. She felt such a

fierce, protective love for him. As far as she was concerned he was all the family she had in the world and he meant everything to her. She'd barely spoken to her mum in months. And neither of them had heard from their dad in years. When her mother had left for Spain it had been a huge responsibility for Crystal; Luke was only thirteen. Throughout his teenage years Crystal had worried about him – worried he would be bullied because they didn't have much money and he couldn't afford the PlayStations, Xboxes, computer games and expensive trainers that his friends could, worried too that he would fall in with the wrong crowd. But Luke had stayed the sweet, open person that he'd always been. When he was sixteen he told Crystal that he wanted to be a garden designer and that's exactly what he'd trained to do. She was very proud of him.

After lunch Luke wanted to show her the garden he was working on. She was bowled over by what he'd done. He'd created such a beautiful space. 'You're so talented!' she exclaimed. 'I don't know what any of these plants are but they look fantastic.'

'Perhaps one day I'll design a garden for you and Jake,' Luke answered, clearly pleased by her reaction.

'For me definitely,' Crystal replied. The mention of Jake's name made her check her watch. It was four o'clock. 'I'd better start heading back now,' she added, feeling her heart racing faster at the prospect of seeing Jake.

'Sure, you need to get ready for your big date,' Luke teased her.

As he drove her to the station Crystal mentally ticked off all the things she needed to do – shower, shave legs, put on nail varnish, and then decide what to wear. Jake had texted her to say that he'd booked a table at Le Caprice in Mayfair for eight o'clock so she wanted to wear something smart.

She caught the 4.49 with seconds to spare, then sat back in her seat; she should be back in London with plenty of time to get ready. Two hours later she was not feeling so good. The train had been stuck outside Haywards Heath. And to make matters worse, she couldn't text Jake to tell him because she had no signal and nor did any one else in her carriage.

She finally arrived back home at eight o'clock, almost crying with frustration. She'd texted and called Jake once she had a signal to tell him she was going to be late but he hadn't replied. She could only hope that he'd got the message. Realising she had no time for a shower, she simply cleaned her teeth, sprayed on some perfume and changed her T-shirt for a long black vest which she wore with a thick black belt. She kicked off her pumps, swapping them for her favourite Christian Louboutin slingbacks, keeping her jeans on. She had to put her make-up on in the taxi. She arrived at the restaurant forty minutes late. It was not the entrance she had planned.

'I'm so sorry I'm late,' she exclaimed when the waiter showed her to the table.

Jake managed a small smile, but she could tell he was pissed off.

He softened slightly when she gave her explanation about the train, but there was a distance between them that hadn't been there the last time they had been together.

'Didn't you get my messages?' Crystal asked.

He shook his head. 'I left my phone at a friend's; I'm crap with mobiles.'

They hardly spoke after the waiter had taken their order. This was not what Crystal had imagined happening, not after their kiss. What was going on?

She looked at Jake. God, he was so handsome, but he seemed so distant, so reserved.

She had another sip of wine, longing for a cigarette, even though she knew he didn't approve.

Their hors d'oeuvres arrived but Crystal's appetite had left her. She didn't want to be sitting in the restaurant with someone who didn't want to be with her. She rearranged the food around her plate and drank more wine.

Finally, Jake spoke. 'I'm sorry, Crystal, I'm behaving like such a shit; it's just that when you weren't here I thought you were standing me up.'

'Why would I do that?' Crystal demanded, stunned that he would think such a thing.

'I'm sure you wouldn't but my ex-girlfriend . . .' he paused, obviously struggling with his feelings, 'did it several times towards the end of our relationship when she'd forgotten that she had arranged to meet me and she was busy shagging her other man. And it's just left me with this feeling that I can't trust anyone.' He ran his fingers through his short blond hair. 'God, I hate being like this! All day I've wanted to see you and now I seem to be doing everything to push you away. I don't blame you if you want to go.'

'And all I was worried about was that I hadn't had time for a shower! I had no idea I would be having dinner with someone who had so much baggage.' Crystal tried to make light of the situation while she tried to understand what had been going through Jake's head.

Jake made a conscious effort to shake off his mood. 'You didn't have a shower!' he said in mock horror, then took her hand and gently kissed the inside of her wrist, saying, 'You smell delicious', sending a shiver of desire through Crystal. She had made a list of reasons in her mind why there was no way she would sleep with him tonight: 1) because she hadn't known him long enough, 2) because she hadn't showered, 3) because she hadn't shaved her legs. But the touch of his lips against her skin and the way he was looking at her made her want to revise that decision.

The rest of the evening was very nearly a perfect

first date. Jake stopped being abrupt, he opened up and they slipped back easily into flirtatious talk. As they left the restaurant Crystal had almost decided to go home with him. And when Jake pulled her into a doorway and started kissing her in the passionate way he had before, Crystal definitely wanted to take things further. But she was in for a surprise when, after a kiss which seemed to be leading to more, Jake hailed a taxi and, instead of following her in, remained on the pavement and said, 'I'd better get my mobile. I'll call you tomorrow.'

Crystal sat back in the taxi in a state of disbelief and frustration. She wanted him and she knew he wanted her, so what was the big deal? Back home she finally showered but was feeling too wound up to go to bed. There was no point in phoning any of her friends as it was too late; besides, Tahlia wouldn't get it, she'd just think he was respecting her by not sleeping with her on the first date. In spite of Jake saying he didn't like game playing, it seemed to Crystal as if that's exactly what he was doing.

Their next three dates followed the same pattern – every one ending in passionate kissing that had Crystal longing to rip his clothes off and get him into bed. Jake was a gorgeous kisser and in Crystal's experience that meant he was bound to be a great lover. But each time Jake pulled away and said goodnight. When she finally told Tahlia, her friend laughed at her and told her to enjoy it and that it was good to take things slowly. Jez was a little more on her wavelength but also told her the best things were worth waiting for. 'Yeah, right,' she told him. 'That means a big fat nothing coming from you seeing as your middle name is instant gratification. How long after meeting Rufus was it before you had sex?'

'Half an hour,' Jez admitted. 'But you hetrosexualists are different.'

By the Saturday she was about to explode with frustration. They'd been to see a film together and everything had been perfect until the end of the night, when Jake yet again hailed her a taxi. She could barely bring herself to say goodnight to him as he shut the door. What was wrong with her? Why didn't he want to take things further? Didn't he fancy her? Back home she threw herself on her sofa and considered whether to get out her Rabbit. But that was the trouble with vibrators; they were great for when you just wanted a quick fix, not so great when you burned with desire for someone in particular . . .

She lit a cigarette instead and switched on the TV. *Big Brother* was on. *Oh well*, she thought, *I may as well watch some people who are getting even less sex than me*. She was just getting into the housemates' bitch fest – the 'he-said-she-said-no-I-fucking-didn't!' routine – when her doorbell rang. Thinking it was probably someone wanting her neighbour, she ignored it. But it went again.

She marched to her front door, intending to give the insistent caller a piece of her mind but she saw Jake on the video screen. She picked up the receiver, and buzzed him in. She opened her front door; arms folded trying to look cool, while inside she was anything but.

'I know it's late, but I had to see you,' Jake said.

Crystal shrugged. 'I wasn't asleep, come in.'

As soon as she shut the door his mouth found hers and his hands caressed her body, undoing the buttons on her black silk dress. They fell on to one of the huge white sofas in a tangle of limbs. Crystal didn't care that he might think she was easy or a slag; she just wanted him and it felt so right. She pulled off his T-shirt, caressed his flat, hard stomach. He slipped off her dress and began kissing her breasts, sucking her nipples in the most tantalising way that had Crystal almost writhing with desire and wishing he would explore more of her body.

'God, I want you,' he murmured. 'I wanted you as soon as I saw you.

Why the fuck have you kept me waiting then? Crystal was tempted to ask; instead she surrendered herself to his touch, to the way his fingers moved further down her body, ending up between her legs and gently, teasingly, he caressed her through her silk underwear. And then he was slipping down the silk and his tongue was on her, hot and knowing, and Crystal closed her eyes and gave herself to the pleasure.

193

Then she was pulling him up to her, kissing him deeply, while she unbuttoned his jeans and eased them down his muscular thighs. Then she was slipping down his black Calvins, revealing his hard cock, caressing it with her hands, with her tongue, then he was stopping her, reaching for a condom. Crystal lay back on the sofa watching him. God, he was so sexy. She closed her eyes in anticipation and it was just as good as she thought it would be. But suddenly she had a flashback to Max raping her. She froze and felt the tears well up in her eyes. She wanted Jake to stop. Every time he tried to kiss her she turned away, not wanting him to see the tears.

All the desire she had felt had gone and she just wanted it to be over, so she could cry on her own. Realising it wasn't going to be unless she put in a performance, she faked it for all she was worth, willing him to come.

'God, that was so good,' Jake panted, reaching out and touching her face, which was by now wet with tears. 'Hey, what's wrong?' he asked, concerned.

'Nothing,' Crystal tried to say, then found herself sobbing. All the pain, humiliation and hurt she'd felt about Max seemed to be pouring out of her and she was powerless to stop it, even though the timing couldn't have been worse.

She tried to get up to go to the bathroom, but Jake held her tightly in his arms, stroking her hair and telling her it was okay. Crystal didn't feel okay; she was mortified.

'I've never had that effect on a woman before,' Jake said lightly as Crystal dried her eyes on a tissue he'd got her. 'Was I that bad?'

Crystal gave a wobbly smile. 'God, I'm sorry, I don't know what happened.'

'D'you want to talk about it?'

Crystal shook her head, dreading that she would start crying again. 'Maybe you'd better go,' she mumbled.

'No way. I'm not leaving you like this.'

In bed Jake put his arms round her and held her tight, telling her how beautiful she was. He was so perfect, and now she'd blown it with him. She couldn't believe he would ever want to see her again. *He must think I'm some kind of frigid nutter*, she thought miserably. She closed her eyes and prepared for a sleepless night of agonising about what had happened. Instead, she fell into an exhausted sleep.

She woke up feeling totally disorientated and turning over to look for Jake she found a note on the pillow. *It's probably to tell me to fuck off after last night*, she told herself grimly.

Hi Crystal, I've had to go to work. How about meeting me for lunch in Soho at 1 p.m.? If you wake up by then! Jake x.

So he wasn't dumping her and she hadn't blown it. He must still like her. *Last night was a one off*, she told herself. *I'm not going to let Max ruin things.*

She showered and changed in record time. She decided to show Jake she wasn't afraid of colour and put on pair of white shorts, a blue and white striped top that she wore pulled in tightly at the waist with a wide red suede belt and a pair of red suede heels. She was feeling pleased with how she looked when she checked her mobile to see if Jake had texted her the address. He had but she'd received another less welcome, text. It was from Max, 'Just checking my favourite ex is okay, be in touch soon.' Her good mood evaporated. *Why was he texting her? She thought when he'd got the money that he'd leave her alone.*

She sat in the taxi fretting about Max. She just couldn't see a way out of the situation. And what made it even harder was having no one to confide in. Her brother would be too upset to think rationally and would probably threaten to beat him up; Dallas would be furious that she had an affair with Max in the first place and she couldn't deal with that right now. She thought of Tahlia. She'd resisted up till now because she didn't want to put her friend in an awkward position, but she was desperate for her advice. She got out her mobile and called Tahlia, leaving a message saying that she wanted to talk to her urgently.

'I thought we could have lunch in a café,' Jake said, draping his arm round Crystal as they wandered out of the post-production office on Wardour Street. 'Unless you're one of those no carbs girls who only lives off macrobiotic crap.'

'Don't worry, I'll eat carbs for lunch and then starve myself for the rest of the month,' Crystal replied, loving the feel of his arm round her. She was expecting to feel embarrassed after last night when she saw him; instead he made her feel so at ease that she almost forgot it had ever happened. Almost, but not quite – every now and then she'd remember and cringe at the memory. As they strolled down Old Compton Street two people sneaked pictures of them with their camera phones.

'That's fucking annoying!' Jake exclaimed.

Crystal shrugged. 'It goes with the territory, I guess. At least I'm not looking minging. I don't ever want to appear in that "Stick it on your mirror" section in *heat* where they show celebs looking shit without their slap on.' Crystal shuddered in mock horror.

'You're hardly wearing any make-up, are you?' Jake stopped to look at her.

And Crystal laughed. 'D'you have any idea how long it took me to put my make-up on, so it wouldn't look like I was wearing much? I'm wearing loads!'

'Well, you look very good.' And to Crystal's delight and to the delight of another passer-by who whipped out her camera phone to capture the moment, Jake kissed her.

Lunch was flirtatious and when they thought no one was looking, they stole lingering kisses. They ate toasted paninis and drank lattes in a cosy Italian café, where no one seemed to recognise Crystal. Jake had some time before he was due back in the edit so they lay on the grass in Soho Square. Crystal couldn't believe how well they were getting on together; there was a real connection between them and an undeniable chemistry. But when he asked her what had upset her last night she felt herself clamming up, and instead of engaging with him she lit a cigarette, even though she knew he hated smoking.

'It's just been a while since I slept with anyone.' Even to Crystal it sounded like a feeble explanation and she knew Jake didn't buy it. But, then, what was she supposed to say? *I had an affair with my friend's boyfriend, who raped me and is now blackmailing me?* He'd think she was such a bad person and she couldn't bear him to think badly of her.

Jake looked at his watch and sighed. 'I'd better get back to the edit.'

The two of them got up and walked out of the park, but this time he didn't put his arm round her.

Oh God, was this going to be it? Would he realise that he'd made a mistake in seeing her? Crystal didn't want to be so pathetically girlie, waiting for him to ask when they were next going to see each other. The old Crystal would have said that she really wanted to see him again. But she no longer had the confidence; Max had seen to that. They walked back in silence, both of them lost in thought. Finally, when they reached the building, Jake spoke. 'I've got to go away tonight for a shoot and I won't be back until next week. How about meeting up on Wednesday?'

'I'd love to,' Crystal replied, thrilled that he wanted to see her again.

He kissed her lightly on the cheek. 'Great, see you later.' And then he was gone.

'I'm not interrupting anything, am I?' Crystal asked as Tahlia opened the door to her.

'No way; Mum and Leticia have gone to see my aunt and Hadley is working. It's just us.'

Crystal followed Tahlia into the kitchen. When her friend had called her back, wondering what was so urgent, Crystal had told her it wasn't something she could say on the phone and Tahlia had asked her to come straight round.

'D'you want a cup of tea?' Tahlia asked, putting the kettle on.

'Actually,' Crystal said, a little shame-faced, 'I don't suppose you've got anything stronger?'

'Glass of wine?'

Crystal needed a double vodka at least before she told Tahlia what was on her mind, but wine would just have to do. Tahlia poured her a large glass, which Crystal quickly knocked back.

'So what's on your mind, Crystal?' Tahlia asked.

Crystal took a deep breath. 'Before I tell you, Tahlia, I want you to know that I really regret what I've done so please don't hate me.'

'I can't imagine it can be anything that bad!' Tahlia exclaimed, and was going to carry on, but she stopped when she saw how serious Crystal looked.

'Okay, just tell me what it is.'

Fifteen minutes later she had told Tahlia everything.

'So I'll understand if you don't want to be my friend any more,' Crystal said, hardly daring to look at Tahlia.

'Crystal! How could you even think that? That bastard raped you!' Tahlia got up and hugged Crystal tightly, and said in a voice that trembled with emotion, 'I'm so sorry, babe. We've got to think of a way of getting him out of your life.'

Crystal shrugged and looked hopeless. 'I just don't know what to do, Tahlia.'

'I wish you'd told me at the time. I could have helped you. We should have gone to the police.'

'And told them what? That a man I was having an affair with raped me? It would have been my word against his. They never would have believed me and now it's too late.'

The two girls went round and round in circles trying to figure out what to do for the best, and by the end of the afternoon Crystal was no closer to knowing how to deal with Max but at least she'd confided in Tahlia. She didn't feel quite so alone any more.

'And what do you think about what happened with Jake last night? Do you think I'm always going to feel like that when I have sex?'

Tahlia shook her head. 'I bet it was just because it's the first time since Max.'

'God, I hope so, Tahlia. I really, really like him.'

Seeing that Crystal's glass was empty Tahlia poured her another. 'Actually there's something I've been wanting to talk to you about for ages.'

Crystal looked at Tahlia enquiringly.

'It's Belle. I've found her really difficult to work with lately to the point of it being unbearable. She just doesn't put the effort in that you and I do and, to be honest, there are more talented singers out there that I'd rather work with.'

'God, Tahlia are you suggesting we drop her? I just couldn't do it.'

'She never needs to know about Max and, yes, I am suggesting it.'

'But Dallas would never agree.'

'Who says we have to be with Dallas? I've been going through our contract with Hadley and it would be possible to fire him. I think we have to give him about three months' notice but then we could manage ourselves.'

'But Dallas has been great for us. Do you really think we could do as well as him?'

'I just don't know if Dallas would ever agree to

get rid of Belle. And the question is, do you want to be in a group with Belle for much longer? I think she's holding us back.'

Tahlia had a point but Crystal thought there was a strong chance they'd be shooting themselves in the foot. Would they really do as well without Dallas? And she knew that Dallas would not give them up without a fight, and God knows what Max would do.

Chapter 11

Closer

'No! I hate it, take it off!' Belle said crossly as Crystal emerged from the changing room in the fifth bridesmaid's dress she had tried on for Belle.

'What's the problem with this one?' Crystal answered back, bored with being at Belle's beck and call.

'It's just wrong, not what I want. Put the other one on.'

'You're not getting married until next April!' Crystal replied.

'I know and I want every detail to be perfect,' Belle snapped back.

Sighing, Crystal returned to the dressing room where the assistant helped unfasten the tiny diamante buttons down the side of the dress. Meanwhile, Tahlia had emerged from the changing room in one of the other dresses, only to receive another negative reaction from Belle.

The trouble was that Belle wanted designer and

although Daddy was coughing up a small fortune to pay for the wedding and Belle had managed to secure a deal with a celeb mag for exclusive coverage, there still wasn't quite enough money for Belle to have the wedding she thought she should have. She wasn't quite famous enough in her own right to get a bigger deal from the magazine. And so Belle was having to settle for off-the-hanger bridesmaids' dresses so that there would be enough money to pay for her own designer wedding dress.

Earlier in the week when the girls were in the studio, Belle had told them how she wanted a midsummer night's dream theme – she wanted to transform the marquee into an enchanted forest with trees, banks of flowers, a chocolate fountain, ice sculptures of nymphs and plenty of moss . . .

'It's very important that I have lots of moss everywhere. Victoria Beckham really likes moss in her arrangements so I want that look as well,' Belle had told Crystal and Tahlia, who both had to struggle to keep a straight face.

'And I want the staff to be dressed as fairies.'

'Even the men?' Crystal asked, trying not to giggle.

'Of course. They can wear green tunics and tights or something like that.'

'Won't there be too much green because of all your moss?' Tahlia put in.

'God, I hadn't thought of that. Maybe they should wear silver.'

'I hope you're getting some fit-looking waiters then, because not everyone can carry off silver tunics. You don't want any porkers, do you?' Crystal said giggling with Tahlia. Belle clearly did not see the joke. 'Yes,' she said huffily. 'I'll get the wedding planner to insist that I only have good-looking, slim waiters.'

'Isn't that discrimination?' Crystal couldn't resist adding.

'Fuck off,' Belle snapped. 'It's my wedding, I'll do what I like.'

Feeling thoroughly pissed off, Crystal put on the final dress – a ballerina-style number with a tight white bodice and a tulle skirt with lots of layers.

'That's it!' Belle squealed as Crystal emerged from the fitting room. She clapped in delight, a huge smile replacing her earlier frown. 'You can wear flat ballet pumps with ribbons. It's perfect. And I can get the stylist to customise the dresses, dye them different colours, and sew pearls and sequins on to the skirts. But you can't have a black one, Crystal!'

Seeing her excitement a wave of guilt hit Crystal. She couldn't remain silent any longer. She had to warn Belle about Max, let her know the kind of man he really was and what he was capable of. There was no way Crystal could stand by and let Belle marry him and say nothing. She couldn't put it off any longer; it would have to be tonight. And Crystal would just have to live with the consequences . . .

'Are we done then?' she asked, 'because Tahlia and I want to take you out for a drink.'

'Okay,' said Belle happily, all sweetness and light now that she'd found the dresses. 'Let's go to Sketch.'

While Belle was relaying her instructions to the assistant, Tahlia whispered to Crystal, 'I really don't want to go out for a drink with her. She's been doing my head in all afternoon.'

'Please Tahlia, I've got to tell her about Max. I've been in denial about it. I kept thinking and hoping that the wedding would never happen, but all of this makes it so real and I can't stand by and let her marry that bastard.'

'Are you sure about this?' Tahlia said. 'She'll go mad'.

'Yes,' Crystal said determinedly, 'I've been putting it off for way too long.'

'Cheers, babes,' Belle said, clinking her glass of pink Laurent Perrier champagne against theirs. 'I'm so pleased we found that dress. I can't wait to tell Max.'

Crystal looked at Tahlia, who rolled her eyes, then she took a deep breath. 'Belle, I really need to talk to you about Max. I should have done it ages ago.' Crystal stared intently at Belle, but she appeared not to have heard her. Instead she was standing up and waving.

Crystal turned round and her heart plummeted

as she saw Max walking towards their table.

'I thought Max was in Ibiza?' Tahlia asked.

'He flew back this morning. Maxy, babe, guess what? I've found the bridesmaids' dresses!' Belle sprung up from her chair and threw her arms around Max. Crystal and Tahlia exchanged appalled glances. Crystal forced herself to look civil as Max come over to her chair and kissed her on each cheek.

'Long time no see, Crystal, how are you?'

'Good, thanks,' Crystal replied, getting a blast of his aftershave, reminding her of things she would rather forget.

He kissed Tahlia then sat down opposite Crystal and smiled at her knowingly. Belle launched into a detailed rundown of how the wedding plans were going. When she had finally run out of steam after updating Max on the food, invitations, flowers and the music, Max said, 'I'm so glad that you two are bridesmaids. It means a lot to Belle and me.' Then he turned to Belle and said, 'We'll have to buy them something lovely, won't we, babe? Something inscribed, so they can always remember our special day. And Belle says you've got a new boyfriend, Crystal. What's he called again?'

'Jake,' Crystal muttered, feeling worse and worse.

'That's it. Jake will have to come too, won't he, Belle?'

'Yes, he's already on the list.'

'Well, I look forward to meeting him, Crystal,' Max said, lighting a cigarette. 'He must be special. You haven't been out with anyone for ages, have you?'

Crystal and Tahlia drained their glasses, both desperate to get out of the bar.

'We've got to go,' Tahlia said, picking up her bag and getting ready to leave.

'Really?' Max sounded surprised. 'I thought we might all go for dinner.'

'No, no, you two hardly ever get to spend time together.' Both girls quickly got up and said their goodbyes before Max could say anything else.

'Fucking hell,' Crystal exclaimed as they waited for a taxi. 'It was like he knew what I was going to say!'

'Don't worry, Crystal, you can do it another time.'

But over the next couple of days Crystal didn't get a chance. Max stayed in London and every day came to the studio to watch the group rehearsing. He didn't let Belle out of his sight. The only comfort for Crystal was that he'd just bought a club in Ibiza and would be flying out there at the end of the week and was likely to stay there for at least three months.

But it left her feeling on edge. Tahlia could see how tense she was. 'Come on, Crystal,' she told her, 'don't let him get to you. Jake's back tomorrow night; don't let Max spoil things for you.'

It was easier said than done. At least they had a day off on Wednesday which meant she didn't have to see Max. Instead she decided to do a bit of retailing. First stop was Agent Provocateur for some new lingerie. She chose a sheer black and pink bra with a matching string; she wanted to feel extra sexy tonight. Then she nipped into Miss Selfridge and bought a black mini skirt. (She must already have about ten black mini skirts, but as far as she was concerned you could never have too many.) Then she dropped into Jez's salon and had a pedicure, wanting her feet to look their best in her new Christian Louboutin metallic heels – you could never have too many pairs of designer shoes either . . .

'Agent Provocateur?' Jez said, spotting the distinctive pink bag. 'Someone's in for a saucy surprise tonight.'

'Maybe,' Crystal replied coyly.

'Oh, come on, darling, we all know you don't buy Agent Provocateur underwear for any other reason than to have it deliciously peeled from your body.'

'Maybe,' Crystal repeated, then blew Jez a kiss and started walking out of the salon.

'I demand to know all the details. I'm your hairdresser; you have to tell me everything, it's in the contract!' Jez called out after her.

That night Crystal was on a mission to seduce Jake. He had offered to cook dinner at his flat. Crystal's culinary expertise only stretched to spag

bol and toast so she was impressed to find him hard
at work in the kitchen making linguine puttanesca.

At first they were slightly awkward with each
other. Crystal was anxious not to have a repeat
performance of last time. She wanted to banish the
memory of her tears. She had tonight all mapped
out – they'd kiss, tear each other's clothes off and
then have the most mind-blowing shag . . . She
didn't want dinner – no matter how delicious – she
wanted Jake. But he seemed perfectly happy to
cook, telling her about the shoot, asking her what
she'd been up to. Crystal sat at the kitchen table,
sipping wine and wondering how to make the first
move. Maybe he was being so cool because of what
had happened.

'This is a great kitchen,' she said looking at the
state-of-the-art appliances, the black marble work-
tops, expensive-looking bespoke wooden cabinets,
and the stone floor.

'I suppose so. We'd just finished doing it up
when Eve left me,' he said abruptly. *Bollocks!*
thought Crystal, *this conversation wasn't going to get
him in the mood, was it?*

She drained her glass. Jake poured her another.
At this rate she'd be pissed.

'Do you want to try the sauce? Let me know if it's
spicy enough for you.' Jake held the spoon to her
mouth and Crystal tasted it. It was definitely spicy
enough for her, but she wasn't interested in the
sauce at this precise moment.

'You've got some there,' Jake said, pointing at her mouth.

Crystal rubbed at her mouth.

'Still there,' Jake told her, bending down to kiss her. And this time it wasn't a casual, take-me-or-leave-me-kiss, it was a I-want-you-and-I-want-you-right-now kiss. Dinner was forgotten as Jake picked Crystal up and carried her into the bedroom.

'Hungry?' Jake asked several hours later as they lay in bed together, arms and legs entwined.

'Hmm,' Crystal couldn't resist kissing him again.

'Dinner's ruined but I could make you a peanut butter sandwich,' Jake said, getting out of bed. Crystal nodded, in a blissful post-sex daze. All memories of her tears had been erased in their passionate, intense lovemaking. It had felt so right and this time, with every kiss, every caress, it felt like she was freeing herself from Max.

He returned from the kitchen with a plate piled with sandwiches and some more wine. Crystal thought she had never seen a man with such a beautiful body; everything was perfect – smooth, tanned skin, muscular body, just the right amount of body hair . . . and –

'Sorry it's only this. I had wanted to impress you with my cooking,' Jake said.

'You've impressed me with far more important things,' Crystal said, taking a look at his perfectly sized cock and wondering if there was any chance of seconds. And she didn't mean the peanut butter sandwiches . . .

'Well?' Jez said two days later as she dropped by at the salon to have her hair washed and blow dried for an interview with a teen mag.

'Very good,' Crystal answered; *fucking fantastic more like*, she thought. She and Jake had spent the whole of Thursday together, only getting out of bed at six in the evening to go for a Thai meal, but they'd even cut that short when desire drove them back to bed once more.

'Is that the best you can do?' Jez said, pretending to be in a huff. 'I was expecting size details, positions, a complete rundown.'

'Okay, I'd say eight, lots, never had such amazing sex before. Will that do?'

'Eight?' Jez said dreamily. 'I could tell just by looking at him.'

'But it's not just the length, the width is perfect,' Crystal said cheekily. 'No one wants a party sausage inside them.'

'You're one lucky girl, Crystal; you've found the Holy Grail of cocks!' Jez exclaimed.

'I really, really like him, Jez,' Crystal answered, suddenly serious. 'I can't stop thinking about him. I've only been away from him for a couple of hours and I really miss him.'

'Oh, my God, you're in love! I'm seeing a winter wedding. You in white fur (fake, of course), diamonds in your hair (real, of course), him in a midnight blue suit to bring out the colour of his stunning eyes. Then you'll honeymoon on a private island in the Caribbean, return to your new house in Notting Hill and retreat to your country estate in Oxfordshire at weekends. A year later you'll have a beautiful baby girl and a chocolate-brown Labrador. You'll be top of the charts, he'll win a Pulitzer for his photographs – or whatever prize you win for photography – then you'll adopt a poor little AIDS orphan from Africa and set up your own organic wine label.'

Crystal laughed. 'You've been reading way too many *OK!* magazines, darling.' But as fantasies went, it was a pretty good one.

For the next two weeks Crystal spent every night with Jake. She was in that delicious loved-up state where he was all she could think about. She just wanted to be with him whenever she could. She pushed her worries about Belle to the back of her mind; she'd tell her everything as soon as Max was safely out of the way in Ibiza. And it was easy to forget when she was with Jake.

When she first met him she had been worried that he might think she was superficial, just another girl band singer, but he soon dispelled her fears when one night over dinner he revealed that he had bought her first album and had been listening to it non-stop while he was working.

'I thought it wasn't your kind of music,' Crystal

teased, secretly pleased that he'd made the effort.

'Well, it isn't usually but it grew on me. I think you're really talented, Crystal.'

'So does that mean you'll work with us again?'

'Yeah, so long as you keep that diva pain in the arse away from me.' Jake rubbed his eyebrow where Belle's shoe had hit him. 'And so long as I get to see plenty of your tattoo.'

'For your eyes only, darling . . . So you don't hate working with bands then? I got the impression you thought there were more important things you should be doing.'

'Shit, no, I love my work and I want to work with different people. Sure, I like doing the serious stuff but I need the music work as well.'

Crystal was relieved. Most of the other men she'd been out with hadn't exactly been renowned for their minds and it hadn't mattered so much to her that those relationships had never really progressed beyond the bedroom. But Jake was different – he was intelligent, he was thoughtful, and she wanted him to see her as an equal, not a bimbo pop tart.

'Shit, I'd totally forgotten I was supposed to be meeting my parents for lunch today,' Jake exclaimed, leaping out of bed. It was midday on Saturday and he and Crystal were lying in bed together *again*. 'Come with me,' he said impulsively.

'Really?' Half of Crystal thought, *Great, that must*

214

mean he likes me if he wants me to meet his parents; the other thought of her own dysfunctional background and thought she would rather keep well away.

'Please? I promise we won't be there for long. And then we can do something you want to do – maybe meet up with your friends at the Soho Hotel.'

'Okay,' Crystal said, pulling him back on to the bed with her, 'on one condition.' She ran her hands over his naked body and Jake got the idea.

'Whatever you say.'

As a result they were even later in meeting his parents and Crystal had no time to go home and change into something more suitable. She was forced to wear the previous night's outfit – a strapless leopard-print Wheels & Dollbaby low-cut top, a tiny black mini skirt and red Gina heels, an outfit chosen entirely for its fuck-me qualities. It certainly did not say meet the parents. Crystal muttered about it in the taxi. 'Oh, don't worry, my parents don't bother with things like that,' Jake said.

I suppose his mum is *Swedish*, Crystal tried to reassure herself. *Aren't Swedes supposed to be laid back? She'll probably be wearing Birkenstocks and jeans.* Her reassurance was short-lived, though, when the taxi dropped them outside Claridge's.

'We're going here?' she demanded. This venue didn't scream out laid-back Swede to her.

Jake sighed. 'Yes, my mother always has lunch

here when she's in town.' As they walked into the vast, marble-floored lobby, Crystal suddenly felt awkward and seriously underdressed.

The mâitre d' greeted them and they were shown to the table.

And there Crystal finally had to abandon any hope that Jake's mother would be easy-going as she was introduced to an immaculately dressed, Chanel-suited, sixty-something woman, who had obviously been a great beauty in her youth and who still looked beautiful now, albeit in a very cold and distant way. Ingrid just about managed a chilly smile when Jake introduced Crystal. Her eyes were the same amazing blue as Jake's but had none of the warmth Crystal saw in his. Crystal caught Ingrid look disapprovingly at her outfit.

Harry, his dad, though, couldn't have been nicer.

'I've been listening to your songs on iTunes, Crystal – they're really very good.'

'Really?' Crystal asked, not quite believing him.

'Dad's obsessed with technology – he was practically the first person I know to get an iPod,' Jake put in. 'And as soon as I told him about you he was straight on to iTunes'.

'Yes,' Ingrid added, tight-lipped. 'He spends all his time on the computer.' Her English was perfect; she only had the slightest accent.

God, so would I if I was married to you, thought Crystal.

Ingrid spent a few minutes telling everyone what they should order, and then interrogated Jake about what he'd been doing. Right before her eyes, Crystal saw her handsome, sexy, talented, charming boyfriend turn into an awkward, monosyllabic teenager. Realising that she had got all she was going to out of her son, she turned her attention to Crystal.

'So how long have you been singing for, Christy?'

'It's Crystal,' Jake said crossly.

'Oh, that's an unusual name, isn't it?'

Crystal had barely managed to explain about her name before Ingrid fired off the next set of questions. Where did she live? Was it a house or a flat? Did she own it? Where had she been brought up? What did her father do?'

'I don't know,' Crystal replied in answer to the last question, which momentarily stopped Ingrid in her tracks. She raised an eyebrow, clearly expecting an explanation.

'My parents divorced when I was eight and my dad remarried and moved away.'

'Oh,' Ingrid answered and was clearly about to launch into a further barrage of questions when Jake said, 'I think that's enough questions for Crystal, don't you? She hasn't had a chance to eat.'

Crystal shot Jake a grateful look, then stared down at her plate in horror – smoked salmon. Yuk! She hated smoked salmon but had been so thrown by Ingrid telling everyone what they should have that she hadn't realised she'd ordered it.

'Do you want mine?' she whispered to Jake.

He shook his head. 'Just leave it, it doesn't matter.'

But it clearly did matter. Ingrid looked disapprovingly at the untouched plate when the waiter came to clear the table.

'Was there something wrong with the salmon, Christy?' she demanded.

'No, I'm just not that hungry,' Crystal replied, too pissed off to correct her.

'Oh, I do hope you're not one of those girls who starve themselves. Jake had such a wretched time with Eve – he's probably told you about her eating disorder. I mean, beautiful girl, from a very good family, but the eating thing drove you insane, didn't it, Jake?'

'Actually, Mum, it was more her infidelity if you recall,' Jake said crossly.

Lunch was turning out to be a nightmare. All Crystal wanted to do was get the hell out of there. Then Ingrid started singing the praises of her goddaughter, Stella. She wanted Jake to take her on as an assistant; Jake was not keen.

'But, darling, she's so talented and I've sort of promised her mother that you would.'

'Well, you had no right to do that,' Jake said angrily. 'I don't want her as an assistant.'

'It would just be for a couple of months, just to give her experience.'

'I've got Gavin,' Jake retorted.

'And Gavin's fine, but he's not very good at the meeting and greeting thing, is he? You need someone a little more polished to interface with your clients. And I'm sure Stella's beauty and charm will do your business no end of good.'

What a cow, Crystal thought. Gavin was one of the nicest lads she had ever met and she thought most people would rather 'interface' with him than some stuck-up girl.

Jake sighed. 'I'll think about it, okay?'

'Please do, darling, I promise she's an utter gem.'

'I'm sorry,' Jake said as they got into a taxi. 'I should have warned you how uptight my mum can be, but I thought you wouldn't have come if you'd known.'

'Too bloody right!' Crystal exclaimed. 'I wish I'd been wearing something different; your mum obviously didn't approve of me at all.'

'My mum's issued to the max,' he sighed. 'As you can see, I don't have the greatest relationship with her. My gran was the one who really brought me up. You'd have liked her.' He looked sad. 'She died four months ago, just before I split up with Eve. I really miss her.'

Crystal found his hand and squeezed it, 'Sorry, that must have been tough.'

'Yeah, well, it definitely wasn't the happiest time of my life. But please forget about my mum; she doesn't approve of anyone.'

'Except Stella,' Crystal corrected him. 'She seems to love Stella. And by the sound of it, who wouldn't, so beautiful and so charming.' She couldn't help being sarcastic; she hated being round people who thought they were better than everyone else.

'Hmm,' Jake was clearly keen not to carry on the conversation about her, but Crystal's curiosity had been aroused and if she was honest she couldn't help feeling a tiny pang of jealousy. She was not at all sure she wanted some beauty hanging out on a daily basis with Jake.

'So is she very beautiful then?' Crystal asked.

'If you like that sort of thing – long blonde hair, perfect skin, pretty face, slim, blah, blah, blah. She's always seemed a bit of a trustafarian to me and I don't happen to find that kind of girl attractive.'

'Oh?' Crystal replied, moving closer to him. 'I expect you like a bit of rough like me.'

'I certainly do,' he answered, pulling her on to his lap and kissing her deeply.

The day improved dramatically after that. As they wandered through Soho, Jake stopped to buy her a bouquet of velvety dark red roses, saying, 'These will do for now. I'll buy you something proper to make up for lunch.'

'Okay, just as long as it's a really expensive piece of bling, you know what us pop stars are like,'

Crystal teased, secretly thrilled by the romantic gesture.

Then they met up with Danni, Jez, Tahlia and Hadley at the Soho Hotel for cocktails. Everyone got on well and conversation flowed easily; there was none of that awkwardness Crystal had sometimes experienced in the past between her friends and boyfriends. Jake went out of his way to be friendly and charming to everyone.

'He's lovely!' Tahlia whispered to Crystal when Jake and Hadley were talking.

Crystal looked over at Jake and her heart flipped. 'I know,' she whispered back and wanted to add that she was falling in love with him but didn't.

But there was something bothering her about Jake – the ex factor. Clearly the break-up had left him feeling bitter and insecure and Crystal couldn't help wanting reassurance that he wasn't still in love with Eve. Maybe she should have left well alone but it had been on her mind ever since they started seeing each other and Crystal just had to know. The night had been perfect. After the drinks Crystal and Jake had gone back to her flat and made love – each time felt better than the last. Now, as she lay with her head on his chest, she asked the question that was starting to bug her. 'Were you really in love with Eve then?'

Instantly she felt Jake tense. 'I don't want to talk about her.'

221

'It's just that every time her name comes up you seem so angry,' Crystal said, ignoring his request.

'I don't want to talk about her,' he repeated. 'Don't fuck up a really good evening.' He sounded distant, abrupt. 'I'm really tired; can you turn the light off now?'

For the first time he didn't hold her as they lay in bed. *Why did I have to ask him about his ex? And why is it still such a big deal to him?* The questions went round and round in Crystal's head, making sleep impossible. At three a.m. she was still wide awake.

'Can't you sleep?' Jake finally asked as Crystal fidgeted yet again.

'No. Sorry, am I keeping you awake?'

He sighed. 'No, it's me. I should be able to talk to you about Eve. It's stupid, but I still find it hard. We were going to get married and then I found out about the affair. It totally threw me. I did love her and I thought she loved me. It felt like the three years of our relationship had been a lie.'

Crystal moved closer to him. 'I'm sure it wasn't a lie.'

'I don't know that for sure. Anyway, because of that I find it really hard to trust people, women. Until I met you.' He turned round to face Crystal and kissed her. And Crystal was so close to telling him about Max.

Lost Angels were away in Paris, Rome and Madrid for the next week promoting their latest single and

222

it was the usual hectic conveyor belt of performing live on TV and radio shows, interviews and photo calls. It was a punishing schedule which meant being up at the crack of dawn and often not going to bed until the early hours. Belle drove Crystal and Tahlia mad with her non-stop moaning about how knackered she was. She also managed to fit in several diva outbursts: when the hotel had put the wrong flowers in her suite – Belle always demanded white roses; when the mini bar hadn't been emptied of all chocolate; and when one of the journalists failed to recognise her. Tahlia and Crystal remained positive – the promotion went hand in hand with the music as far as they were concerned, though Crystal was starting to be wary when she was interviewed, especially when she was asked about Jake. It was early days and she didn't want to scare him off by sounding too keen. But it was now public knowledge that she was seeing him. Pictures of them together had already appeared in the tabloids and in *heat* and all the other celeb mags. Crystal tried to give as little away as possible, however persistent the questions, but it was hard not to let on how much she liked him.

And then there was the matter of finally telling Belle the truth. Jake's revelation that he trusted her had been the final spur. The trouble was, it never seemed to be the right time. Crystal didn't want to tell her just before they went on TV or before an interview. She thought she might have a chance on their last night in Madrid, the final European city in their schedule. The girls were VIP guests at the opening of a hot new club. It had been designed to look like an underwater paradise – the walls and floors were glass aquariums filled with brightly coloured tropical fish and what looked like miniature sharks; the guests could recline on waterbeds while the waitresses, who all wore designer bikinis and looked like models, fetched their drinks. It reminded Crystal of a Bond movie set and she kept expecting to see Blofeld sitting in a black leather chair, stroking his white Persian cat, pressing a secret button and opening up the floor to send some unfortunate sod to meet the sharks.

'Max would love this place,' Belle said. 'He's trying to make his new club as spectacular as possible, to attract the celeb crowd.'

'How is he?' asked Crystal, steeling herself for what she was about to say.

'Really good; of course we miss each other, but actually I quite like being able to do my own thing and then catching up with him every other weekend,' Belle said breezily.

'And he hasn't been like he was that time in Ibiza when he got so angry about the contracts?'

'No!' Belle exclaimed. 'He's got a temper on him, but I just ignore him when he's like that.'

'He's never hurt you, has he, Belle?' Crystal asked tentatively

'God no!' Belle replied, sounding shocked. 'What makes you ask that?'

Gathering all her courage Crystal was about to make her confession when they were suddenly surrounded by photographers who wanted them for a photo call. By the time they'd finished posing and chatting it was late and Belle was pissed after one too many Bellinis. Crystal had missed her chance yet again.

'God, Tahlia', Crystal sighed as she got into bed (the two of them usually shared a suite when they went away; Belle insisted on her own), 'when am I ever going to be able to tell her?'

'Don't worry, babe, there'll be time. But maybe you're worrying too much. You heard what Belle says; he's never hurt her, she doesn't get upset by his moods. Maybe you shouldn't rock the boat.'

'No, I've got to tell her. I'm sure he wasn't like that just with me. I couldn't sit back and let her marry him.'

As soon as Crystal got off the plane the next morning she called Jake and was surprised to hear a posh female voice on the line. 'Jake Fox's office'.

'Hi, can I speak to him, please,' Crystal asked, wondering who the hell the woman was.

'I'm afraid he's busy at the moment. Can I take a message?'

'No, he'll want to speak to me, it's Crystal,' she said impatiently.

'I'm sorry but he did say—'

Crystal cut across her angrily. 'I'm his girlfriend. Please go and give him his mobile.'

It must be Stella. Crystal instantly disliked her just from the plummy sound of her voice and arrogant manner alone.

'Crystal, is there a problem?' Jake came on the line, sounding distracted.

'No, I just wanted to let you know that I'm back. Shall I come over?'

'Sure, I'll be done in a couple of hours.'

Crystal wanted him to say that he'd missed her and couldn't wait to see her and was slightly put out that he hadn't. Still, maybe he was surrounded by people and couldn't talk. She was knackered from the trip but sleep couldn't have been further from her mind. She had missed him so much and now all she wanted to do was make up for lost time.

As soon as Jake opened the door to her she wrapped her arms round his neck and kissed him, slipping her hands under his T-shirt to get her fix of his smooth skin.

'I missed you,' she murmured, pulling back to look at him.

'I missed you too,' he replied, kissing her again, unbuttoning her shirt and caressing her breasts.

They stopped mid-kiss at the sound of someone coughing quietly behind them. Jake turned round.

'Oh, yeah, Crystal, this is Stella.'

Jake stepped to one side to reveal Stella – all five

foot eight of her – slim figure, waist-length white-blonde hair and stunningly pretty face.

'Nice to meet you, Crystal,' Stella stepped towards her with an outstretched hand. Crystal held her shirt together with one hand and shook Stella's with the other. It was definitely not nice to meet Stella, who was every girlfriend's worst nightmare. Stella was dressed in a pair of low-slung tight white jeans and a white vest that ended just above her naval to reveal an enviably flat, brown stomach.

'I put a bottle of champagne in the fridge earlier, so it should be chilled by now,' Stella told Jake. 'I thought you guys might be in the mood for celebrating.'

'Cheers, Stella, I'll see you in the morning.'

'Bye. It was lovely to meet you, Crystal.'

Crystal forced herself to smile and through narrowed eyes watched Stella's tiny pert bum going out of the door, her long hair cascading silkily down her back.

'I thought you didn't want her as an assistant,' she tried to say as casually as possible as Jake expertly opened the champagne and poured them each a glass.

'It's not for long and actually she's been really useful and sorted out all my paperwork and my bookings. I hadn't realised how disorganised I'd been.'

'So will she be working with you every day then?'

Crystal asked, not liking the thought of Stella parading round Jake's flat one little bit.

'No, just a couple of days a week, I guess. Can we stop talking about Stella now?' Jake said impatiently, handing her a glass. 'I thought we had better things to do.'

'Like?' Crystal said flirtatiously.

'Like get into the bedroom and get your kit off.'

Apart from Stella's arrival, Crystal couldn't have been happier. Her relationship with Jake seemed to be getting more serious by the day. And although he hadn't said he loved her, Crystal thought there was a chance he might . . . She was certainly head over heels in love with him. She had never really believed in the idea of 'the one' but with Jake she was having to revise that view – physically they were a perfect match and emotionally she had never felt so close to a man before.

'What time are you expecting Jake?' Tahlia asked. The two girls were meeting for cocktails at the Blue Bar at the Berkeley before going on to Scott's in Mayfair to celebrate Hadley's birthday.

'He should be here any minute now,' Crystal answered, looking at the beautiful new Chanel watch Jake had bought her to celebrate their first month together. Crystal had never been given anything so gorgeous before.

'Is that the watch?' Tahlia asked. Crystal nodded

and Tahlia exclaimed, 'He *really* likes you. And here he is!'

Crystal turned round, a big smile on her face which faded when she saw Stella walking next to him. *What the fuck was she doing here?*

'I hope you don't mind me coming along,' Stella said after everyone had said hello, 'but I've just broken up with my boyfriend, Xavier' – Stella sniffed and looked as if she might cry, prompting Jake to put a reassuring arm around her – 'and Jake really sweetly asked me along. I just didn't want to be alone.'

If it had been any other woman Crystal would have been immediately sympathetic and loved Jake all the more for being so considerate. As it was, she was fuming because, while Stella might claim to be heart-broken, Crystal had never seen anyone look so pleased with themselves and so together. If she had been crying earlier, she'd been careful not to smudge her make-up, and in the middle of her heartache she'd managed to put on a gorgeous turquoise silk tunic and Jimmy Choo heels.

Because Stella didn't know Tahlia, after a short conversation involving all four of them inevitably Stella talked mainly to Jake. It was noisy in the bar and Crystal couldn't hear what they were saying and couldn't join in. She felt sidelined and jealous. She scowled at Tahlia, who shrugged sympathetically. Her mood did not improve when they left the bar and looked for a taxi to take them on to the restaurant. She'd hoped that Stella would leave them now but she looked so miserable when Jake asked if she was going to be okay that, to Crystal's fury, he said, 'Well, you're welcome to join us for dinner; that's okay with you, isn't it, Tahlia?'

Tahlia could hardly turn round and say no, but Crystal interrupted: 'Well, the reservation is only for four.'

'It'll be fine; they can always put an extra chair round the table,' Jake said casually. In the taxi Stella managed to sit next to Jake, with Tahlia and Crystal sitting opposite them, and Crystal couldn't help noticing how, even though there was plenty of room, Stella's bare legs were just inches away from Jake's. As they got out of the taxi Tahlia whispered, 'Don't look so pissed off, Crystal, Jake was just being nice.'

'It's not him I'm worried about. It's obvious she fancies him,' Crystal whispered back.

'Yeah, but he fancies *you*, so chill babe.'

It was easy enough for Tahlia to tell her to chill but Crystal felt on edge for the rest of the evening. Over dinner Stella continued to monopolise Jake and Crystal barely got to speak to him, though when Stella went to the bathroom Jake said, 'Sorry, Crystal, I couldn't leave her; she was really upset.'

'It's okay,' Crystal said grudgingly. 'It's just she's not really my kind of person.'

'She's not mine particularly, but I feel kind of

responsible for her now she's working for me. And she's only young.'

'She's twenty-two! That's the same age as me!' Crystal retorted.

'Oh, I thought she was much younger.'

Crystal wanted to say, 'That's because she's a spoilt little rich girl, who's never done a proper day's work in her life and has never struggled for anything', but saw Tahlia give her a warning look and kept her mouth shut. She tried to snap out of her resentful mood for the rest of the meal, not wanting to spoil Hadley's birthday. But it wasn't easy and by the end of the night she was desperate to shake off Stella and be alone with Jake. Unfortunately they had to share a taxi back as Stella owned a flat just off the very swish Kensington Church Street. Crystal was sure it had been bought for her by Mummy and Daddy. But this time, Crystal made sure *she* sat next to Jake, snuggling up to him. *Back off bitch,* her body language screamed, *he's mine.* Stella managed to squeeze out a few tears when it came to say goodbye but clearly Jake felt he had done enough by spending the evening with her.

'You'll be all right over the weekend, won't you?' he asked as she got out of the taxi.

'I'll be fine,' Stella replied. 'And thanks again for rescuing me, and thanks for putting up with me, Crystal.'

'No problem,' Crystal answered. 'Take care.'

'You were a bit off-hand with Stella,' Jake observed as the taxi drove away.

'Was I? I just didn't want Hadley's birthday spoiled, that's all.'

Jake laughed. 'Don't have such a chip on your shoulder about Stella, Crystal.'

Crystal wanted to say that she hadn't, that there was just something about Stella that she didn't like, but as she didn't want Jake to think she was being a total bitch she said nothing.

However, over the next couple of weeks her dislike for Stella deepened as she watched her flirt with Jake – touching him at every opportunity, sucking up to him, constantly telling him how great she thought his work was, how talented he was. She was politeness itself to Crystal and Jake never flirted back, but it drove Crystal wild. July ended in a scorching heat wave – it was over thirty every day and Stella took full advantage of it, wearing as little as possible, or so it seemed to Crystal. The final straw was when she arrived at Jake's one afternoon to find Stella in a pair of tiny denim shorts and white halterneck – showing off far too much of her slim, tanned body. The only consolation to Crystal was that Stella had tiny tits.

'I'm telling you,' she said to Danni and Jez through gritted teeth as she got ready for a magazine shoot the following day, 'the shorts were so far up her bum cheeks, it must have felt like she was flossing her arsehole every time she sat down!'

Danni and Jez exploded into giggles.

'It's not funny,' Crystal protested, 'she's round Jake all the time, and who's to say that one day he won't crack.'

'Crystal, according to you her crack has been on display for some time now and he hasn't "cracked" so far, so I think you're okay,' Jez said, laughing.

'Relax, she's just some stuck-up little rich girl. Jake doesn't fancy her; I've seen what he's like with her. He treats her like a kid sister.' As usual Danni tried to reassure Crystal.

'Well, you wouldn't stand for it, would you?' Crystal appealed to Jez.

He shrugged. 'Danni's right. Don't let her wind you up.' This was unnaturally reasonable for Jez.

'What's the matter with you?' Crystal demanded.

'I've got a hideous hangover and I'm feeling too ill to be mean, but you're right. I'd see the bitch off.'

The question was how? Should she have it out with Jake or just bide her time? The latter sounded more dignified, but, *Jesus Christ Almighty*, she thought, *I'm not a saint!*

Two nights later Crystal was forced to act. She and Jake had gone out to dinner and as they ordered he said, 'God, I mustn't eat too much, I had a huge lunch.'

'Oh? Was it a business meeting?' Crystal asked.

'No, Stella made this amazing mushroom risotto. She's an incredible cook. And I'm afraid I stuffed my face.'

Crystal felt her lip curling. 'Did she learn that at finishing school then?' she said sarcastically.

'Now, now, just because you can't cook. Though didn't you know that's the way to a man's heart?' Jake teased her.

'Really? I thought it was by giving him great blowjobs, but if you like I'll stop doing those and concentrate on my cooking instead,' Crystal shot back.

That shut Jake up. 'You don't need to cook,' he said quickly.

'Seriously Jake,' Crystal couldn't help saying, even though she felt she'd scored one victory over Stella, 'don't you realise that she fancies you?'

Jake laughed, 'Crystal, I've known Stella for years – she's just a family friend. She doesn't fancy me – she's like that with all men, I promise.'

A day later, though, Stella was definitely not behaving like a family friend. Crystal and Tahlia had been working on a new song and had recorded a demo which she wanted to play to Jake. But when she went round to Jake's, Gavin answered the door.

'Is he in the studio?' Crystal asked.

'Nope, the bedroom, he's done his shoulder in and' – he paused, and avoided looking Crystal in the eye – 'Stella's giving him a massage.' Even laid-back Gavin obviously thought this was out of order.

With a feeling of mounting anger, Crystal marched straight to the bedroom where she was confronted with the sight of a half-naked Jake lying on the bed, with only a towel round his waist, being massaged by Stella.

'What the hell's going on?' she demanded angrily

'Oh, hi, Crystal,' Stella replied, all butter-wouldn't-melt-in-her-mouth, 'Poor Jake's hurt his shoulder and I'm just giving him a massage.'

'I can see that,' Crystal said icily. 'Are you sure you know what you're doing? You don't want to make it worse, do you?'

'She's doing a great job,' Jake said, turning his head to look at Crystal and, seeing the furious look in her eyes, added, 'it's feeling much better. You can probably stop now, Stella.'

'Don't worry, Crystal, I've done a massage course so I know exactly what I'm doing,' Stella said, getting up from the bed, dressed in one of her revealing numbers, yet again – an off-the-shoulder white silk tunic that only just covered her bum. 'I'll go to the chemist now for those painkillers.'

'Thanks, Stella,' Jake muttered.

'You're welcome,' she called back sweetly, making Crystal long to deck her. *How dare she do that to my boyfriend!*

Crystal shut the bedroom door after her and stood, hands on hips, looking at Jake.

'What?' he demanded. 'It was only a massage.'

'So if it was the other way round and I was lying on the bed practically naked, being massaged by my sexy male assistant because I'd hurt *my* shoulder, you wouldn't have a problem?'

'Of course not,' Jake said, but Crystal was pretty sure he was lying and he knew he was in the wrong.

'And is this what you get up to with all your family friends,' Crystal continued, still outraged at his behaviour.

Jake sighed and then winced as he moved, obviously playing for the sympathy vote. 'It was an emergency. I was in agony and Stella offered.'

'Yeah, I bet she did. Well, it better not happen again. And you'd better not have a stonker on,' she muttered, marching towards the bed, and attempting to whip the towel away from his waist.

'Get off,' he protested, trying to hold on to the towel. 'I'm injured and if I do have one it's from seeing you looking so sexy.'

Crystal knew that jealousy was not an attractive quality, but she couldn't help it. She was still furious with Stella but instead of continuing the argument decided to channel her anger into something more satisfying.

'I'm sorry if you're injured; is there anything I can do to make it better?' she said in her best smoky and seductive voice, getting on the bed beside him. 'Anything apart from your shoulder that needs kissing?' she asked, running her hands down his chest, over his flat, hard stomach and gently pulling away the towel.

'I can think of one thing,' Jake said, playing along.

Some time later there was a knock at the door. Crystal ignored it and carried on what she was doing. Jake was in no state to talk. The door opened.

'Oh my God, I'm so sorry!' Stella exclaimed, hastily shutting the door. Crystal resisted the urge to laugh as Jake murmured, 'Don't stop now.'

That's round two to me as well then, thought Crystal.

Chapter 12

The Fall Out

'I'm going to really miss you,' Crystal murmured, wrapping her arms round Jake and pulling him back on to the bed and kissing him.

'It's only for a week,' he replied surfacing from the kiss.

'Do you know that's the second longest time we've been apart since we met?' Crystal said, wondering how she would survive without him. For the last four months they had become practically inseparable. She'd even stopped worrying about Stella because no matter how much she flirted with Jake he really didn't show any interest in her beyond that of an employee and a friend. Jake didn't even seem hung up about his ex any more and to Crystal's delight he talked about getting rid of the tattoo of Eve's name on his wrist, saying maybe he should get someone else's name on his arm instead. 'Okay,' she'd replied, 'maybe I'll get one too.' They didn't have to say that they meant each other's names. Crystal had fallen for him hard. She was in love. There was just one problem. Even though she thought they could not have been closer, Jake still hadn't said he loved her and that stopped her from telling him. Tahlia advised her to be patient, and that he would tell her in his own time; Crystal just hoped that she was right.

Jake smiled. 'Just think what a good time we'll have catching up when I get back.' And with that he kissed her again, got up from the bed, grabbed his bag and walked out of the door, pausing to turn round and blow her another kiss.

Crystal sighed as she curled up under the duvet, and, holding one of his T-shirts, she fell asleep. She was woken by her mobile, and, thinking it would be Jake texting her from the airport, she reached for it. But it was Max.

'Back in London on Wed have to see you. Will call with time.'

Crystal felt as if she'd been punched. She'd almost forgotten about Max. Almost. She'd allowed herself to believe that he must have decided there was nothing more to be gained from blackmailing her. She'd obviously been wrong. She'd been burying her head in the sand about Max for too long. This couldn't go on. She had to do something.

The girls were rehearsing the dance routines with Tash for the final two songs from their album – one would be their Christmas single, the other two would be released the following March. They'd all grown in confidence since their first single and now their videos were known for their sexy dances and slick concepts. Usually Crystal would have been full of enthusiasm. She was often at her happiest when she was working but that Monday morning she felt sick with dread and anxiety. Her mind was made up. There could be no more excuses: she was going to see Max and tell him that his hold on her was over, she would tell Belle what had happened. She was expecting her to be angry and to hate her for what she'd done but somehow she hoped that they could work together on the final tracks. It all seemed so simple in her head, so clear-cut, but she knew in her heart life wasn't like that.

To distract herself she booked into a tattoo parlour. She decided on a simple black design of the Chinese character for J on the inside of her wrist. It bloody hurt! Though not as much as her love heart, and every time she looked at the tattoo somehow it made her feel closer to Jake, feel that she would be able to deal with Max . . .

On Wednesday, just as she was leaving the studio, Max called her: 'I'm at the club, I need to see you now.'

Just hearing his voice after so long sent a shiver of apprehension down her spine. 'What do you want?' she demanded.

'I'll tell you when I see you.'

Crystal had vowed never to go to Max's club

again and thought about suggesting they meet somewhere else. Then she checked her watch; it was half eight, there'd be plenty of Max's staff already there and she wanted this over and done with. When she got there she'd insist on meeting him at the bar, tell him it was game over, and leave.

'I'll be with you in twenty minutes,' she replied, ending the call. She usually rang Jake around this time, but she didn't want to put on an act and pretend that everything was okay. She'd call him after she'd seen Max.

The door to Max's was shut which wasn't unusual at this time of night. She rang the bell and waited for someone to answer but there was no reply. Instead the door swung open. Music was pumping out from the downstairs club. She hesitated for a few seconds, gathering her courage, then walked down the stairs, dreading the moment when she would see Max. At the bottom of the stairs she pushed open the heavy door that led into the club and stepped inside. But immediately she sensed something was wrong. The place was deserted; she couldn't see anyone. The bar had been emptied of drinks, except for one bottle of vodka. The expensive black velvet couches and glass tables were covered in dust sheets. She quickly turned round to go and screamed when she saw Max standing in front of the door, blocking her exit.

'I don't look that bad!' he laughed at her. 'Good

241

to see you too, babe.' He moved forward, obviously intending to kiss her, and she took a step backwards. He laughed. 'I thought you might have mellowed, thought you might have missed me.'

'Where is everyone?' she demanded, fear pulsing through her at being alone with Max.

Max looked angry. 'The club's shut; the bastard bank stopped my overdraft. But, anyway, let's not talk about that. Come and have a drink and we can get down to business.'

When Crystal didn't move, he grabbed her arm and led her over to the bar, his fingers digging into her skin.

'Now you just sit here,' he said pulling out one of the few remaining stools, 'and I'll get us a drink.'

Crystal sat down, while Max climbed over the bar and poured out two large glasses of vodka. Her heart was racing and her mouth felt dry. She had planned to tell him that she was going to tell Belle the truth but now she couldn't risk it. She just wanted to get out of there. She'd go along with whatever he said.

'I know I said I wouldn't ask you for any more money, and this really is the last time, I promise,' Max told her, sliding her drink across the dusty bar to her. Then he once more climbed back and sat down next to her.

'How much?' Crystal asked quietly, thinking the quicker she agreed, the quicker she could get out of there.

'Just twenty.'

'Fine, I'll transfer it tomorrow. Can I go now? I'm meeting someone in ten minutes.'

'Have a drink first,' Max insisted, 'I haven't seen you for ages.'

It was so eerie the way Max acted as if he had never raped her in Ibiza, as if he had never blackmailed her, as if they were friends. Crystal took a small sip of vodka.

'It's funny seeing you at the club again; all those memories. We were good together, weren't we?' Max said. And Crystal wanted to shout, *No we weren't! You're a psycho*. Instead she muttered, 'It seems like a long time ago.'

Suddenly the front doorbell rang, 'Who the fuck's that?' Max said irritably, going to answer it. Crystal waited until he had gone out of the door, then got up and followed him, reasoning that if there were people there he wouldn't be able to prevent her leaving. But she stopped, hearing Max shouting. Instinctively she moved towards one of the corners of the club which wasn't lit and waited, listening, wondering what was going on. There was a lot of shouting followed by the sound of someone falling down the stairs. And then Max was shoved through the door by two heavy-set men.

Max was pleading with them. 'Tell him I'll get him the money, I can do it by the end of the week.' He sounded scared. Crystal shrank further back into the shadows, crouching behind one of the tables, praying that she couldn't be seen. It didn't exactly look like a social call.

'You do that, and we're here to make sure you don't forget. Not like last time.'

Max tried to make a run for it, but the two men, although beefy, were surprisingly quick and he only got as far as the bar when they both grabbed him. From her hiding place she couldn't see what was happening but it didn't sound good. She put her hand over her mouth to stop herself from crying out, as she heard Max being thrown against the bar and viciously punched and kicked. He screamed out in agony and pleaded with them to stop. Crystal was terrified. She contemplated running out and trying to stop them but they didn't sound like the kind of men who would listen to reason. It went silent; she couldn't hear a thing. 'He'll have a headache tomorrow,' one joked as they walked out of the club.

Crystal stayed still for a few minutes, fearful that the men might come back. She tentatively got up and made her way to the bar, dreading what she was going to find. Max was lying on his back, his face a bloody mess. He was barely recognisable. She clasped a hand over her mouth to stop herself retching. Then she forced herself to bend down. 'Max,' she called urgently, 'can you hear me?' He gave no sign that he could, and his breathing sounded rattled and shallow. Frantically she searched in her bag for her phone and with a voice shaking with emotion she called for an ambulance.

The next couple of hours were like a nightmare – the paramedics arrived and tried to revive Max before rushing him to hospital. Crystal sat in the ambulance willing him to be all right. She hated him for what he'd done to her but there was no way she had wanted this to happen.

'I came as soon as I could,' Tahlia said, immediately running over and hugging Crystal, where she sat curled up on the sofa in the waiting room. She'd been there for over an hour on her own, believing the worst and tormenting herself further by thinking that she should have intervened.

'Are you okay?'

Crystal had held it together up until then, but as soon as her friend hugged her, she gave in to the shock and fear, sobbing, 'No I'm not.'

Through her tears she told Tahlia about the attack.

'Jesus,' Tahlia exclaimed, looking horrified. 'What kind of people had he got himself involved with?' Crystal was just about to answer when Belle burst into the room.

'What the hell happened?' she demanded, standing in the middle of the room, hands on hips.

For months Crystal had been rehearsing what she was going to say to Belle in her head. She had thought of a million ways to explain it. She knew it was never going to be easy, but she hoped at least it could be done calmly. There was no chance of that now.

Crystal ignored her question. 'How is he?'

'Several broken ribs, a broken nose and concussion. He's been given a CT scan but apparently it's all okay. It looks worse than it is. Tell me what happened,' she repeated. 'Max said you'd gone round there to talk about a promotional idea of his and then these two thugs turned up out of the blue and attacked him. Did you see them?'

Crystal shook her head, and braced herself. *Here goes.* 'No, that's not what happened. I wanted to tell you ages ago about me and,' she paused, trying to summon all her strength, 'and Max.' She looked apprehensively at Belle.

'I had a fling with him last year and I know it was wrong but I thought I was in love with him, I couldn't think straight.'

For a few seconds Belle was speechless, then she let rip: 'You bitch!' she yelled. 'You fucking bitch, I can't believe that you would do that to me!'

Crystal tried to explain how she'd ended it and how Max raped her in Ibiza and had been blackmailing her ever since. But Belle wouldn't have it, even when Tahlia backed up Crystal. 'She's telling you the truth Belle, you've got to believe her.'

'Bullshit,' Belle shouted back, 'Max wouldn't do any of those things. You're just saying that because you're jealous that he proposed to me. I bet he realised he'd made a mistake and tried to call it off and you're the one who went all psycho bunny boiler on him.'

'No, please Belle, it wasn't like that. I should have told you before. You can't marry him, he's a really bad person.'

'And what does that make you then?' Belle was screaming hysterically. 'You're a fucking two-faced whore. What about my wedding? You were supposed to be one of my bridesmaids. You've ruined everything!'

It was no good Crystal trying to say anything else. Tahlia tried to back her up but it was hopeless.

'You wait 'til I tell Dallas. He's going to have plenty to say to you!'

'Oh, please Belle,' Crystal begged, 'let me tell him.'

'No way! I'm not having you poisoning him with your evil little lies. I'm calling him right now.'

Crystal pleaded with her, but Belle had already flipped her mobile open.

'Are you sure you're going to be okay? You can always stay at mine,' Tahlia said as Crystal got into a taxi.

'I'll be fine. I just need to get my head together for when I see Dallas,' Crystal replied wearily. Back at home, she flung herself on the sofa, feeling emotionally and physically drained. Then she suddenly realised she hadn't spoken to Jake. She would finally have to come clean about Max and she was dreading it. She reached for her mobile, which she'd switched off in the hospital. There were ten messages, most of them from Jake wanting to know if she was okay, wondering why she hadn't called. And several from a journalist wanting to know what she'd been doing with Max at the club. Her stomach went into free fall as she realised the press were already on to her. She called Jake, but his phone went straight to voice mail. She left a message asking him to call her as soon as he could, that it didn't matter how late. She found herself longing for a cigarette and ended up ransacking her wardrobe until she found the packet that she'd stashed away weeks ago, in case of an emergency. If this didn't count as an emergency she didn't know what did. Jake had been so proud of her when she told him she'd given up, but she tried to banish that thought as she lit up. Five cigarettes and a large vodka later and if anything she was feeling worse. She couldn't understand why Jake hadn't rung her back. She called him again, but he was still on voice mail.

She paced round her flat, unable to relax, dreading what the next day would bring. Her mobile rang and she leapt for it, hoping it was Jake, but it was the journalist again. She switched the TV on and flicked mindlessly through some magazines, but nothing could distract her. She ended up going to bed at half four. *Please call me, Jake*, she prayed, pulling the duvet round her and hugging his T-shirt.

She'd only just fallen asleep when her mobile rang at eight. Hoping for Jake, she was bitterly disappointed when it was Dallas's PA, Jenny, summoning her to his office for ten. Crystal's spirits plummeted further still – she didn't know if she felt strong enough for a showdown with Dallas. She showered, put on a long black cashmere jumper, jeans and boots, and just about managed to apply some make-up, though her hand was shaking so much she smudged her mascara and had to do it twice. She was feeling too jittery to eat breakfast; instead she had a coffee and two cigarettes. She'd stop the minute Jake called her, she told herself. She tried his mobile again but he was still on voice mail. In desperation she called Gavin who had stayed in London. She apologised for waking him and told him she needed to speak to Jake urgently.

'I expect he's just finishing off the edit – sometimes when he gets really busy he switches his phone off. Don't worry, Crystal,' he added sleepily, 'I'm sure he'll call you later.'

Crystal didn't feel reassured. She logged on to her laptop and checked out a couple of tabloid websites. There was just a brief mention in one of Max having been rushed to hospital after being beaten up. Crystal's name wasn't mentioned but she didn't think it would stay that way for long. The journalist called again, leaving another message. Crystal felt sick; the press obviously thought they were on to something. Would Belle have said something to them already? Would Max? She felt horribly alone. She thought of phoning her brother, but didn't want to worry him. She was going to have to face this on her own.

'What I want to know is what the fuck did you think was going to happen?' Dallas was shouting now, leaning over Crystal where she was cowering into the sofa, after she'd told him everything. 'How could you screw your friend's boyfriend? What was going on inside that head of yours?'

'I don't know,' was all she could think of to say.

'You don't know!' Dallas was even more enraged, 'Well, shall I tell you what you've done, princess? You've wrecked your friend's relationship and you've destroyed the group and possibly your own singing career. I hope that all those secret fucks were worth that.' He walked away from her, shaking his head in disbelief.

'Should I go to the police? Tell them about what Max did to me?' Crystal asked, hardly able to take in what Dallas was saying.

Dallas sighed, and this time his voice wasn't so hostile, 'Crystal you should have gone to the police straight after it happened. It's too late now. What he did to you was appalling and I'm really sorry but do you seriously think a jury would believe that he raped you? You were having an affair with him. It just doesn't look good.' He paused, then said, 'I really thought you had something, Crystal. Belle and Tahlia are good but you were special. However, I just don't know if the group can recover from this.'

'But we've still got the other singles to release, and I'll do whatever it takes to make them do well,' Crystal pleaded. She'd had no idea that Dallas thought so highly of her. 'And there's the second album; Tahlia and me have written some great material.'

'You don't get it, do you? I've been in this business a long time and I know the public; they don't like women who have affairs with their friends' fiancés.'

'But no one needs to find out, do they?'

'I'm afraid Max, the charming little shit, has sold a story. He was on the phone to a paper, minutes after Belle finished with him.'

'There must be something I can do?' Crystal said, feeling distraught. *This surely couldn't be the end of her singing career.*

'The only thing I can think of is that you have to apologise for what you did. You'll be interviewed by the press tomorrow. That way we might be able to salvage the last singles.'

Crystal was about to say that there was no way she could do that when Dallas said bluntly, 'I understand that you don't want to do it, but you have to – think of Tahlia, think of Belle. Anyway, you look exhausted, go home, chill out, switch off your phone for now. Jenny will call you later to let you know your appointments.'

Feeling totally shell-shocked, Crystal got up and walked out of his office, trying to blink back the tears.

Outside it was raining hard and Crystal had to wait twenty minutes before she was able to get a taxi. By the time she managed to hail one she was drenched. In her anxiety about seeing Dallas she'd forgotten to bring a coat or an umbrella.

'Aren't you that girl from Lost Angels?' the taxi driver asked her, as she got in, soaked through and shivering.

'No, I get that all the time, but I'm not her,' Crystal answered, thinking, *Wouldn't it be good not to be her now?*

When the taxi pulled up outside her flat the press were already camped out in force. Just as Crystal was telling the driver to drive straight on to north London, a journalist caught sight of her and suddenly the cab was surrounded by photographers shouting her name and trying to get a picture of her through the window.

'Bloody hell,' the cabbie said. 'I thought you said you weren't that girl!'

'Please, just drive,' Crystal begged him. 'I'll give you a hundred if you can get me there without anyone following us.'

The cabbie fortunately didn't talk to her because he was busy concentrating on taking the most indirect route to north London to shake off the paps. Crystal phoned Tahlia to warn her she was on her way. Jake still hadn't called and she was desperate to call him, but she didn't want the driver overhearing her conversation.

At least one thing seemed to be going her way. The driver got her to Tahlia's without any of the press following her.

'You're freezing, Crystal,' Tahlia said, giving her shivering friend a hug. 'Go and have a hot shower and I'll get some dry clothes out for you.'

Crystal tried to protest that she needed to speak to Jake first but Tahlia hustled her into the bathroom.

Twenty minutes later Crystal was sitting on the sofa, clasping the hot chocolate Tahlia had made for her; she'd laced it with brandy to calm Crystal. Tahlia had lent her jeans and a jumper so she was warmer now, but still felt wobbly and weak.

'What am I going to do, Tahlia?' she asked, her eyes glistening with unshed tears. 'I really don't want to talk to the press about what happened. What's Jake going to think of me, and why hasn't he called me back?' As soon as she'd got out of the shower she'd tried to call him but he was still on voice mail.

'I'm sure he'll understand,' Tahlia said soothingly. 'It happened way before you met him; it's got nothing to do with your relationship.'

Crystal wasn't at all sure that Jake would see it that way. She could only hope that she got to speak to him before a journalist did.

A couple of hours later, the press pack had tracked her down to Tahlia's flat and Jenny called her to let her know that she should check into the Dorchester that night – her interviews with the press were going to be starting there at nine the following morning. The police also wanted to speak to her; they wanted a statement about what had happened at the club.

'Don't go there until tomorrow,' Tahlia said, seeing how overwrought Crystal looked.

'No, I must, it's not fair on you and your family having the press here. It's my problem and I've got to sort it out.'

They were brave words, but Crystal didn't feel brave; she felt as if her world was falling apart around her. She knew that she had to do as Dallas said; she couldn't see beyond that. She ached with longing for Jake, just to hear his voice, for him to tell her that none of this mattered, that he was there for her. Tahlia might try and persuade her otherwise, but she thought his silence spoke volumes.

She hugged Tahlia and prepared to face the press, putting on her sunglasses and pulling the hood of Tahlia's white parka down over her face. At least Dallas had sent a car for her. As soon as she opened the front door the journalists started shouting, 'Crystal, tell us about you and Max', 'Where's Jake? Come on, Crystal, talk to us.' She put her head down and pushed her way through the wall of people, with cameras flashing wildly around her.

'So, Crystal, tell me about your affair with Max. Did you really think he was going to leave Belle for you?'

Crystal looked at the female journalist sitting opposite her, leaning forward as if she couldn't bear to miss a single word, an eager gleam in her eye. She was obviously loving getting all the gossip. More than anything Crystal wanted to tell her to fuck off. It was her fifth interview of the day and she was finding the whole thing excruciating – it was like being on a conveyor belt of misery. Dallas had insisted on sitting in on all the interviews, no doubt to make sure Crystal behaved herself.

Crystal sighed, took a deep breath and said mechanically, 'I thought I was in love with him. It was a moment of madness, which I regret.'

Of course that wasn't enough to satisfy the journalist and Crystal had to go through the whole story again – when she first met him, what it was like when they first had sex, how she felt about deceiving Belle. She didn't mention the rape or the blackmail, knowing that no one would believe her, that they'd think she was just trying to get revenge on Max.

Half an hour later the woman had got what she wanted and left. Crystal lit another cigarette and her gaze fell once more on the tabloid lying on the coffee table in front of her which had run Max's story. Crystal couldn't believe how far he had twisted the facts of their ill-fated fling – laying the blame squarely at Crystal's door. According to him Crystal had relentlessly pursued him, done all she could to poison his relationship with Belle and finally, when Max was feeling depressed about the end of his racing career, he had relented and they'd become lovers.

He'd spared no one's blushes in the juicy, salacious descriptions of their lovemaking. Crystal was depicted as an insatiable, demanding lover, who liked dominating and being dominated. To add authenticity he'd given the papers her text messages and they'd also printed the photograph of her lying naked on his bed. It was a complete character assassination. If Crystal had been reading about someone else who had behaved like this she would have hated them too.

'Can't I sue?' Crystal had asked Dallas in despair. 'Most of it isn't even true.'

'But some of it is, isn't it?' Dallas replied.

Next the two police officers, a female DC and a uniformed male PC, turned up to interview Crystal. She was tempted to tell them the truth about Max, but she realised that if she did, the whole business would drag on even longer and occupy even more space in the tabloids. Crystal just wanted to be shot of it. She could tell that they weren't convinced by her story – she told them she'd been in the area and decided to drop in on Max and that she had absolutely no idea why the men had attacked him. Even though they pressed her on the details, Crystal stuck to her story and they left, telling her she might have to identify the two men or be called as a witness in court. Crystal was certain the case would never get that far – Max was bound to keep his mouth shut about it.

After that she had three more interviews with various celeb magazines, all wanting the juicy details and when they were over she was finally free.

'Okay Crystal, I'm sorry you had to go through that, I wish there could have been something else we could have done but I don't think there was. You better go home now. I suggest you keep a low profile for the next couple of weeks, maybe get Jake to take you away somewhere. Jenny will let you know where we're filming the video for the final single.' And with that Dallas headed for the door.

'Dallas,' Crystal called out. He turned round. 'I'm sorry.'

'Yeah,' he replied wearily. 'So am I.'

Dallas had made her switch off her mobile during the interviews and the first thing she did when he left was to switch it back on. But to her bitter disappointment there was still no word from Jake. He was due back that night. She took a taxi home. The last thing she wanted was to be alone. She hoped that he might come and see her. There were still a couple of photographers staking out her flat, but with Crystal doing all the interviews today some of the heat had gone out of the story. She got out of the taxi and raced into her flat, not wanting them to get her picture. The lights were on inside. 'Hello?' she called out tentatively, convinced that she hadn't left them on.

'In here,' Jake called out from the living room.

Thank God, Crystal thought, running into the room. Jake was sitting on the sofa, and she was about to run over and throw her arms around him but something in his eyes stopped her. He gave no sign that he was pleased to see her. Her heart sank.

She sat down next to him. 'Didn't you get any of my messages? I've been calling and calling you.'

He shrugged and avoided looking at her. He looked exhausted; he had dark shadows under his eyes and hadn't shaved for days.

'I've been thinking about what to say, I suppose.' Jake said, staring straight ahead. 'Was it good, then, your affair? Must have been for you to have risked so much. What was I, then, your rebound fuck or your cover so you could carry on seeing him?'

'No!' Crystal exclaimed, 'I had a two-week fling with Max last year, that's all. It was way before I met you. I would never be unfaithful to you.'

'Oh? You just sleep with your friend's boyfriend. That's some moral code you've got, Crystal,' Jake said icily.

'I know it looks bad, but it was a mistake and I really regret it. He told me he was going to leave

258

her, and I thought I was in love with him, but he was lying to me and I wasn't really in love with him.' Crystal was gabbling now, frantic to make Jake believe her. 'It has nothing to do with our relationship.'

'Our relationship?' Jake said, getting more heated. 'You call *this* a relationship when you hadn't even told me about your affair! How many other things have you kept secret?'

'Nothing,' Crystal pleaded with him, 'I swear.'

Jake got up from the sofa and walked to the other side of the room, where he leaned against the wall and finally looked at her.

'I just don't trust you any more, Crystal, and I can't be with someone I don't trust. I told you that right from the start.'

'*Please*, Jake, let me explain, there's so much you don't know,' Crystal pleaded. But she had lost him; she knew it in her heart.

'I don't want to know, Crystal. It's bad enough that it happened. You're not the person I thought you were.' He paused to take something out of his pocket and put it on the mantelpiece. Crystal knew it was the key to her flat.

'Please don't go, Jake, please don't leave me,' she cried out in anguish, unable to stop the tears. She covered her face with her hands, not wanting to watch him go. He paused in the doorway.

'Goodbye, Crystal.'

It sounded so final.

Chapter 13

Escape

The next week passed in a blur of misery. The press attention didn't let up. Crystal was portrayed as a sex-mad maneater, an unfeeling bitch who cared nothing about betraying her friend. Dallas's insistence that Crystal tell her story only added fuel to the fire. Max responded with even more salacious details of their affair, most of it made up, but Crystal knew that everyone would believe what they read. She'd taken coke with him once and that was turned into their 'crazy drug-fuelled sex'; he claimed that she was insatiable and made him have sex with her up to five times a night (in his dreams, she thought) and how she gave him the best oral sex of his life (well, maybe that much was true). Everyone wanted to stick the knife in – people she'd barely known from school claimed she'd been a bitch back then; even her father who she hadn't seen or spoken to for twelve years, sold a story saying that he was ashamed of her. At least her mum didn't talk to the press, but she didn't give Crystal any support either, telling her that she'd been a fool to get involved with someone else's boyfriend. Meanwhile, Max's other women crawled out of the woodwork and sold their stories. It seemed Crystal hadn't been the only woman he'd betrayed Belle for – there was a waitress from his London club, a glamour model and a lap dancer in Ibiza.

Crystal stayed holed up in her flat, chain smoking and drinking, feeling like a prisoner, unable to face the world. There were still a few photographers lurking outside. Tahlia called round every day, bringing her a home-cooked meal from Rosie. Crystal would thank her for it but only throw it in the bin the minute she left, her appetite gone. Jez and Danni made frequent calls leaving messages of support and love and asking to come round and see her, but Crystal could only bring herself to see Tahlia. Gavin left a couple of messages as well but she didn't pick up the phone. She couldn't bear to speak to anyone. She had lost everything she had ever wanted and she felt she had nothing left. Jake didn't call her. She knew he wouldn't.

'Pack a suitcase, we're getting you out of here,' Tahlia said, walking into the flat on Saturday morning.

'I don't want to go anywhere,' Crystal said

stubbornly, lighting another cigarette. Her fifth of the day, and it wasn't even eleven.

'You need a break,' Tahlia insisted, 'a chance to get your head together.'

'What for?' Crystal said bitterly. 'So that I can face the fact that Jake's left me and that I'm probably finished as a singer?'

'You're not. I'm sure when you've taken some time out and Dallas has calmed down we can sort something out.'

Crystal shook her head. 'I doubt it. I reckon he'll drop me after we've recorded the final song. And if he doesn't want me then no one else will.'

Tahlia sighed; she realised it was pointless trying to argue with Crystal. All she wanted to do now was get her friend out of London, out of the way of the press and give her a chance to regain her fighting spirit.

'Luke wants you to go and stay with him in Brighton. I'm going to drive you into central London, and we'll meet him and hopefully you can switch cars without the press seeing you. That way they won't know where you've gone. What do you think?'

'I haven't had any better offers,' Crystal replied, but she was touched all the same, that Luke and Tahlia wanted to look after her. 'I'm sorry I'm being like this, Tahlia, it's just I really love Jake. I can't believe I've lost him.' Her voice trembled with emotion and she struggled to hold back the tears.

'I know, babe,' Tahlia, replied hugging her friend.

Two hours later, Crystal had successfully switched cars, and she and her brother were on their way to Brighton. Crystal felt completely light-headed, after a week of eating practically nothing other than a few slices of toast.

'You look shit, Chrissy,' was the first thing Luke said to her when he saw her. 'But don't worry, I'm going to look after you and you're going to be okay.'

Not wanting to disappoint her little brother, Crystal simply nodded and looked out of the window at London flashing past her. She was leaving behind the man she loved, saying goodbye to her singing career. She felt as if she was leaping into the dark and there was nothing and no one there to save her.

Luke shared a seafront flat with his girlfriend Ruby. On Crystal's first night, when the others had gone to bed, she put on her coat, wrapped herself up in a blanket and sat outside on the balcony, looking out at the black sea and the lights of the pier flashing on and off garishly in the distance. There, in the cold November air, she wept for all that she had lost.

'Chrissy, I've made you a cup of tea. I think you should get up now.' Crystal opened her eyes to see her brother. 'What time is it?' she mumbled, hungover and bleary-eyed.

'Eleven.'

She groaned and pulled the duvet over her head. She'd been at Luke's for three days now and had been spending most of her mornings lying in bed, getting up around lunchtime and watching mindless daytime TV curled up on the sofa. She'd start drinking wine around six and then stay up until two, drinking, smoking, listening to music and watching DVDs. Luke and Ruby kept trying to persuade her to come out with them, but she still couldn't face seeing anyone.

'Get your lazy arse out of there,' Luke said, whipping the duvet off her head. 'You've got songs to write. I've set up my computer so you've got your own log in.'

'No, I can't do it any more,' Crystal groaned, trying to pull the duvet back over herself.

'Yes, you bloody can! But before you get started, I'm making you breakfast. You're making yourself ill with all this smoking and drinking. You've got to stop.'

It was a complete role reversal – in the past Crystal had always been the one looking out for Luke, getting him up in the morning, making sure he had breakfast before he went to school, being like a parent. Part of her wanted to protest that she'd always been the strong one and didn't need him. But she knew she could do with being looked after. She felt emotionally battered after the events of the last few weeks.

And so she dragged herself out of bed, showered

and for the first time since she'd arrived at the flat got dressed in something other than her black Juicy Couture tracksuit. She put on a denim mini skirt, which practically slid down her hips because she hadn't been eating, and a black jumper, but she couldn't be bothered putting on any make-up. She could barely bring herself to look at the pale girl in the mirror, with dark shadows under her eyes. She wandered into the kitchen where Luke was busy chopping up fruit.

'Right, sit down, I've made you a fruit smoothie and you can have croissants, cereal and fruit salad.'

'I'll never be able to eat all that!' Crystal protested.

'Start with the smoothie and then see what you feel like. I've got to build you up,' he said, hugging her. 'You've lost too much weight.'

'Thanks, Luke,' Crystal whispered, willing herself not to cry. In the end she only managed the smoothie and a croissant but she did feel better for it. And then to please Luke she sat down at the computer for most of the afternoon. At first she put off writing, looking instead at Jake's website which had several pictures of him and an audio download of him talking about his work.

Jake, where are you now? she wondered, *Are you thinking about me?* And then she found herself writing the lyrics to a song about losing the love of your life. As she thought about Jake, the words poured out of her.

Crystal

It had been one week and three days since she last saw him. *Had he already met someone else*, she hated the thought of him with another woman. She could just imagine how happy Stella would be at the news of their split. Oh my God, perhaps she'd made a move on him already? On top of the heartbreak she felt, Crystal suddenly experienced such a violent rush of jealousy that she thought she'd be physically sick. She got up from the desk and paced round the bedroom, ending up at the window, staring out at the slate-grey, forbidding sea. The weather was miserable, overcast skies, and a bitingly cold wind, as if in tune with Crystal's mood. But staying in all the time and obsessing about Jake was doing her head in. She was fearful of going out in case she got spotted and she didn't think she was strong enough to deal with the whole media circus again. She rummaged in her suitcase and found a baseball cap and, putting it on, she looked at herself in the mirror. No, that just looked ridiculous, like she was trying to hide her face, and she didn't want to draw any attention to herself. She drew her long hair back into a ponytail and then had an idea.

She wandered into the living room where Luke's girlfriend, Ruby, was drinking beer and chilling out after a long day at the hairdressing salon where she worked. Ruby was nineteen, pretty, feisty and changed the colour and style of her hair every other month. This month she'd taken to wearing her flaming red hair in plaits.

'Ruby, will you cut my hair for me?' Crystal asked, flopping down next to her on the sofa.

'Sure, I'll give it a trim; it doesn't look as if it needs much taken off,' Ruby replied.

'No, I want you to cut it all off,' Crystal said. 'I want it really short.'

Ruby shook her head, 'No way – you'd be gutted if I did that. And what about that video you've got to film for the last single?'

'I'll wear a wig,' Crystal answered.

'It's a really bad idea to do anything that drastic to your hair when you're feeling down,' Ruby said sympathetically. 'We're always getting women in who want to do something radical with their hair after a break-up and nine times out of ten I guarantee they regret it, especially if they've got long hair like yours.'

Crystal sighed. 'This isn't about Jake, I just want to be able to go out and not get recognised.'

Ruby seemed to consider her request more seriously and she looked at Crystal as if weighing up the options. 'What about a bob? I could cut it just below your jaw line, and give you a fringe. That would look different and at least if you hated it, it wouldn't take too long to grow out.'

Crystal hesitated for just a moment. She'd always thought her long hair had been one of her best assets, then replied decisively, 'Okay, let's go for that.'

An hour later, after Ruby had finished cutting

her hair, Crystal had a tough time pretending that she liked the new style, but as she'd begged Ruby to do it she didn't want to hurt her feelings by letting on how she felt. She locked herself in the bathroom and studied her new hair. She thought she looked ugly and wanted to cry. She wanted to wallow in looking bad, reasoning that as everyone thought she was a bad person she may as well look crap. But however low she felt it wasn't in her nature to keep being a victim so, instead of hiding away, she forced herself to put on some make-up, and to get changed into a short black skirt, a sexy, tight black cardigan, unbuttoned to show off some cleavage, and her black cowboy boots.

'Come on,' she called out to Ruby, 'I'm taking you and Luke out for dinner. We'll pick him up after football.'

She didn't want to go anywhere flash, opting instead for an unpretentious Italian restaurant that had been open for years. She chose a table in the darkest part of the room and made sure she had her back to the other diners. Luke and Ruby kept telling her how good she looked but Crystal shrugged off their compliments and drank just enough wine to stop her feeling paranoid about being recognised and to numb the pain she felt over Jake. The night was a success – she wasn't spotted and that gave her confidence that she could go out. But her longing for Jake just grew more intense. Crystal felt that she was just going through the motions of living, but she had no purpose. She was drifting.

Luke's gardening work had finished for the winter and to keep the money coming in he worked in a friend's bar. Every morning he made Crystal come to the gym with him and in the afternoon he would go to the bar and Crystal would email her friends, write song lyrics – misery was apparently good inspiration, because the words really flowed – and try not to think about Jake. She knew from the emails she'd exchanged with Gavin that the two of them were working in Australia for the next month. There were so many times Crystal wanted to call Jake and beg him to listen to her explanation, beg him to come back to her. But she never did. Every night she slept with one of his T-shirts which still carried the faint scent of him and his aftershave. She felt lost without him, as if nothing in her life had meaning any more. Although they'd only been seeing each other for six months, Crystal knew in her heart that he was the one and that she'd never meet anyone like him again.

Dallas called her to let her know that he was adding an extra song to the album and that he needed her to record her part – separately, of course, from Belle and Tahlia. Crystal had sent Belle several text messages and a letter begging for her forgiveness, or at least asking her to under-stand that she was genuinely sorry for what had happened, but Belle hadn't replied to any of them.

Tahlia told her that Belle was still furious with her and couldn't even bear to have Crystal's name mentioned.

Belle had also sold a story to one of the celeb mags about how betrayed she had felt by Crystal and Max. Crystal came out of it far worse than Max. Belle made out that they were best friends and had shared everything, when the truth was they had never really been close – not that that excused what Crystal had done. Belle's story was another nail in the coffin for Crystal's reputation. Then Dallas sent her the lyrics and music of the new song 'Betrayal', which was all about a girl who stole her best friend's boyfriend. It didn't take much to work out who had inspired that particular number.

'So it's not enough that every tabloid has printed stories about me being a bitch. Now I've got to sing about it as well!' Crystal said to Tahlia during one of their daily phone calls. 'I'm really tempted not to do it,' she added.

'You can't, Crystal,' Tahlia said quickly. 'I already told Dallas that we shouldn't sing it and he pulled out the contract – he has the final say on all the songs on our album.'

'Fuck him,' Crystal exclaimed. That was one piece of small print she hadn't thought would matter when they signed up.

She spent the next few days rehearsing the song. In spite of the lyrics it felt good to be singing again but she missed being part of a group.

At the recording studio Phil, the producer who had worked with the Lost Angels from the beginning, was very sweet, telling her he thought all the press stuff about her had been a load of bollocks, but Crystal found it soul destroying having to sing on her own. She was gripped by the fear that this might be the last song she would ever record.

'Don't worry, Crystal,' Phil reassured her, 'you've got such a great voice, I'm sure if things don't work out with Dallas someone else will want to sign you.' Crystal wasn't so sure – her phone hadn't exactly been ringing off the hook with other record companies fighting to offer her a deal.

She'd been in Brighton for three weeks and had almost forgotten to be concerned about anyone spotting her. She made sure she always dressed down and swapped her designer shoes and clothes for Timberlands, jeans and a parka – the weather was too bad to wear anything else anyway – though even on cloudy days she never went out without her sunglasses on. One morning she was wandering through the Lanes on her way to the gym when someone called out her name. Instantly she panicked; she spotted a photographer following her, his camera aimed directly at her. She didn't know what possessed her but instead of ignoring him or slipping into a shop, she bolted. She ran as fast as she could but the photographer was still right behind. In her desperation to escape him, she rushed straight across a busy road without looking. She heard the screech of a car braking suddenly and felt a searing pain in her shoulder, then nothing.

She came to in A&E, lying on a narrow hospital bed with Luke bending over her, white with anxiety. 'Thank God, Chrissy, are you all right?'

'I think so,' Crystal answered, wincing in agony as she moved her arm. 'What happened?'

'You got hit by a car; you were really lucky,' Luke's voice trembled and he held his sister's hand tightly. 'You've got a broken collarbone, concussion and a nasty cut on your left arm.'

'I was trying to get away; there was a photographer after me,' Crystal replied, feeling groggy from the concussion.

'Just promise me you'll never do anything like that again,' Luke said urgently. 'Let them take their pictures, it doesn't matter, you're the only thing that matters.'

Not wanting to worry him any more Crystal whispered, 'Okay,' and closed her eyes. Did she matter? It didn't feel like that any more.

She was kept in hospital overnight. They gave her a CT scan, which was all clear, and she was discharged the following evening. She arrived back at Luke's flat to discover his living room full of flowers from friends sending their love and wishing her a speedy recovery. There was even an exquisite bouquet of white lilies from Dallas, which made Crystal feel that maybe he was softening towards her. As Crystal looked through the labels she couldn't help hoping one of them was from Jake. Luke told her that he'd phoned Jake's office and left a message with Stella, who promised to let him know what had happened. Crystal spent the next couple of days resting in the flat and fantasising that Jake would call her and tell her that it had all been a terrible mistake, that he loved her. On day three when there was still no word from him, she realised that he was never going to call. *He must really hate me*, she thought miserably.

All she wanted to do was curl up on the sofa in her pyjamas, with her iPod – she'd taken to listening to the Red Hot Chili Peppers as she knew they'd been Jake's favourites – and gazing at the stormy sea. But after four days of seeing his sister in that state, Luke insisted that she get dressed.

'Come on, let's go out and have a coffee. It's not good for you to spend so much time inside. You need fresh air.'

'Have you seen the state of me?' Crystal objected. Her left arm was bandaged, and her right was in a sling to support her broken collarbone. She also had a black eye and a cut lip.

'I promise you, you'll feel so much better if you come out.'

'But what if there are photographers?' Crystal asked anxiously.

'They'll have me to deal with,' Luke said, sounding as if he meant business.

Crystal

Very reluctantly Crystal hauled herself up to get dressed – which took ten times longer than usual because of her arm.

For the first time in ages, the sun was shining. Outside the safety of the flat everything around Crystal seemed so much brighter, the sounds so much louder than usual. The sky appeared bluer, the white Georgian houses in the elegant squares were so white that it almost hurt to look at them; the cars roared by, making her feel dizzy and the harsh cries of the seagulls overhead jarred her nerves. They walked slowly by the sea and when they got too cold they stopped at one of the cafés for coffee to warm up. Crystal was just thinking that she'd done okay when a large group of students arrived at the café and it went from being deserted to packed. Crystal felt panicky all of a sudden, as if she couldn't breathe; she felt giddy and sick. Everywhere she looked people were talking loudly and laughing and it felt as if their voices were pressing into her head, their words hammering into her brain . . .

'What's the matter?' Luke asked, sounding concerned.

'I don't know, I feel really odd,' Crystal gasped.

'Put your head between your legs, and breathe deeply,' Luke ordered. She did as she was told and gradually the horrible feeling of anxiety and fear subsided. After a few minutes she raised her head and looked at her brother.

'What's wrong with me? I'm such a fucking wreck.'

'I think you had a panic attack,' he replied. 'Come on, we'll go home.'

'Belle's got a new boyfriend, a footballer,' Tahlia said, as they drank coffee in the living room while Leticia drew yet another picture of a princess in a tower, waiting to be rescued by a prince. Crystal resisted the temptation to tell her not to bother – there were no princes, only men who broke your heart. It was two days after her panic attack and she was trying to put a brave face on things.

'Look, there's a piece about them in *heat*.'

She passed the magazine to Crystal who read that Belle had been seeing Lee Raven, who played for Spurs, and was apparently getting very cosy with him. The piece said how pleased everyone was that Belle had found happiness after her recent heartbreak, and how much she deserved it. Crystal skipped over the next paragraph which was all about her own part in the break-up of Belle and Max. God, would the press ever let her forget it? Then she considered the photograph of the boyishly good-looking footballer, who, judging from the fake tan, shaped eyebrows and carefully tousled and highlighted hair, was obviously as dedicated to personal grooming as Belle. 'Um, not bad, not really my type, but maybe he looks better in the flesh.'

'Crystal!' Tahlia said, clearly horrified.

Crystal laughed. 'Tahlia, it was a *joke*.'

'Oh, yes, sorry,' Tahlia muttered, embarrassed by her mistake.

'If my best friend thinks I'm capable of fancying another of Belle's boyfriends, no wonder the tabloids are giving me such a hard time!' Crystal exclaimed. Not even her recent accident had brought her any sympathetic headlines. Instead the press seemed to revel in her fall from grace, commenting that she'd swapped her luxurious West London pad for a small rented flat in Brighton and her designer clothes for the high street. Just before the photographer had chased her, he'd got a picture of her and much had been made about how her clothes came from Topshop. It was all bollocks, of course; Crystal had always mixed designer clothes with the high street. There were quotes from 'friends' saying that they were worried about Crystal's mental health, that her drinking was out of control, and that she was on the verge of a nervous breakdown.

'Anyway, I'm glad Belle's met someone else. What's he like?' Crystal asked.

'Sweet, not the sharpest tool in the box. Plus he's got the money to keep her in the style she thinks she deserves.'

'I always saw Belle as a WAG in waiting,' Crystal answered, then changed the subject. Thoughts of Belle always ended up making her feel guilty.

It did her good, though, to spend time with Tahlia and Leticia. Crystal felt tense when the time came for them to say goodbye. She knew that the next time she'd see Tahlia was for the video shoot in the New Year, something she was dreading. Tahlia had tried to brush off her worries, telling her it would be fine, but Crystal had a strong suspicion that it wouldn't.

Chapter 14

Face the Music

'I'm sorry, there must be some mistake,' Crystal said to the smiley stewardess at the check-in, whose cherry-red lipstick was the exact shade of her uniform. 'I seem to be in economy and I should be in first.'

The stewardess tapped away again at her keyboard, looked up at Crystal and said sweetly, 'I'm sorry, Ms Hope, you are definitely booked into economy.'

'Can't I upgrade?' Crystal pushed, feeling frazzled, 'I'll pay extra.'

'I'm sorry, Ms Hope, the flight is fully booked.'

Crystal was aware of the queue of people waiting impatiently behind her and realising that she would have to accept the situation, she grudgingly replied, 'Well, is there at least a window seat?'

'I'm sorry, they've all gone, you're in the central aisle.'

What a perfect start this was proving to be to her

twenty-third birthday. She'd had to get up at the crack of dawn and she hated getting up early. Then she'd had to leave before the post arrived so she hadn't received any cards. Crystal couldn't help wanting the day to be a little bit special, but so far the only way it was proving to be special was in being exceptionally crap. As Crystal grabbed her hand luggage and marched towards departures, she felt furious. It wasn't the lack of luxury she objected to, it was being surrounded by people – people who were likely to recognise her. At least in first, people didn't stare as much or if they did, it didn't feel like they were crowding her because there was more space. It was already happening as she wandered through the departure lounge. She could see people's eyes lighting up with recognition, see them pointing her out to their friends. One of the celeb mags had recently published a picture of her with her new hairstyle and her cover had been blown. The others would be protected from all this sitting in the VIP lounge, Crystal thought bitterly, as someone took a picture of her with their camera phone. Suddenly, as she looked around for somewhere to sit, she felt the familiar sick feeling of a panic attack coming on. She couldn't breathe, her vision seemed to blur, her heart was racing and she thought her legs would give way. She somehow stumbled to the ladies where she locked herself into a cubicle. Frantically she rifled through her luggage until she found a paper bag. She put it over her mouth and nose, trying to remember what her doctor had told her about taking deep breaths.

You're all right, she told herself over and over again, *Just breathe*. As she sat there, Crystal lost all track of time, but then she heard her flight being called. To her horror she realised that it was the last call. Still feeling wobbly and light-headed, she grabbed her bag and started running for the gate. Just as she felt her luck couldn't get any worse she realised that her gate was the last one. She got on the plane with minutes to spare and then had the humiliation of walking the length of the aircraft with everyone staring at her and hating her because the pilot had warned them that they may have lost their slot for take-off because of the final passenger boarding so late.

'About bloody time too,' she heard someone say, and another adding, 'Stupid bitch.'

Finally she reached her row and did a double-take because there, sitting in the seat next to hers, was Jake. Her stomach flipped. She hadn't seen or heard from him in three months. He looked up at her briefly and muttered 'Hello' before turning his attention back to his book. Crystal was too stunned to speak. She nodded then tried to shove her bag into the overhead locker. It was already crammed with other passengers' luggage and she was struggling to squeeze hers in. Just as she thought she would cry with frustration, with the stewardess threatening to take her bag somewhere else, Jake got up to help her and managed to force the bag in and shut the locker.

'Thanks,' Crystal mumbled, too overcome with emotion to look at him. She sat down in her seat, fumbling with the seat belt.

'What are you doing on this flight?' she asked.

'I'm shooting the video. Didn't you know?' Jake replied. 'It was part of my contract otherwise—' he shrugged and he didn't need to finish the sentence. She knew this was something he didn't really want to do.

'Hiya, Crystal.'

She turned and saw Gavin sitting next to Jake. 'Oh hi, Gavin. I'm sorry, I didn't see you there.' Crystal managed a smile and Gavin beamed back at her. For a moment Crystal thought he must be taking the piss. She wasn't used to people smiling at her, then she realised it was genuine. Jake had his head buried in his book again, so Crystal leant back and pretended to watch the safety display by the stewardess.

She experienced the feeling of panic she always had during take-off. Usually she'd have been with Tahlia and she would have held her hand tightly. Now all she could do was grip on to the handrest so tightly her knuckles went white. She closed her eyes and prayed – not that she believed in God, but in times of stress it was useful to pretend.

After a few minutes she heard Jake say, 'It's okay, we're up. You can open your eyes now.'

For a moment Crystal thought she must have imagined his voice, but she opened her eyes and Jake was looking at her.

'I didn't know you were scared of flying.'

'Just taking off and landing. I read somewhere that's where most accidents happen.'

'Well, if anything did go wrong, I don't think we'd have that much time to worry about it,' Jake said dryily.

'Yeah, I'm sure you're right,' Crystal answered and was about to ask him how he was but he'd gone back to reading his book.

Crystal's own book was in the overhead locker and she didn't like to ask Jake to get it down for her so she picked up the in-flight magazine and flicked through it, trying not to think about Jake sitting next to her – Jake who looked so incredibly gorgeous. He was still tanned from his trip to Australia which made his blue eyes look even more intense. His hair had been bleached blond by the sun and was cut close to his head, making his handsome face look even more striking. There was hardly enough room for his long legs and Crystal shifted in her seat, so hers couldn't brush against his. She had thought – foolishly, she now realised – that she was starting to get over him but sitting next to him she felt the full force of her feelings for him return. If anything she wanted him even more because she knew she couldn't have him.

The in-flight movie was some schmaltzy rom-com about true love prevailing in the end. Yeah, right, thought Crystal bitterly. It was the last thing she felt like watching, but as she had nothing else to do she bought a set of headphones and pretended to be engrossed. She couldn't believe that Jake was sitting next to her. What the hell was it going to be like working with him? The prospect of filming the video filled her with dread. She was only doing it because she was bound by contract and because maybe, just maybe, if she did it well, Dallas might forgive her. She wasn't expecting to stay a part of Lost Angels but perhaps another group, a fresh start?

'Oi, aren't you that girl from that group?' Crystal looked up as someone prodded her on the shoulder. She saw a large man in his forties, dressed in an England football shirt, leering down at her.

Fuck, this is all I need.

She shook her head and carried on watching the movie.

But the man persisted. 'You are her, aren't you? The one who shagged her friend's boyfriend,' he laughed. 'Cheeky cow!'

Crystal ignored him, willing him to go away. But instead he shook her shoulder again, this time harder. 'I'm talking to you! My daughter loves your group and I want an autograph.'

'Piss off,' Crystal muttered, turning her head away from him.

'I heard that!' the man's voice became more aggressive and louder. 'I'm not moving until you give me an autograph.'

Judging by the alcohol fumes on his breath he'd been hitting the duty free for some time.

'Look, mate, why don't you just go back to your seat and leave her alone.' It was Jake.

'Fuck off!' the man shouted back. 'It's none of your business!' But Jake was already unfastening his seat belt and standing up as two of the cabin crew were approaching them. And drunk and belligerent as he was, the man realised he was outnumbered and backed off, but not before delivering his parting shot. 'It's the blonde one's autograph I really wanted, not that slag's.'

Crystal felt tears of humiliation fill her eyes. She never should have agreed to make this final video. Whatever it cost her she should have said no. Her self-esteem was already in tatters. She really didn't know how much more she could take. Next to her Jake had sat down again, and muttered, 'You okay?'

She nodded, not trusting herself to speak.

'Why don't we swap seats? You won't get hassled in the middle.'

'Thanks,' Crystal managed to reply.

'There's more leg room for me at the end anyway,' Jake answered.

Still, thought Crystal, *it had been nice of him to rescue me; he couldn't still hate me, could he?*

He barely spoke to her for the rest of the flight. Instead Crystal found herself chatting to Gavin. She had always got on well with him. Luckily she didn't have to do much of the talking as Gavin had recently fallen in love and was desperate to talk about Lara, his new girlfriend who he'd met while he and Jake were working in Australia. He'd obviously bored all his friends stiff and needed a fresh audience. Crystal was only too happy to oblige, anything to stop her obsessing over Jake.

'So what do you think?' Gavin said eagerly at the end of his glowing description of his girlfriend.

'She sounds great,' Crystal answered.

'And you'll have to meet her; she's flying over when I get back from Ibiza and I'm having a party.'

Crystal smiled; partying was the last thing on her agenda.

'And if you're seeing anyone, you can bring them too,' Gavin added.

Crystal shook her head. 'I'm not seeing anyone.'

That got Jake's attention. He turned to Crystal. 'That must be a first for you.' There was an edge to his voice that made Crystal wince; she'd been wrong earlier. He obviously did hate her.

She shrugged. 'Not at all.' Not wanting the attention to be on her, she asked Gavin if he had any photographs of his new girlfriend. She regretted asking as Gavin proceeded to show her what seemed like a hundred snaps. With every picture of the two of them wrapped in each other's arms, or of his girlfriend smiling away happily at the camera, Crystal felt a wave of sadness and regret rise up inside. She couldn't ever imagine being that happy and in love again.

She handed the photographs back to Gavin, repeating how lovely his girlfriend looked, and as she did so the sleeve of her jacket slipped back revealing the long scar on her right arm.

'What happened to your arm, Crystal?' Gavin asked, sounding concerned.

'It was from my accident,' Crystal answered, assuming he knew.

'What accident?' Jake put down his book and turned to look at her.

'You know, when I got knocked over by the car, in December.'

Jake shook his head. 'I didn't know.'

'Oh? My brother left a message for you with Stella. She said she would call you.' She dared herself to look at Jake. For a few seconds it looked like he actually cared, before he said: 'There must have been a mix-up. I never got the message. You're okay, though?'

Crystal nodded and Jake went back to reading, while Gavin wanted to know all the details.

She hung back from the group when they landed. She didn't want to see Belle or Dallas but he sought her out.

'Good flight, Crystal?' he asked.

'It was great, thanks. I must travel economy more often; you meet such interesting people. You should try it, Dallas,' she answered sweetly, determined not to let him get to her.

He laughed. 'I'm sorry, you were meant to be in first class, there was a mistake in the bookings. I'm not *that* mean. Anyway, good to see you looking so well.' He walked off, then seemed to remember something else. 'But by the way, you'll be staying with the crew in the guesthouse. It's nothing personal, it's just I can't risk Belle getting upset by seeing too much of you. You do understand, don't you?'

'Whatever you want, Dallas,' Crystal answered, thinking, *shit, I'm staying with Jake. What's that going to be like?* Just then Gavin called her; 'Hey, Crystal, the car's waiting, come on.' Crystal picked up her bag and walked swiftly to the exit. *If I can get through the next week,* she told herself grimly, *I can get through anything.*

The guesthouse turned out to be a spacious, luxurious villa next to Dallas's mansion. No expense had been spared in its lavish decor, and it even had its own pool and hot tub. There would be five of them staying there – Jez, Danni, Jake, Gavin and Crystal. After the car dropped them off they all wandered into the house and into the open-plan lounge, with its stunning view of the Med.

'There are five bedrooms – three face the sea and

two are at the back. So shall we draw straws to see who gets what?' Gavin asked the group. Crystal could tell that Jez and Danni really wanted a sea view, and as she didn't care where she slept she said, 'I'm happy to have one of the back rooms, if that makes it easier.' The others seemed okay with that, so she picked up her bag and wandered upstairs. It had been a very long day and she felt emotionally strung out. All she wanted to do was have a shower, a beer and crash out. She smiled to herself as she checked out her bedroom – she made sure she chose the smallest of the two, not wanting the others to think she was grabbing the best one for herself – but it was still a huge room and shared a bathroom with the other double. She'd almost forgotten that Dallas never settled for anything less than full luxury all the way. The view from the balcony was of a beautiful garden filled with purple and orange bougainvillea and palm trees. She took a long shower, put on a pair of denim shorts and a black vest and went downstairs to grab a beer from the fridge, intending to sneak back upstairs, sit on her balcony and celebrate her birthday quietly. Most of the others were outside by the pool drinking beer and chatting.

'Come and have a drink, Crystal,' Danni called out. Crystal hesitated; she could go back upstairs and be on her own, or she could join them. It was going to be a tough week and she'd missed her friends – at least they still liked her.

'Okay,' she shouted back. 'Anyone want another beer?'

'I'll have one.' Crystal started at the sound of Jake's voice behind her. She turned round. He'd also had a shower and swapped his jeans for cut-off combats and a white vest. He looked seriously good.

'Sure,' she answered, getting two beers out of the fridge. Just being this close to him made her so nervous she couldn't even work out how to use the bottle opener. After a few minutes of watching her fumbling around uselessly Jake took the opener from her and expertly prised the tops off both bottles.

'A man could die of thirst waiting for you,' he said, handing her a beer and walking past her and out on to the terrace. She followed him out, taking a slug of beer for confidence.

As she sat down Jez held up a bottle of champagne and said, 'Surprise! Happy birthday, Crystal!' He cracked it open and poured everyone a glass.

'Oh my God!' she exclaimed, self-conscious about being the centre of attention. 'You didn't have to do this.'

Jez came over and kissed her. 'You didn't think we'd forget our favourite girl's birthday, did you?' he said, handing her a present and a card. He was followed by Danni, who handed her another parcel, and by Gavin, who gave her a big hug and said, 'Jez

289

only told me when we landed, so I couldn't get you anything.'

Jake remained sitting some distance away but at least he raised his beer and said, 'Happy birthday, kid.' Crystal smiled, then quickly looked away. It was too bitter-sweet seeing him. Jez bossily ordered her to open her presents.

He'd bought her some gorgeous lingerie from Agent Provocateur, which Crystal hastily wrapped up again as she felt awkward looking at it in front of Jake.

'I thought you deserved a treat, my darling,' Jez said as she thanked him. Danni had bought her some lovely spa products.

'Thank you so much,' Crystal said, hugging both her friends. 'I feel really spoiled.' She was touched that they'd remembered her birthday. She didn't want to be the centre of attention any more but her friends hadn't seen her in months and were keen to catch up with her and bombarded her with questions.

'How was your Christmas?' Danni asked.

'Oh, you know, pretty quiet, it was just my brother, his girlfriend, a few of their friends and me.' The truth was it had been awful – everyone was so full of festive spirit and Crystal had never felt more miserable. She'd put on a brave face for everyone else's sake but hated every minute. It was meant to have been her and Jake's first Christmas together and he had talked about hiring a cottage somewhere where they could celebrate it, just the two of them. When Crystal had said that she didn't particularly like the countryside he had told that she didn't have to go out, and that they'd spend the time making love in front of the fire . . .

'You should have come to my New Year's Eve party,' Jez said. 'It was fabulous, wasn't it, Danni?'

'It was unforgettable,' Danni replied. 'Jez had a beach theme and everyone had to go in their swimsuits. Jez wore the tiniest pair of white trunks and more fake tan than everyone else put together.'

'Well, I had to show off my new body,' Jez said. 'I've lost nearly a stone, haven't you noticed, Crystal?'

'I had and you look great,' Crystal smiled, enjoying being back with her friends.

'Though if you don't mind me saying so, darling, you've lost a little too much weight. You're not going all anorexic on us, are you?' Jez said, a note of anxiety in his voice.

Crystal tried to shrug off the comment. 'I haven't really, Jez, I've just been going to the gym a lot. I've got to wear a bikini for most of the shoot and I didn't want to be worrying about my belly and having to hold my breath in the whole time.'

'All right, but I'll be keeping an eye on you to make sure you eat. Size zero is *so* last season. Anyway, I love the hair, it looks sensational, though I wish you'd come to me, darling, I am a little hurt.'

'Sorry,' Crystal answered. 'It was a bit of a spur of the moment decision.'

'It really suits you, Crystal,' Danni put in. 'I just can't believe you were brave enough to have it all cut off.'

'And what's this?' Jez pointed at the delicate black tattoo on her wrist.

'Oh, it's nothing,' Crystal mumbled. 'Just the Chinese character C,' she lied, *really* wishing they would talk about something else. Jez looked as if he was about to say something else, so Crystal quickly got in first and asked Danni about her recent trip to France. As Danni talked about her stay in Paris, working on one of the fashion shows, Crystal sipped her champagne and took surreptitious glances at Jake. He was talking to Gavin and he looked relaxed and happy. The last time she'd seen him was when they broke up. He'd looked so angry and hurt.

God, I've missed him so much. Not wanting to think about it, she had another sip of champagne and lit a cigarette. Immediately Danni was on her case.

'I thought you'd given up, Crystal,' Danni exclaimed.

'I did for ages, and then I cracked,' she answered. Jake looked over at her and frowned. Smoking was one of the few things they'd argued about. He thought it was a disgusting habit and gave her a really hard time about it. She had managed to give up when they were together and then when the Max situation came into the open, she went straight back to her bad habit.

'Well, you should try again, shouldn't she, Jake?' Danni asked. Jake looked over but avoided eye contact with Crystal.

'I'm sure Crystal will give up when she wants to.' He looked away again. Crystal took another drag of her cigarette and found she didn't really want it any more.

'Hey, Jake, isn't that a new tattoo on your arm?' Jez exclaimed. 'You and Crystal are getting into them, aren't you? Next thing we know you'll have a giant crucifix on your back à la Beckham.' Crystal looked over. Jez was right. On Jake's right shoulder there was a tattoo that she hadn't seen before.

Jake nodded, clearly not wanting to talk about it. Crystal shot Jez a warning glance as she could see he was about to ask him more.

Jake stood up. 'I've got a couple of calls to make. I'll see you later.' And he walked back into the house.

'Why did you give me that look?' Jez demanded.

'Because I could see he didn't want to talk about it. It's probably the name of his new girlfriend,' Crystal said bitterly.

'Actually, it's your name, Crystal. He had it done when he was filming in Spain; he wanted it to be a surprise and then—' Gavin trailed off awkwardly.

'Then we broke up,' Crystal finished the sentence for him. She wondered if there was any hope to be gleaned from the fact that he hadn't had it removed yet, and then remembered he still had Eve's name tattooed on his wrist.

'Yeah, he says he's not going to get anyone else's name tattooed and that if he does it will only be after they've been married for at least ten years. Oh God, sorry Crystal. I didn't mean to say that.' Gavin looked mortified.

'It's okay,' Crystal reassured him, feeling anything but okay.

'That doesn't mean C, does it?' Danni asked quietly, pointing at Crystal's tattoo.

Crystal shook her head and willed herself not to cry. 'No, it's J.'

'Oh sweetheart!' Jez said, getting up and giving her a hug. 'I'm sorry.'

That night one of Dallas's chefs came over to the house and cooked a delicious Thai green curry for them. Danni, Jez and Gavin all hit the booze and ended up quite drunk. But the last thing Crystal wanted to do was lose control so she just had a couple of glasses of wine then stuck to the water. As for Jake, he outdrank all of them, but didn't seem at all drunk. By the end of the night she realised with surprise that, even given the awkward situation with Jake, she'd actually quite enjoyed herself. When Jake was out of the room, she'd even managed to find out through Gavin that he didn't have a girlfriend. But she was jolted out of her good mood when Danni whispered, 'How are you feeling about seeing Belle tomorrow?'

'I can't bear to think about it if I'm honest,' Crystal answered. 'I haven't seen her since . . .' she trailed off. 'I just know it's going to be awful, Danni. She hates me and I can't tell you how bad I feel about what happened.'

She suddenly became aware that Jake was listening to their conversation and looked away awkwardly.

'Anyway, I'm going to bed. What time are we starting?' She looked at Danni, who shrugged and asked Jake.

'I want to start filming by ten at the latest,' he replied abruptly.

'Okay, Crystal, I'll need you at half seven if that's okay. Dallas said to do your make-up and hair first.'

'Fine,' Crystal answered, getting up. 'See you all in the morning.'

The morning came round too fast for Crystal. She didn't get to sleep until four, as she was obsessing about Jake. She slept straight through her alarm and only woke up when Danni knocked loudly at her door at seven fifteen.

'Oh God, Danni, sorry, I'll have a really quick shower.' Crystal leapt out of bed and raced to the bathroom, only to find that there was someone in there. Just as she was about to knock on the door and ask them to hurry up, the door opened and Jake walked out. He was wearing just a white towel wrapped round his waist. He looked so incredibly sexy, it took all of Crystal's willpower not to stare. When they'd been together he'd had a great body, but in the last three months it looked as if it'd got even better; his abs and pecs were even more toned and his skin was a beautiful golden brown.

'Morning,' he said cheerfully. 'You'd better hurry up; I want you on set in a few hours.'

Mumbling 'Okay', Crystal dashed into the bathroom. Jake was obviously in the other back bedroom. *Why did it have to be him?* she fretted, as she took the quickest shower ever. But even in her haste she couldn't resist taking the lid off Jake's bottle of aftershave and experiencing a rush of desire and longing as she breathed it in.

In the end she was only twenty minutes late for Danni, and Jez sweetly brought her coffee and croissants as she'd had no time for breakfast. She felt so secure with the two of them. But it was strange being made up again. She hadn't worn this much make-up in months. Danni had gone to town on her eyes, giving her a vampy, smoky-eyed look, with long false eyelashes. Then it was Jez's turn to do her hair. That was one good thing about having a bob, she thought: all it really needed was a good cut and blow dry, but secretly she missed her long hair. *After this video*, she told herself, *I'm growing it back*.

The video was mainly going to be shot on the beach and at Dallas's mansion. He wanted this video for 'Betrayal' to be their sexiest yet, so all three girls had to wear bikinis for most of it. He'd also brought in three attractive male dancers. (He was obviously banking on people downloading the video on to their MP3 players and phones.) Surprise, surprise, Crystal was playing the villain of the piece – the girl who had stolen someone else's man. She really didn't want to do it and thought if Dallas had any kind of imagination he'd have played them against type and made Tahlia the villain. But she was in no position to say anything. She had to go along with what he wanted, however much she hated it. She wasn't at all happy when she came to try on the first bikini, though. It was a tiny black number; the top barely covered her breasts, and the bottoms were so brief she felt they were almost non-existent. She was sure that the top of her love heart tattoo must be visible. Round her waist she wore a gold chain and that was all.

'Wow, you look great,' Jez told her, just as he was about to go over to the other house to get Belle and Tahlia ready.

'I don't want to wear it!' Crystal exclaimed. 'I wouldn't even wear it on a private beach. My arse is wobbling about all over the place.'

'Honestly, you look fab, stop worrying. Anyway, you know it's pointless to say anything to Dallas. He'd just say if you don't like it take it off and do it naked.'

Crystal sighed. Jez was right but it didn't make

her feel any better. She grabbed a sarong and followed Jez. It was time to meet Belle.

Fortunately Tahlia was the first person she saw. She was sitting by the pool with Leticia. As soon as she spotted Crystal, Leticia raced over and threw her arms round her waist. 'Crystal come in the pool with me please!' she begged.

Crystal laughed. 'I promise I will when we've finished filming, but I can't right now. If I get my hair and make-up wet Jez and Danni will go mad!'

Tahlia got up and hugged her, stepping back to look at Crystal's bikini. She raised her eyebrows. 'God, I hope mine's bigger than yours!'

'Oh no,' Crystal groaned, 'is it that revealing?'

'Do you really want me to answer that?' Tahlia replied. 'Put it this way, it looks like you've gone way beyond Brazil, if you know what I mean.'

'Yeah,' Crystal answered, 'I've been to Hollywood, and it bloody well hurt. Never again.' She tied the sarong round her waist.

Tahlia laughed and even Crystal managed a smile. Then a familiar voice said, 'Danni's ready for you now, Tahlia.'

Crystal turned round and found herself face to face with Belle. She hadn't seen her for three months, but there hadn't been a day when she hadn't thought of her. She cleared her throat nervously. 'Hi, Belle.'

Belle seemed to look through her. 'Let's get one thing straight, Crystal. I'm only doing this because

Dallas threatened to sue me if I didn't. After this week I never want to see you again. As far as I'm concerned you're just a girl Dallas got in for the video. I don't know you any more.' She turned away from Crystal and marched back into the house. Not even the fact that her footballer boyfriend had recently proposed to her had softened her attitude. It was only to be expected though.

'Are you okay, babe?' Tahlia asked sympathetically, having heard what Belle had said.

Crystal nodded. 'It could have been worse, I suppose.' But inside she felt awful. She had a week of this to endure and she didn't feel in the strongest emotional state.

'Leticia, will you come with me now. I've got to get ready,' Tahlia asked her daughter.

'No, I want to stay with Crystal,' Leticia pleaded.

'Is that okay?' Tahlia asked.

'Sure, we'll go to the beach,' Crystal said, wanting to spend as little time as possible at Dallas's mansion. It brought back too many bad memories.

But no sooner had Crystal left one awkward encounter than she walked bang into the middle of another as she ran into Jake and Gavin getting ready for filming. They'd been joined by three cameramen and a sound engineer and were busy marking out where they wanted to film. Leticia immediately went running over to Jake while Crystal trailed behind.

'Hey you,' Jake said, bending down, and

scooping Leticia into his arms, making her giggle.

When Crystal and Jake had been together they'd spent a lot of time with Tahlia, Leticia and Hadley. Leticia had adored Jake and clearly still did. Crystal hung back watching him talking to Leticia. Being close to him was like being slapped in the face. Why was it that everything about him was so perfect? Not only did he look great and have a great personality, he was also great with kids, good dad material judging by his rapport with Leticia. And she had lost him. *Fuck*.

Finally Jake seemed to register that Crystal was there. He straightened up and Crystal was aware of him taking in her revealing bikini. She folded her arms and looked defiant.

'Come on, Leticia, let's go and look for shells. I'm sure Jake's got work to do.'

'See you later small stuff,' he said to Leticia. And just as Crystal thought he was going to ignore her altogether he called out, 'And we'll start in about an hour and half, Crystal' as she walked away.

'Okay,' she called back without turning round.

'Let's get one thing straight,' Crystal hissed at the cocky young lad grinning at her as they both lay on a towel at the water's edge. 'When I kiss you I don't want your tongue rammed into my mouth!'

They were shooting the beach scenes. All three girls had been paired with a good-looking dancer but, while Belle and Tahlia were able to stroll along the beach hand in hand with theirs, Crystal had been directed, by Jake – *how fucked up was that?* – to kiss hers. She kept trying for innocent kisses, but Kyle had other ideas and forced his tongue into her mouth and groped her breasts.

He just shrugged and said that's what he'd been told to do.

Crystal looked up at the wall of people surrounding her. Jake raised his eyebrows as if he couldn't see what her problem was.

'Dallas,' she shouted out, 'I need to talk to you.'

Dallas strolled over, immaculate in a cream linen suit. Crystal got up from the towel she was lying on and tried to make herself look taller, but it was hard to assert her authority in a teeny-weeny bikini.

'I don't like the way he's kissing me, and he shouldn't be touching my tits,' she hissed.

Dallas raised his eyebrows. 'Well, it's supposed to look sexy, you can't just be lying there reading a book. But perhaps he is going a little far. I don't want to end up with a parental advisory warning on the video.' He addressed Kyle, 'Hey, no tongues and no touching her tits, okay?' Kyle shrugged. *God he was vile*, just being near him made her skin crawl, so she went on, 'If you want it to look sexy, then I need a drink.' She lowered her voice so Kyle wouldn't hear and said, 'I can't do it sober with this creep with everyone staring at me. I want champagne.' Crystal didn't particularly want a drink but she knew the alcohol would help make her feel slightly less inhibited.

Dallas laughed again. 'I always knew you had it in you to be a diva. Okay, Crystal, vintage Cristal suit you?'

For the next hour Crystal was filmed writhing on the sand with Kyle. She'd acted before and often had to kiss other actors but this went way beyond anything she'd ever had to do. Not only did Kyle kiss her lips, though thank god he cut out the tongues, he was also directed, by Jake, to kiss the rest of her body, moving further and further down while the camera focused on Crystal's face, a shot which they kept having to retake as Crystal looked less than ecstatic. Then she was directed to straddle him. The champagne took away some of the edge but Crystal couldn't help feeling humiliated. There she was simulating a sex scene in front of her ex-lover and ex-friend. In between takes, Jez and Danni were the only ones who made her feel better, telling her she was doing great, that it would look fantastic in the video. Finally, Crystal was able to take a break while the action moved to Belle and Tahlia. She slipped on the white shirt that Danni handed her, wishing she could become invisible.

Gavin called over, 'Great job Crystal, you'd be such a good actress, you know. Doing those kind of scenes is the hardest thing, but you got it straight off.'

Crystal was about to thank him, but Jake cut in with a sarcastic smile: 'Oh, I don't know if Crystal was even acting. Behaving like that is probably second nature to her.'

Both Jez and Danni looked shocked by the comment, and Gavin muttered, 'That's a bit out of order, mate.'

Jake turned away abruptly and walked off to talk to one of the cameramen.

Crystal was so stunned that for a moment she couldn't say anything. She'd never known Jake to be deliberately cruel before. But now she was furious; how dare he say that to her! She marched over to where he was standing and without caring who was listening, she said, 'Fuck you, Jake. I would never humiliate someone like that. I'm doing this because I have to, not because I want to.'

He looked as if he was going to say something, but Crystal had already turned away and was running down the beach, back to the guesthouse. Angry with herself because she couldn't stop the tears.

She raced upstairs to her bedroom and threw herself on the bed, sobbing. She lost all track of time; she was more humiliated and unhappy than she had ever felt. It had been bad enough when Jake left her, but somewhere deep down she'd always hoped that one day she would be able to put right what had happened. Today was the final proof that she couldn't. That she'd lost him forever.

'Crystal?' Danni was knocking at the door. 'Are you in there?'

Wiping her eyes and sniffing, Crystal mumbled for her to come in.

'Are you okay?' Danni asked, sounding concerned. 'We've got an hour and then they need to film you again. Are you up for it? I could tell Dallas you're sick or something.'

Crystal shook her head miserably.

'And ignore Jake, it was a shitty thing to say and it's not true.'

'Isn't it?' Crystal answered. 'He only said what everyone else must be thinking.'

'Nobody thinks that, Crystal, and I don't believe Jake thinks it either. You and him have got unresolved business. It's obvious that he's still got feelings for you.'

'Yeah, feelings of hatred,' Crystal said bitterly.

'No, that's not what I meant. So shall I tell Dallas you can't do it?'

Crystal shrugged. 'I don't have a choice, Danni. I have to do this, even though I know it makes me look like the biggest slag in the world. I'm never going to live it down, am I?'

'Look, the song's great and people will just see the video as a bit of fun.' Danni did her best to reassure her.

Crystal lit a cigarette, still smarting from Jake's comment.

'I've got your costume for the second scene and

you'll be pleased to know it's a little less revealing,' Danni continued.

Crystal watched, hardly caring as Danni held up a white costume. It was more like a bikini than a swimsuit. There was just a single strip of material linking the top and bottom, with a gold ring in the middle. It was the same as Belle's costume. The idea was that Crystal would be filmed on the beach with Belle's dancer. They'd lead everyone to believe it was Belle, because Crystal would be filmed from the back wearing a blonde wig, but it would become clear that it was Crystal stealing Belle's man. *How subtle was that*, Crystal thought miserably.

'I'll get all your old make-up off; we haven't got long.'

Crystal felt completely drained as Danni got to work, wiping off her ruined eye make-up and giving her a sun-kissed look.

There was another knock at the door and this time it was Jez, holding a long blonde wig.

'Hiya, darling,' he breezed in. 'Don't let the bastards get you down. What was Jake's problem back there? I couldn't believe it when he said that to you. I'm so glad that you told him to fuck off. He totally deserved it.'

Crystal definitely did not want to talk about Jake, she just muttered, 'Yeah, well, I just can't bear that he obviously hates me.'

'I'm sure he doesn't,' Jez answered, and was

about to continue but, seeing the look on Crystal's face, changed the subject. 'Now let's get this wig on you.'

'I know I'm going to look minging with blonde hair,' Crystal moaned.

'Rubbish, you're going to look gorgeous.' Jez fiddled about with the wig, tugging it this way and that, until finally he was satisfied and let her look in the mirror.

Crystal stared back at an unfamiliar woman. It wasn't as bad as she'd thought; in fact even she could tell that she looked good. She was a different kind of blonde to Belle who looked wholesome and fresh-faced like Claudia Schiffer. Crystal was more a Kate Moss kind of blonde, a bit unpredictable, a bit naughty, very sexy.

'You see?' Jez said, 'you look fabulous. Now get back out there and wow those bastards and then tonight we'll all go out on the lash.'

The second dancer Crystal had to get up close and personal with was called Marcus and he was a hundred times nicer than Kyle.

'Don't worry,' he whispered, when they met, 'I'm gay, so if you don't mind when I'm kissing you, I'll be thinking of Daniel Craig.'

'And if *you* don't mind,' Crystal replied, 'I will as well.'

The two of them laughed and for the first time since the shoot began Crystal felt relaxed.

'Okay, Crystal and Marcus, I need you by the sea now,' Jake called over.

Without acknowledging him, Crystal flicked back her long blonde hair and sauntered to the water's edge.

The scene with Marcus was much more comfortable for Crystal. They had to kiss and caress each other but Marcus made it feel like he was being professional and just doing his job, whereas, with Kyle, Crystal felt as if he really did want to have sex with her. As a result they hardly had to do any retakes and Crystal was spared the humiliation of hearing Jake tell Marcus to kiss her and touch her body.

As they walked off the set Marcus said, 'A few of us are going out clubbing tonight. Do you fancy coming?'

'Kyle isn't going, is he?' Crystal asked; she definitely didn't want to see him again unless she had to.

Marcus laughed. 'No, he's probably got an appointment with his mirror – don't worry, we all hate him too.'

'Okay, I'll bring Jez and Danni along as well.'

'Cool, see you later.'

Given how hard the day had been for her, Crystal was in the mood for kicking back. Jez and Danni agreed to come; Jez needed no encouragement, having developed a massive crush on Marcus. The other people were all from the crew and were lovely and down to earth. For the first time in ages she didn't feel self-conscious in company, paranoid that everyone was staring at her and thinking she was a bitch. As her hair had been flattened by the wig, she decided to keep it on. Ironically, looking different made her feel she could be herself again – her old self, the cheeky, lippy Crystal, who wasn't afraid of anything, who was up for a laugh. They all ended up downing tequila slammers and dancing crazily in Manumission until four in the morning.

'Tell me we haven't got an early start,' Crystal said as they stumbled back into the house.

'No, we're not filming until tomorrow night,' Danni answered.

'In that case,' Jez put in, 'who wants to have another drink?'

'Yes!' Crystal and Danni shouted back together, as Jez grabbed a bottle of Bacardi.

The three of them had lost all inhibitions and awareness that there might be other people nearby – other people who were sober and trying to sleep. They put on an eighties compilation CD and were continuing with their wild dancing and singing along raucously to 'Relax' when Jake appeared in the doorway, looking extremely pissed off.

'Hey, turn it down will you?' he shouted over the music.

'Okay,' Jez managed to reply and started

staggering over to the stereo only to trip and fall flat on his face.

Danni and Crystal burst out laughing hysterically. Jez was groaning about his leg, which only made them laugh harder. Jake strode across the room and switched the music off.

'I've got to be up early to start the edit, so I'd appreciate it if you kept it down,' he said angrily.

'You're the boss,' Crystal said cheekily, deliberately blowing her cigarette smoke at him.

Jake looked at her coldly. 'I thought we'd agreed there shouldn't be any smoking inside the house.'

Crystal shrugged and took another drag. After his comment today he could go and screw himself. As he walked out of the room she and Danni gave him the finger before collapsing in giggles again.

Crystal was not feeling quite so full of herself the next day. She woke at midday with a raging hangover and it was a real effort to drag herself out of bed. Downstairs the living room was trashed – there were overflowing ashtrays, empty bottles and glasses, someone had spilt their drink on the white sofa and the room stank of cigarette smoke. At some point they'd been hungry and had made themselves toasted cheese sandwiches, and the plates were strewn around the room. There was no sign of Jez and Danni – probably still in bed, she thought. Jake and Gavin must be at the edit. Before she could face tidying up she just had to clear her head, so she poured herself a Coke, made some toast and went and sat by the pool, wincing in the bright sunshine, even in her dark glasses. She closed her eyes, wishing that the thumping in her head would stop. The one good thing about being hungover was that she couldn't actually summon the energy to be worried or stressed about anything else. After half an hour she decided to go for a swim. She managed ten lengths and was starting to feel slightly better when she became aware of someone standing by the pool. She looked up. It was Jake. She carried on swimming. She had nothing to say to him. But he called out, 'Nice of you to leave the house looking such a mess last night, Crystal. Are you waiting for the maid to clear it up?'

He sounded so hostile. Crystal swam to the side and looked up at him. 'I'm going to sort it out in a minute. I just wanted to have a swim and clear my head.'

He didn't move. And he looked furious.

'Look, what's your problem? I said I'd do it and I will. What's the big fucking deal anyway?'

She was angry now. Why did he have to keep picking on her? She swam to the steps and pulled herself up, and marched over to the sun lounger to grab her towel.

'The big fucking deal, Crystal, is that you only seem to care about yourself. You don't give a shit about anyone else, do you? Last night you decide to get pissed and turn up the music, and stuff anyone else. It's the story of your life.' He had followed her to the sun lounger and was standing over her, shouting.

Feeling at a disadvantage in her wet bikini, Crystal wrapped the towel round her waist and then squared up to him. 'It wasn't just me making a noise last night and I'm sorry if we woke you up. We'd all had a long day and needed to unwind.' She tried to keep her voice steady.

'That's right, blame someone else. That's you all over, you never take responsibility,' Jake said harshly. 'It must be so easy to be you, Crystal, riding roughshod over everyone else. So long as you're okay that's all the matters, isn't it?'

'You don't know what you're talking about, Jake! I know you hate me so it's pointless me saying anything because I know you're not going to listen. But you're completely wrong about me. And I've had enough of you judging me and criticising me. I'd never do that to you, so why don't you fuck off and leave me alone!'

She was absolutely furious now. This wasn't about last night, this was about Jake offloading all his anger on her and she couldn't take any more. He never wanted to listen to her side of the story. He went to say something else but Crystal muttered, 'Forget it, I'm not listening', and ran into the house before he could say anything else to upset her.

Back inside, she quickly got dressed and headed

downstairs where she set to work on the living room. She straightened furniture, put away CDs, loaded the dishwasher, collected the empty bottles, emptied the ashtrays and did her best to get rid of the drink stain. When she'd finished, Jez and Danni wandered downstairs, both moaning about their heads. Feeling better herself, Crystal made them breakfast. All three were in the kitchen chatting when Jake and Gavin turned up for lunch.

'Sorry we woke you last night,' Danni said to the two men.

'It's okay,' Gavin said, 'I didn't hear a thing.'

Jake shrugged. 'No worries. I just didn't like coming downstairs to a room that stank of smoke and was a tip.' They all looked into the living room, now back to its pristine condition, and then back at Jake.

'Well, it looked a mess.' Jake looked questioningly at Crystal, but she turned away.

'Sorry, we just got a bit carried away,' Jez answered. 'We wanted to cheer up Crystal because she'd had such a shit day, having to be groped by that creep Kyle.'

'What about that creep Marcus?' Jake asked sarcastically.

'I didn't mind being groped by him,' Crystal replied. 'He was cute. In fact I'm looking forward to later; don't I have to pretend to give him a blowie?'

Jake was the only one who didn't laugh. Crystal

was just about to go upstairs and have a lie-down when Tahlia and Leticia turned up.

'Hope you don't mind us coming over. Belle's in a mood, Dallas is working and we felt a bit lonely.'

''Course not,' Crystal said warmly. 'It's great to see you; d'you want to go swimming, Leticia? I've got a while before Danni needs to put my make-up on.'

Squealing 'Yes!', Leticia raced to the pool and jumped in, closely followed by Crystal. Playing with Leticia helped Crystal forget her argument with Jake. It was impossible to stay angry when you were with an energetic seven-year-old. Leticia floated around on a lilo while Crystal pretended to be a shark. At some point Gavin and Jake wandered past but Crystal ignored them.

For the evening filming Crystal was dressed in another extremely revealing outfit – a tiny pair of black sequined hot pants, a black sequined bikini top and a pair of strappy sandals with killer heels. She could barely walk in them, never mind dance.

'Honestly,' she grumbled as Danni glued on a set of sparkly false eyelashes, 'all I need is a sign round my neck saying how much I charge.'

Danni laughed. 'You look great; stop obsessing.'

The filming was taking place round the luxurious pool at Dallas's mansion; the three girls had to recline on the loungers while the men danced around them, then the positions switched and the men lay down while the girls danced for them. Typically, Crystal's moves were more racy than Tahlia and Belle's. They simply had to kiss their partners and hold hands, while Crystal had to sit on Kyle's lap and act seductive. Having to touch his oiled body again made her want to throw up and when he leered at her suggestively it took all her willpower not to slap him one.

It was the first time all three girls had been on set together and Crystal knew Belle wasn't going to make it easy for her. Once the filming started, Belle stopped it several times, complaining that Crystal was getting the moves wrong (she wasn't, but Crystal knew Belle wanted to make her feel bad). The fifth time Belle complained, Crystal snapped. She was hot, she was tired, she was hungover, and she was sick of people being horrible to her. 'Belle, I know you've got a problem with me, but please can we get this shoot over and done with? Everyone's knackered and you're making it hard for them as well.'

'Oh,' Belle said, in her best snooty voice, 'did *it* speak? Well, I don't speak to *it* because I don't usually have anything to do with whores.'

'Come off it, Belle,' Tahlia tried to intervene. 'Let's just get this finished.'

'No, I won't fucking come off it,' shouted Belle, working herself up into one of her diva fits – Dallas wasn't there, so she obviously knew she was safe from a bollocking. 'I shouldn't have to be anywhere near *it* – *it* makes me feel sick.' She shouted over to Jake, 'Can't you film our bits separately and do *its* some other time?'

Jake shook his head and said wearily, 'Can we please get on with it, Belle?'

But Belle had lost it big time, screaming back, 'I would have thought you of all people would have understood how I feel! How do you know she didn't two-time you!'

Jake walked over to Belle and lowered his voice. 'Don't presume to tell me how I should feel; you'll never know how I feel and I'm warning you that if you don't get on with the shoot right now, I'll call Dallas.'

Belle looked as if she had plenty more to say but realising she'd gone far enough she stomped back to her position, pausing only to mouth 'fuck you' at Crystal.

Crystal didn't know how she got through the next two hours – she felt so humiliated and power-less to do anything about it. Only Tahlia's smiles of encouragement and the sight of Danni and Jez's friendly faces kept her from running away. They finally finished filming at one in the morning. Immediately Jez gave her a hug. 'Come on, let's go back to the house. You need a drink after all that.'

'Actually, I'm just going to go to bed,' Crystal replied, desperate to be on her own, so she could stop having to hide how she felt, and without waiting for anyone else she took off her heels and ran back to the house. She grabbed a bottle of wine from the fridge and went straight upstairs. More than anything she wanted to run away, but she knew she had another day's filming to get through. She decided to drink herself into not caring. She poured herself a large glass of wine and curled up on the chair on the balcony smoking, listening to music on her iPod to try and distract herself from the feelings of hurt. Two large glasses later she was starting not to care quite so much. After downing the bottle, she was pissed and decided she didn't give a shit about anything. She was almost succeeding when something caught her eye and she looked up to see Jake on his balcony, looking over at her. She prepared herself for another ear bashing, but instead Jake said gently, 'Rough night?'

Crystal took her headphones off. 'I'm used to it so if you've got anything you'd like to add, go ahead. I'm pissed enough not to remember in the morning.'

'Belle was out of order speaking to you like that.'

'I'm sure she was just saying what you were feeling too,' Crystal said.

'I don't feel like that,' Jake replied.

'Oh, come on, you didn't even care when you were told about my accident. And I know you hate me, but I just want you to know that I was never unfaithful to you. I never would be. And I wish you would believe me.' Unable to carry on the conversation without crying, she got up and stumbled into the bedroom, where she collapsed on the bed, burying her face into her pillow. It was all too much. She couldn't put on a brave face and pretend that none of this mattered any longer; it did matter and she couldn't take any more.

She heard a knock at the door but ignored it; Jake knocked a couple more times before opening the door anyway. He came and sat down next to her on the bed.

'Hey, don't get upset,' he said softly.

'Please', she sobbed, 'just leave me alone.'

'I'm not leaving you like this,' he insisted and he lay down beside her and put his arm around her. 'I'm sorry for being so horrible to you. I didn't mean any of those things I said. And I swear I didn't know about your accident,' he sighed and went on. 'I don't know, Crystal, seeing you again has brought back so many feelings . . .' He trailed off.

Hearing his words and feeling his body next to hers only made Crystal cry even harder. She pressed her face into his chest, not wanting him to see her tears while he gently stroked her back. And suddenly, in the midst of her tears, she felt such intense, overwhelming desire for him. She found herself sliding her arms round his neck and pressing her body against his, willing him to respond. For a few seconds it seemed like he was going to, as he held her tight in his arms, but then he pulled away. 'I'll get you some water.' He got up from the bed as she lay back down and then she must have passed out.

She woke up to the sound of Jake opening the wooden shutters in her room and letting the early morning sunshine stream in. He turned and said, 'How are you feeling?'

Crystal groaned. 'Crap, my head is killing me.'

'Well, what do you expect sinking a bottle of wine on an empty stomach,' Jake replied, but he didn't sound unsympathetic. 'Drink this water, you'll feel better.'

Crystal sat up and reached for the glass he held out. She felt so rough she didn't even care what she looked like.

'I'm due on set now, but we need to talk. Can you meet me for dinner tonight?'

Crystal nodded. Suddenly her headache was forgotten, and in its place the butterflies started up. Surely it was a good sign? If he still hated her he wouldn't suggest they talk.

It took her several attempts to get out of bed. She still felt drunk but for the first time in months she felt a sense of excitement. It was just as well because when she arrived on set, dressed in the Belle swimsuit and blonde wig, Belle continued her campaign against her, deliberately moving away whenever Crystal came anywhere near her, loudly declaring, 'Not everyone can get away with being blonde. Some people just look like the whores that they are.'

'She should get over herself,' Jez muttered when Belle was out of earshot. 'You've said you're sorry. What more can you do? Anyway, she should be grateful. If it wasn't for you she'd have married that bastard and then she'd never have met that gorgeous footballer and be having her dream wedding – even though I suspect he's gay.'

'I'm sure she doesn't see it that way,' Crystal said, longing for the day to be over so that she could see what Jake wanted to talk to her about.

The first scenes they shot were of Crystal and Marcus locked in a passionate embrace by the pool, which went according to plan. Now that the filming was nearly over and there was the prospect of seeing Jake that night, Crystal was actually enjoying herself. Dallas had been a little vague about what was to happen next; he just said that Belle would discover the affair, have a go at Crystal and Marcus and storm off. The scene didn't quite go according to plan, though. Crystal was just laughing with Marcus when Belle grabbed her arm and yelled, 'Get off him, you bitch!'

'Calm down,' Crystal answered, thinking that actually Belle was quite good at acting after all. Her anger was very convincing.

'You're just a cheap whore,' Belle carried on her tirade, 'a two-faced bitch. You were supposed to be my friend and then you betrayed me. I hate you.'

It was suddenly all very real. Belle meant what she was saying.

'Please Belle,' Crystal said quietly, 'I told you what he did to me.' She looked over at Jake intently.

'Those lies again!' Belle seemed to have lost control. And before Crystal had the chance to defend herself Belle smacked her hard in the face. Crystal, who was wearing the killer heels, lost her footing and fell back, hitting her head on one of the ornate marble pots by the pool. For a few seconds she lay there, stunned.

'Crystal!' Jake shouted, racing over to her.

'I'm okay,' she answered, struggling to sit up, but as she put her hand up to her head and felt the sticky warm blood everything went fuzzy and she passed out.

She was underwater, looking up at the blue sea above her. She felt so peaceful floating there but someone was calling her, pulling her back to the surface. She opened her eyes, then shut them again, dazzled by the light.

'Crystal, can you hear me? Squeeze my hand if you can.' It was Jake.

He sounded upset. Making a huge effort, she opened her eyes again, wincing in the bright sunshine.

'Are you okay? Speak to me.'

'I'm okay,' she said slowly, though her mouth felt as if it was stuffed with cotton wool and she felt very disorientated. 'I think I just fainted. I hate the sight of blood.' She made as if to get up but Jake stopped her.

'No way. You're not moving. I've called Dallas and his doctor will be here any minute. I want him to check you over. It's only been two months since your accident.'

Crystal was about to protest that she felt fine when Jake put a towel under her head and another one over her body. Then he knelt back down by her side and held her hand. Even though her head was throbbing, there was something so lovely about being looked after by him.

Belle came over, looking anxious. 'I'm really sorry, Crystal. I didn't mean for that to happen. Are you okay?'

'We won't know until the doctor arrives,' Jake said coldly.

'Sorry,' Belle said again.

'I'm fine,' Crystal said.

'Please leave Crystal in peace now, she needs to be calm.' Jake's voice was so firm.

As Belle walked away, Crystal said, 'I'm sure I can get up now, you don't need to worry.'

Jake looked serious and held her hand more tightly. 'Yes I do and I want to make sure you're okay.'

Dallas's doctor arrived and spent the next few minutes checking Crystal over, asking her how she felt and doing a few tests to check her reflexes and reactions. Everyone was still standing around watching her and Crystal felt like a right idiot just lying there.

'Everything seems fine but as you said she's recently had a head injury,' the doctor addressed his comments to Jake, 'I think it would be a good idea to have a scan at the hospital.'

Four hours later Crystal was lying on the sofa back at the guesthouse. The hospital had given her the all clear but advised her to take it easy for the next twenty-four hours. She felt perfectly okay, apart from a dull headache. She wanted to go to the beach but Jake wouldn't hear of it.

'You heard what the doctor said.'

Crystal tried to argue but gave up. It was too wonderful spending time with Jake again. He hadn't left her side, insisting on taking her to the hospital, staying with her when she had the scan and when they got back to the house he made her a bed on the sofa, fixed her a sandwich and ordered everyone else to leave her alone.

But when he left the room to take a call Jez and Danni sneaked in.

'How are you, darling?' Jez said, rushing over to give her a kiss.

'I'm fine, honestly. I don't know what all the fuss is about,' Crystal answered.

'Are you sure?' Danni asked, coming over and giving her a hug. Crystal nodded and Jez flopped down on the sofa next to her.

'Well, Jake has been an absolute tower of strength,' Jez declared, always fond of a cliché in a crisis. 'When Belle hit you and you fell it was like watching a scene from *ER* – Jake totally took control, he wouldn't let anyone else touch you. He ordered Dallas to get hold of the best doctor on the island. I tell you, girl, that man *really* likes you.'

Crystal shook her head. 'He doesn't, that's just the kind of person he is. He'd have done the same for either of you.'

Danni smiled. 'No he wouldn't, Crystal. He still has feelings for you, it's obvious.'

Crystal was about to say no way when Jake walked back in.

'We should leave you two together,' Jez said, looking meaningfully at Jake and then back at Crystal. Typical Jez, thought Crystal: all the subtlety of a herd of charging elephants.

He and Danni left the room, but when Jake's back was turned Jez mouthed *he loves you!* and drew a love heart in the air and pointed at Crystal. She giggled.

'What?' Jake asked, sitting down on the sofa next to her.

Crystal shook her head. 'Nothing.'

'Thank God you're all right, Crystal,' he said, and to her surprise and delight he picked up her hand and gently kissed it. *Wow*.

'I must get hit on the head more often if it has this effect on you,' Crystal said softly.

'Don't say that. I don't know what I'd have done if—' he was interrupted by another knock at the door and the arrival of Belle.

For once Belle did not look her super-confident self; she looked less than immaculately groomed and she hadn't brushed her hair or reapplied her make-up since the shoot.

'Jez told me you were okay,' she said tentatively. 'And I just wanted to say sorry again.'

'I think Crystal needs to rest now,' Jake said protectively.

'It's okay, I'd like to see Belle,' Crystal replied. 'Can you give us a minute?' Very reluctantly Jake got up and left the two girls together.

Belle stood in the centre of the room, looking awkward. 'I'm sorry, Crystal, I never meant for that to happen. I felt so bad when you hit your head, I thought I must have really hurt you when you passed out.' Suddenly Belle was crying and they weren't the usual stage tears that she would turn on whenever she wanted sympathy. These were heart-felt sobs.

'Belle, I'm all right. I don't blame you for what you did. I would probably have done the same if I'd been you.'

Belle came and sat down on the sofa, opening up her designer bag and searching for a tissue.

'I was angry with you for ages and even when I met Lee I was still bitter about what happened. I blamed you for everything but I know Max was just as responsible, more so really, because I know now what a manipulative bastard he can be. And it's stupid because I'm a thousand times happier with

Lee than I ever was with Max. All those times you asked me how he treated me, I lied. Everything wasn't okay. It was like being with Jekyll and Hyde. I never knew what mood he would be in from one moment to the next.' Belle paused to blow her nose.

'I know we can never go back to how we were, but please let's not be enemies any more,' Crystal said softly.

Jake walked back into the room. 'Belle, that's long enough.'

Belle stood up to go. 'Okay, Crystal,' she said slowly, 'I agree,' then she turned and left, flicking her hair back, the confidence returned to her step.

'We still need to talk,' Jake said, sitting down next to her, 'but I want you to rest now. I've got to go back to the edit but I want you to promise that you'll go to bed at nine.'

'Okay, doctor,' Crystal replied in what she hoped was her best seductive voice, 'but we could talk now.' She was reluctant to let him go.

'We'll talk tomorrow.' Then he kissed her forehead, and just feeling his lips on her skin gave Crystal a jolt of desire so powerful that even though her head still hurt the rest of her body felt up for anything . . .

'Okay, that's a wrap.' It was four o'clock the following afternoon and Crystal and Belle had just re-enacted their fight scene. This time Belle used the technique she'd learnt from stage school when she went to slap Crystal and Crystal didn't get hurt. Jake had been dead against Crystal working but Dallas had pleaded with her, saying it would cost him a fortune if they didn't finish filming today. For the first time in ages Crystal could actually use a bit of bargaining power. It was a good feeling, so she let him sweat for a bit before saying, 'I'll do it on one condition.'

'How much?' he asked.

'I don't want any money, Dallas, but I would like to borrow the guesthouse for a couple more nights after everyone else has flown back and I'll need two first class plane tickets.'

Obviously thinking he'd got off lightly, Dallas agreed.

After filming, everyone had to race back to the guesthouse and get packed for their flight that evening. Jake was about to join the exodus when Crystal called him over. She took a deep breath, suddenly feeling nervous: what if he turned her down? Well, so what if he did? She'd never know if she didn't ask. 'Dallas has let me have the guesthouse for a couple more days; how do you feel about staying on?' She paused. 'With me.'

'Yes, we need to talk, don't we?' Jake said. For the first time since they'd broken up he gave her his sexy grin which sent her stomach into free fall.

Half an hour later Crystal was frantically rifling through her clothes for the outfit that said, I still want you, take me back. Thinking that she was going to be spending most of her time filming or in a bikini, she hadn't packed much and her choice was limited. In the end she settled for the only dress she had brought with her – a slinky black backless number – but to make it look like she wasn't trying so hard she put on flat gold gladiator sandals instead of heels and kept make-up to a minimum.

Let him still want me, she prayed, making a final check on her appearance in the mirror.

She met Jake downstairs in the guesthouse but he didn't make any comment on her appearance. Instead, he asked how she was feeling.

Horny – Crystal was tempted to say because Jake looked delicious . . . but she kept that opinion to herself as they travelled in the taxi to the restaurant.

The first thing Crystal wanted to do when they sat down at their table was to order a bottle of wine – she needed a drink to give her confidence – but just as the waiter handed her the wine list Jake said, 'We'll just have water, thanks.' And to Crystal he added, 'I think you should leave it another twenty-four hours before you have a drink.'

'Whatever you say, doctor,' Crystal said, and she couldn't resist giving him a flirtatious look from under her lashes. Unfortunately Jake seemed oblivious and studied the menu instead. *Oh God, maybe he just wanted us to clear the air and to be friends . . .*

For the first part of the evening it felt like they were making polite conversation, as if they were just acquaintances. Jake asked how her work was going (that was a short topic as she hadn't worked at all); he asked after her brother and about her stay in Brighton. She in turn asked about his work and the trip to Australia. Finally, Crystal couldn't stand the pretence any longer – as far as she was concerned there was a fucking great elephant in the room, the reason why they split up – and if they didn't talk about it soon she thought she would explode.

She blurted out, 'So you said you wanted to talk?'

Jake smiled. 'You're right; enough of this small talk. Okay, here goes. When we split up,' ("correction", Crystal wanted to say, "when you left me", but she let it go) 'I didn't want to know anything about what had happened between you and Max. I decided to think the worst. But seeing you again has changed everything. I want to know the truth. Will you tell me? And this time I promise to listen.'

And not judge, Crystal wanted to say, instead she took a deep breath, knowing that everything hung in the balance. She told the whole sorry story of her fling with Max.

'Bastard!' he exclaimed, hitting the table with his fist when she told him of the rape and subsequent blackmail. 'Where is he now? I'm going to teach that lowlife a lesson. How could he do that to you? You should have told me!' Then he added, 'Of course, I didn't give you the chance, did I? If he ever tries to contact you again, I want you to tell me. I don't want that shit anywhere near you.'

Crystal had never seen Jake look so angry before – *did that mean he still cared? Or would he be like this if it was any other woman?* Jake looked as if it was taking all his self-control to calm down.

'It's all over now,' Crystal replied. 'He knows he can't get anything from me any more.'

Jake ran his hand over his short blond hair and gazed at Crystal. 'I'm so sorry Crystal. I totally let you down, didn't I? I suppose when the Max thing broke it just took me back to what happened with Eve. I missed saying goodbye to my gran in hospital because I was so caught up in my relationship and I don't think I've forgiven myself for it. So instead of dealing with difficult situations, I run away. When I heard about Max, I thought it was easier to cut it all out of my life.'

He looked so sad. Crystal reached out and held his hand and as she did he saw the tattoo on her wrist.

'So what does your tattoo mean then?' he asked.

Crystal hesitated before answering. She really didn't want to frighten him off – 'It's a J.'

Jake raised her wrist to his lips and lightly kissed her tattoo, then said, 'You know what mine says, don't you?' He rolled up his T-shirt, revealing the tattoo across the top of his arm. She couldn't resist running her fingers across it. *He hadn't had it removed. Did that mean there was a chance?*

By now they were the only couple left in the restaurant and their waiter kept looking at his watch in a very obvious way, but Crystal didn't want to break the spell of intimacy between them, worrying that a change of scene might cause Jake to back off again.

'We should go,' Jake said, signalling for the bill.

Crystal reached for her wallet to pay her share, but Jake shook his head.

'Let's go back to the house and maybe I could let you have one brandy. I think we could both do with a drink.'

During the taxi ride back, Crystal's mind went into overdrive analysing his words – *why could he do with a drink?* He was so shocked by what he'd heard? Or was it just that he felt sorry for her? Did he feel anything for her still? Was he concerned for her just as a friend? Or did he feel something more for her? She had no idea. God, he could be so frustrating! She'd forgotten how unreadable he could be at times. But after he'd shut the door behind them he reached out and gently put his hand up to her face, tracing a finger along her jaw line, down her neck and then up round her mouth, and then he dipped his head down to kiss her, and as their kiss became more passionate and more intense he didn't seem so hard to read any more. They didn't make it up to the bedroom, only as far as the elegant marble staircase. Desire had overtaken both of them and to wait even a second longer to touch, taste each other's bodies, and to make love, wasn't possible.

'I missed you so much, Crystal,' Jake whispered afterwards, gazing into her eyes.

Crystal's heart leapt. Okay, he hadn't said he loved her, but he missed her, that meant something. 'I missed you too,' she whispered back, thinking that the words didn't even come close to the intensity of her feelings for him. And then, because she didn't want to reveal how emotional she felt, she joked, 'I wish Dallas didn't have such a thing about marble. What's wrong with a nice bit of carpet?'

Jake stood up and held out his hand to help her up. 'Let's go to bed.'

Chapter 15

Starting Over

'Come back to mine,' Jake said as they waited to pick up their luggage at Heathrow. They'd spent two idyllic days together. It was almost as if the break-up had never happened – they'd made love for hours and lay in each other's arms, talking, seamlessly slipping back into their old relationship, or so it felt to Crystal. She longed to ask if these two days meant that they were together again, but fear of rejection kept her silent.

'I should unpack,' Crystal started to say, wanting to go with him, but wondering if she should play it cool.

'Come back,' Jake repeated. 'I'll make you dinner.'

'And what should I do?' Crystal asked flirtatiously.

'You can provide dessert.'

But it seemed someone had already started cooking at Jake's flat – when he opened the front door, the first thing they both noticed was a delicious smell of roast chicken.

'Wow, I am impressed,' Crystal said. 'You can cook remotely?'

'Shit,' Jake said, running his hand over his head in exasperation. 'I'd forgotten. Stella's here.'

Crystal looked at him questioningly and he went on, 'Yeah, she's staying here while her flat is redecorated.'

'I thought I heard you.' Stella came into the hallway. She looked pretty in a figure-hugging blue cashmere sweater dress and understated make-up, far too pretty for comfort.

'Crystal – nice to see you again,' Stella said, walking over and kissing Crystal on each cheek. Crystal thought she sounded insincere. She'd obviously been planning a cosy little dinner with Jake.

'Jake didn't tell me to expect you; so sorry, I've only cooked enough for two.'

She was acting even more possessively round Jake than she had before. 'That's okay, Stella, we'll just shower and then I'll take Crystal out,' Jake replied.

For a second, Stella looked sulky, not doing herself any favours, then she snapped back into her Little Miss Perfect routine.

'I'm sure it will keep for lunch. I've written down all your messages. You've got a shoot first thing tomorrow.'

'Thanks, Stella,' Jake said, carrying the luggage through to his bedroom.

There was plenty Crystal wanted to say about Stella staying at Jake's, but she reasoned she was probably on shaky ground to start making any demands. Instead, when the bedroom door was safely shut behind them, she wrapped her arms round Jake and said, 'Let's have a shower together to save time', which really meant *let me seduce you in the shower so you can forget about how good Stella looked* . . .

'I thought this was meant to save time,' Jake said a while later as they lay on the bed entwined in each other's arms in a post-sex haze.

'Would you rather have gone straight to the restaurant?' Crystal demanded.

'No, I would not.' He paused to stroke her hair and then delivered a blinder. 'You really are the blowjob queen, aren't you?'

For a split second Crystal thought she must have imagined what Jake had said. 'Blowjob queen' had been one of the things Max had said about her in the press. Her face must have betrayed how upset she was because he looked rather sheepish and said, 'Sorry, that came out wrong.'

Crystal pulled out of his embrace and started searching for her clothes which were strewn all round the room. She had vowed to herself that, after the way Max had treated her, she would never let a man make her feel like shit again, not even Jake.

'What are you doing?' Jake said.

'I'm getting my stuff together and going. And you can think about how I would never say something so cruel to you. I told you what he did to me! Why do you have to bring him up now? Don't you think I want to forget all about him?! And I'm not going to sit here and act like what you said didn't hurt because it fucking well did.'

Crystal wanted to stay cool but in her emotional state couldn't help raising her voice. No doubt Miss Goody fucking Two Shoes would be listening in and loving it.

'Crystal, I'm sorry, please don't go. I was totally out of order. I know it's irrational but I can't help hating what happened between you and him. I should have never have read the details but I did. Jesus Christ. He's the one I want to hurt, not you!'

'Well, you've got to find a way of dealing with it,' Crystal said more softly, 'or what chance do we have?' She was still tempted to leave, but Jake got up and held her tight, murmuring, 'Forgive me. I want us to get back together again, I really do.' But his comment took some of the shine off their reunion and Crystal had so wanted everything to be perfect.

That night was just the beginning of the problem Jake had with Crystal's past. She felt as if she was walking on eggshells whenever the subject came up. Jake often muttered about sorting Max out for what he did to her, which caused conflicting emotions in her – half of her thought it showed that Jake must be committed to her even though he never said it, and the other half was terrified that he'd do something stupid. And in a weird way, Crystal felt as if Jake was trying to compete with him in some way, which was crazy as Crystal only felt disgust for Max and she'd told Jake that enough times.

But he was always trying to push the boundaries when they made love; they never seemed be able just to go to bed any more. When they went out for dinner or went clubbing, he'd suggest a quickie in the bathroom. And in just one week they'd clocked up a shag in the men's loos at Sugar, a chic club in Mayfair; once in the front seat of Jake's car; a freezing cold one in St James's Park, which Crystal hadn't enjoyed one little bit, thinking someone would see them at any moment or they'd get arrested for indecent exposure, and such anxiety was not likely to lead to an orgasmic experience, well not for her anyway. Crystal was no prude but Jake's exploits were starting to unsettle her.

And if that wasn't enough Crystal had two other major problems – a career and cash crisis. *Why was it that problems always seemed to come in threes?*

The day after she flew back from Ibiza Dallas called her. He was typically blunt.

'Crystal, we both know it's not going to work for you to carry on in Lost Angels. I really appreciate the effort you put into the video but you and Belle

– there's too much history and I can't have any conflict in my groups.'

Crystal had been expecting this for months now but it was still a shock to hear it. 'Is there any chance you could keep me on as a solo artist or in any of your other groups?' she asked struggling to hold back the tears.

Dallas sighed and said, 'I wish there was, but I'm afraid I can't. I just don't have any confidence that the public would buy your records. Jenny will be in touch to let you know how much money you can expect from the termination of your contract. Good luck, Crystal, and goodbye.'

That was it, then. The dream was over. If Dallas didn't want her, then she was pretty certain that no one else in the industry would.

And as for the money, Crystal thought she had been careful but the blackmail money she'd paid out to Max, as well as a loan she'd given her brother, had made a large dent in her savings and if she wanted to keep her flat in London she had to earn some money pretty fast. Pride prevented her from revealing her precarious financial state to Jake and her friends but one night when she'd gone out for dinner with Jez, Danni and Tahlia and she'd handed her credit card over to pay she'd been forced to come clean.

'I'm sorry, Ms Hope, but your card has been declined,' the waiter said.

'Really?' Crystal replied. 'There must be a

mistake. I'm sure I had plenty of credit left. Oh well, I'll just give you another card.' She held out her hand for the card and was shocked to discover that the waiter had cut it in half. 'At the orders of the credit card company, Miss,' the waiter said quietly.

Crystal felt her face burn with embarrassment as she fumbled for another card. 'Take it off mine,' Jez said, handing his card to the waiter.

'No way,' Crystal said, outraged. She always paid her way. 'I can get it.'

'It's not a problem, Crystal; you can buy me dinner next time,' Jez answered.

Crystal took a deep breath. 'Actually, Jez, I probably can't. I'm totally broke.'

'Why didn't you say?' Tahlia said, looking concerned. 'I'll lend you some money, babe. You only have to ask.'

Crystal shook her head. 'No, I've got to sort it out myself. I need to get some work but I haven't got an agent and Dallas is hardly likely to do anything for me, is he?'

'Have you thought about doing some modelling?' Jez asked. 'I reckon you could easily do some lad mag shots and that's quite good money.'

Crystal pulled a face. 'Yeah, and I bet I know exactly how they'd want me to be – a right slapper.'

'You wouldn't. Think of Angel – she never looks like that.' Angel Summer was a top glamour model, a close friend he worked with. Jez was in full flow now. When he had an idea he was pretty much unstoppable. 'I tell you what. Why don't I speak to Angel's agent, Carrie Rose, and see if she'll meet you? She's always looking for new clients.'

'Why not? I've got nothing to lose.'

'Well, at least I know why you haven't been coming to me to have your hair done,' Jez added. 'I was beginning to think you'd found someone else.'

'I'd never go to anyone else,' Crystal said. 'I'm sorry. I'm just trying to be really careful with money at the moment.'

'Babe, you know I'd do your hair for free.'

'Thanks, Jez,' Crystal said gratefully, but knowing she would never ask Jez to do that.

Three days later she was sitting in the office of Carrie Rose, the legendary modelling agent who had been behind the careers of several famous glamour models including Angel Summer. Carrie was a straight-talking, hard-as-nails, fifty-something American with an addiction to plastic surgery, Botox, money, toyboys and coke, or so it was rumoured. According to Jez, she had once been enormously fat but ten years ago had had her stomach stapled and extensive plastic surgery to get rid of the excess skin. 'If she gives you a hard time, just imagine her when she was fat,' he advised her.

Carrie flipped through her publicity shots with a practised eye, drumming her perfectly manicured acrylic red nails on the glass table, and then delivered her damning verdict. 'I wouldn't usually take on a girl like you, Crystal, your boobs aren't big enough.' She pushed the portfolio away and took a sip of her fresh pomegranate juice, flicking back her long blonde highlighted hair extensions. She looked like mutton. Crystal had always thought that when women got to a certain age they should say goodbye to long hair. She did not have a good feeling about Carrie; however, she knew she couldn't afford to be picky.

'But I'll probably be able to get you some glamour shoots off the back of you leaving the band. You'd have to do topless, of course.'

'Would I really have to?' Crystal asked, her heart sinking at the prospect.

'Darling, in your situation you'll be lucky to get any work at all, so I suggest you prepare to get your tits out. And if the modelling works out in the next few months you should get a boob job. I can give you the name of my Harley Street surgeon. He's done me and several of my girls, including Angel. It did her career no end of good. He's absolutely the best and hardly leaves a scar.'

'Thanks,' Crystal muttered; then she quickly changed the subject, not wanting to discuss her assets – or, rather, her lack of them – with Carrie any more. 'I've done some acting in the past as well. Is there any chance that you might be able to get me any auditions?'

Carrie sniffed dismissively – maybe it was just her coke nose, but she seemed to sniff a lot – then said,

'Possibly, but I wouldn't hold your breath. And before you go you'd better sign the contract. I take thirty per cent.'

Crystal was about to protest that it was way too high but Carrie simply said, 'It's that or I don't represent you, Crystal.'

Crystal would love to have told her where she should shove her percentage, but unfortunately beggars couldn't be choosers and Crystal had too many bills to pay so she was left with no choice but to sign.

A week later she was booked for her very first shoot. When she told Jake about it and confessed how worried she was, he reassured her, saying she'd find it a breeze. But he did express surprise that she wanted to model. 'What about your singing career?' he had asked, seeming puzzled.

'It's not going very well,' she replied, trying to sound casual.

'Something will come up,' he told her. Crystal just about managed a smile, but the truth was her singing career was over and she wasn't at all sure what she was letting herself in for by agreeing to model. She didn't want to have any secrets from him but then what if he didn't like the idea? *God, her life was complicated.*

'Okay, Crystal, now I want you naked on the Harley, but keep your boots on.'

Crystal stared at Vince, the photographer, in

disbelief. She'd been posing for the last half-hour in a tiny gold bikini in a variety of positions on the bike – straddling it, standing up on the pedals, lying on the saddle, perched on the handle bars – she'd never realised that glamour modelling would be such hard work or required such gymnastics. And all the while she knew that she would have to take her top off eventually but that was supposed to be all.

'My agent said topless, but she didn't mention anything about nudity,' she answered.

'Actually she agreed it with us.'

Crystal looked across the studio at the male journalist from the lad mag, a right cocky looking twenty-something, all flash in a designer suit. Gross. Crystal had no intention of getting her kit off in front of him.

'It's no big deal, baby, I'll be shooting you from the side,' Vince said, sounding bored.

Crystal raised her eyebrows at Danni and Jez as if to ask what the hell she was supposed to do. They shrugged. She decided to play for time.

'Could you give me a few minutes?'

'Whatever,' Vince replied. *Miserable bastard*, Crystal thought, *he definitely hadn't been to charm school*. She marched into the dressing room followed by Danni and Jez.

'What the fuck!' she exclaimed angrily. 'Carrie never mentioned this.'

'Just stay cool, Crystal; so long as you put your

leg in the right position no one will see anything,' Danni said calmly. 'Jez and me will stand next to Vince and give you the thumbs up when you're in a safe position.'

'It's just because you're not used to glamour modelling,' Jez replied breezily. 'When you've seen as much tit and arse as Danni and me you get used to it.'

'We're talking about *my* tits and arse, thank you!' Crystal shot back. 'And I don't want everyone getting an eyeful of my la-la! I'm calling Carrie.'

She didn't hold out much hope that Carrie would back her up; knowing her, she'd probably say lie there and spread 'em. She was right to be pessimistic. As soon as Carrie had heard her out she replied smoothly, 'It really isn't a big deal, Crystal, just be a good girl and do as Vince says.'

'Well, it is a big deal for me,' Crystal answered. 'I thought topless was as far as it would go.'

Carrie laughed. 'Darling, stop being such a baby. No one is going to be able to see your C U Next Tuesday. It will be very tasteful. Just think of the money. I find that makes most things bearable. Bye now.'

'No luck?' Danni asked as Crystal slung her phone down in disgust.

Crystal shook her head, 'I shouldn't have expected otherwise from the Cocaine Queen; she's probably already snorted the percentage I've earnt her up her nose.'

'It'll be okay, Crystal. Just get it over and done with then Jez and me will take you out to celebrate your first shoot,' Danni answered, holding out a white robe for her. Sighing, Crystal took off her bikini, put on the robe and walked back into the studio.

'Everything okay now?' Vince asked, sounding patronising.

'Fine,' Crystal snapped back. 'But I'm not having an audience, so can *he* please leave.' She pointed at the journalist, who looked pissed off, then sauntered out of the room. Crystal got on to the bike, slowly slipped off her robe and handed it back to Danni, trying to reveal as little as possible. She felt incredibly self-conscious. She knew there were models who were able to switch off and not think of anything but getting the pose right, shedding their inhibitions as easily as they shed their clothes. But all Crystal could think was that she was stark naked on a very large motorbike, in front of four other people.

Vince started barking out instructions. 'Right then, Crystal, lean forward, hold on to the handle-bars and look at the camera.'

Reluctantly Crystal did as she was told, checking with Danni that she wasn't revealing more than she should. Danni gave her the thumbs up, but Vince shouted, 'You've got to look more relaxed, babe, like you're enjoying yourself. Come on. What girl doesn't like to have a big throbbing engine between her legs?'

344

'Ha fucking ha,' Crystal spat back. She took a deep breath and adopted the pose once again, this time remembering to look seductive as she stared into the camera.

'Much better,' Vince called back. 'Hold it. Now stick your boobs out more, good, nice one.'

After what seemed like hours of posing on the bike, Crystal was finally able to put her robe back on, dismount and get ready for her final series of shots. This time she had to wear a tiny pair of denim shorts and a pair of thigh-high denim boots and the studio had been transformed to look like a seedy motel room. Vince asked Crystal to lie on the unmade bed.

'I want you looking like you've just had sex,' Vince demanded.

'In this room? You've got to be kidding. I only shag in five-star hotels on Egyptian cotton,' Crystal shot back.

'You know what I mean; and I want you to unbutton your shorts and give us a flash of your tattoo,' Vince continued.

'Now that is where I draw the line,' Crystal replied.

'Oh come on, you've had your kit off, what's the big deal?'

'The answer's no,' Crystal answered and deliberately looked at her nails as if she was bored with the conversation.

She heard Vince mutter 'fucking prima donna'

under his breath, but he knew he'd pushed his luck far enough and he didn't ask again. For the rest of the shoot Crystal did as she was told, leaning seductively against the pillows, kneeling, lying on her front and towards the end she did actually begin to feel slightly more relaxed, but she definitely wasn't a natural in front of the camera.

'God, that was such hard work!' she declared, safely wrapped in her white towelling robe and back in the dressing room.

'Well, considering you've never modelled before, you did really well,' Jez answered. 'And, God knows, Danni and me have seen enough shit models to know a good one.'

'Yeah, you shouldn't be looking so down, Crystal, you're bound to get other work after these pictures come out,' Danni added. But as Crystal took off her make-up and looked at herself in the mirror all she could think about was how much she missed singing – how, although by the end of the shoot she knew she'd done as good a job as she could, it didn't come close to the high she got when she'd been on stage or recording in the studio. Singing was her passion, it was what she felt she was born to do.

'Anyway, tomorrow night there can be no long faces, except mine, because I'm the one who's going to be thirty,' Jez said theatrically, putting his hand on his heart and sighing.

Crystal and Danni knew the drill. 'You don't look it,' they said in unison.

'How old?' Jez demanded. Crystal and Danni looked at each other, neither remembering what Jez's ideal age was supposed to be.

'Twenty-five?' Crystal said uncertainly.

'How *very* dare you!' Jez said in mock horror. 'I'm twenty-four!'

'Jez, you were twenty-four last year,' Crystal said, trying not to laugh. 'Don't you think it's time you grew up, just a little?'

Jez shook his head and said in all seriousness, 'Rufus is twenty-one. He cannot, I repeat CANNOT, find out that I am thirty. No one wants to fuck grandpa.'

'Haven't you considered that he might find older men attractive? Jake's thirty next month and he's gorgeous,' Danni put in.

'He's straight, so he doesn't count,' Jez muttered, picking up his hair dryer and putting it away in its leather case. 'I thought at least I could depend on you two to back me up,' he said sulkily. 'You're supposed to be my friends.'

Crystal let him sulk for a minute; it was just so funny seeing him bustle around the room in a huff, then she put him out of his misery, 'Okay Jez, you can be twenty-four again.'

'Thank you,' Jez replied, the sulk forgotten. 'Just make sure Rufus hears you say that.'

As soon as Crystal left the studio she was on

347

the phone to Jake. 'I've finished, can we meet?'

'Crystal, I'm sorry, I'm still in Paris, I won't finish until Thursday. The video's taking much longer than we thought, because the lead singer is off his face ninety-nine per cent of the time.'

'Oh,' Crystal answered, disappointed that she wouldn't be seeing him. She felt in need of reassurance that only he could give her, and she wanted to explain about the shoot. She had a feeling he wouldn't approve of some of the shots.

'Why don't you fly out tomorrow and see me?' Jake suggested.

'I'd love to but it's Jez's thirtieth and he'd never forgive me if I missed it,' she replied. She was telling the truth, that was the main reason, but she also knew she couldn't afford to fly to Paris.

'Well see you Thursday night, miss you.'

'Miss you too,' Crystal answered; wishing for the thousandth time that he'd said 'love you'. Was he ever going to say those words to her? And if she said them to him would he run away?

Jez was holding his thirtieth/twenty-fourth at the Royale, a plush club frequented by the celeb crowd in Mayfair. Jez had been a hairdresser for years and worked with a number of stars, all of whom adored him, so when he hinted that he wanted his birthday at the Royale, the club owner jumped at the chance, knowing that he'd be guaranteed a host of celebs, from Angel to the

WAGs, and they would attract some great publicity.

Ideally Crystal would have liked to buy a new outfit for the party, but there was no way she could afford to. Instead she went for one of her favourite designer dresses, a simple purple silk number, which showed off her curves. Fortunately her hair still looked good from when Jez had trimmed it for the shoot and by the time Crystal had finished with her make-up she was pleased with how she looked. But even though she knew she'd mainly be among friends, she was still nervous of being out in public. Since the Max story had broken, and since her accident, she had avoided crowds if she could, scared that someone might have a go at her or that she'd have a panic attack. But there was no way she could let Jez down. She just wished Jake could be with her as she walked past the queue of clubbers waiting to get into the Royale. Someone had obviously tipped off the press about the party and the likely arrival of celebs because the paparazzi were out in force, something Crystal was not prepared for. As the flashes went off around her and the photographers shouted out her name, she felt she was back at the time when the press were hounding her and she almost bolted. But then she thought, *Fuck them, I'm going to Jez's birthday and I'm not going let anyone spoil it for me*. So instead of putting her head down and running into the club, she shook back her hair and sauntered in as if she didn't have a care in the world. With any luck the photographers would have so many other stars to photograph that her picture wouldn't be of any interest to any tabloid or celeb mags.

'Darling, happy twenty-fourth birthday,' she said, once she was safely inside the VIP lounge, hugging Jez and handing over her present. 'I'm sorry it's only small.'

'I'm sure it'll be perfect,' Jez replied. 'Now, grab yourself a drink and party! There are Slippery Nipple shots and champagne cocktails. Who says I'm not classy!' In the far corner of the room she noticed Belle and her fiancé, Lee and Belle waved at her. Crystal was relieved that things between her and Belle had moved on since their last meeting, but she wasn't going to push her luck by going over to see her. Instead, when she saw Tahlia, Hadley and Danni, she made her way over to them.

Two cocktails later and Crystal was feeling relaxed; no one was looking at her, she was with her friends, having a great time. Lots of people who Crystal hadn't seen in ages – acquaintances rather than friends – came up and said hello to her, commenting on how good she looked. It was nice to get compliments again, Crystal thought – it wasn't so long ago that people wouldn't even speak to her – but she could have done without all the questions about what she was doing now and how her singing career was going. In the end it all got a bit much and after the fifth person asked her if she had a record deal, she retreated to the ladies for a bit of peace. For one night at least she wanted to be able to forget her worries. However, just as she was checking her make-up she heard a snide voice behind her: 'Ooh, look who it isn't – Crystal Meth, the very *ex*-member of Lost Angels.'

She turned round and saw Kimmi, the lead singer of @ttitude, shooting her a filthy look, though how Kimmi could make out anything through the layers of mascara was a miracle, Crystal thought, determined to ignore her. She went to walk past her but Kimmi stood her ground, blocking her exit.

'Surprised *you* can show your face in public after what *you* did. No one in our group would ever behave like that. And Belle had the nerve to call *us* trailer trash. You're the trash.'

'Okay, you've had your say. Now please can I get past?'

'Or what? Are you going to call security again?'

'God, you're pathetic,' Crystal suddenly snapped. 'Why don't you just piss off and leave me alone. You weren't even invited to the party so what the hell are you doing in the VIP area?'

'I've got my contacts,' Kimmi said, still trying to be cocky. 'I'm surprised you were invited. I would have thought you'd be staying in crying over your lack of a record deal. Did I tell you that we've just recorded our second album?'

'Yeah, and remind me where the first one went? Wasn't it straight in at three hundred?'

'Five hundred, I think,' said a voice from one of the cubicles, then the door opened and Angel Summer, Britain's most famous glamour girl, walked out.

Kimmi had obviously been about to tell the person to fuck off but once she saw who it was her whole manner changed, and instead of the scowl on her heavily made up face, she was doing her best – but failing – to look sweet.

'Hiya, Angel, how are you?' Kimmi said in a lick-arse kind of voice.

Angel, who had never looked more stunning in a white cat suit, unzipped several inches to showcase her impressive cleavage, looked at Kimmi as if she was a piece of garbage, and said icily, 'I heard what you were saying to Crystal and I don't appreciate bullying.'

'But I wasn't!' Kimmi started to say, but Angel cut across her.

'This is the VIP cloakroom and I suggest you get your arse out of here before I call the management.'

Kimmi tried to make a dignified exit, which was ruined by the fact that she had a piece of toilet tissue impaled on her stiletto heel.

When Kimmi had gone Angel turned to Crystal and said warmly, 'Hi, nice to meet you at last. I've heard so much about you from Jez.'

'Hi,' said Crystal back, wondering what she'd heard.

'Don't look so worried!' Angel exclaimed seeing her face. 'It's only good stuff. And forget about all that bollocks in the press, I know most of it is made up. Come on, let's go and have a cocktail.'

The girls hit it off instantly and spent the rest of the night together. Crystal chatted to Angel about her fiancé, Cal, the gorgeous footballer who played for Chelsea. He was away in Italy as there was a strong possibility that AC Milan were going to bid for him.

'So would you move over there?' Crystal asked.

Angel pulled a face. 'I guess I would but I'd want us to keep our London house, because all my work's here and all my friends. To be honest, it's a bit of an issue between us at the moment. Cal thinks I should live there full time with him, but I'm not sure I want to.' Angel sighed. 'So it's nice to be able to come out and forget about it. God, men can be difficult sometimes.'

'They can be very high maintenance,' Crystal agreed and looked at Angel – it was hard not to look at her, her beauty was almost mesmerising. She reminded her of a young Marilyn Monroe; she had the screen goddess's beauty and sensuality but also her vulnerability.

'And how are the wedding plans going?' Crystal asked, changing the subject. Cal and Angel were going to be married early next year, in what was already being talked about as the celebrity wedding of the decade.

'Okay, I think. We finally got a wedding planner because it was taking over my life and I couldn't think about anything else. It's going to be a total fairy-tale wedding, in a castle, and I'm going to arrive in a carriage pulled by six white horses. But I can't tell you what I'm wearing because I want it to be a surprise. No one knows.'

'It sounds wonderful,' Crystal said wistfully, wondering if she and Jake would ever get married.

'I'm so glad you two have finally met!' Jez joined them, along with Rufus, his handsome twenty-two-year-old boyfriend who looked as if he was in the gym 24/7.

'My two favourite girls in all the world!' Jez had clearly been knocking back the cocktails.

Crystal had met Rufus a few times now, but couldn't say that she knew him as he hardly ever spoke. But then Jez's ability to talk could win him an Olympic medal, leaving no one else a chance to get a word in. Besides, he probably wasn't attracted to Rufus because of his conversational skills.

'Seeing you together has given me an idea. Why don't you suggest to Carrie that you do a shoot together? It would look fantastic!'

Angel had recently had her naturally brunette hair dyed platinum blonde again.

'A kind of angel and devil scenario, you mean?' Crystal asked. 'Do I get to wear horns and carry a pitchfork?'

'Don't be silly. I just meant the contrast between

your raven-haired beauty would look striking alongside Angel, a blonde bombshell.'

'It's not a bad idea,' said Angel. 'I'm probably not going to be blonde for much longer so it would be good to make the most of it. I'll mention it to Carrie if you like.'

But it will make my tits look tiny, thought Crystal, surreptitiously checking out Angel's cleavage again and comparing it with her own.

'Don't worry,' said Angel, 'I'll do the topless bit and you can flash your bum which is much perter than mine.'

Chapter 16

Three's a Crowd

'I've just got back, Crystal, so why don't you come over, and—' Jake paused over the phone and said huskily, 'wear something extra sexy.' He'd just returned from Paris and Crystal couldn't wait to see him.

She rifled through her wardrobe, considering what to wear – if Jake wanted extra sexy, she would deliver. She chose her shortest, most revealing black dress, her highest heels, and left her underwear at home.

'Wow,' he said, as he opened the door to her. Crystal immediately wrapped her arms around his neck and whispered, 'Will I do then?'

'Umm,' Jake murmured back, kissing her neck and running his hands over her back and her bum. He slid his hands under her dress and caressed her naked skin.

'I hope this is what you wanted,' Crystal whispered, enjoying what he was doing to her, when suddenly she heard Stella call out from the living room, 'Do you want some more wine, Jake?'

Crystal pulled out of the embrace. 'What's *she* doing here? I thought it was going to be just us,' she hissed.

Jake avoided her eye and answered a little too casually, 'Oh, didn't I tell you? I've got some people round for dinner.'

She was about to ask why the hell he wanted her dressed like this when Gavin popped his head round the living room door and said, 'Hi.'

Crystal forced herself to smile and say hi back, and walked into the living room where Gavin's girlfriend Lara, Stella and another photographer friend of Jake's were sitting on the sofas, drinking wine. They were all casually dressed in jeans, which made Crystal feel even more self-conscious in her bum-skimming dress and heels.

'Crystal!' Stella exclaimed, sounding as if she couldn't have been happier to see her. 'So glad you could join us.' *She's so fake,* Crystal thought. She knew perfectly well the feeling of loathing was mutual.

'We were just talking about the new Mario Testino exhibition. You know, he's the photographer who takes all those amazing pictures of celebrities.' *God, she was a condescending cow!* Crystal was about to say that she knew perfectly well who he was, when Jake said dryly, 'Crystal knows who he is, Stella.'

'Oh, I was just checking,' Stella gushed back. 'I didn't want Crystal to feel left out. Nice dress, by the way.'

Fuck off, Crystal so wanted to say, hating the way that Stella acted as if she owned the place. Crystal sat down carefully on the sofa opposite Gavin, desperate not to give him a Sharon Stone *Basic Instinct* flash. The dress had been for Jake's eyes only and she really didn't feel comfortable revealing so much of her body to everyone else. Fortunately Gavin's girlfriend Lara was as unpretentious and down to earth as Gavin and chatted easily to Crystal. But as they talked about what films they'd seen, Posh's new hair cut and what Lara made of London after Sydney, Crystal couldn't help being aware of how Stella kept offering to help Jake in the kitchen and how she was behaving as if *she* was his girlfriend.

'Actually, Stella, you sit down and relax. Crystal can help me,' Jake answered, forcing Crystal to make another careful manoeuvre up from the sofa, smoothing down her dress as far as it would go as she walked to the kitchen. As soon as she got there Jake pulled her into his arms.

'Did I tell you how amazingly sexy you look tonight?' he murmured, kissing her before she got the chance to reply. Then he slipped the straps from her dress and ducked down to kiss her breasts. They'd been apart for a week and Crystal wanted him as much as he wanted her but, turned on as she was, she couldn't relax knowing that everyone was next door. Maybe if he had told her about the dinner party she would have enjoyed the thrill of a secret fuck in the kitchen. As it was, she felt as if Jake was trying to prove a point yet again. He seemed to be ticking off another box on his invisible list of their sexual exploits – *number 5: have sex in kitchen while guests are in next room.*

'Save it till later, honey,' she whispered as Jake put his arms round her waist and lifted her on to the table, pushing her legs open and unbuttoning his jeans.

But he acted as if he hadn't heard. Crystal repeated what she'd said and this time Jake snapped back, 'I bet you never said that to him, did you? No? I bet you were open for business with him 24/7.'

Crystal pushed him away and jumped down from the table, furious. 'You don't know what you're talking about! I've told you everything you need to know about me and Max. Jesus Christ, I've even told you how many times we did it! What more do you want to know? Did he make me come? Yes, he did. Did I suck his cock? Yes, I did. Did I enjoy it? Yes, I did at the time. But then he raped me and that's all I remember now. Will you stop bringing him up in conversation? I'm with you now and I have the best sex of my life with you. I love you! I don't know what more I can say to make you believe me!' Without meaning to, Crystal had raised her voice, and even though there was music playing in the living room she realised that the guests would have heard everything. Jake went to speak but Crystal cut him off. 'I've had enough of these games you're playing. When you decide to stop, let me know.' And she ran out of the kitchen, into the hallway and out of the flat.

It was still early when she got home. It had been a very brisk walk back, holding her dress down all the way and praying there wouldn't be a sudden gust of wind. She was so angry, she didn't want to stay home wondering if Jake would call or not. And she couldn't believe she'd told him she loved him. To say it like that! In the middle of a row, what shit timing. *That's probably the final nail in the coffin of our relationship.* She angrily pulled off her dress and threw it on the bed, then pulled on a black jumper dress, tights and boots and called Tahlia, asking if she could come over to see her.

'I feel like he's trying to punish me,' Crystal declared, on her third glass of wine.

'Maybe he's just really insecure because of his last relationship,' Tahlia suggested, still sipping her first glass.

'But I haven't done anything to make him feel insecure!' Crystal said passionately. 'God I need a cigarette.'

'Don't give in,' Tahlia warned. 'You'll regret it if you do. You need to talk to him. Why don't you call him?'

'I'm not calling him,' Crystal said stubbornly. 'Anyway, that witch Stella is round there. God, I can't stand her. I wish she'd bugger off back to her flat. I can't believe it still isn't finished.

'She isn't the nicest person in the world,' her friend agreed in a typical Tahlia understatement.

'And I told him I loved him,' Crystal groaned, putting her head in her hands. 'He's going to leave me for sure now.'

'Don't you think there's a chance that he loves you?' Tahlia answered. 'Remember what he was like in Ibiza, how he looked after you, how he was the one who wanted to get back together? He's definitely in love with you.'

'Do you really think so?' Crystal asked hopefully. 'God, *I wish*. I've never felt like this about anyone.' She paused, wondering if Tahlia was right, then realised how self-centred she was being. 'And now I'm going to stop going on about myself. I've come round here and ranted away at you, drunk all your wine and I haven't even asked you how you are.'

Tahlia smiled, 'I'm great, Crystal. It's going really well with Hadley; we're looking at houses together tomorrow. But you never have to apologise, babe, you're my best friend.'

Crystal felt slightly calmer in the taxi ride home. Tahlia was right; she should talk to Jake. They would work through it. But her feeling of calm deserted her the minute she got out of the car and

361

saw Jake sitting on her front step. *What if he's come here to finish with me?* she thought anxiously, strongly tempted to run away. But he'd already spotted her. She took a deep breath and walked towards him.

Jake was the first to speak. 'I've been a complete dickhead. Please say you forgive me.'

He sounded so genuine that Crystal's anger melted away. She sat down next to him. 'I forgive you, so long as you promise not to be like that again – you were doing my head in!'

Jake put his arm round her and pulled her to him. 'I promise,' he murmured.

'Good,' Crystal replied. There were times when a hug and a kiss would do to make up but this was not one of them, and Crystal knew that only a class A shag could help them move on. 'Now get inside and fuck me.'

Jake did not disappoint.

Over the past months, Crystal had written the lyrics for over ten songs and even though she didn't have a record deal she wanted to record them. They were intensely personal, heartfelt songs about love, loss, betrayal. She negotiated a special studio rate with Phil, who had worked with her when she was in Lost Angels. He owned a recording studio in west London and told Crystal she could use it when they weren't busy. That often meant going there late at night. Tahlia had written the music for several of her new songs and Crystal had shelled out her last few grand for three musicians to record it. She'd finish each session with such a mix of emotions – exhilaration that she was singing again and deep frustration that her career had hit a dead end. Phil had heard some of her new material and offered to play it to some of his friends in the business. He was sure that they would offer her a record deal, but she turned him down. 'I know they're not going to be interested and I just don't think I can take rejection at the moment. I'm just doing this for myself right now.'

Phil raised his eyebrows. 'If that's what you want, Crystal, but I think you're making a mistake; you're really talented. I'm certain you'd get another deal.'

Crystal shook her head. 'I don't think so; the public still have such a negative image of me.'

'Come on, Crystal, stop beating yourself up. It doesn't suit you.'

But Crystal was already walking out the door. 'I'll call next week to see when you've got free studio time.'

However, while she was still fearful of what people thought of her, she did want an audience for her songs again. Without telling any of her friends, she started her own page on MySpace and uploaded her new songs on to it. She called herself Pearl and, instead of posting up her photograph, she put up a picture of a black rose with a pearl at its centre. She also started writing a blog, which she found strangely therapeutic, though for obvious reasons she had to be economical with the truth. She could talk about her songs at least and what they meant to her; she also used the blog to vent her frustration about having Stella constantly round at Jake's (she didn't use their real names) and the fact that she was in love with her boyfriend and she wasn't sure if he loved her. The first few times she logged on, she could hardly bear to go to her page in case someone had posted a nasty message about her music, or had realised who she was, but the messages she received were all complimentary – something which gave her such a thrill. It was a small thing but a confidence boost she badly needed.

Things were definitely going more smoothly between Jake and her too. He seemed more relaxed, less uptight and almost back to the Jake she first knew. He didn't talk about Max any more, and it no longer seemed as if he felt he had something to prove when they had sex. He had never mentioned her 'I love you', though, which made Crystal think that either he hadn't heard it or it was so far from what he felt that he didn't want to talk about it. She tried to hold on to Tahlia's words that he did love her and so many times she was convinced he was going to say it – times when they'd just made love, times when they spoke on the phone when he was away – but he didn't. It was deeply frustrating. They'd been back with each other for three months but it felt like their

364

relationship could only go so far before Jake put the brakes on it. And having Stella around all the time certainly didn't help.

'Doesn't she have any friends?' Crystal demanded when Stella was hanging out in the flat and expecting to have dinner and watch a DVD with them, again. If it had been anyone else, Crystal wouldn't have minded so much, but as it was Stella she hated not having Jake to herself – especially since she knew Stella had spent most of the day with him in the studio.

'I know it's a real pain and, honestly, I'm as fed up with it as you, but she'll be gone soon. And I know she's still feeling really down about her ex. He's going out with one of her friends now and I think it's really knocked her confidence,' Jake replied.

'Jake, I've really had enough of her! She needs to give us some privacy, for God sake!' Crystal exclaimed, pacing angrily round the room.

'Okay, how about I say to her that's she got till the end of the week, then she's got to go and stay with someone else. Will that make you happy?' Jake asked.

'Hmm,' Crystal replied. She'd only be happy when Stella, pert bum and all, walked out of the door for the last time.

To Crystal it seemed that Stella's number one hobby at the moment was making her feel inadequate. Practically every time she saw Crystal she'd assume a look of false concern and say, 'How's work going, Crystal?' The week running up to Jake's thirtieth birthday was no exception. Crystal arrived at his flat to find Stella wearing a vest and tiny Lycra shorts and practising her yoga moves in the living room. Crystal muttered 'Hi' and went to seek out Jake but Stella called out from the lotus position, 'You should try this sometime, Crystal. It's so good for getting rid of aggression and tension.'

Crystal wanted to reply that the only way to get rid of any tension would be to get rid of Stella, but instead she muttered that she preferred going to the gym.

'I see that Lost Angels have got a new singer now. So does that mean you'll definitely not be going back to them?' Stella asked, trying her best to needle Crystal.

Bitch. 'Actually I'm doing some modelling at the moment,' Crystal answered. 'So I've been too busy to think about it.'

'Fashion?' Stella asked, her interest piqued.

'Mainly glamour. In fact I've got a shoot in a couple of weeks with Angel.'

'Oh,' Stella did not sound impressed. 'Won't you mind taking your clothes off?'

'No,' Crystal lied.

'And what does Jake think of your new line of work?'

'What new line of work?' Jake asked, wandering into the living room. He'd just had a shower and was wearing only a towel round his waist. Crystal shot Stella a look which said *he's mine and only mine*. And then, not caring that his skin was still damp, she put her arms round him and kissed him.

'My modelling,' she replied. The magazine with her naked Harley poses was coming out next week and she was not looking forward to Jake seeing the pictures.

'So what do you want to do for your thirtieth?' Crystal asked when they were finally alone together lying in bed that night.

'Let's just go out for dinner. I hate big parties and I hate being the centre of attention,' Jake said gently stroking her shoulder.

'Truthfully? You really don't want me to organise you a party?'

'Definitely not,' Jake replied. 'I would be so pissed off if anyone did.'

'Okay, well, I'll book us somewhere really exclusive for dinner.' Crystal already had an idea what she was going to do. Jez had given her a crash course in cooking a delicious meal of grilled monkfish with new potatoes and salsa verde and grilled peppers, with chocolate soufflé for dessert – she would surprise Jake with a romantic dinner at her flat. It certainly would be a surprise as the only thing Crystal had cooked for Jake so far was toast and she'd even managed to burn that. That sorted, she had to decide what to buy him. Recently Jake had lost his watch and she thought a new one would make a perfect present. She roped Jez into coming to the jeweller's with her, so she could see the watch on a male wrist, though, as Jez pointed out, Jake's wrist was quite a bit more masculine than his.

'That one's divine,' Jez said, pointing out a watch that cost over three grand.

Crystal's face fell. 'There's no way I can afford that.'

'Okay,' Jez said briskly. 'Well, he's into his diving, isn't he, so why don't we look at some TAG Heuers? You could get a really good watch for under a grand.'

'Have you ever thought about a job on QVC?' Crystal joked as Jez picked up watch after watch, checking out their qualities, and weighing each one up.

'I like that one' – she pointed out one with a stainless-steel and gold-plated strap – it looked classy but understated and it came in at nine hundred, which was all the credit Crystal had left on her card.

Jez modelled it for her, holding out his wrist as if to check the time, getting up from his chair and walking round the shop, then pausing again to check the time for effect.

'That's a very nice watch, madam, but have you considered one with the diamonds on the face,' asked the male assistant who obviously recognised Crystal and assumed she'd be loaded.

'No, this one is perfect,' Crystal replied, handing over her credit card and praying it wouldn't be declined.

Chapter 17

Birthday Boy

'Now, are you sure you don't want me to come over and help you cook?' Jez asked Crystal over the phone. It was the morning of Jake's thirtieth and Crystal wanted everything to be perfect. Jake had taken the day off work and she planned to take him to a spa hotel for an afternoon of pampering treatments and then back to hers in the evening for dinner.

'Thanks, but I've got to do it on my own,' Crystal replied, mentally ticking off all the things she had to do – clean flat – for the first time in longer than she cared to remember – buy flowers, set out candles and prepare the food. As soon as she put the phone down she raced round the flat tidying up and working through her list. Two hours later she was letting herself into Jake's flat.

He'd got back very late from a shoot the night before and she wanted to surprise him with his present. 'Happy birthday,' she said slipping off her shoes and getting into bed with him.

'Hi,' he said sleepily, putting his arm round her.

'Don't you want to open your present?' Crystal asked as Jake began untying her wrap dress.

'In a minute. I'll have this one first. That's if you want to shag an older man.'

Crystal looked as if she was considering it, then cheekily reached down under the covers and grabbed him. 'Only if he's got a rock-hard cock.'

'It's your lucky day, princess,' Jake said, rolling on top of her.

'Okay, open it now,' Crystal demanded, handing him the gift-wrapped box some time later. He'd bought her such lovely things – the Chanel watch and some gorgeous animal-print Roberto Cavalli lingerie – and she really wanted him to like her present.

To her delight, Jake seemed genuinely pleased with the watch, putting it straight on. 'That is so great, and I love that I can wear it when I go diving. Thanks, Crystal,' he said as he kissed her.

'Right, you stay exactly where you are because I'm making you breakfast in bed – freshly squeezed orange juice, champagne and croissants suit you, sir?'

'That'll do nicely,' Jake said, lying back in bed, smiling at her.

'By the way,' Crystal said, pausing in the doorway in Jake's white towelling robe, 'is Stella here?'

371

'Oh, I meant to tell you. She's moved back home; the decorators have finally finished.'

'Okay,' Crystal said nonchalantly before doing a little victory dance on her own in the kitchen.

The rest of the day went exactly as Crystal had planned. They swam and hung out in the hot tub, steam room and sauna. At the end of the day they each had an aromatherapy massage in the same room which left them both feeling totally blissed out.

'I wish we'd booked to stay at the hotel,' Jake said as they lay by the pool, 'then I could take you upstairs right now.'

Crystal smiled; she was thinking the exact same thing herself. Lying next to Jake and seeing his half-naked body turned her on and brought out her naughty streak. 'Well,' she whispered, 'if you'll follow me, sir.' She got up, took Jake's hand and led him away from the pool. She paused outside the disabled loo and then, checking no one was watching, she opened the door and pulled him inside.

'Why, Miss Hope,' he said in a Texan drawl, 'you sure bring me to the nicest places.'

'Be quiet,' Crystal ordered, 'and get your kit off.'

'Anything you say, ma'am,' he replied, unfastening the string ties of her bikini.

So far, it had been a perfect day and Crystal was looking forward to seeing the expression on Jake's face when he saw the meal she had cooked. But as they travelled back to Notting Hill, Jake's mobile rang.

'Are you sure it can't wait?' he said irritably to the person on the other end. 'Okay, well, I'll drop round now, but I really can't stay as I'm going out for dinner with Crystal.'

'Who was that?' Crystal asked, as he snapped his phone shut.

'Stella,' he answered rolling his eyes. 'She says she got some documents which have got to be signed urgently. I'm going to stop off at her flat. But don't worry, I'll just sign them and be out of there.'

'Okay,' Crystal answered, 'but promise you won't be long. I've booked a very exclusive restaurant and I don't want us to lose our table.'

'I promise; see you very soon, gorgeous,' Jake said, kissing her as the taxi pulled up outside her flat.

Inside Crystal walked into the kitchen and studied step one of Jez's neatly written instructions: 'Chop onion finely and have a large glass of white wine to steady nerves.'

Ha, she thought, there's nothing to it. She happily chopped, peeled and sliced and made the sauce for the next thirty minutes, so that when Jake came round all she would have to do was grill the fish. She checked the time; she had an hour to get ready. She was just applying lip gloss when her phone went. It was Jake. He sounded as if he was in a room full of people.

'I'm afraid there's going to have to be a change of plan. Stella's organised a surprise party for me. I'm really sorry, Crystal, but I can't get out of it.'

'But what about dinner?' Crystal asked, not able to disguise the disappointment in her voice.

'I know, I'm really sorry, but she's gone to so much trouble and got caterers in and everything, I can't just leave. Come over. You've got the address, haven't you?'

Bitch, Crystal thought, remembering quite clearly telling Stella that she was planning to take Jake out for a special birthday meal. 'Okay,' she replied, unenthusiastically, 'I'll see you in a bit.' She spent the next twenty minutes searching everywhere for her gold Gucci sandals. *Oh well, I must have left them at Jake's*, she thought, slipping on a pair of non-designer sandals which always ended up pinching her feet.

When she arrived the party was in full swing and Crystal couldn't see anyone she knew. She gazed round Stella's luxurious penthouse, which was about five times the size of her own flat. The redecoration must have cost a small fortune – every piece of furniture, every soft furnishing, looked as if no expense had been spared. No Ikea sofas and flat packs for Princess Stella, Crystal thought. The enormous living room had been decorated with an oriental theme – green and gold patterned silk curtains hung at the side of the vast windows and there were several huge velvet sofas in different shades of green, strewn with beautiful silk cushions in jade, gold and silver. An intricately patterned screen stood at one end of the room and a real fire blazed in the enormous fireplace at the other. On one wall hung a huge black and white photograph of Stella in the iconic Christine Keeler pose – sitting naked astride a chair. Crystal could only hope that Jake hadn't taken it. Immaculately dressed waiters and waitresses weaved their way round the guests with trays of champagne and delicious-looking canapés. Crystal thought of the meal she had planned at home and her heart sank. She took a glass of champagne when she was offered one, but turned down the canapés, having totally lost her appetite. She sipped her champagne and anxiously scanned the room for Jake. Eventually she saw him. He smiled and walked over to her straightaway.

'Hi, gorgeous,' he said, kissing her. 'I had no idea she had planned this.'

'I thought you hated surprise parties.' Crystal said moodily.

'I do, but you can see for yourself that it would be really awkward to walk out. I'll make it up to you, I promise. Come on, I'll introduce you to some people.' Crystal could tell from the way he spoke that he was already slightly pissed.

'Tell me you didn't take that picture.' Crystal pointed at the photograph of Stella.

Jake laughed. 'No way, that's such a cliché.' They were halfway across the room when Stella called him over and he walked off, telling Crystal he'd be with her in a minute. But Crystal felt abandoned. *Thanks a lot*, she thought bitterly, hating the party and wanting to leave. Unfortunately the next person she bumped into was Ingrid, Jake's mother. They'd only met a couple more times since that first disastrous meeting in Claridge's, and each time Crystal had got the distinct impression that Ingrid didn't think she was nearly good enough for her son.

'Crystal, how nice to see you,' Ingrid said offering a cool cheek for Crystal to kiss. 'Isn't it a fabulous party? Stella's done an amazing job, and it's a great PR exercise. A lot of these people are very important movers and shakers, you know.'

Tossers and wankers more like, Crystal wanted to say, thankfully spotting Jake's dad and going over to say hello to him.

'How's the singing going, Crystal,' he asked. He was being genuinely nice but it was a harsh reminder of the one thing that she was always trying to forget, namely that her singing career was at a dead end.

She shrugged. 'Not great.'

'Don't worry,' he said kindly, 'I'm sure it won't be long before it's back on track. You're very talented, and talent always wins in the end.'

Gavin and Lara then joined her and she spent a few minutes chatting to them – like her they hardly knew anyone.

'Everyone seems so up themselves,' Crystal said quietly. 'Are they really Jake's friends?'

'A few of them are – the ones who look down to earth, but most are business contacts, magazine editors, people like that,' Gavin replied, adding, 'I expect Stella only asked me and Lara because she had to.'

'Well, I certainly wasn't at the top of her guest list,' Crystal answered grimly.

Gavin was about to say something else when Jake wandered over and put his arm round Crystal. 'Sorry about leaving you. There was an editor I needed to talk to. God, this feels more like work than a party. Are you okay, Crystal?'

She nodded. 'It's just that it was supposed to be our day, wasn't it?' she whispered, hugging him close as if to protect herself from the other guests.

'I know, and you've given me a perfect day.'

Crystal smiled, pleased to hear he'd enjoyed it so much. But her happiness was short-lived.

'Hi Crystal.' It was Stella, looking stunning in a short gold-sequinned dress. It looked like a Chloé dress and it probably was a Chloé dress – no high street rip-offs for Stella. Crystal nodded back, not quite able to bring herself to speak to the creature.

'I've just got a little something for the birthday boy,' she said handing a silver gift-wrapped present to Jake.

'Stella,' he groaned. 'You didn't have to get me anything, not after organising the party.'

'It's not much, just to say thank you for letting me stay at the flat and being so lovely after I split up with Xavier.'

Go on, thought Crystal, *see if you can squeeze out a tear*. But instead Stella smiled, as if she was being very brave and watched Jake open the present. He ripped off the silver paper to reveal a very expensive-looking box, inside which was an extremely flash watch, a Breitling, the three grand watch she'd seen on her trip to the jeweller's with Jez.

'Stella, that's far too generous,' Jake exclaimed. 'Please, I can't accept this.'

'You have to; I'd be so upset if you didn't,' Stella said, pouting in a way which would have upstaged even Victoria Beckham.

'Well, thank you, Stella, I've wanted one of these for ages,' he replied, giving her a quick kiss on the cheek.

Crystal's mood became even fouler. Along with the conversation she'd had with Stella about her plans for Jake's birthday, Stella had also asked her what she was going to buy him and Crystal had told her that she was buying him a watch. The nasty cow had deliberately upstaged her. She bit her lip; not wanting to make a scene she looked down at the ground. As she lowered her eyes, she saw her gold Gucci sandals on Stella's perfectly pedicured feet.

'Are those my Guccis?' she said accusingly.

'Oh, yeah,' Stella drawled in her posh rich-girl

voice. 'I meant to ask you if I could borrow them. I found them at Jake's and as they go so perfectly with this dress I thought you wouldn't mind.'

Suddenly all Crystal's intentions to play it cool deserted her. 'I do fucking mind, actually. I looked everywhere for those shoes tonight. I wanted to wear them.'

'Sorry.' Stella didn't seem at all sorry.

'Take them off,' Crystal said.

'What?' Now Stella was looking less composed.

'Take them off and give them to me.'

'But what about my outfit?'

'I don't give a flying fuck about your outfit. Take my shoes off,' Crystal repeated through gritted teeth. Jake had been caught up talking to other guests, oblivious to the heated exchange; he turned round just as Stella had unfastened the sandals and slung them at Crystal. Giving Crystal a filthy look, she marched off.

'What was that about?' Jake demanded.

'Stella was just returning my shoes which she'd borrowed without asking,' Crystal said, expecting him to take her side.

'Oh, come on, Crystal, you could have let her keep them, couldn't you?'

'I only lend things to my friends,' Crystal snapped back.

'You're being a bit childish, aren't you?' Jake retorted and turned away from her again.

'Don't ignore me,' Crystal said, grabbing his arm.

'Ever since I met her, Stella has gone out of her way to be nasty to me. Can't you see that she fancies you? She knew that I was taking you out for dinner tonight so she arranged your party; she knew I was buying you a watch so she bought you one too, though I expect Mummy had to help her out.' Crystal knew that she sounded bitchy but couldn't help it; she was sick of pretending that she couldn't see what Stella was up to.

Jake just laughed. 'I've told you, Crystal, she really doesn't fancy me! Chill out! I'll get you another drink.' He walked away, leaving Crystal fuming.

Crystal didn't think the evening could get any worse but then she found herself trapped by one of the posh pissed male guests, who was holding – she could hardly believe it – the magazine with her photo shoot in it.

'I must say,' he slurred, 'looking at these pictures Jake is one very lucky guy.'

'Where did you get that?' she demanded, snatching the magazine away from him. 'There's a stack of them over there; thought Jake must have put them out to show you off. Bastard.'

Crystal looked in the direction he was pointing and there was a pile of about five magazines on one of Stella's elegant little coffee tables. There could only be one person responsible for this. Crystal marched over to the pile of magazines and grabbed them, intending to take them out of the room. She was just weaving her way through the guests, when Stella stepped in front of her.

'Oh, you found the magazine, Crystal. I was just going to show it to Jake.'

'If anyone is going to show it to him, it should be *me*. Stop interfering,' Crystal snapped back, trying to get past Stella. But Stella was tougher than she looked and, standing her ground, reached out and tried to grab a magazine.

'Fuck off, Stella!' Crystal hissed.

'This is my house. Don't speak to me like that!'

'Or what? You'll call Mummy and Daddy and say someone's being nasty to you. Just get out of my way.' Crystal tried to get past her again.

'You shouldn't be with him,' Stella snapped, 'I'm much more his type than you are. I could really help him with his career, whereas all you ever do is drag him into the tabloids.'

By now other guests had overheard them and stopped their own conversations to listen.

'I'm not going to argue with you, Stella, just let me get past,' Crystal said, trying to stay calm but feeling the rage reach boiling point inside her.

'No, I won't; he needs to see what you're really like, a cheap little chavvy tart who'll do anything for money. God, you even slept with your friend's boyfriend. How low is that?'

Crystal made one last attempt to get past her but Stella decided to play dirty and, grabbing a large hunk of Crystal's hair, pulled it sharply, causing

Crystal to cry out in pain and drop the magazines. Swiftly Stella grabbed one and, before Crystal could stop her, she ran to where Jake was standing and handed him the magazine. She saw Jake's jaw tighten and his eyes grow serious as he flipped through the glossy pages. Then he came striding towards Crystal, took her arm and practically pulled her out of the room and into the hallway. Drink had made him unreasonable.

'I thought you were supposed to be a singer,' he said with barely restrained anger, leaning over her as she stood against the wall.

'I am a singer but I needed to earn some money,' she shot back, furious that he was having a go at her.

'These are really tacky pictures, Crystal. God, if you wanted to do some modelling, I'd have photographed you. I don't understand why you did them.'

Crystal was about to try and explain when he added sarcastically, 'Did you have a shoe bill you couldn't pay or something?'

'Actually my rent,' she said bitterly.

He didn't seem to have heard her. 'All the guests have seen these. Do you know how that makes me feel?'

'Well, they wouldn't have seen them if Stella hadn't bought all these copies,' Crystal shouted back. 'Didn't you hear her having a go at me?' She'd had it with Jake taking Stella's side. Tonight had been more than she could take. 'I didn't want to do the modelling, but I had to, and I don't think I've got anything to be ashamed of. The pictures might not fit in with your arty style but they're not tacky either.'

Jake was about to reply but Crystal pushed his arm out of the way and marched towards the front door.

'Don't think I'm going to run after you,' he shouted.

'I wouldn't want you to,' she called back, trying to ignore the burning tears filling her eyes.

Why couldn't he see what Stella was trying to do? she thought bitterly as she walked home. It seemed that each time she and Jake overcame one problem in their relationship, something else always got in the way. First it was his ex-girlfriend, then Max and now Stella. Back home even the flat seemed to mock her, as she saw all the ingredients painstakingly laid out for the romantic meal and the table set for dinner for two. Crystal poured herself a large vodka and tonic; she'd lost count of the number of drinks she'd had that night but was so angry that she felt oddly sober. She curled up on the sofa and picked up her mobile. She had a text message. It's not going to be from Jake, she told herself, but all the same she couldn't help feeling disappointed when she saw it was from Jez asking her how the meal had gone. She felt too miserable to reply.

Part of her wanted to call Jake and argue her case, but her pride wouldn't allow her to. She'd done nothing wrong; it was Stella who had ruined everything. God she hated her. She sat there fuming, then picked up a pen and paper and wrote down the lyrics for a song called – '24-carat Bitch'. Writing down her feelings made her feel slightly better; she'd probably think the lyrics were crap in the morning but at least she'd got some of the poison out of her system. She wandered into the kitchen, grabbed all the ingredients and chucked them into the bin. Then she ripped up the little menu cards she'd written out so carefully. She was just about to climb into bed when her doorbell went.

She opened the door to an extremely drunk Jake. 'I didn't realise you were cooking dinner for us,' he slurred. 'Just got a text from Jez asking me how dinner went. I didn't realise.' He staggered in and put his arms round her. 'Sorry, Crystal, I didn't know. I'll have some now if you like.'

'It's in the bin,' Crystal told him sharply. She couldn't forgive him easily for his earlier treatment of her.

'I'm sorry about Stella laying into you, as well. Gavin told me what she'd said and she was well out of order. And you're right; she does have a thing for me, she just tried to kiss me as I was leaving. She even told me that she was in love with me. It was very embarrassing.'

He held Crystal tighter. 'God, Crystal, it seems all I ever do is say sorry to you. And I want you to know that you're really special to me.'

Crystal looked up at him. In spite of his apology, she was tempted to make him suffer a little longer. But her heart ruled over her head and she gave in and hugged him back. 'Come to bed. You're drunk.'

'Not so drunk I can't make love to the sexiest woman in the world.'

For the first time all night Crystal actually smiled. 'Come on then,' she said. 'What are you waiting for?'

Chapter 18

The Morning After

Crystal woke up with a pounding headache. She opened her eyes, winced at the bright morning sunshine and quickly closed them again. *I didn't drink that much, did I?* She tried to remember, then realised that the reason she felt so rough was that she had barely eaten anything the day before. She'd been saving herself for dinner, the dinner which had ended up in the bin. Beside her, Jake was still fast asleep. She snuggled up next to his warm body, replaying the events of last night in her hungover brain. She remembered the scene with Stella and marching back home in a fury. She remembered Jake coming over and apologising and they'd made love. Suddenly she sat up in bed. 'Shit,' she exclaimed out loud. In their drunken passion, they hadn't used a condom. 'Shit, shit, shit.' She dragged herself out of bed intending to go straight round to her local chemist's and get the morning after pill. But as she emerged from the bathroom, wrapped in a towel, her mobile rang. 'Is that Crystal Hope?' a male voice asked.

Great; surely it wasn't another journalist hassling her.

'Yes,' she said wearily. 'But I've got nothing to say, so just piss off.'

She was about to hang up when the man said quickly, 'I'm not a journalist, I'm Sadie Park's assistant, she wants to speak to you.'

That got Crystal's attention. 'Okay,' she answered, instinctively pulling her towel round her more tightly to protect herself. What the hell was Sadie Park doing calling her? She hadn't seen or spoken to her since the end of *Band Ambition* last year.

'Crystal, is this a good time to talk?'

'This is fine,' Crystal replied cautiously, wondering if it was a wind-up. But it definitely sounded like Sadie.

'I'll get straight to the point. One of my assistants showed me a MySpace site yesterday of someone called Pearl and I listened to the songs. It's you, isn't it?'

'Why do you want to know?' Crystal couldn't help being defensive. Sadie Park was a force to be reckoned with.

'I want to know because I want to sign up whoever is behind the music. I want to offer them a record deal and make them a star.'

Now Crystal felt stupid. 'Yeah, it is me,' she mumbled.

'So are you interested in what I'm saying?' Sadie demanded.

'Of course I am,' Crystal replied. It was the understatement of the decade.

'Good. Well, next we need to meet, but I don't want anyone to know about this yet, Crystal. Certain things have happened in the past and I don't think we need to go over them again. But I think those things would affect you so we should release your first single anonymously. That way we can build up your fan base before people know it's you.'

'Because of the Max thing?' Crystal asked, wondering when she would ever be allowed to forget.

'The Max factor certainly plays a major part,' agreed Sadie, laughing at her own pun. 'I'm going to hand you back to Claude, my assistant, to fix a time for you to come in. In the meantime, don't tell anyone about this, Crystal, not even that divine boyfriend of yours.'

In a daze Crystal arranged to meet Sadie the following day at the Dorchester. Was this for real? Was there a chance that her singing career could start again? She immediately called Jez's salon and booked herself in for a cut and blow dry and a manicure. She hadn't spent any money on herself in ages and she wanted to look her best for her meeting with Sadie. As she raced round her flat getting ready her hangover was forgotten, as was her planned trip to the chemist. Jake was still fast asleep, so she left him a note telling him where she'd gone and saying she'd call later.

Jez was clearly expecting her to be down in the dumps after the failure of her romantic dinner for two. 'You're not too disappointed?' he asked as she sat down in her usual chair in front of the mirror.

'What about?' she asked, thinking only of tomorrow's meeting.

'The dinner,' Jez asked, obviously taken aback at her lack of concern.

'Oh that,' Crystal answered, trying to bring herself back down to earth. 'I was but then Jake apologised and he said he was going to give Stella her notice too.'

'Result!' exclaimed Jez. 'Stuck up Park Avenue Princess nil, Sexy Street Girl Crystal one.'

'I'm not a street girl! That makes me sound like a prostitute!' Crystal bantered back.

'Oh, you know what I mean. I meant rough diamond, people's champion, blah blah blah.'

They spent the rest of the appointment gossiping and giggling and all the while Crystal couldn't stop thinking about Sadie's offer.

It was torture not being able to tell anyone the news, especially Jake. She was almost dreading his call suggesting they meet up, as she didn't think she'd be able to see him and not tell him, but when he rang it was to say he'd forgotten he had a shoot in Manchester and he'd be away overnight, so at least she didn't have to lie. But she felt bad about not telling him. When they'd got back together they had both agreed to be 100 per cent honest with each other.

'I'm here to see Pippa Scarlet,' Crystal told the receptionist at the Dorchester, trying not to giggle as she gave the made-up name Sadie had insisted she use.

'She's in suite 505,' the receptionist told her, after she'd called Sadie to let her know she had a guest. As Crystal made her way up, she tried to stay calm, but it was hard. After six long months, when she had thought there was no chance of turning her career around, Sadie was throwing her a lifeline. *This is just a meeting*, she told herself sternly; *until you've signed a contract with her, don't expect anything*. She stood outside Sadie's door for a few seconds, took a deep breath, then knocked.

An extremely good-looking young man, dressed in a sharp pin-striped suit, opened the door.

'Crystal!' Sadie called out from the huge sofa where she was sitting, drinking coffee. She was in her usual rock-chick uniform – tight black jeans, pointed suede stiletto ankle boots and a black D&G sequinned top. Her blonde hair was long and tousled and in the same style it had been twenty years ago. It was a look which would have had Trinny and Susanna screaming *mutton!* But, actually, Crystal thought, if anyone could carry it off, Sadie could.

'Hi, Sadie,' Crystal replied, suddenly feeling shy. She was about to shake Sadie by the hand, but Sadie got up from the couch and hugged her as if she was an old friend. 'That's Claude, by the way, my assistant.' Claude shook Crystal's hand and as he walked away Sadie whispered, 'He'll do anything for me, but he won't do *that* – he's gay.' She sighed wistfully as she watched Claude's perfect body walking away. Then her tone switched to business mode. 'Now, sit down. I want to know everything that you've been doing since you left Lost Angels. Dallas is such an arsehole for getting rid of you. But his loss is going to be my gain. I mean *our* gain,' she quickly corrected herself.

Crystal had forgotten what a strong rivalry there was between Dallas and Sadie and she worried that Sadie was only using her to score points. As if reading her mind, Sadie reassured her. 'This has got nothing to do with Dallas; it's everything to do with you. I think you could be a big star.'

After a meeting which lasted two hours and then became lunch, where the champagne flowed freely, Crystal pushed any worries out of her head. Sadie had everything mapped out. She wanted Crystal in the studio and recording her songs by the end of the month; she was having a contract drawn up that she'd be able to show Crystal the following day and she had booked Crystal a singing coach and a dance instructor to get her back to her best. In just four months time she wanted to release Crystal's first single, closely followed by the album. It seemed too good to be true, but there was just one thing bothering her.

At the end of the meal, Crystal asked, 'Are you sure I really can't tell anyone?'

'You're thinking of Jake, right?' Sadie asked.

Crystal nodded.

'I know it's a tough one but I want you to keep this between us. I'm sure you trust him but you just never know. He's in the business as well; it's too risky. He could say something to someone by mistake and then they tell someone else, and then before you know it, it's all over the papers and we've lost our surprise – it would totally blow the deal. And, of course, it would give the press the chance to rake up all that crap about you. So that we know where we both stand, I've drawn up a confidentiality agreement, that I want you to sign, that stipulates you tell no one about our deal.'

Reluctantly, Crystal agreed. She didn't want to have any secrets from Jake but surely he would understand when she was finally able to tell him the truth?

That aside, in the weeks that followed Crystal couldn't have been happier. Every day she woke up with a feeling of energy and purpose she hadn't had since she'd left Lost Angels. It felt like she was being given a second chance to prove herself and this time she was not going to blow it. Jake was away filming most of the time so fortunately she didn't have to invent any excuses about what she was up to. When he asked, she admitted that she was writing songs again and had taken up singing lessons. He was so supportive that she couldn't help feeling guilty that she hadn't told him her big news. She was also secretly over the moon that he'd given Stella her notice. She had taken it extremely badly and walked out there and then, and, despite Ingrid calling Jake to plead Stella's case, Jake stood firm and refused to have her back. When he told Crystal she had to use all her willpower not to gloat.

'Oh, right,' she'd said, then quickly changed the subject. She didn't want Jake to think she was being bitchy. However, as soon as she was on her own she called Tahlia and Jez to tell them the news and spent a very therapeutic half-hour bitching non-stop about Stella and celebrating her departure.

'I feel like opening a bottle of champagne,' Crystal told Tahlia. 'To think I'll never have to see her smug, spoilt face again, or have to watch her flirting so outrageously with Jake or see her skinny little arse parading around in those shorts.'

'Hi, Jake it's just me. I've left a message on your mobile but I'm leaving one here as well to let you know I'm going to be late. See you later. I'm out with Jez, by the way.' The studio session was lasting much longer than she had anticipated; she should have remembered these things always overran. It was eleven at night and she had promised to go round to Jake's. Now it looked as if she wouldn't get there until well after midnight. She just hoped he wouldn't ask any awkward questions. She'd finally had to ask Jez to be her alibi for any late nights.

'You know I'll do anything for you, Crystal, but I'm not lying for you if you're having an affair,' he'd said to her when she'd asked him, for once a serious expression on his face.

'Jez, I swear on Jake's life that I'm not having an affair. I'd never cheat on Jake,' Crystal said passionately. 'I just can't tell anyone about this thing yet, but it's nothing bad, I promise. But I understand if you feel you can't cover for me.'

'Okay,' Jez said slowly. 'Well, so long as it's not an affair or you've become a crack whore, then I'll do it.'

Crystal didn't want Jez to have to lie for her, and hoped it wouldn't come to that.

At two, she let herself quietly into Jake's flat. Thinking he was asleep, she jumped at the sound of his voice. 'Where have you been?' He stood in the doorway, dressed in a white towelling robe, looking extremely pissed off.

'Didn't you get my message?' she asked.

'Yeah, but it's really late. Where have you been?'

'I was out with Jez. He needed to talk to me because things aren't going too well with Rufus,' Crystal lied. It was always a safe bet to imagine some drama in Jez's love life.

'Things must be really bad to keep you out so late. We haven't seen each other all week.'

'I know, babe, and I'm really sorry. Jez was really upset,' Crystal said, hating herself for lying, but also surprised at the accusing tone in Jake's voice.

'Well, I'm going to bed. I've got a really early start,' he said moodily.

'Okay, I'm coming too,' Crystal said, wondering why he'd got the hump. In bed, instead of cuddling up to Crystal as he always did, he turned away from her, after muttering a very grumpy goodnight, and moved to the opposite edge of the mattress. And for the first time they spent a night together without making love.

Perhaps that night wouldn't have mattered so much except it happened again the following week, when Crystal had to leave yet another message, again blaming her lateness on Jez. This time Jake was really angry.

'If there's something you want to tell me, I'd rather know now,' he said angrily when she walked in at four a.m., after having spent the last twelve hours in the studio.

'I told you in the message, I was seeing Jez,' Crystal pleaded, her throat was sore, and she felt exhausted.

Jake sighed heavily. 'God, this is déjà fucking vu.'

'I'm not Eve!' Crystal said passionately. 'Please stop comparing me with her.'

'Well, all the signs are there. You're back late; we haven't made love for a week. I've been there before, Crystal, and I don't want to go there again.'

'Hang on a minute; you're the one who gets into bed and turns away from me,' Crystal said angrily, hardly believing the way the conversation was going. 'Phone Jez if you don't believe me.' She selected Jez's number and held out her phone to Jake.

'Crystal, Jez is one of your best friends. He would always protect you,' Jake said wearily, the fight suddenly gone out of him. 'I'll see you in bed.'

For a few minutes Crystal stood in the living room, too emotionally strung out to do anything. She hated not being able to tell Jake the truth. Then she forced herself to move and, even though she was exhausted, she got into bed and wrapped her arms round Jake, kissing him and pressing her body against his.

'What's this,' he murmured, 'a mercy fuck?'

'Yes, a mercy fuck for me,' replied Crystal. 'I want you; don't be cold with me.'

She wanted to tell him that she loved him, but since that one time, she didn't dare say it again.

In the morning, Crystal woke up feeling guilty about lying to Jake. She spent longer than usual in the shower trying to work out the best thing to do. In spite of Sadie's order to stay quiet, Crystal didn't think she could carry on the pretence without jeopardising her relationship. She didn't want to lose Jake again and she could see that if she wasn't honest with him there was a very strong chance that she would. By the time she returned to the bedroom her mind was made up.

Jake was still half asleep so she got back into bed beside him.

'Morning,' he said sleepily turning over and putting his arm round her. 'Sorry about last night. I thought I was getting over the paranoia but apparently not.'

'Actually, Jake, there *is* something I need to tell you,' Crystal said anxiously.

'Oh?' Jake was wide awake now, sitting bolt upright in bed.

'It's nothing bad, it's actually really good news.' And she went on to tell him all about Sadie Park and the record deal. Jake couldn't have been happier for her, telling her it was fantastic news and that she deserved it.

'I'm sorry I didn't tell you straightaway, I really wanted to. It's just that Sadie made me sign a confidentiality agreement.'

'You can trust me, Crystal. And I'm sorry for even thinking you were seeing someone else. You're right; you're definitely not Eve. '

Crystal traced her finger over the tattoo of her name on Jake's shoulder. 'Does that *really* say my name?' she asked. It was a question she'd asked several times before.

'I think so,' he answered, 'unless the tattooist was having a laugh and it really says wanker.' He paused and said more seriously. 'There's no one else's name I would want.'

Crystal

He still may not have told her he loved her but hearing him say that was the next best thing and Crystal felt a huge surge of happiness.

Now she had come clean with Jake, Crystal felt she could really enjoy the relaunch of her singing career. She would have liked to be able to tell her brother and her close friends but knew it was best to keep quiet. Confiding in Jake had made all the difference though – to be able to share her excitement with him, to be able to tell him all about her day in the studio and to know that she had his support gave her such a boost. Everything seemed on track. Sadie had secured her record deal with one of the leading labels. The feedback she was getting from her MySpace site continued to be extremely positive. It looked likely that in a few months she would have a number one single. But sometimes life has a way of dealing you a wild card . . .

Chapter 19

Don't Leave Me This Way

'I'm sorry, babe, I don't feel up to meeting in town, I've got chronic period pain. Do you think you could come over?' Tahlia was on the phone to Crystal; they'd planned a girls' night out as they hadn't seen each other for ages.

'No problem. I'll pick some food up from M&S on the way,' Crystal replied.

As she slipped on her jacket, she had a sudden thought which sent her on a frantic search for her diary. She flipped through the pages. Christ, *her* period was over three weeks late and she was never late. She sat back down on the sofa for a few minutes, too shocked to move. In the frenzy and excitement of signing up with Sadie she had completely forgotten about the night she and Jake had been careless. *Maybe I'm all out of sync because I've had so much going on*, she told herself. She'd have to pick up a pregnancy test kit on her way to Tahlia's.

'I've got to use the bathroom,' she said the second Tahlia opened the door to her, too anxious to say hello. She raced into the house, past a stunned Tahlia, into the bathroom, and then, with trembling, clumsy fingers, Crystal ripped open the packet, not even giving herself time to think, just desperate to know.

Less than two minutes later she was staring at the strong blue line forming in the tiny square window. There was no doubt: she was pregnant. Then she threw up in the loo.

Tahlia was knocking at the door. 'Crystal are you okay?'

Crystal ran the cold tap, splashed her face with water and rinsed out her mouth, looking at her face in the mirror in disbelief – this couldn't be happening, could it?

'You can come in,' she called back, sitting down on the edge of the bath as she feared her legs were about to give way.

Tahlia came into the room. 'Are you okay, babe?' she asked again.

'I'm pregnant,' Crystal said quietly.

'Crystal, that's fantastic!' Tahlia exclaimed, hugging Crystal. 'It *is* fantastic, isn't it?' she asked again, seeing Crystal's grim expression.

'Oh God, Tahlia, I don't know. Jake's never said he loves me; he might just think it's all too much.

And there's something else going on that could be ruined by this news. I just wish I could tell you but I can't.' Crystal was babbling now.

'Come into the kitchen and I'll make you a drink. You need to sit down and be calm, babe.'

Crystal followed Tahlia into the kitchen, feeling numb. She sat down at the kitchen table and watched Tahlia making the tea.

'I'll put some sugar in it, Crystal, it's good for shock.'

'Okay, nurse,' Crystal replied, managing the smallest of smiles.

'How did it happen?' Tahlia asked, sliding a mug of tea in front of Crystal and sitting down at the table opposite her.

'Well, I would have thought you'd know about the birds and bees by now . . . you see, the man puts his penis into the woman's vagina and—' Crystal attempted humour, but she felt as if a metal vice was pressing round her head.

'Very funny. I meant were you trying for a baby?'

'No. The night of Jake's thirtieth we were both really drunk and forgot to use a condom. It is the only time in my life I've ever been careless. I can't believe it!' She put her head in her hands and groaned. 'What am I going to do?'

'Well, you've got to tell Jake. There are two of you involved in this. He needs to know,' Tahlia said calmly.

Just then Leticia skipped into the room, dressed

in her pink checked pyjamas and clutching a huge toy Dalmatian which was nearly as big as her.

'Leticia,' Tahlia warned, 'it's way past your bedtime.'

'I just wanted to show Dotty to Crystal,' Leticia said, bounding over to Crystal and holding the toy dog up for inspection.

'He's so cute,' Crystal forced herself to sound normal. 'Tell you what, why don't I come and tuck you up in bed and you can show me where Dotty sleeps.'

'Okay,' Leticia said happily, giving Tahlia a hug and then skipping back out of the room.

'Don't let her keep you too long,' Tahlia said as Crystal followed Leticia upstairs.

Leticia's bedroom was like a little girl's dream come true. Practically everything in her room was a different shade of pink, Leticia's favourite colour – she had a pink bed with a loveheart-shaped headboard, pink fairy lights hung round the room, the curtains had pink princesses on them, there was a pink wardrobe and a pink rug in the shape of a flower . . . Crystal's nausea returned as she took in all the different pink objects, but she forced herself to perch on the end of Leticia's bed as she climbed under the duvet and carefully laid Dotty next to her. Crystal remembered what Leticia's bedroom used to be like, before Tahlia made it as a singer, how she'd had to share a room with her mum and how few toys she had back then. It seemed Tahlia had more than compensated for that now.

'D'you like my room?' Leticia asked.

'It's great; it's very pink. I just hope you don't suddenly change your mind about liking pink.'

Leticia looked at Crystal in amazement. 'Why would I do that? I love pink.'

'I'm sure you won't,' Crystal said, suddenly feeling exhausted. 'Now I'm going to tuck you and Dotty up and say goodnight.'

It wasn't as easy as that. Leticia wanted a story and Crystal ended up reading three to settle her, but eventually Leticia was ready to snuggle down with her toy dog. As Crystal crept out of the room she paused at the doorway and looked back at the child curled up in bed. *I'm having a baby*, she thought, and it seemed unbelievable. It was the most natural thing in the world but Crystal felt as if she'd been beamed into a parallel universe where everything had been turned upside down.

'Thanks for settling her,' Tahlia said as Crystal walked into the living room. 'I'm sure it was the last thing you felt like doing.'

Crystal sat down on the sofa next to her and sighed. *God, what a mess.*

'I think I've made it hard for you to talk to me,' Tahlia said slowly. 'When you told me you were pregnant I just assumed that you'd want to have the baby, but I guess there might be reasons why you might not be able to.'

Crystal appreciated the effort Tahlia was making. She knew her friend would never consider having an abortion; in fact she knew that she was desperate to have another child, and worried that she couldn't because of her polycystic ovaries.

'I've already had one abortion,' Crystal said quietly. 'I really don't want to have another.' She paused. 'After that time with Max, I discovered I was pregnant. There was no way I wanted to keep the baby, not after what he did. But I still felt so bad about it, Tahlia.'

'Oh, babe,' Tahlia moved across the sofa and hugged her. 'I can't believe that you never told me. Please, Crystal, whatever you decide to do, tell me. I won't judge you, I would never judge you. It's your decision and only you know what to do for the best.'

She stayed the night at Tahlia's; Jake was away and she didn't want to be alone. They talked about how she should break the news to him. Tahlia said that she shouldn't wait for a time, that she should just come out with it, that she was sure he would be happy. 'Often men don't realise that they want a baby until they know they're having one, but I bet when the news has sunk in he'll be over the moon.'

Crystal tried to hold on to that thought the next day. Jake sounded stressed out when they spoke on the phone; he also said he wouldn't be able to see her that night as Simon, one of his best mates was about to leave his girlfriend and needed to go out for a drink.

'I'll just crash at home as it's bound to be a long session. They've been together ten years and he wants out and she doesn't.'

'Do *you* think they should split up?' Crystal asked. Somehow she didn't like the thought of Jake being around someone who was about to end a relationship.

'God, yeah, she's a total nightmare. I've been telling him to leave her for months. She's desperate to have a baby and he doesn't want one. I think he should get out now.'

'Maybe he just doesn't know that he wants a baby,' Crystal said, repeating Tahlia's line.

Jake laughed. 'That's bullshit; how would he not know? He doesn't want one with her and that's it.'

Crystal didn't feel brave enough to ask Jake if he wanted one.

A week later she still hadn't been able to tell him – she was even busier than ever working on her album and Jake had a major fashion campaign to shoot and they hardly saw each other. By the week-end Crystal was desperate to get it out in the open. She'd suggested that the two of them have a chilled-out Saturday night at her place but Jake had barely walked in the door when his mobile rang and he disappeared into the bedroom to take the call. He was gone for twenty minutes and when he walked back into the living room he looked stunned.

'I don't fucking believe it!' Jake exclaimed, throwing his mobile on to one of the armchairs in disgust.

'What's up?' Crystal asked from where she sat curled up on the sofa, trying to convince herself that she didn't feel sick. Morning sickness had kicked in with a vengeance and Crystal was sick at least five times a day.

'Simon's girlfriend has just told him she's pregnant. He was about to tell her he was leaving and she came out with that. I reckon she knew that he was going to leave her and she got pregnant to hold on to him.'

'Oh come on, that's a bit calculating, isn't it?' Crystal asked, realising with a sinking heart that tonight was definitely not going to be a good time to tell Jake the news.

'She *is* calculating. God, I feel so sorry for him; he's too decent to leave her now, he's well and truly shafted. Poor bloke – he's trapped now.'

Jake spent the rest of the night drinking wine and going on and on about 'poor Simon' until finally Crystal snapped, 'Look, it took two of them to get pregnant. Stop having a go at her.'

'He thought she was on the pill! She claimed she'd forgotten to take it, but I think she did it deliberately.'

Crystal was feeling nauseous and stressed and this was the last thing she wanted to hear. Jake was so busy ranting that he fortunately hadn't noticed that she hadn't drunk her wine and instead was on peppermint tea.

'I'm going to bed,' she announced. Anything to stop the tirade.

'Fine. I'm going to ring Simon again, to see if he's okay.'

He didn't come to bed for the next two hours, and when he did he was apparently in the mood for some loving. Crystal was most definitely not – along with the nausea and sore breasts, she'd suffered a dramatic loss of libido. All she wanted to do was sleep. But sleep was not on Jake's mind. He kissed her neck, then slipped his hands under the T-shirt Crystal had taken to wearing in bed, so he didn't notice how swollen her breasts looked, and caressed her skin.

'Ouch,' Crystal couldn't stop herself exclaiming when he touched her breast. 'Jake, I'm sorry, but I really don't feel well. Can't we just have a hug?'

He sighed then put his arms round her. 'Hope you feel better in the morning,' he said slightly grudgingly.

'I just don't know how to tell him,' Crystal groaned to Tahlia. The two had met for dinner – not that Crystal felt like eating. Toast was all she could manage at the moment.

'He's now in New York for two weeks and I can hardly come out with something like that over the phone, can I?'

'You've just got to tell him – you're having his baby!' Tahlia exclaimed.

'You make it sound so easy, but since he found out about that friend of his, I'm really worried that he'll think I've done it deliberately to trap him.'

'That's mad and you know it, babe. Jake wouldn't think like that. Anyway, he's just as responsible for the situation you're in as you are.'

Crystal knew that Tahlia was right, but her hormones were making her feel irrational and insecure and she was afraid of losing Jake again, at a time when she wanted him the most.

She was also really anxious about telling Sadie her big news. Her single was coming out in three months' time and by then she'd be six months pregnant, which wouldn't be ideal, given the promotion she would have to do around it. What if Sadie decided it wasn't worth the risk and dropped her? Sadie was such a brilliant manager, she didn't want to lose her. She had great ideas but always listened to Crystal and took on board what she said. It felt much more like a partnership than it ever had with Dallas – he usually ended up imposing his ideas and refusing to listen to hers. Sadie had even agreed that Crystal could tell Jake the good news and that he could shoot the cover of her album and the video to accompany the first single.

'I told you it wouldn't be too long before you were snapped up by a label,' Jez said as he arranged

Crystal's hair for the shoot of the album cover. She'd finally been able to let him and Danni know her news. The look was full-watt glamour. Unfortunately, Crystal had chosen the outfit before she knew she was pregnant – something she was regretting now as Danni helped lace her into the tight black satin corset which she was wearing with a figure-hugging black pencil skirt. She was paranoid that her bump was starting to show. But at ten weeks her stomach was still flat – all those hours in the gym had obviously done wonders for her abs. She completed the look with black velvet over-the-elbow gloves and gold and black patent leather Christian Louboutin's platforms. Crystal managed a smile and slipped another piece of gum into her mouth – trying not to think about how nauseous Jez's musky aftershave was making her feel. Her sense of smell seemed to have intensified and practically every strong smell – perfume, food, petrol fumes – made her want to throw up.

'It's brilliant news, Crystal,' Danni said warmly.

'We've got to celebrate after the shoot!' Jez said. 'We could all go clubbing. We need to toast your success, Crystal, in vintage Cristal!'

Just the mention of champagne triggered another wave of nausea in Crystal. 'Actually, can we make it another time? I'm on antibiotics and I really shouldn't drink. And I'm not bloody going out with you lot if you're going to be pissed as farts!'

409

'Okay, but make sure you book a date very soon,' Jez said.

'Ready, Crystal?' Jake wandered into the dressing room. 'Wow, you look amazing,' he exclaimed walking over to her and embracing her.

'Are you sure?' Crystal said anxiously. 'You don't think I look fat?'

'What! You look gorgeous.' Then he whispered, 'I'm looking forward to unlacing that corset later', adding, 'see you in the studio' as he walked out of the room.

So am I, thought Crystal, but not for the same reason. She'd read in one of the pregnancy books Tahlia had lent her that some pregnant women experienced a surge in their sex drive but it definitely hadn't happened to Crystal. She still thought Jake was the sexiest man in the world; she just had absolutely no desire to shag him at the moment. Given a choice between a cup of tea and hot sex, the cup of tea won hands down . . .

Tahlia then turned up. Crystal had asked her along for a bit of moral support. 'Hey, babe, you look beautiful,' she said, coming over to give Crystal a hug.

'Are you sure no one can tell?' Crystal whispered.

Tahlia shook her head and whispered, 'How are you feeling?'

'Sick, my boobs are killing me, I feel bloated, I don't want to have sex; it's like the worst PMT in the world, except that I can't even eat chocolate.'

'Yep, sounds about right.' Tahlia smiled at her friend. 'You'll probably start to feel better after fourteen weeks.'

'What are you two whispering about?' Jez demanded. 'I hope you're not planning a secret celebration without the rest of us.'

'I was just asking Crystal if her thrush had cleared up,' Tahlia replied.

That shut him up. Jez had plenty to say on most things, but gynaecological problems was not one of his specialist areas.

In spite of Crystal feeling so rough, the shoot went well. It was great working with Jake – he was such a fantastic photographer and knew exactly how to get the best out of Crystal. And it was lovely having her old team around her. While it lasted, she even managed to forget about the pregnancy, but as soon as it was over, it was back to reality and the nausea.

'Are you sure you don't want to go out for a drink with the others?' Jake asked as they called it a day. All Crystal wanted to do was curl up in bed with a cup of tea.

'I'm totally knackered. Do you mind if we don't?' Crystal asked, thinking she might cry if she didn't get the corset off soon.

''Course not. I've got a couple of calls to make and then I'll come over. Someone from New York has been trying to get hold of me all day apparently.'

By the time Crystal got home it was nine, and she was too exhausted even to have a bath. She just about managed to pull off her clothes and crawl into bed. An hour later Jake let himself into the flat.

'Are you okay?' he asked, walking into the bedroom.

'Not really,' Crystal mumbled. 'I think I might have a bug, I feel really sick.'

'Do you need anything?'

'No,' she replied, feeling very sorry for herself.

Jake sat on the bed next to her and gently stroked her hair. *Tell him now*, she thought, but before she could get the words out, Jake stopped her. 'I've just had the most amazing news.'

'Oh?' He had Crystal's full attention and she managed to sit up.

'I've been offered a fantastic seven-month assignment in America – travelling round the country and capturing images of life today for a new book.'

'Oh?' Crystal replied, her throat suddenly dry.

'Yep, and they want me to start next week. Can you believe it? The photographer who was going to do it has just put his back out.'

Crystal could not believe it. *Somebody up there definitely doesn't like me. Talk about bad timing.*

'And I figure as you're going to be so busy with the album it's a good time for me to go. What do you reckon?'

There was a pause while Crystal tried to think what she could say. Of course she didn't want him to go; it was the last thing she wanted. 'I don't know,' she finally answered. 'Is it something you really want to do?' Thinking *please say no, please say you'll stay*.

'It's a great opportunity and we could still see each other at least once a month. And it's not for that long.' It seemed to Crystal that Jake had already made up his mind.

'Well, then,' Crystal said quietly, 'you should do it.' And to try and hide her true feelings she pretended that she needed to sleep, lying down and pulling the duvet round her.

'Are you sure I can't get you anything?' Jake asked.

Crystal shook her head and muttered from under the duvet.

'Okay, well, I'm too wired to sleep yet, hope you feel better,' Jake said switching off the light and walking out of the room.

Well, Crystal thought bitterly, *I can hardly feel any worse*.

She couldn't help thinking it was a sign that he didn't feel as much for her as she did for him. For her it was a really big deal for them to be apart regardless of her pregnancy, whereas Jake seemed to take it all in his stride.

She hoped that they might at least be able to spend the next week before he left together but both their schedules were crammed. She started in the studio at ten and often didn't finish until ten at night. Tahlia kept insisting that Crystal had to tell Jake now more than ever. But something stopped her. What if he gave up the chance to go to America because of it and then resented her? And what if he felt trapped, staying with Crystal and the baby out of duty and not because he loved them? He still hadn't said he loved her and he had never said that he wanted a baby with her. She couldn't bear it if he only stayed because he felt he had to. While she was struggling to keep a lid on her emotions, Jake was over the moon about his job and kept telling her that it would be fantastic when she came over, how much she would love America and how it might be useful for her career too, that he might be able to introduce her to some influential figures in the business. It was so hard to pretend to be pleased for him, so very hard to pretend that she wasn't filled with sadness at the prospect of his leaving.

But the day before Jake was due to fly out Crystal realised that she just had to tell him, whatever the consequences. She was having his baby! He had to know! She was in the studio and desperate to finish the session, so desperate that she kept making mistakes.

'Something tells me that you don't want to be here,' Sadie teased her as Crystal came in early for the fifth time.

'God, I'm really sorry, but Jake's going to the States tomorrow and I really need to see him.'

Dallas would have made her work on, but Sadie took pity on her and told her she could go early.

'You're a star,' Crystal said, hugging Sadie and racing for the door.

Outside the studio she checked her mobile. She had a voice mail from Jake: 'Crystal, I hope you get this message. I'm at the airport. There's a strike tomorrow and I need to fly out today. Call me as soon as you can, maybe you could come to the airport and say goodbye.'

Frantically Crystal called up his number which went straight to voice mail. Then she checked her text messages and there was one from Jake: Sorry I didn't get to say goodbye properly, am at the departure gate. Will call you when I get in. Jxxx

All Crystal's earlier excitement drained away. Jake had gone and he didn't know about the baby.

Chapter 20

All By Myself

'That's the baby's spine – can you see? Come on, little fella, turn round so we can see you.' The sonographer pressed the ultrasound to Crystal's belly, causing the tiny baby to wriggle around.

'Oh no, he's cross with us for waking him up. I think he wants to go back to sleep.'

'Can you tell it's a boy then?' Crystal asked, staring transfixed at the screen which showed her baby. *Her baby!* Until now, she'd been preoccupied with feeling so physically awful and so emotionally stressed that she'd almost forgotten what this was all about – but there it was, her baby. Her eyes filled with tears, and she felt an amazing surge of love.

'No, no,' the woman replied. 'I just call all the babies boys at this stage. We can't tell the sex for sure until the twenty-week scan.'

'That's my baby,' she said in awe to Tahlia, who had come with her. 'Look he's sucking his thumb!'

As they left the hospital Crystal kept looking at

the picture of the scan. The baby was in profile and she was convinced s/he had Jake's nose. Jake had been in the States for two weeks now. Crystal had so hoped that by now he would know about the pregnancy and that he would be the one holding her hand at the scan, looking at their baby. There were many, many times when they were talking on the phone when she had thought – right, this is the time to tell him, but he was so full of news about his work that somehow she couldn't. Later that day she could only get his voice mail. *I saw our baby today,* she longed to say. *He's got your nose and he was sucking his thumb.* Her real message simply said, *Call me, I miss you.*

Sadie's assistant, Claude, called. 'Hi Crystal, can you come by the studio later on today?'

'Is there something wrong?' she asked, suddenly worried that Sadie wasn't happy with her work.

'Not at all. It's not to do with you; I think Sadie wants you to meet someone.'

After the call Crystal spent twenty minutes going through her wardrobe and wondering what on earth to wear. She couldn't do her jeans up any more. She was going to have to get some maternity clothes and she was going to have to face the fact that she couldn't hide this pregnancy from the world much longer. In the end she settled on an Empire line green summer dress, which disguised her growing bump.

Fortunately when she met up with Sadie she seemed too preoccupied with work to notice that Crystal looked different. She gave Crystal a hug and then said, 'Honey, we have a problem. I've listened to the final version of the album and I'm just not happy. Oh, it's not you, darling,' she added, seeing how upset Crystal looked. 'No, you're fabulous. It's the production; I really think it needs to be sharper. So I've arranged for Jim Savage to come in and produce it. You may have to rerecord some of the tracks, but that isn't a problem, is it? I still want the album out in two months. He's coming by in a minute.'

Sadie paused and looked questioningly at Crystal. 'Is everything okay, honey? You don't quite look yourself.'

'Oh I'm fine,' Crystal lied. 'I'm just missing Jake.'

'Of course, I forgot. Love's young dream.' Sadie smiled at her and Crystal forced herself to smile back. Crystal was just debating whether to come clean to Sadie about the pregnancy when Claude buzzed through to say that Jim had arrived.

As he walked into the room, Crystal felt unexpectedly shy. She was totally in awe of him because he'd worked with some of the biggest stars in the business and it seemed incredible that he was now going to be working with her. She soon relaxed though: Jim was, quite simply, lovely – unpretentious, straight-talking, totally bullshit free.

He was in his early forties, casually dressed in baggy combats and a T-shirt, with long dark-brown hair that he wore tied back, a ruggedly handsome face and the warmest pair of brown eyes. Halfway through their conversation about what needed doing he suddenly gave an enormous yawn. Sadie arched an eyebrow at him and he exclaimed, 'Sorry. My baby son Otis had us up all night. I've only had three hours' sleep and I'm not firing on all cylinders.'

'How old is he?' Crystal found herself asking. Now that she was pregnant she had discovered a new obsession with babies – a complete turn-around for her. Until now she'd had zero interest – apart from Leticia – dismissing them as an alien species who made noise in restaurants, were bloody annoying on planes and, frankly, were mostly ugly. Sure, she thought she probably would have a baby one day, but she'd never imagined being pregnant at this time in her life.

'He's four months and he's taken twenty years off my life expectancy already – no, just kidding, he's fantastic.'

'Your first?' Crystal asked.

'Third, actually. I've got an eight-year-old daughter, and a five-year-old son. You'll have to come round for dinner. Mia, my daughter, is dying to meet you. She loved Lost Angels and she was ecstatic when I told her I was going to be working with you.'

'Well, you can all meet up at my party,' Sadie put in. 'You haven't forgotten, have you, Crystal?'

It had totally slipped Crystal's mind. Every year Sadie hosted an extravagant fancy-dress ball for her favourite children's charity.

'Of course not,' Crystal replied, thinking, *shit what the hell am I going to wear?* The party was less than three weeks away. *Were there such things as maternity fancy dresses?*

During the next couple of weeks Crystal felt happier than she had in a while. Working with Jim took her mind off missing Jake. He was so talented and enthusiastic – he seemed to care about the music as much as she did and she quickly felt at ease with him, as if she'd known him for years.

She told Jake all about him, not thinking anything of it, but Jake was unusually quiet during the conversation and she couldn't understand why, until a sudden thought had her saying, 'I don't fancy him. He's just a friend.'

'Yeah,' Jake replied, 'I'm sure he is.'

But Crystal couldn't help thinking as she put the phone down that he didn't sound so sure.

'Are you thinking of having a baby then?' Jim asked one day when they'd taken a break from recording and had nipped out to a café. Tahlia had been right – after fourteen weeks she had started to feel slightly better; the nausea had stopped but she was still off caffeine, sticking to peppermint tea, and the thought of alcohol still made her want to be sick. It was an obvious thing to ask because whenever they weren't talking about work, Crystal bombarded Jim with questions about babies – he and Tahlia were the only people she knew who had children.

Crystal was about to trot out a lie about one of her friends being pregnant when she thought, *Hang on, I don't want to lie any more. I want to be able to talk about my baby.* She looked at Jim and considered it for a minute. She knew she could trust him.

'Actually, I'm pregnant, but please don't tell anyone. I still haven't told Sadie.' *Wow!* She'd said it! And it felt really good.

'Congratulations!' Jim said warmly and, leaning over the table, gave her a kiss and a hug.

'Do you think Sadie will be mad with me?' Crystal asked anxiously.

'Are you kidding? She loves babies! And you've done the hard work; we've nearly finished the album. You'll be able to promote it; you're pregnant, not ill. My wife carried on working up until a week before she had Otis. How does your boyfriend feel about it?'

Crystal put her head in her hands and groaned. 'I haven't told him yet', and went on to tell Jim exactly why. When she had finished, he said, 'Crystal, you've got to tell him. He's not going to freak out; he's going to love it. It's what we're here

421

for! There is nothing in my life more wonderful than being a father. And I'm sure Jake will feel the same.'

Crystal nodded, feeling too emotional to speak. She wasn't going to put it off any longer – she was going to fly out as soon as she could. Jake was going to be a father. He needed to know and she wanted to tell him face to face.

As they left the café, Jim gave her a huge hug again and as he did so he said, 'You're going to be okay, Crystal, more than okay. I promise.'

Crystal hugged him back but was startled to hear the sound of a camera clicking away behind her. She turned round and stared straight into the lens pointed by a paparazzo just a few metres away.

'What the hell?' she said angrily. Ever since her mauling by the press over Max, she hated being photographed, even though her reign in the tabloids as the scarlet woman of England seemed to have come to an end. A member of a very successful boy band had taken her place in the tabloids when he had been exposed for shagging his fiancé's twin sister just days before his wedding.

'They must be interested in you,' she told Jim as they walked back to the studio.

He shook his head. 'I doubt it.'

'Well,' Crystal shrugged, 'he's not going to be able to sell that picture for very much, is he?' But she was about to be proved wrong.

*

Belle had recently been interviewed for a glossy woman's magazine, where she talked about Crystal, saying that while she couldn't quite forgive her completely, she had moved on and regretted slagging her off so much. She even said that she was grateful to Crystal, because she was a hundred times happier with Lee than she could ever have been with Max. As a result, Crystal's name was back in the press and the following morning she opened several papers to find the picture of herself and Jim with an accompanying article speculating that she had a new man in her life. Fortunately Jim and his wife Helen were able to laugh about it, but deep down it left Crystal feeling slightly unsettled. She knew that once she was revealed as the voice behind Pearl she'd have to face the press full on but, until then, she wasn't really ready to let them back into her life.

Later that day she told Jake about the story. 'It's so stupid, we're just friends, like I told you. I don't know why they have to print that shit.' She'd expected Jake to shrug off the story as well but he sounded distant and, after she'd told him, he quickly ended the call saying he was too busy to talk more.

It'll be okay, I'll see him this weekend, she told herself, lying on her sofa and gently stroking her belly. In spite of Jake sounding distant she was starting to think they'd be okay. Jim's enthusiasm about the joys of fatherhood had won her over. She let herself think about the future. She hoped that once she'd given Jake the big news he might cut his work short to be with her in London. Then she could move into his flat and they could start behaving like a couple who were having a baby. He'd hopefully be back in time for the next scan – when they'd find out whether they were having a boy or a girl. Crystal didn't mind either way; she just wanted the baby to be healthy. So far all the tests had shown that her baby was well, but that didn't stop her wanting Jake there with her, to share the anxiety, to reassure her that everything would be all right. Tahlia was a fantastic support, but she wasn't there at three in the morning when Crystal was worrying that the baby would have something wrong with it, or that it might die. She'd been reading too many pregnancy books and read some devastating stories of women whose babies had been stillborn. She'd gone from hardly knowing whether she wanted the baby or not, to wanting nothing else in the world more.

'I've got to get some maternity clothes,' she told Tahlia when they met up in central London for some retailing. 'I can't do up my jeans any more. But I don't want to look like some earth mother in a long flowery skirt and sensible shoes. When I see Jake again, I want him to fancy me and not see his whole life flash before him when he realises he's stuck with a frump.'

'Well, lucky for you Topshop do maternity clothes now so you won't have to look as crap as I did when I was pregnant.'

'I bet you didn't even show,' Crystal retorted.

'No, you're right, I didn't really,' Tahlia replied, 'but I had some horrible clothes for the last couple of weeks – some baggy leggings and a vile mustard-coloured T-shirt.' Tahlia shuddered and Crystal couldn't help laughing at the vision of beautiful, fashionable Tahlia in such an outfit, though knowing Tahlia she probably still looked like a supermodel in it.

After an hour and a half of power shopping, where Tahlia kept having to steer Crystal away from the mini skirts and back to the maternity section, they emerged from the store laden with bags and headed along Oxford Street. Suddenly Crystal heard her name being called. She turned round to be confronted with someone she never thought she would have to see again – Stella. Stella looked sickeningly gorgeous and very, very slim in a pretty black and white strapless summer dress, white pumps and Dior shades.

'Oh, it's you,' Crystal said flatly, wondering why the hell Stella had bothered to say hello to her.

'I hear Jake's getting on well in America,' Stella drawled in her posh voice, which set Crystal's teeth on edge.

This was bullshit. She didn't want to make conversation with Stella; the last time they'd seen

425

each other Stella had called her every name under the sun and physically assaulted her, not to mention the fact that she'd made a pass at Jake. Did she seriously think Crystal would have forgotten? She made as if to carry on walking but Stella called out, 'Have you got a message for Jake then? I'm flying out to New York next month. I'm going to be living there for a year and we're bound to meet up.'

So that was why she had stopped Crystal – just to needle her about her trip.

'I don't need you to give him a message for me; I'm seeing him this weekend. Come on, Tahlia, let's go.'

'How's Jim Savage, by the way?' Stella wouldn't let her walk off. 'You looked very cosy together in the papers. Are you hoping that he'll jump-start your singing career if you shag him?'

Crystal was about to tell Stella to fuck right off, but Tahlia gave her a warning look, and whispered, 'That's exactly what she wants, babe. Ignore her.'

Summoning all her self-control, Crystal picked up her bags and walked away from Stella.

'God, I thought I'd never have to see that bitch again!' she exclaimed. 'Can we go to a café now? I'm knackered. I don't think I can shop any more.' Stella had ruined her afternoon. And she hadn't even managed to get an outfit for Sadie's party which was only three days away.

That night she couldn't get hold of Jake. He'd been in America a month and she missed him so much – the phone calls, emails and texts weren't enough – and she longed to feel his arms round her, to see his face . . .

After much discussion with Tahlia, Crystal decided to go to Sadie's party as Scarlett O'Hara from *Gone with the Wind* and hired an amazing red silk Southern-belle-style dress with an enormous skirt and corset top, which gave her an impressive cleavage and managed to disguise her bump.

'Are you sure I don't look fat?' she whispered to Tahlia while Danni was out of the room. She'd just finished Crystal's make-up and Jez had done her hair and was on the phone to Rufus.

Tahlia sighed. 'For the hundredth time, babe, you're not fat, you're pregnant. And, no, you look fantastic.'

Crystal studied herself in the mirror. Jez had pinned her hair up in an elaborate style with ringlets framing her face; Danni had given her a pale complexion with just the hint of a blush in her cheeks; her lips were the same deep red as her dress, and her naturally long lashes had been made even more striking with false ones.

'It's just that I don't want anyone to know before I tell Jake and there'll be loads of press there tonight.'

Just then Jez walked back into the room.

'What do you think?' Crystal said, twirling round and causing the silk skirt to billow out around her.

Jez looked her up and down and declared in his best Rhett Butler voice (which sounded a little too camp to be convincing), 'Frankly, my dear, I don't give a damn! You look as stunning as ever, but are you sure you haven't had a little bit of work done recently?' He stared meaningfully at her chest. 'I don't mean to be personal and as you know I never usually look at that area, but your boobs are looking – how can I put this delicately – fucking massive.'

'It's the corset,' Crystal said, avoiding Tahlia's eye. She was saved from further explanation by her phone ringing. It was Jim.

'Hey, Crystal, I wondered if you fancied coming with me tonight. Mia's got a bug and is running a high temperature and Helen doesn't want to leave her with the babysitter.'

'I'd love to,' Crystal answered, pleased that he'd offered. She still felt nervous in crowds and hadn't been looking forward to arriving at the party on her own.

Half an hour later, she was in a taxi with Jim, who was dressed as a dashing Adam Ant, in his Prince Charming days, heading for the ball. Crystal's costume took up most of the back seat and Jim was in danger of being swamped by the layers of red silk.

'Tell me honestly,' she asked, 'do you think I look pregnant?'

Jim smiled. 'Honestly, yes, but that's probably only because you told me. You've got that glow all pregnant women have when they reach a certain stage.'

'And do you think that Jake will still find me attractive when I see him?' she said anxiously. She felt so at ease with Jim that she was able to ask him things that usually she only confided in to Tahlia.

He smiled again. 'Oh yes, more than ever, I'm sure.'

Buoyed up by his words, Crystal didn't find the red carpet experience as much of an ordeal as she feared. She happily posed for the photographers when they called out her name. The only downside was when a journalist shouted, 'Are you a couple now then?' Jim laughed and pointed to his wedding ring; Crystal shook her head and hurried into the hotel. But she quickly forgot the comment – everyone who was anyone in the celebrity world was at Sadie's. It was one of *the* parties of the year. The ballroom had been decorated to look like the inside of a huge circus tent and as the guests sipped their champagne cocktails – Crystal stuck to water – they were treated to trapeze artists swinging elegantly above their heads; acrobats performing feats of strength and balance on the stage, and jugglers strolling round the ballroom. After mingling for an hour it was time for a lavish meal, followed by an auction for charity. Crystal was enjoying herself, but just as Jim was leading her on to the dance floor she suddenly felt faint. She gripped his arm and whispered, 'I think I'm going to pass out.' He put his arm round her waist and managed to get her to a chair, where she collapsed, feeling as if she couldn't breathe; the corset was pressing into her and she felt a rising feeling of panic.

'Are you okay?'

'No,' she gasped, 'I can't breathe. Could you please undo the corset.'

He quickly did as she'd asked, but unfortunately he loosened it so much that it practically slipped off her.

She clutched the top to her, concentrating on taking deep breaths. 'You don't think there's anything wrong with the baby, do you?' she asked anxiously.

'I'm sure everything's fine. I think you were just laced in too tightly. Come on, I'll take you home. I think it's time for Cinderella to have a rest.'

'You don't have to,' she said, not wanting to spoil his night.

'It's no trouble. I want to get you home safely and, besides, I want to get home myself to see if Mia's okay.'

And taking off his jacket, he slipped it round Crystal's shoulders and put his arm round her waist. She was grateful for the support; she really did feel wobbly.

She didn't stop to think about how the two of them might look to the paparazzi camped outside but as soon as they walked through the hotel door, the cameras started going off around them. Crystal put her head down and held on tighter to Jim's arm. She just wanted to be home.

She was woken the following morning by her mobile. Hoping it might be Jake she picked it up. 'Hello,' she said sleepily.

'Hi, Crystal, that looked like quite a night,' said a female voice that she didn't recognise.

'Who is this?' she demanded, certain it was a journalist.

'What does Jim Savage's wife think of your affair then? And does Jake know?' the voice went on.

'Oh, piss off,' Crystal shot back, ending the call. She lay back in bed trying to collect her thoughts but was interrupted by the ringing of her doorbell. *What the hell was going on?* she thought anxiously, reaching for her robe and walking to the front door. She checked the video monitor and to her horror saw several journalists and photographers crowding on to her front step. Her mobile rang again but this time it was Jim. 'Are they outside your flat as well?' he asked sounding concerned.

'Yes,' she replied, suddenly feeling tearful. She really didn't think she could handle the press attention right now. 'Is Helen okay?'

'She's livid, but not with you, with them. Don't worry: she can hold her own. I'm not so sure about you, it's not what you need right now. I'm going to call Sadie and see what she can do.'

Sadie's suggestion was that Crystal got on a flight

to New York to see Jake as soon as she could. The story about her so-called affair with Jim had made nearly all the tabloids. There were pictures of them laughing together on the red carpet and then details of how they spent the evening locked in each other's company, how they'd been discovered kissing passionately in the corridor, and then seen stumbling out of the party, and getting into the same taxi. It was all lies. Crystal couldn't believe she was back here again . . .

Hardly able to focus on what she was doing she started flinging clothes into a suitcase. Sadie had insisted on sending over one of her drivers to take her to Tahlia's, saying that Crystal shouldn't be alone. Journalists kept calling her and in the end she had to switch her phone off. She was desperate to call Jake but it was only five a.m. in New York. She'd leave it an hour, and then call him; she didn't want him to hear about the story from anyone else.

Tahlia was supposed to be rehearsing but she cancelled, so that she could spend the day with Crystal.

'You don't have to do that,' Crystal told her, when she arrived at her house.

'Listen, babe,' Tahlia said, hugging her, 'I can sing those songs in my sleep. I'm not the one who needs the rehearsals and I want to be with you, make sure you're okay. Now, have you had breakfast?'

Crystal shook her head, and Tahlia tutted, taking in her friend's pale face. 'Right, come into the kitchen. I'm going to get you something, you need to eat.' While Tahlia prepared a bowl of muesli and fresh fruit for her, Crystal checked her mobile, deleting yet more messages from journalists and worrying about Jake.

'Don't worry,' Tahlia told her, 'this will blow over in a day. It's got to, they've not got anything else to print, it's all lies.'

But Crystal didn't feel reassured and knew she couldn't be until she'd spoken to Jake. But at seven when she tried him she just got his voice mail. She left an urgent message for him to call her, but two hours later there was still no reply. She called his office but they said he was on a shoot and could only be contacted on his mobile – if only he'd turn it on.

She tried him throughout the day, with a rising feeling of panic but she kept getting his voice mail. Tahlia did her best to try and distract her, suggesting that they made a list of all the equipment and clothes she would need for the baby and check out some baby sites online. Crystal was grateful to her friend but she was unable to concentrate on anything, and when Tahlia asked what kind of buggy she wanted Crystal could only look at her blankly, while unanswered questions were flying around her mind. *Why wasn't he returning her calls? Had a journalist already got hold of him, poisoning him with their lies?* At three, Tahlia went to pick up Leticia from school and take her to ballet class and Crystal spent a miserable three hours on her own, pacing round Tahlia's lovely house and willing Jake to call. A day had never gone by so slowly. When Leticia and Tahlia returned Crystal did her best to put on an act, pretending to be enthralled by the ballet moves Leticia insisted on showing her.

Somehow she got through the evening but there was no word from Jake and it wasn't until midnight that she finally got hold of him. Instantly she knew something was very wrong. He didn't sound pleased to hear from her, nor did he explain why he hadn't returned her calls.

'I need to talk to you because of this stupid story the press has made up about me,' she gabbled.

'You mean the story about your affair with Jim? Oh, I've read all about it, I've even seen the pictures. Stella emailed me.'

'It's bullshit, you do know that, don't you?' she went on frantically. *Why was he being so cold?* 'Anyway, I'm flying out to New York tomorrow; I *really* need to see you.'

She waited for Jake's reply but there was a long pause before he spoke. 'Actually, Crystal, this is a really bad time for me.'

'What do you mean?' she exclaimed, on the verge of tears.

'I think I need some space. I thought I could

434

handle the whole long-distance relationship thing but I can't.'

'But you're the one who said it would be good!' she protested. 'I didn't want you to go.'

'Well, you didn't try and stop me, did you?' he retaliated. 'I keep imagining what you're up to and it's doing my head in.'

'I'm not up to anything, Jake. That story about Jim and me is all lies, you know that, don't you? Please say you do.' She was crying now.

Jake sighed. 'Yeah, I know it probably is, but when I saw those pictures of the two of you together, I don't know . . . you can't deny you're close to him.'

'But not in that way, for fucksake! He's married; he's my friend, that's all.'

It was like history repeating itself. Crystal remembered only too well the tone of Jake's voice when he finished with her last time and, just like then, he sounded cold and distant, like a man who had already made up his mind.

'Please, Jake,' she sobbed, 'let me come and see you. We can work this out, I know we can.'

'I don't think we can. I know myself too well. Take care and good luck with the album. I'm sure you're going to be a star.' His words sounded so final.

She was about to beg him to change his mind, but he'd already hung up.

Last time they'd broken up she'd tried to numb

435

the pain with alcohol. At sixteen weeks pregnant, she didn't have that option. She curled up on the bed sobbing, huge sobs that wracked her body. 'Sorry, baby,' she said through her tears. 'Sorry for crying like this. Sorry you haven't got a daddy.'

Chapter 21

I Will Survive

Much as Crystal wanted to lose herself in her grief over Jake, she couldn't. She had a baby to think of and after crying for two days, somehow she found the strength to pull herself together, for his sake. She got dressed, forced herself to eat and went to the studio. She told everyone she was fine when her pale face and red, bleary eyes told a different story. But while she felt as if her heart was breaking, she realised that she wouldn't have to face life as a single mum on her own. She finally told Luke and he was over the moon, promising that he would help her in whatever way he could. He wanted her to move down to Brighton but Crystal wasn't ready to leave London yet. It was her home, it was Jake's home too and, as irrational as it seemed, as long as she was there it felt like that was a connection between them. She didn't want to turn her back on the city. Tahlia promised to come to the antenatal classes with her and offered to be her birthing partner. And she told Jez and Danni her big news too when they met up at Tahlia's for a barbeque.

'I've got something to tell you,' she told them, as they sat in Tahlia's garden. She was expecting Jez to be his usual over-the-top self and start speculating wildly about what it could be. Instead he was subdued and said quietly, 'Please tell us then.'

'I'm surprised you haven't guessed by now,' she replied, looking down at the bump, which she'd given up trying to disguise. 'I'm pregnant!'

'Crystal, that's wonderful!' Danni said, straightaway getting up and giving her a hug.

Crystal looked over expectantly at Jez and was surprised to see that he had tears in his eyes. 'It's not that bad, Jez! I'm still the same person; I'm not going to turn into one of those women who can only talk about their children, and I promise I'll never wear ugly shoes and floral dresses.'

'It's not that,' Jez answered. 'I'm just so relieved. I thought you were ill. I thought you might have,' he lowered his voice and whispered, 'cancer.'

'Jez!' Crystal exclaimed. 'Why the hell did you think that?'

'Well, you stopped going out, stopped drinking. Every time I called you, you were in bed, and I just assumed the worst. It never occurred to me that you might be pregnant.'

Crystal studied his face, checking he wasn't taking the piss, but he looked serious. 'I'm so sorry

that you thought that, babe. But you're stuck with
me a bit longer – me and my baby.'

'Thank God!' he exclaimed, leaping up from his
chair and rushing over to embrace her. And now
the Jez she knew and loved kicked in. 'I'm going to
be an uncle! I'm seeing a spring christening – you
and the baby dressed in white and silver, lots of
gorgeous *petit cadeaux* for the little *bébé*, champagne
and a white chocolate christening cake in the shape
of a cherub.' He paused. 'Or would it be weirdly
cannibalistic to eat cake in the shape of a baby; oh,
you could always have a swan or something.'

'Don't you mean a stork?' Crystal asked, smiling
at him. 'And don't you think it might be odd to have
a christening when I'm not sure I believe in God.'

'*Dahling*, you don't seriously think people get
their child christened because they believe in God!
I bet you the majority do it for the presents and the
party and in your case it would be a great magazine
photo opportunity.'

'When you've finished, Jez, do you think you
could open the champagne?' Tahlia finally
managed to get a word in.

For the first time in her pregnancy Crystal
allowed herself a glass of champagne to celebrate
with her friends. And as they sat chatting in the
warm September sunshine she thought, *My baby
might not have a dad but I've got all these people who love
me and who'll love him. We're not on our own. I think
we're going to be okay.*

439

*

Once she'd told Jez and Danni she knew that she would have to come clean with Sadie. She was dreading it, despite Jim's reassurance that Sadie would be happy for her. After agonising about when to do it, she finally blurted out her news when she and Sadie were going through the publicity schedule in her office. Sadie's office totally reflected her personality – it was like a cosy boudoir, red velvet curtains hung at the windows, thick purple sheepskin rugs were scattered over the floor, Jo Malone candles burned, filling the room with the fragrance of tuberose and, while Sadie had a beautiful antique desk, she conducted most of her meetings lounging on an enormous zebra-print sofa, using her laptop. She was clicking away at it now.

'So, Crystal, once the first single is out and doing well, as it's sure to, we'll leave it a month and then reveal you're Pearl. I thought maybe we should do it live on air, say on Radio 1. What do you reckon?'

'I'm pregnant,' Crystal replied.

'I know,' Sadie answered, smiling and looking up from her laptop. She didn't seem at all surprised. 'I wondered when you were going to tell me.'

She laughed at the look of shock on Crystal's face and said, 'Honey, it doesn't take Einstein to work it out. You're a size eight usually and you've blossomed quite a bit, haven't you? And you've gone from wearing mini skirts all the time to tunics and leggings. And I even saw you in a poncho last week. I can't remember the last time I saw you have a drink. You may as well have hung a sign round your neck saying *I'm pregnant.*'

'Are you really pissed off with me?' Crystal asked tentatively. 'I know the timing's bad.'

At that Sadie put down her laptop and leaned across the sofa to hug Crystal.

Then she looked at her, and Crystal was touched to see that she had tears in her eyes. 'I'm really happy for you; a baby is a blessing and there's never a right time. We can work round it; it just means we'll release the single earlier. Even pop stars have babies. Jake must be so thrilled.'

At that Crystal's own eyes filled with tears. 'He doesn't know, Sadie. It's over between us. He doesn't love me.'

'Oh come on!' Sadie exclaimed. 'Sure he does. I've seen the two of you together, he *adores* you.'

Crystal shook her head and even though Sadie continued to protest that Jake loved her, eventually, in the face of Crystal's resistance, she stopped.

'Well, we'll see, but you'll be okay, Crystal. My husband left when our girls were three and one and at first I thought I'd never be able to cope as a single parent. But I did and so will you and you'll be a wonderful mother.'

*

Sadie was true to her word and fast-tracked the release of the single. It went straight to number one. The interest had been steadily building while it was only available on MySpace and once it was released it reached fever pitch. Everyone wanted to know the identity of Pearl – the woman with the beautiful, soulful voice. While Sadie had always insisted that the song would be a hit, in her heart Crystal had never really believed her but now practically every time she switched on the radio she heard *her* song – 'U Can't Break Me'. She was amazed at her success but it didn't mean what she thought it would mean. She had always imagined that if she made it as a solo artist she would feel that she had achieved all her ambitions and she would feel fulfilled, but she found it wasn't enough. She longed for Jake with all her heart, with every part of her being. He completed her and without him she felt an emptiness inside that the success could not fill . . .

'I feel sick,' Crystal groaned as Danni applied the finishing touches to her make-up. She was about to go on air and reveal her true identity at last and was crippled with nerves. 'And I look terrible! Nothing to do with your make-up, Danni,' she quickly added. She hadn't even wanted to be made up for the interview but Sadie had pointed out that there was bound to be press waiting outside the Radio 1 building once the world found out that

Crystal was Pearl. So Crystal had dutifully made an effort, putting on a black and silver wrap dress, black leggings and silver pumps. She thought she looked like the most enormous pregnant woman ever.

'You look blooming,' Danni told her.

'I need to look sexy and sharp,' Crystal groaned. 'Who is going to want to buy a record by a great fat porker like me?'

'You're not fat, you're pregnant!' Danni and Jez chorused back – they had to say it to Crystal at least five times a day. 'And,' Jez added, 'your video is seriously steamy. People are going to be too busy lusting after you in that to think about you being pregnant.'

Crystal gave a small smile, but it hurt to think of the video, to think about Jake directing her, to remember how happy she'd been back then . . .

'How's my girl?' Sadie asked, breezing into the room. In honour of Crystal's big day, she'd swapped her usual skin-tight jeans and T-shirt combo for an Yves Saint Laurent black trouser suit and put on some of her bling – a dazzling diamond cross pendant, and a seriously huge sapphire ring.

'God, Sadie, I hope we don't get car-jacked because of you!' Crystal joked.

Sadie shrugged. 'Well, I thought it was a day for flaunting it, and I've a little present for you.' She handed Crystal a velvet pouch in the distinctive Tiffany pale blue, which she opened to reveal a

443

stunning platinum and diamond Tiffany heart necklace.

'Wow,' Crystal exclaimed. 'Thank you so much, it's beautiful.'

'I thought you deserved to wear something special today – jewels for Pearl,' Sadie replied, fastening the necklace round Crystal's neck.

Sadie had booked extra bodyguards who were all built like tanks to help smuggle Crystal into the building unobserved. Crystal also had to put on dark glasses, a floor-length coat and, to Jez's horror, a long blonde wig.

'Do you know how long I spent blow drying her hair this morning?' he said huffily.

'Relax, Jez, she's only wearing the wig for a few minutes. I'm sure her hair will look perfect,' Sadie assured him.

Sadie's plan worked perfectly and Crystal got into the building and into the studio without anyone recognising her. Now there was just the interview to get through . . .

Damon Williams, the DJ, had no idea that Pearl was Crystal either. When Sadie had set up the interview, she hadn't told anyone. His surprise made for great radio. Once they started chatting, Crystal's nerves left her. She was here because she wanted to make a success of her music and it wasn't just for her, it was for her baby, a fact that Damon was quick to pick up on.

'So it's going to be Crystal plus one soon?' he

asked halfway through the interview, having already played several tracks from the album and raved about them.

'It is,' Crystal answered, her heart sinking because she really didn't want to give anything away. Damon wanted a lot more detail than that and asked about the father, mentioning Jake's name, but Crystal firmly but politely declined to reveal the father's identity or even when the baby was due, and he was forced to change the subject. The minute she left the building the cameras went off all around her and the press were everywhere, calling out her name, demanding a comment. But for the first time in what seemed like ages the questions didn't seem hostile and Crystal held her head high and posed away for the cameras.

The next few weeks were a whirlwind of interviews and photo shoots. The media couldn't get enough of Crystal; she was on the cover of every magazine, she appeared on chat shows, music shows, kids' TV shows. Sadie kept checking that the schedule wasn't too much for her, but the truth was, she wanted to be busy. She didn't want to have time to think, because when she was alone that's when the sadness caught up with her, that's when the thought of being a single mother, of a future without Jake, almost seemed too much. She knew that Tahlia and Sadie had coped, but it wasn't what she would have chosen. She wanted her baby to have a dad. She kept remembering her own

445

childhood – of how much she had missed her father when he left. Was that how her child would feel? Would he have the same sense of loss that Crystal had had or would he feel even worse because he didn't even know his dad? And what would she tell him about Jake? Maybe, in spite of everything she had thought, in spite of her fears that he might end up staying with her because he felt he had to, she had a duty to tell Jake – not for her and not for him, but for the baby. She spent a week agonising about what to do. Every night when she lay in bed, she would pick up her mobile, select Jake's number and be on the verge of calling him, and every night she would come up with a reason not to. But by Friday she decided that, whatever her reservations, she would make the call.

Tahlia and Jez were both round her flat that evening. Jez had taken to coming over at least once a week to cook supper for her. At first Crystal had told him that she was perfectly capable of doing it herself, but Jez wouldn't take no for an answer. 'This baby cannot flourish on a diet of baked potatoes. You need more protein; I've been checking the baby book,' he declared. So Crystal gave in. It was lovely having home-cooked food – she was tired of eating out, bored of ready meals, which were all she could manage to shove in the microwave in the evening when she returned home. And it felt good being looked after.

The three of them were chilling in the lounge

while Jez's fish pie – his finest yet, he boasted – was cooking. Tahlia and Crystal were chatting while Jez flipped through a copy of *Grazia* magazine and commented on the different styles and fashions he came across, delivering damning verdicts on many of the celebs he saw – 'Frocky horror show!' and 'I wouldn't go to the corner shop to buy a pint of milk looking like *that*' were just two of his favourite put-downs.

'God, I hope we'll always be friends,' Crystal joked. 'Because there is nothing crueller than a gay fashionista passing judgement.'

But Jez didn't appear to have heard her; he looked shocked, muttered 'shit' and then shut the magazine.

'What's the matter Jez?' Tahlia asked. 'Did you see someone wearing last season's colours?'

'No, no, it was nothing,' Jez replied, but he looked uncomfortable.

'Jez, you are the worst liar,' Crystal said, grabbing the magazine from him.

'It was nothing,' Jez insisted, trying to wrestle it back from her. 'Come on, I think dinner's nearly ready.' But by now Crystal's curiosity was aroused and, ignoring Jez, she began flipping through the pages.

'Please don't,' Jez said quietly. But it was too late. Crystal had found the page. It was coverage of an exclusive masked ball in New York for a leading designer. There were photos of various A list actors and supermodels. But it was one supermodel in particular who held her gaze, or rather the person she was with, because on the arm of Phoebe, the stunning Australian model, was Jake. Feeling as if she'd been punched, she read the captain underneath – *'Has Phoebe got a new man? The gorgeous and talented Jake Fox? The two were inseparable at the ball.'*

'It doesn't mean anything,' Jez said quickly. 'They're just friends.'

'They don't look like friends,' Crystal said numbly. 'Look at him smiling and the way they're standing so close.'

'Pictures can be misleading,' Tahlia told her gently. 'You know that – look at how Jake got the wrong idea about you and Jim.'

Crystal shook her head and said miserably, 'Thanks for trying, but I think they're probably together.'

Tahlia and Jez carried on trying to reassure her, but all Crystal could think was that Jake was lost to her forever. He had obviously moved on. *How stupid to think I could tell him about the baby and that we might be together again.* It had been a fantasy, nothing more.

'The first stage of labour is when the cervix opens out fully or dilates to let the baby's head pass through,' the midwife explained, holding up a rather battered looking toy baby and what Crystal had initially taken to be a scarf, but now seemed to be a uterus and birth canal, made out of knitted pink wool, *Were NHS cuts that bad that they couldn't afford a model?* 'The cervix is fully dilated when it's approximately ten centimetres in diameter,' the midwife continued, holding up the pink woolly uterus to demonstrate what ten centimetres looked like. *And this was just the first stage?* Crystal looked at Tahlia, and whispered, 'Bloody hell, I don't like the sound of that!' It was her first antenatal class and she'd been dreading it, thinking that she'd be the only one without a partner, but there were two other women in the same position – one of whom was there all by herself – so Crystal counted herself lucky to have Tahlia.

'That's nothing,' a woman sitting next to her said grimly. 'You wait till she starts talking about the second stage when you have to push that baby out. And you don't even want to know about episiotomies.'

'What's that?' Crystal asked nervously.

'That's when they cut you down below to deliver the baby,' the woman replied. 'A friend of mine had to have one, never the same again.'

Oh God. Crystal had been so preoccupied with Jake that she hadn't given the birth much thought, but now she was feeling very apprehensive.

The midwife caught the mood and said, 'I know it seems scary but the thing to remember is this is just a day in your life, hopefully less than a day, and at the end of it you'll have your baby.'

She beamed at the group, still holding up the knitted uterus, with the baby bulging inside it. Crystal made a mental note to get rid of the pink scarf she had at home; she didn't think she'd ever be able to wear it again.

'Don't you think it might be better to have a Caesarean?' Crystal whispered to Tahlia.

'No, I do not!' Tahlia said sternly. 'You should only have one if there is a good medical reason. It takes longer to recover from a C-section.' Tahlia's aunt was a midwife and Tahlia had a very firm grasp of the subject. In fact, she was a bit of a hardliner when it came to natural versus Caesarean births.

'Anyway, you're not too posh to push. If I can do it, so can you.'

'Yeah, but what about my pelvic floor,' Crystal groaned. 'What kind of state is it going to be in after I've pushed an eight-pound baby out? Wouldn't a Caesarean keep it – what's that expression – honeymoon fresh?'

Tahlia softened. 'Well, I can't pretend it won't be different but if you do your exercises, then it does tighten up again.'

'I know you think I'm being really superficial – and the most important thing to me is that my baby is okay – but maybe one day I will want to have sex again and all I'm saying is that I don't want a vag like a multistorey car park.'

Tahlia was about to reply when, to Crystal's

450

horror, the midwife asked what was concerning her. Crystal was all set to answer that everything was fine when Tahlia said, 'We were just talking about what your vagina is like after childbirth and about what sex is like once you've had a baby.'

Crystal looked at Tahlia in disbelief; her friend was usually so modest about such things.

'Well, that's a really good subject for us to talk about,' said the midwife enthusiastically. 'But as we're running out of time, we'll have to cover it in our next session.'

'Yeah, right,' muttered the woman next to Crystal. 'They're never going to let on what really happens – it's a total conspiracy of silence, mark my words.'

Crystal smiled nervously. *God, this childbirth stuff was scary.*

As Crystal and Tahlia waited for a taxi Crystal said, 'I can't believe you Tahlia! You said vagina in public!"

'Well, I think it was important. You saw how much everyone wanted to know about sex after childbirth. I was doing a public service,' she replied.

'You go, girlfriend,' Crystal replied, relieved now more than ever that Tahlia had promised to be her birthing partner. 'Come on, I'll buy you a hot chocolate as a reward for saying vagina in front of twenty people. I can't wait to hear what you're going to come out with next week.'

451

Crystal

*

Very suddenly, or so it seemed to Crystal, who felt as if time was on fast forward, it was December and her baby was due on the 28th. She had decided not to find out whether she was having a boy or girl, but was convinced that she was having a boy. She was too heavily pregnant to work any more. She had wanted to keep singing but the baby made that difficult because of the way he was lying across her diaphragm, but she had the satisfaction of her album still being in the top ten. The days could feel lonely. She tried to keep busy by shopping for baby things but it was a real effort – and instead of walking she was reduced to waddling slowly everywhere. Plus she hated going into baby shops where every other pregnant woman seemed to have a partner with her. She felt like there was a big arrow pointing down at her saying 'Single Mum, Failed Relationship'. She would meet friends for lunch; go to antenatal yoga and antenatal aqua classes. Tahlia kept nagging her to ring up some of the women from the antenatal group and meet up for coffee, but Crystal was reluctant. She didn't want to explain to a stranger why there was no man in her life.

Gavin had gone travelling for six months with Lara so she couldn't check whether or not Jake was with Phoebe, and she hardly wanted to phone Jake's parents. She found that her world suddenly contracted to just her, the baby and her closest friends. She spent her evenings curled up by the fire watching DVDs with Jez, Danni and Tahlia. Luke and Ruby came up for a weekend and took her shopping to buy the cot and the buggy – tasks that she'd put off for so long. She very nearly had everything ready for the baby.

'I think we should have a baby shower,' Jez declared on one of his visits. 'There hasn't been enough celebrating around this baby.'

Crystal groaned. 'I don't think so, Jez.'

'No, I insist – I'll sort out the food and the drink – all you need to do is decide who to invite.' Once he had set his mind on something, Jez was pretty much unstoppable. And so, two weeks before her due date, Crystal found herself at her own baby shower. Jez had ordered her out of the house while he and Rufus got to work. When she returned several hours later, she couldn't believe the transformation. Jez had bought a huge Christmas tree which they'd decorated with white and silver ribbons and feathers, icicles and cherubs – Crystal hadn't felt like buying a tree just for herself – they'd hung up silver streamers and balloons with a picture of a pregnant Crystal printed on them – she wasn't quite so keen on those as the shape of the balloon made her look huge – and they'd put scented candles on the mantelpiece, lit the fire and hung fairy lights all around the room.

Crystal was touched by the effort they'd gone to. 'It looks fab,' she said, hugging Jez and Rufus, or rather attempting a hug because her huge bump made that kind of contact impossible.

'And we've got baby quiches, smoked salmon, canapés and chunky chips,' Jez went on.

'That sounds divine, but do you know, even though I look the size of a house, I can't eat that much any more,' Crystal moaned. 'I get terrible indigestion, just another horrible side-effect of pregnancy.'

'Well, you've got to eat something. Rufus and I slaved over these for hours. I had to miss spinning to get them done.'

An hour later the guests had arrived and the conversation and champagne were flowing.

'Crystal, will you open the presents now?' Leticia said, twirling round in her pink velvet party dress.

'I will if you help me,' Crystal said, not really wanting to be the centre of attention. Leticia was only too happy to help, and gleefully ripped off wrapping paper to reveal cute cuddly toys, sweet baby blankets, a mobile, Babygros, a music box and, last but not least, a sex toy. Crystal was surprised to find Jez's present was a pink vibrator, complete with marabou feather trim and a gold stand.

'Yes, it's called a Minx,' he said knowledgeably – 'the ultimate chic pleasure maker.'

'This isn't a very baby-shower-type of present, is it?'

'Well, I was thinking of mama. Look, it's got all those different speeds.'

'Okay, Jez,' Crystal said, hastily shoving it back in its box, away from the curious eyes of Leticia.

'And that's not all,' Jez said meaningfully, checking his watch. He was rewarded by the door-bell ringing. 'I'll get that,' he said leaping from his seat and rushing to the door. He returned with a young, extremely good-looking uniformed police officer in tow. Well, he was dressed as one, but frankly everything from his fake-bake tan to his super-buff body screamed stripper.

'Crystal, this officer says he needs to talk to you urgently,' Jez said, his mouth twitching.

'Oh really?' Crystal replied, thinking that Jez really was the worst liar in the world.

'Yes, miss,' the young man replied. 'I hear you've been a very naughty girl.'

'Well, before you get started, can children please be allowed to leave the room?' Crystal asked.

Smiling Tahlia stood up and coaxed her daughter out of the room with the promise of chocolate cake, followed by Jim and his daughter Mia. As soon as the door was safely shut, Jez turned up the music and Crystal said, 'Okay, officer, show me what you've got.' And to whoops of delight from the guests the stripper whipped off his helmet, tore off his jacket, pulled off his trousers, posed for a while in an indecently small gold G-string – the contents of which had Jez nailed to the spot – before slipping that off, and giving everyone quite an eyeful . . .

Crystal hadn't laughed so much in ages. Maybe it hadn't been the most traditional baby shower but she had loved every minute of it. After the stripper had gathered up his things and gone, Jez insisted that everyone fill up their glasses for a toast to Crystal.

'She's gorgeous, we all love her to bits, and I know she's panicking like mad, but she is going to be a fab mum.' He raised his glass and said, 'To Crystal', and everyone raised theirs and echoed, 'To Crystal.'

Crystal was too overcome with emotion to make much of a speech in reply but she managed a thank you. 'And now, will everyone please stop making me cry!'

After the guests had gone she put the baby presents away, pausing to put on the musical mobile which played 'Twinkle, Twinkle Little Star', and the baby who had been sleeping during the shower woke up and started moving around. Crystal put her hand on her belly – as an arm or perhaps a leg moved against her. 'Not long now,' Crystal whispered, 'I can't wait to meet you and I *hope* I am going to be a good mum. I know I'll love you, because I love you now, little one, so very much.'

Chapter 22

You've Got the Love . . .

At just two weeks before her due date, Tahlia insisted that Crystal come and stay with her. At first Crystal refused, saying that she was fine on her own, but one night when her Braxton Hicks contractions were stronger than usual and she thought she might be going into labour she panicked and called Tahlia. And when the offer was repeated, Crystal decided to take it up. She had tried to put on a brave face and said she could cope on her own, but inside she was terrified – not just of the birth but also of afterwards, of being a mum. Would she know what to do? It's not like her own mum had been much of a role model. All she had done was set an example of everything Crystal did *not* want to be as a mother.

'We're all going to help you, Crystal,' Rosie told her on her first night at Tahlia's. 'You mustn't think you're alone.'

Crystal couldn't help comparing Rosie's attitude

with that of her own mother's. When she'd told her about the baby, her reaction had been typically negative, 'I would have thought you'd have wanted to concentrate on your singing career,' she said. 'It's not going to be easy having a baby as well. Especially as you're going to be a single mother, and I should know,' she added bitterly. Crystal obviously couldn't expect any support from her, not that she'd want it.

After Tahlia and Rosie had gone to bed, Crystal stayed downstairs a little longer, staring into the dying embers of the fire and wondering where Jake was and what he was doing. Was he still in the States or back in London? Was he with his new girlfriend? Maybe he'd taken her away to the country cottage that he'd promised to take Crystal to. Maybe they were lying by the fire making love . . . For the past few months she'd tried so hard to suppress her feelings for him, to tell herself that she was over him, that if he didn't love her then he wasn't worth her love, but suddenly the pain she felt at losing him felt as raw as it ever had. And she knew that she loved him still. The baby kicked and she found herself whispering, 'I wish your daddy was here.'

But being with Tahlia and her family reassured her, made her feel less afraid of the future, and for a change Crystal was the one cheering up Tahlia. Hadley couldn't spend Christmas with her, as his

mum was ill, which had bitterly disappointed
Tahlia. Crystal had been relying on Tahlia for so
long that it felt good to look out for her friend. She
also got caught up in the Christmas preparations.
She went to see Leticia in her Nativity play, where,
to Tahlia's pride, she had the starring role as the
Virgin Mary. She bought presents and helped to
decorate the house, or rather watch Leticia do it.
Tahlia had given Leticia a free hand to do what she
wanted and the result was a living room that looked
like Santa's grotto – an enormous Christmas tree
dominated the room, with fairy lights changing
colour every few seconds and every branch laden
with tinsel, glittery stars, angels, reindeers and
baubles – seven-year-old girls clearly did not do
minimalist. Giant silver and gold stars were hung
from the ceiling and snowmen and snowflakes had
been sprayed on to the window in fake snow.
Outside Leticia insisted that the two trees in the
front garden were decorated with flashing fairy
lights and there was an inflatable Father Christmas,
sleigh and reindeer in the porch. 'This is
Hampstead!' Tahlia said in mock horror to Crystal.
'People are going to think we're so common!'

'Let them. Look how happy Leticia is,' Crystal
replied, thinking that her pregnancy hormones
were definitely affecting her as usually she would
have agreed with Tahlia. In fact, she would have
been the first to point it out.

*

On Christmas Eve Crystal thought she'd better drop in at her flat, check it was okay and pick up any post.

'I just can't believe that this time next year I'll have a one-year-old,' she said to Tahlia as her friend drove them across London.

'Never mind a year! In less than a week you'll have a baby!' Tahlia exclaimed.

'Wow! he heard you!' Crystal touched her belly where the baby had just delivered a powerful kick.

'You know that you can stay at mine as long as you want when you've had the baby,' Tahlia told her.

Crystal smiled, 'Thanks, but you've got Leticia and Hadley to think of and we've got to learn how to be on our own, haven't we?'

Crystal had a large pile of post waiting for her outside her flat door. Tahlia picked it up for her and carried it into the flat. It was cold inside and Crystal shivered as she walked into the living room. She sat down on the sofa and went through her post, then froze as she came across a large flat parcel.

'Oh my God, this is Jake's handwriting,' she exclaimed, staring at the parcel.

'Open it then!' Tahlia ordered.

Crystal ripped off the paper to reveal a book of photographs. Her heart suddenly felt as if it was beating faster as she gazed at the cover – a black and white picture of herself. She was kneeling up in bed, naked except for the white sheet she was clutching, her hair wild and tumbling down her back, laughing at the camera. She remembered Jake taking it, how she'd begged him not to, saying that she needed to put on some make-up, but he'd taken it anyway and afterwards when he'd printed it he said that it was his favourite picture of her. Wondering what this must mean, she opened the book. Inside there was a message written by Jake, in his bold handwriting – *For my beautiful Crystal, yours forever Jake x*

'Oh, my God!' she said again. Then she started urgently flicking through the pages, amazed to see that every single photograph was of her – from the moment they met at the first video shoot, to the week before Jake went to New York when they'd gone out for a picnic and it had taken all her willpower not to beg him not to go. The final photograph was of the pair of them together – one of the very few pictures, as Jake hated being photographed. They'd gone down to Brighton for the day to see Luke and Ruby; Luke had taken the picture of them as they sat on the beach, arms round each other, drinking beer. Underneath Jake had written – *You and me – how about it? I can't believe it's taken me so long to say it but I love you, I always have done, and I always will. You mean everything to me. Do I still have a chance? Call me. Jx*

'He loves you!' Tahlia said happily. 'I knew he did! And the book is like a love letter to you. He's loved you all this time.'

461

'But when did he post it?' Crystal checked the postmark. 'Two weeks ago! He must be wondering why the hell I haven't called him. He's going to think I don't love him.' It was too cruel a twist of fate.

'Call him now!' Tahlia urged her and Crystal scrambled through her bag for her phone. But when she called him he was on voice mail. 'It's Crystal; I've only just got the book.' She paused; finally she could tell him how she felt. 'I love you too, Jake. Will you call me, please, it's urgent.'

'He could be anywhere,' she said despairingly, getting up from the sofa, because she couldn't bear to sit still. 'He could have gone back to the States for all I know, because he hasn't heard from me.'

'You don't know that,' Tahlia tried to reassure her. 'He'll call. He loves you!'

Jake loved her! He'd said it at last, it was what she'd longed for all these long, lonely months, when she thought she had lost him, but where was he? Suddenly Crystal was seized by a powerful contraction that left her gasping for breath. 'Tahlia! I think I'm going into labour!'

'Okay,' Tahlia replied calmly, 'remember the breathing: breathe in through your nose and let it out slowly as the contraction goes.'

'I've got to tell Jake about the baby!' Crystal cried. 'I want him here, he's got to be here.'

'Calm down, babe, you mustn't get too emotional.'

Crystal wanted to shout that of course she felt emotional. Her world had just been turned upside down!

'I'll run you a bath, it'll help with the contractions,' Tahlia said. 'And I'll call the hospital.'

Crystal tried Jake again, but he was still on voice mail.

She lay in the bath for forty minutes, fretting about Jake – what if he didn't have his mobile with him? What if he had left the country? After all these months when she thought he was out of her life, and she had resigned herself to having the baby without him, now she wanted him with her, wanted it more than anything. She didn't think about how he would react to the news; all she knew was that he had to be by her side when their baby was born.

But he didn't call back and when she got out of the bath the contractions were coming more frequently and were becoming more powerful. 'Bloody hell!' she exclaimed. 'This really hurts; they don't get worse than this, do they?' she asked Tahlia anxiously, suddenly feeling frightened and overwhelmed at the prospect of what was to come.

Tahlia avoided answering the question, saying instead, 'You'll be fine, babe. I'll just time them and if they're three minutes apart we'd better get to the hospital.'

At that moment Crystal felt warm liquid trickling down her leg. 'Oh my God, I'm not bleeding, am I?'

'No, no,' Tahlia reassured her, 'it's just your

waters breaking. That's good, you won't need them broken by the midwife, but I think we should definitely get you to the hospital now.'

Crystal insisted on calling Jake while they waited for a taxi, but he was on voice mail still. She was going to have to leave a message about the baby. She hadn't wanted to tell him like this, but time was running out. 'It's Crystal again. I know this is going to come as a shock but I'm in labour. I'm having our baby, Jake. I'm going to be at St Mary's Hospital. Please, please, can you get here.'

'I'll phone Gavin,' Tahlia offered. 'He's bound to know where he is.'

'He's travelling!' Crystal exclaimed, feeling more and more desperate.

'She's not going to give birth in here, is she? I've just had it valeted,' the cabbie joked as he drove Crystal and Tahlia to the hospital.

'No,' Tahlia answered, rolling her eyes. Crystal couldn't speak. She was suddenly gripped by a contraction and this time the pain was appalling.

'Remember the breathing,' Tahlia urged her, as Crystal felt overwhelmed with agony.

'Try Jake again,' she panted, when the pain had passed. But Tahlia just got his voice mail again.

'Will that man ever learn to switch on his bloody phone?' Crystal cried in exasperation and desperation. 'He might be at his parents. I haven't got their number but can you get it, *please*.'

Tahlia got the number just as they arrived at the hospital.

'Babe, let's get you in first and then I'll call.'

Tahlia booked her into the maternity suite, helped her change into a large white shirt and then went outside to make the call. 'Don't be long,' Crystal called after her, fearful of being left on her own. The midwife was lovely and calm. 'You're dilating really well,' she told Crystal after examining her.

'The baby's not going to come right now, is he?'

The midwife smiled. 'No, I think it will be a while yet.'

'Good,' Crystal replied and adding when she saw how surprised the midwife looked, 'it's complicated, but I want the dad to get here in time.'

'I'm sure he will,' the midwife replied soothingly.

Just then Tahlia walked back into the room.

'Well?' Crystal demanded.

'I'm really sorry, babe, there was no one there. I left a message.'

'They must be away!' Crystal said, her heart sinking. 'He's not going to make it here, is he?' And she couldn't stop the tears from sliding down her face.

Tahlia held her hand, and said, 'Okay, you need to tell me the names of all Jake's friends and then I'm going outside to call them. Someone will know where he is.'

'But it's Christmas Eve; everyone will be away,'

Crystal said miserably. 'And you should be with Leticia.'

'I'm not leaving you, babe. I'll make these calls and I'll be right back.'

Tahlia was gone for the next half hour, leaving Crystal feeling increasingly frightened as the contractions grew more powerful. She paced round the room, trying to find positions in which to cope with the pain, willing Jake to come, and willing the baby to wait. Finally, Tahlia returned but she still hadn't managed to track Jake down.

'I'm really sorry, babe. I've tried everyone you mentioned but none of them know where he is.'

'Oh no!' Crystal sobbed, feeling totally defeated.

'Come on, you've got to forget about Jake and concentrate on the baby now,' Tahlia said, seeing that her friend needed to pull herself together and save her energy for labour. Crystal was about to protest that she couldn't forget Jake when the contractions went up a gear painwise and she couldn't speak. Her survival instinct kicked in and it was just about getting through the pain. Tahlia was brilliant with her, encouraging when she needed to be, stern when she felt Crystal wasn't breathing properly. Crystal had foolishly said in her birth plan that she didn't want any drugs – she had been inspired by Tahlia who had given birth using just gas and air – but after four hours of sheer agony she had forgotten all about her birth plan and was screaming for an epidural. She lost all track of time; the pain just seemed to be going on and on. In between contractions she obsessed about Jake, wondering if he had got her message, worrying that it might freak him out and that she might never see him again.

And then suddenly she remembered that there was someone else they should call. 'Simon, his friend, I totally forgot about him,' she gasped. 'Call Simon, he might know.'

Tahlia really didn't want to leave Crystal but she insisted. She returned with some good and some not so good news. Simon told her that Jake was staying in a cottage on the Sussex Downs. There was no phone and no mobile signal so there was no way of getting hold of Jake, but when Tahlia explained the urgency of the situation he offered to drive there and pick Jake up and bring him to the hospital – it would be a three-hour round trip. Even if Simon found Jake it really looked like they wouldn't get back to London in time.

Tahlia squeezed her hand. 'I'm sorry, babe.'

Crystal felt too emotional to reply. The anaesthetist had just given her the epidural which, thank God, had temporarily stopped the pain of the contractions. She closed her eyes, full of regret that Jake was going to miss out on the birth of his child. It was all her fault; she should have told him months ago. She closed her eyes and must have drifted off into an exhausted sleep.

She didn't know how long she slept but suddenly

she became aware of someone standing by the bed. She opened her eyes and, for a second, thought she must be dreaming, because there was Jake.

'Hey, how are you?' he asked, the same handsome Jake with those blue eyes that melted her heart.

'Is it really you?' Crystal asked, overcome with emotion at seeing him again.

By way of an answer he leant down and kissed her and took her hand in his, whispering, 'It's really me. Is that really you?'

'I should have told you,' Crystal replied, gazing into his eyes. 'I'm sorry, Jake.'

'No, I'm the one who's sorry; I didn't give you the chance to tell me.'

'Do you mind about the baby?' she asked apprehensively.

'Mind?' he exclaimed. 'I think it's the most wonderful thing ever! I was a fool to push you away; I can't believe you've had to go through all this on your own. I love you, Crystal.' She looked into his beautiful blue eyes and they were full of tears.

Finally he had said the words that she had feared he never would. 'I love you too,' she whispered back. But by now the epidural was wearing off and the pain was starting up again. She winced and tried to carry on speaking but Jake said, 'Don't talk now.'

When the contraction finished, Crystal whispered, 'Please don't leave me.'

Jake shook his head, and said seriously, 'I'm yours, Crystal, you have me for keeps.'

'Okay, Crystal, I need you to push now,' the midwife ordered her. 'Come on, Crystal, push!'

'I am fucking pushing!' Crystal screeched back, past caring that she sounded like a fishwife.

'You can do it, Crystal!' Jake told her. Crystal gripped his hand as hard as she could, she just wanted to get her baby out! The midwife was praising her.

'You're doing really well, Crystal. I can see the baby's head, it's just going to take two more pushes. Just two more, *come on*!

Using what felt like the last of her strength Crystal pushed with all her might, experiencing an excruciating, burning pain that was almost as bad as what had gone before, but then she knew she'd done it.

'Is the baby all right?' she managed to ask as the midwife quickly checked the newborn over.

'Absolutely perfect. Congratulations, you have a baby boy! Happy Christmas!'

Wanting to hold her son more than anything, Crystal struggled to lift her head from the pillow to watch as the midwife helped Jake cut the cord. She couldn't believe how tiny her baby was. He gave a cry that pierced her heart; it was her baby, calling for her. The midwife carried him to Crystal, laying him gently on her chest and covering him with a blanket, so Crystal could feel her son's warm, new born skin against hers. She put her arm up to support him and make him feel safe and looked in wonder at his face. He was still covered in the white gunk that had protected him in the womb and his eyes were tightly shut against the bright lights but she could see he was perfect. She reached down and touched his tiny hand, feeling a rush of intense and overwhelming love.

'Look at him,' Jake said in awe, lightly touching his son's head. 'He's so beautiful. Then he looked at Crystal and this time the tears were falling down his face. 'You're amazing. I love you *so much*, Crystal.'

Christmas Day, 6.30 a.m. – a year later

'Has Joel settled?' Crystal asked sleepily, moving closer to Jake as he slipped into bed beside her.

'Yeah, he's fast asleep. Happy Christmas, gorgeous,' Jake said, putting his arms around her.

'Happy Christmas,' Crystal replied. 'So how long do you reckon we've got?'

'At least an hour,' Jake replied.

'Well then, what are we waiting for?'

'Do you want to open your present now?' Jake asked afterwards.

'I thought I'd just had it,' she replied, smiling.

'That was just your stocking filler. Here's your real present; close your eyes and hold out your hand '

Crystal did as she was told.

'You can open your eyes now.'

She looked at what she was holding – a black leather ring box, a box that she was dying to open! *It won't be what you think it is,* Crystal told herself sternly, willing herself not to be disappointed. Since they'd got back together Jake no longer held back from telling her he loved her. He revealed that he always had, but was so scared of everything going wrong again that he hadn't dared admit it. But during that year he hadn't mentioned marriage, even though Crystal was secretly longing for him to ask. Hardly daring to breathe she opened the box and then let out a gasp of joy, seeing the beautiful antique diamond engagement ring that she knew had been his grandmother's.

'So will you?' Jake asked.

'I will,' Crystal whispered back, gazing at him as he slipped the ring on to her finger.

They kissed, then, as they lay in each other's arms, Crystal traced her finger across the tattoo on Jake's shoulder.

'I promise I'm not just asking so I don't have to get the tattoo removed,' Jake told her smiling. 'Seriously, Crystal, I want to spend the rest of my life with you.'

'And I with you,' she answered, gazing into his blue eyes and feeling like the luckiest girl in the world.

Angel

Katie Price

A sparkling and sexy tale of glamour modelling, romance and the treacherous promises of fame.

When Angel is discovered by a model agent, her life changes for ever. Young, beautiful and sexy, she seems destined for a successful career and, very quickly, the glitzy world of celebrity fame and riches becomes her new home.

But then she meets Mickey, the lead singer of a boy band, who is as irresistible as he is dangerous, and Angel realises that a rising star can just as quickly fall . . .

'The perfect sexy summer read' *heat*

'A page-turner . . . it is brilliant. Genuinely amusing and readable. This summer, every beach will be polka-dotted with its neon pink covers' *Evening Standard*

'The perfect post-modern fairy tale' *Glamour*

arrow books

ALSO AVAILABLE IN ARROW

Angel Uncovered

By Katie Price

Angel Summer looks as if she has found her happy ever after. She's married to the love of her life, sexy footballer Cal, they have a beautiful baby girl and Angel is Britain's top glamour model. But all is not as it seems and there is heartache in store.

When Cal is transferred to AC Milan, Angel feels isolated being so far away from her family and friends instead of embracing the WAG lifestyle of designer shopping and pampering. Surrounded by beautiful people, will Angel and Cal pull together or will they turn elsewhere to seek comfort? Angel's worst nightmares come to life when an old flame of Cal's comes back on the scene and suddenly Angel is fighting to save her marriage, and herself . . .

'Glam, glitz, gorgeous people . . . so Jordan!' *Woman*

'A real insight into the celebrity world' *OK!*

'Brilliantly bitchy' *New!*

arrow books

Paradise

Katie Price

It's six months since beautiful model Angel Summer found herself having to choose between a life with Ethan Turner, the laid-back Californian baseball player, or giving her marriage to football star Cal Bailey another go. Her friends and family were stunned when she picked Ethan, but it looks like Angel made the right decision: Ethan loves her and she loves him.

But nothing is perfect. Ethan has secrets in his past that could threaten their relationship and when he faces financial ruin the couple are forced to star in a reality TV show about their life together. Despite everything, though, Angel is convinced that Ethan is the man for her. So why can't she stop thinking about Cal?

As the tabloids have always been quick to point out, the path of true love has never run smoothly for our sexy celebrity, and when her dad falls dangerously ill Angel rushes back to England to be by his bedside, throwing her and Cal back together. But Ethan loves her, Cal has a girlfriend, and Angel has made her choice. It's too late to go back now . . . isn't it?

'A fabulous guilty holiday pleasure' *Heat*

'Peppered with cutting asides and a directness you can only imagine coming from Katie Price, it's a fun, blisteringly paced yet fluffy novel.' *Cosmopolitan*

arrow books

THE POWER OF READING

Visit the Random House website and get connected with information on all our books and authors

EXTRACTS from our recently published books and selected backlist titles

COMPETITIONS AND PRIZE DRAWS Win signed books, audiobooks and more

AUTHOR EVENTS Find out which of our authors are on tour and where you can meet them

LATEST NEWS on bestsellers, awards and new publications

MINISITES with exclusive special features dedicated to our authors and their titles

READING GROUPS Reading guides, special features and all the information you need for your reading group

LISTEN to extracts from the latest audiobook publications

WATCH video clips of interviews and readings with our authors

RANDOM HOUSE INFORMATION including advice for writers, job vacancies and all your general queries answered

Come home to Random House

www.rbooks.co.uk